BRUTAL KING
KINGS OF TEMPTATION

SIENNA CROSS

Copyright © 2024 by Sienna Cross

All rights reserved.

No part of this book may be reproduced in any form or by any electronic or mechanical means, including information storage and retrieval systems, without written permission from the author, except for the use of brief quotations in a book review.

Paperback ISBN: 9798320035345

Cover Design: Joy Design Studio

❀ Created with Vellum

To all the women who find it perfectly acceptable for a gorgeous Italian mobster to stalk you until you fall hopelessly in love...

~ Sienna Cross

BRUTAL KING

CONTENTS

1. Come Closer, Little Fox	1
2. Just Behave	7
3. Back in Business	12
4. The Most Dangerous Thing	18
5. A Lamb & A Lion	24
6. In Lust	32
7. Psychos	39
8. Happy Pills	46
9. The Best Dream	53
10. You Again?	59
11. Toying with My Prey	66
12. A Vile Present	74
13. Obsessed with Me	83
14. I'm Coming for You	89
15. Stay	95
16. All About You	101
17. This Was a Bad Idea	107
18. Enough to Break Me	116
19. He's Back	122
20. An Impossible Ultimatum	128
21. Inescapable	134
22. A Surprise Proposal	140
23. Read Between the Lines	147
24. My Total Undoing	155
25. Scars	161
26. What Did He Do to You?	167
27. Sleep Now, Fight Later	175
28. Into Submission	182
29. Inside Me	188
30. Never Been Taught	194
31. It Was Love	199
32. A Night You'll Never Forget	205
33. I'm Not Going Anywhere	212
34. All Ours	218
35. Ain't Love Grand?	224

36. My Greatest Work	231
37. You Are a Masterpiece	237
38. A Reluctant Apology	244
39. Find Me	251
40. When You Know, You Know	259
41. Flames	267
42. A Coffee and a Kidnapping	273
43. Another Trophy	281
44. Unalive You	287
45. A Shot Rings Out	293
46. Finally Perfect	300
Epilogue	306
47. Sneak Peek of Wicked King	314
Also by Sienna Cross	321
Acknowledgments	323
About the Author	325

CHAPTER 1
COME CLOSER, LITTLE FOX

Nico

Come closer, little fox. Closer…

My heart taps out a frantic rhythm as adrenaline rushes my veins. The mad flutter drowns out the rumble of engines and sharp blasts of horns just beyond the lush tranquility of Central Park. A sanctuary amidst the chaos.

My gaze settles on *her*. The object of my desire, the reason my cock strains against my slacks. The thrill of the chase is seductive, addictive, a narcotic far more potent than any available on the market. Crouching behind the shadows of the towering oak, my prey is oblivious to the predator lurking only a few feet away.

The alluring redhead clutches a white paper bag in her hand, her delicate fingers obscuring the name of the franchise. I only know there's a salad inside because I trailed her from the moment she left Palestra. The exclusive gym is nestled within the bowels of the Plaza Hotel. Thanks to my newfound success with Gemini Corp, I was finally granted entry to the high-end facility. Not only would it provide me with unfettered access to the enticing female, but it would also serve as a strategic location to network with the high and mighty of Manhattan.

The only downside is being forced to endure the occasional presence of my half-brother, Dante Valentino, the insufferable *capo* of the Kings. He and his brother Luca rule the streets of lower Manhattan with their underground dealings, while their aboveboard business affairs are conducted through King Industries. Thanks to a few key moves, Gemini Corp is now poised to overtake both parts of their enterprise.

My half-brothers have everything, while my brother, Marco, and I grew up penniless at the cruel hands of the foster care system. Now all of that is about to change.

The crackle of footsteps across brittle twigs returns my attention to the task at hand. The mesmerizing female settles down on a bench, folding one leg over the other. Wisps of brilliant auburn hair lash across her face as a chilly spring breeze sails across the oak trees. I've always had a thing for redheads, but this is different…

The beautiful Maisy Jordan captured my attention three long months ago. I've waited patiently, looming in the shadows but *cazzo*, I can't watch her from afar any longer. It's time for me to make my move.

I step out from behind the thick trunk of the ancient oak but before I make it far, a man appears and with a cheesy smile, sits beside *my* little fox.

A wave of fury lashes at my insides as he strikes up a conversation. She smiles politely, as they discuss the weather. Clearly, this man has no idea what he's doing. She brings the plastic fork to her mouth, and her full pink lips close around the verdant leaves of lettuce. Irrational jealousy flares at the nerve of that fork, of that salad to experience those lips. I've dreamt of them since that day in the container at the shipping yard when I had Maisy at my mercy.

She wasn't supposed to be there. It was my half-brother's girlfriend I'd been targeting. Maisy had been collateral damage, but only a few hours with that woman and I was hopelessly obsessed.

I've never stalked a woman before, but with every passing day, the roots of obsession grow deeper. I was content with keeping my distance at first, but now, the urge to touch her is overwhelming.

A bubbly laugh jerks my attention to the pair still chatting on the park bench. The blonde guy has his phone out now, and he's clearly trying to get her number. That rage ignites, and my nails curl into my palms.

My feet propel me forward before I can stop myself. I emerge from behind the trees, and Maisy's gaze lifts almost instantly. Her deep emerald irises latch onto mine, and a faint gasp escapes those pretty pink lips.

It's the first time I've let her see me since all those months ago at the airport. I'd tracked my half-brother and his fiancé to JFK and again, Maisy had simply been at the wrong place at the wrong time. But so right for me.

I stalk closer and that mouth curves into a capital O. I can just imagine her lips wrapped around my cock, sucking and licking me into oblivion. Fuck, I'm so hard now it hurts.

The blonde guy's head swivels in my direction, and I imagine twisting it farther, until it snaps. The satisfying crunch of bones sends a rush of gratification through my hollow chest.

"Nico Rossi…" she whispers on an exhale, and fuck me, my name on her lips only fuels the fire raging below my belt. I've never had such a visceral reaction to a woman. Maybe it's the months I've spent watching her, keeping myself at a careful distance. It's an entirely new experience for me.

"Good afternoon, little fox." I dip my head into a slight bow, my eyes fixed to hers. To her body's reaction to mine.

Her cheeks are flushed, her chest rises and falls more quickly, her lips parted in invitation. I'm not imagining it; she's startled by my presence but there's something more there too.

The male stands to his full height, still half a head shorter than me, and offers his hand. "Jack Dawson, and you are?"

"Not interested," I growl, my gaze intent only on Maisy.

"What are you doing here?" she asks, the slight tremble in her voice doing illicit things to my cock.

"Simply enjoying the beautiful scenery." I inch closer so that her tantalizing scent reaches my nostrils. It's a heady mix of orchids and warm vanilla. I can only imagine what she tastes like.

Her eyes taper at the edges as if she doesn't quite know what to make of this situation. She's frightened, yes, but there's more, too. Pressing the plastic lid atop the salad container, she drops her chin. The moment her eyes leave mine that vacant chasm in my chest deepens.

Maisy hastily shoves the remains of her lunch in a plastic bag and stands, swiveling toward the grinning idiot. "It was nice meeting you, Jack, but I have to get back to the office."

"Oh, sure." He rises and holds out his hand again, his fingers closing around her small palm. "The pleasure was all mine. I'll call you tomorrow then."

A light crimson flushes her cheeks, but now I'm the one seeing red. The urge to rip that phone from his hands and smash it into a million pieces is overwhelming. I swallow hard, reining in the ravenous demon.

She starts to walk down the pathway without so much as a goodbye. I move into step beside her, and she quickens her pace.

"Why are you running, little fox?"

"I'm not... And don't call me that."

I lengthen my stride to keep up with her. I'm nearly a foot taller than her, and still, I'm nearly at a jog. She is most definitely running away from me. "Do I frighten you?"

"Um, geez, I don't know... you kidnapped me and my friend and held us at gunpoint just a few months ago. Why would I ever be scared of you?" She keeps her gaze fixed straight ahead and jabs a chipped fingernail at the crosswalk button.

"I've already apologized for that."

"Somehow that's the sort of thing that sticks with you, Mr. Rossi. Despite apologies."

The light turns green, and she steps onto the crosswalk without looking, presumably in such a hurry to escape my company. A bike whizzes by, blasting a bell, and I just get my hand around her arm and jerk her back onto the sidewalk before the bike runs her over.

She lets out a gasp, her palm flying to her chest and drops the plastic container. The lid pops off and a mess of lettuce, tomatoes, and a myriad of other vegetables splatter across the asphalt. "Slow down, you butthole!" she shouts once she's steadied herself against the metal crosswalk pole.

I don't think I've ever heard an adult use that turn of phrase. It brings an unexpected twist to my lips. My hand is still wrapped around her upper arm, and she's clearly still too flustered about her salad to notice.

"Unbelievable." She bends down, jerking free of my grasp and tries to collect the sad remnants of her lunch.

"What are you doing?" I watch her incredulously as she picks up the dirt covered tomatoes and places them back in the plastic container.

"I can't just leave them on the sidewalk. The pigeons will try to eat them, and they could choke."

I don't think a single inhabitant in the city would miss those rats with wings. "I think they'll be just fine." I reach for her again and try to force her up, but she glares up at me, those deep green eyes ablaze.

Fuck, that look. It goes straight to my dick.

"No one asked you to wait." She continues her painstaking

task until every leaf of lettuce and pulverized vegetable is back in the plastic bowl.

I eye her completely mesmerized. After months of watching her, I still don't understand this woman. How this sweet, innocent, rather bumbling female could have been married to a psychopath like Jasper Whitaker is beyond me. She must have a dark side, one I am desperate to find and let loose. And if she doesn't, even better. There is nothing I want more than to corrupt her, defile that purity and drag her into the dark depths of my world.

A deep grumble turns my attention to a now standing Maisy. She stomps across the street, and I barely race behind her in time before the light turns red again.

We're only a few steps from the Plaza now, and I'll miss my chance if I don't make my move. "Have dinner with me tonight."

She spins around, her eyes impossibly wide. "Excuse me?"

"You heard me."

A nervous laugh titters out. "I can't…"

"Why? Because of that Jack Dawson asshole?"

Her brows slam together as she regards me. "No, because you kidnapped me, and to be perfectly honest you scare the bejesus out of me."

I barely suppress the chuckle that time.

"Now, please, leave me alone. I have to get back to work." She spins away, but my hand catches her wrist before she makes it to the first step.

"Do not go out with that Jack guy."

"Right, whatever," she mumbles over her shoulder.

"I'm serious, little fox. I don't like it when others try to play with *my* plaything."

She doesn't even acknowledge my final comment as she races up the steps of The Plaza Hotel.

Rage simmers in the center of my chest. If I can't have Maisy Jordan, no one else will.

CHAPTER 2
JUST BEHAVE

M*aisy*

The clang of dumbbells mixes with the tune of ragged breaths and thump, thump of sneakers on the treadmill, but none of that distracts from the maddening tempo of my pulse roaring across my eardrum. One encounter with Nico Rossi and my insides are in a twisted mess.

I glance over my shoulder for the tenth time since I walked into the hotel, then descended the steps to the exclusive gym where I work. Walking across the crowded workout floor toward my office, I still can't help but hazard a peek back to make sure he's not behind me.

Relax, Maisy, he can't possibly do anything to you in the middle of all these people. And not just any people, but the upper crust of Manhattan's high society. At Palestra, senators, diplomats and C.E.O.'s mix and mingle over sweat and sweatshirts. I noticed Nico here for the first time only a few days ago. My heart had nearly jumped out of my chest at the sight of the dark haired, tattooed gangster-slash-C.E.O. The worst part was the reason he'd caught my eye within the sea of bare-chested men: I found him attractive.

Like crazy, scorching, panty-dropping hot.

One look at that long, midnight hair pulled into a tie at the back of his neck, dark wisps falling over a massive phoenix tattoo across his broad shoulders had my entire body perked up in attention.

It was only when he turned around and those hypnotic blue eyes met mine, I realized I'd been ogling the man who'd captured my friend and me at gunpoint, drugged us and tossed us into a shipping container a few months earlier.

Nico Rossi is a bad man. A very bad man, and I needed to stay far away.

If only someone could get the message to my lusty cooter.

"Hey, Maisy!" Becca, one of the girls at the reception desk, waves with a smile. "Good lunch break?"

Ha. "Uneventful." Total lie. I dart past her before I start spilling completely embarrassing information and move down the hall to the administrative offices. I've been working as the human resources assistant for almost six months now. Ever since my divorce was finalized.

Jerking my office door open, I squeeze my eyes closed as thoughts of my ex-husband flood my mind. Jasper Whitaker a.k.a. Mark Rattinger. As it turns out, not only was my ex an abusive mother trucker, but he was also living a double life assaulting innocent women under an assumed name.

Thank goodness that son of a biscuit is finally out of my life for good.

Or is he? That niggling dark voice echoes in the back of my mind, and goosebumps cascade down my arms. He was never caught.

I settle into my desk and try to shoo the dark thoughts to the far corners of my mind. Something to discuss with my therapist at a later time.

Only they keep surging to the surface.

Darkness consumes my vision. My rapid breaths setting my lungs on fire as I sit in the backseat of a van, gagged, and with a hood over my head.

"Everything's going to be okay, Maisy." Or at least I think that's what my friend, Rose, says around her gag. Somehow, she must have loosened hers because I can't get a single word out.

A man sits beside me, his firm thigh pressed against mine and the spicy scent of his cologne filtering through the hood and invading my nostrils. He spouts off directions to the driver. Some in Italian which I don't understand but the majority in English. Apparently, we're headed to some shipping yard in lower Manhattan.

"Where's Max?" The male beside me growls, the deep tenor of his voice amplifying my rioting heartbeat.

"He's already on his way. He'll meet us there with the package."

"Good. I'm sure it's only a matter of time until Dante shows up. I cannot wait for our big surprise."

The car begins to slow, and another rush of fear ices my veins. I want to believe Rose's boyfriend, Dante, will save us, but we're caught in a freaking mob war right now, and who knows what will happen once the bullets start to fly. I'm a magnet for disasters. Poor Rose is never going to survive this with me by her side.

The van door jerks open, and another male voice ushers us out. I take a step from the car and pitch forward, tripping on who the heck knows what. Probably my own dang feet. An arm laces around my waist and tugs me into a firm chest so I don't fall flat on my face since my wrists are bound.

I recognize the man's spicy scent from a second ago in the van. He holds me flush against the hard planes of his body for another instant, and my body rages at his touch. I'm hot and cold all at once, a deadly mix of fear and something else I will never admit to. Good golly, how long has it been since I've been touched by a man? My stupid, traitorous body is all confused.

"Relax, little fox. No one's going to hurt you." That deep voice, even through the thick material of the hood sends chills down my spine. He finally releases me, and another big hand jerks me forward. "Careful with her, fuckhead." The snarl from behind me instantly loosens the hold around my upper arm.

"Sorry, boss."

A faint sea breeze hangs in the air, and the crash of water lapping over the docks signals to my brain we've arrived at our destination. Rose and I are walked another few yards before a sharp squeal echoes in the tense silence.

"Step up." A male voice says, not the deep one I've now come to recognize.

I do as I'm told while Rose puts up a fight just ahead of me. I wish I could see what's happening, but I can't make out anything with this darned hood over my head. The asphalt beneath my sneakers is replaced by metal, and it only takes me a second to realize where we are now. Inside one of those huge metal containers in the shipping yard.

Panic grips my chest, and I try to scream but nothing more than a muffled moan seeps out. Oh God, please, I don't want to die today.

Firm hands press down on my shoulders, and my knees give way despite my best efforts. My butt lands on a seat instead of the metal floor as I'd imagined.

"Just behave and everything will be fine, little fox." That familiar voice appears beside me again.

I try to draw in a steadying breath, but my lungs are rioting. I'm terrified I'm going to pass out. My chest is heaving, and darkness invades the corners of my vision, and this time it's not just from the hood.

Rose screams beside me, muttering something. Help her? Oh, me. She's talking about me.

The hood is ripped off my head, and I blink quickly, until my pupils adjust from the pitch black. A pair of mesmerizing sapphire orbs drill into me.

"Are you having trouble breathing?"

I can barely make out the man's words over my thundering heart.

Finally, I focus on the movement of his lips, on the thin scar that bisects the upper one. My head bobs up and down.

"Do you promise to behave if I remove the gag?"

I nod again.

His hands come around my head and untie the knot. I draw in a lungful of blessed air, and my manic pulse begins to settle. He remains standing in front of me, those piercing irises razing over me.

Fudge, now my heartbeat is ratcheting up again.

A door creaks open, flooding the container with light. I take a quick look at Rose who sits beside me and whisper, "Are you okay?"

She nods quickly, the hood still over her head.

The clang of approaching footsteps jerks my attention to the two males walking toward us. All the blood in my veins ices over.

Jasper, my ex-husband.

"What are you doing here?" I splutter. Rose and I had only just discovered his dirty little secret moments before we were snatched.

Jasper opens his mouth to respond, but the other guy gags him before he can get a word out. Then the hood comes next.

The man with the scar on his lip who I'm now starting to understand is the head of this whole operation crouches in front of me. "It's almost over, little fox. I must say I'm so thrilled to finally meet you in person. After all these months spending quality time with Jasper, I feel as if I know you."

Before I can respond, he slips the gag around my mouth again. My eyes go wide, my lungs constricting once more.

"Just breathe through your nose, and you'll be fine. It's the panic that's not letting you breathe. Not the gag or the hood. Understand?"

I nod slowly, trying my best to temper the fear. When all I really want to do is kick the son of a biscuit in the family jewels.

He drops the hood back over my head, and everything is black once again.

CHAPTER 3
BACK IN BUSINESS

Maisy

My knee bounces up and down beneath the table at the corner café, a nervous flutter vibrating my entire body since my encounter with Nico Rossi yesterday. With spring here, a few of the restaurants have already set out tables and chairs on the bustling sidewalks. A cool breeze passes, raising the hair on the back of my neck. I hazard a quick glance over my shoulder. Nothing. For months now, I've felt this unnamable presence lurking in the shadows.

And now after my encounter with the brutal mob boss, the feeling of unease has only intensified. No way he's been following me all these months, right? Why would he? It makes no sense…

I take a sip of my Chai Latte, hoping the soothing warmth will chase away the anxiety filling my chest. I place it back on the colorful tablecloth, but my trembling fingers knock it over and the fragrant liquid spills across the table.

"Sugar!" I mutter.

A sharp cackle forces my gaze up to my approaching friend. "Oh, Maisy, man, I've missed your ridiculous curse words."

A smile curls my lips, and I stop sopping up the mess and stand to give Rose a hug. Even wearing my chunky heels, she towers over me, her long blonde hair cascading across her shoulders. She's a total Barbie, and I'm a cute little Skipper with crazy red hair. "I've missed you too!" I hold her out at arm's length and scrutinize her chic, floral jacket and skinny jeans. "Wait, there's something different about you."

A huge smile stretches across her face, and she flashes me the back of her hand. Stacked beneath her whopping diamond engagement ring is a diamond-studded wedding band. "Dante and I got married!" she squeals.

"No freaking way, you did not!" I gasp and clap my hand over my gaping mouth. I love my friend and I know Dante is crazy about her, but everything has been moving so fast with them. "How did this…? When did you…?" My rambling tongue gets all tied up with the excitement.

"Sit and we'll talk." Rose steers me to my seat and flops down beside me. Then she waves down the waitress and has her clean up my mess. Golly, I'm worse than a toddler with this cursed clumsiness.

My friend is beaming as she stares at her gorgeous rings, and I'm so happy for her, but also, I'm sad for me, which is stupid and mean-spirited, but I'm tired of being alone. I should totally return that Jack Dawson guy's text… No, I'll do one better, I'll call him. Despite Nico's warning. I mean he wouldn't really do something to some random stranger, right?

"So Dante surprised me with a trip to Atlantic City." The enthusiasm in Rose's voice drags me out of my funk. "Then when we get there, he takes me to the penthouse suite at the Ocean Casino Resort, which has a jacuzzi in the middle of the room by the way…"

Heat flushes my cheeks just at the mention. Dante and Rose screw like bunnies, and she is not shy about the details. It's fun hearing about her crazy sexcapades with the foul-mouthed mafia god, but I'm not sure I could ever do it. I'm such a bumbling, rambling idiot, I could never get that dirty talk down.

I nod and smile as she details their hours-long sexual encounter across every inch of the suite, and heat begins to build between my legs. Yup, it's definitely time for me to get back in the game. Jasper and I have been apart for over a year now, and I'm afraid I'm minutes away from reinstating my V card.

"Anyway, then he pulls this gorgeous white mermaid gown from the closet and tells me we're going out for some fancy dinner."

"And instead, he took you to one of those quickie wedding chapels?"

"Yup!" Her head is bobbing up and down and that smile only grows wider.

My heart is brimming with joy for my friend. "I wish I could've been there."

She reaches for my hand and squeezes. "I know, me too. It was all so quick and such a surprise. Only *Mamma*, Luca and Stella were there, and they only stayed for the ceremony before they jetted back to wherever the hell they've been hiding out. Anyway, I doubt Dante would've even let them come if we didn't need witnesses. Plus, his Ma would've probably murdered him if she wasn't invited."

"I bet Dante couldn't wait to get you back to the hotel room to rip the dress right off."

Rose laughs, a wicked cackle bursting from her lips. "Pretty much. We've only been married for a few days and already he wants me off the pill. I mean he's wanted me off it for months now, and I've been fighting him every step of the way. Now that we're married, I don't know how much longer I can hold him off. I'm not sure I want to either... which is insane."

"Gosh, Rose, it all sounds beautiful and so perfect. I'm really happy for you guys."

"Me too." She casts a dreamy gaze in my direction as she twists the rings around her finger. Rose and Dante sure had a rough start, and despite my reservations about the guy, I've never seen my friend so happy.

The waitress reappears, and we each order, a cheeseburger for Rose because with her perfect yoga instructor body she can eat whatever she wants, and a salad for me because I swear if I look at a carb I gain a pound.

"So, what's been going on with you?" Rose asks around a slurp of water.

I briefly consider telling her about my encounter with Nico, but I hate to ruin her great mood. Things between the Kings, Dante's underground organization, and Nico's Geminis have been teetering on a knife's edge for months. "Nothing much," I finally grumble.

"Oh, come on, Maisy, you can't just bury yourself in work. You're not some forty-year-old divorcee, get out there and have some fun."

"Ugh, easy for you to say. It's hard to meet quality guys in the city."

She pulls out her phone and starts typing away. Then she flashes me the screen with some dating app pulled up.

"No way. I said quality, remember?"

"You can look for quality after you get laid." She shoots me an evil smirk. "Tell me the truth, how long has it been?"

That dang heat rises up my neck, coating my cheeks, and I'm sure my freckles are so bright they're glowing against my pale skin. "A long time," I finally mutter.

"Please tell me you practice self-care at least?"

I shake my head, my cheeks flaming. I'd tried a few times, long ago, when I was with Jasper. The truth is I'd never been able to have an orgasm from traditional sex, so I was getting desperate. "It doesn't really work for me."

"Did you use a vibrator, a dildo? What?"

"Oh, geez, no, I don't have one of those." I giggle like a schoolgirl. It took me the better part of college to be able to say penis with a straight face.

"Okay, we're putting an end to this insanity right now." She jabs her finger at her phone then turns it to me once again. "This one is my favorite. Well, honestly, I haven't had to use it since Dante and I got together because he keeps me more than satisfied." Her eyes take on that dreamy quality again. Lordy, she is so in love. "And one-click." She shoots me a smirk. "It'll be arriving at your place by tomorrow night."

"Rose!" I groan.

"Don't knock it till you've tried it, sister." Then she swipes at her phone, and we're back on another dating app. "Now back to Love Roulette…"

"What?" I snort on a laugh.

"The dating app where hearts take a spin." She lets out a cackle, and I can't help but laugh along with her.

"I can't do this."

"Yes, you can." Rose scoots her chair beside me so we can both ogle the scantily clad men. "Oooh, how about this guy?" She swipes past the half-naked ones and stops on a blonde guy in a business suit. "He looks very GQ."

"I guess."

"Not your type? No problem, we have hundreds of eligible bachelors." She smirks as she continues to scroll.

I squeeze my eyes closed, and a pair of piercing blue eyes swim across my vision. Then wisps of dark hair fall across a sharp jawline. And those lips, constantly twisted in an arrogant smile. Even the scar across the top one is oddly enticing.

No… No! My eyes snap open, and I shake my head out. Oh, sugar, I've clearly lost my mind. How could I be lusting after the man who held me hostage all those months ago? It must be some sort of post-traumatic stress disorder. I'll have to bring it up with Dr. Winchester at my next appointment.

"Oh, what about him?" Rose waggles her brows. A dark-haired male with long hair pulled up into a bun fills the screen. Tattoos peer out from beneath his t-shirt, and an embarrassing sigh slides through my clenched teeth. "Oh, my gawd, Maisy, you like Mr. Dark and Dangerous? I was totally joking. I never thought you'd go for that type."

I shrug, mortification flooding my cheeks. "I guess I just want something completely different from Jasper."

Rose nods, her lips pressed in a tight line. "I get that." She reaches across the table and squeezes my hand. "So, let's give this guy a thumbs up."

I heave in a breath and nod slowly. "Okay."

And I resolve to answer Jack Dawson's text as soon as I get home. It's time to resurrect my divorced, dusty cooter. We're back in business, girl.

CHAPTER 4
THE MOST DANGEROUS THING

Nico

A crisp breeze whips wisps of brilliant auburn across my muse's face. She wrinkles her nose and bats it away, pinning the errant strands behind her dainty ears. Dipping my brush into the paint, I imagine it's my cock sinking into that warm pussy.

A feral growl rumbles my chest, and I dip the brush in too deep. When I pull it out, the ferrule, the metal band that connects the bristles to the wooden handle is coated in crimson. Fuck. What is it with this girl that has me so out of control?

I reach for the rag on the grass and wipe the brush down, the deep red paint stretched all the way up to the handle in my mad thrust. If I'd done that with a paintbrush, I could only imagine what would happen when I finally sank my cock inside her. I'd rip her apart.

I'd only spent a few hours with Maisy that day three long months ago. There was something about her fiery spirit wrapped in a beautiful, yet bumbling package, and those ridiculous curse words… A silly smile curls the corner of my lips.

I'd never met a grown woman who was at the same time sexy as sin and as pure as the driven snow. And damn, all I wanted to do was corrupt her, fuck her so hard she screamed one of those ludicrous curses.

My cock strains against my slacks at the vivid images my mind has conjured. I consider scrapping the canvas of Maisy in her prim little black dress on the park bench and painting her nude sprawled across my bed. But I have a feeling whatever vision my thoughts could conjure would never be as good as the real thing. No, I'd have to see her completely bare before me so that I could accurately paint every perfect detail.

Soon.

I haven't been inside her house yet, but I think the time has come. Watching her from afar without ever being able to touch her is growing tiresome. I hadn't meant for her to see me the other day at the park, but when that guy showed up, I simply couldn't help myself.

The same urges are coming over me today. I need to see her up close, hear that melodic voice. Maybe she'll drop something again and blurt one of those colorful curses I'm quickly becoming obsessed with.

I glance at my pocket watch, the long gold chain hanging from my slacks and mutter a curse. Maisy's lunchbreak is nearly over and if I plan on finishing my portrait, I must work quickly.

Focusing on my muse once again, I bring the bristles to the canvas and capture the smattering of freckles across her nose. She seems distracted today. Every few bites, she glances at her phone. Whose call is she awaiting?

Shit. What if it's that Jack guy from the park the other day?

Would she have dared to disobey me?

If that asshole thinks he can touch what's mine and live to tell about it, he's got another thing coming. My fingers curl around the brush handle, my knuckles white from the strain. I've been in a foul mood for weeks now, and it isn't only this unquenchable, burning desire for my little fox. Ever since Jianjun, the leader of the Chinese Triad sold me out and joined forces with my half-brothers, I've been seething. I'm so close to bringing down the King's empire I can practically taste it. Which is exactly why I don't need this distraction…

Maisy has become an obsession in the past few months. I need to get her out of my system before she costs me what I've spent my entire life working toward. Annihilating King Industries.

My half-brothers inherited everything from our father, while Marco and I got nothing. We fought tooth and nail for everything we have today. We clawed our way up from dark alleyways to rub elbows with Manhattan's elite.

I've come so far, I won't lose it now.

A sharp squeal jerks my attention to Maisy. A dog has gotten loose, and the giant creature is jumping on her lap, dragging its filthy tongue across her face. Between bouts of giggles, she tries to shove the animal off.

Its owner comes running, an older man, his cheeks rosy from the exertion. The moment the dog sees the man, he takes off, straight toward me.

Shit.

Maisy's gaze trails the mangy animal to my spot beneath the towering oak. Despite my best attempts at ducking behind the canvas, her eyes lock on mine. Damn it. One would think after months of this, I'd be better at remaining concealed.

But maybe a tiny part of me wants to be discovered.

Her mouth curves into a capital O as I straighten to my full height, and she takes me in. The big golden dog races past me with its owner hot on its heels. By the time I look up again, Maisy has packed up her lunch and is making her escape.

Dropping the paintbrush, I take off after her, deserting my masterpiece to weave between bicycles and a jogger who curses me out. Maisy had gone further into Central Park today giving her endless amounts of space to run from me, and more time to catch her.

"Maisy," I shout.

She hurries over the small stone bridge and dips behind a towering rock formation. I'm practically jogging now to keep up with her, my tie flapping on the light spring breeze.

"Maisy, wait!"

She doesn't even pause, the click-clack of her kitten heels matching the rapid tempo of my pulse. Fiery excitement surges through my veins. Has no one ever taught this woman never to run from a predator?

I circle the massive boulders and find Maisy on the ground, wincing. Her dress has ridden up to her thighs, exposing milky white legs. Her hand is wrapped around her ankle, and her lunch is splattered across the grass. Slowing my frenetic pace, I drag my hand through my hair, forcing the errant strands back.

"Are you hurt?" I keep my voice neutral despite the thrill coursing through my system.

"No!" She winces again as she holds her foot out and tries to wiggle her ankle. "Ugh, ow, that hurts like a mother trucker."

I barely restrain a laugh at her absurd choice of words and instead, focus on the odd twist of her joint. I drop to the ground beside her and examine her foot. She lets out a squeak as my fingers gently graze her flesh. "It doesn't seem broken, hopefully just a sprain."

"Are you a doctor now? I thought your extracurricular activities were limited to stalking and kidnapping women."

A smirk creeps across my lips. "I also like to paint."

"How multi-talented of you."

"Thank you. I've been working on a rather difficult piece today. My muse simply won't keep still."

Her eyes widen, and a faint gasp escapes through those

perfect pink lips. I inch closer and breathe her in. The scent of orchids and sweet vanilla floods my nostrils.

"Why do you do that?" she snaps and falls back on her ass with a muffled *oomph*.

"Do what?"

"Are you sniffing me?"

"I'm committing your scent to memory for my own personal use in the privacy of my home."

Her auburn brows slam together, and horror etches into her expression. "You think of me like *that*?"

Something else sparks through those expressive emerald orbs. Not just revulsion but curiosity? Dare I say, excitement?

"Only every time I stroke my cock."

A sharp gasp erupts, and her eyes grow impossibly wide. "Oh, my stars..."

She crawls back but hits the jagged boulder and lets out a whimper.

"I'm not going to hurt you, Maisy. As long as you behave."

"I just need to get back to work," she murmurs.

"Can you walk?"

"I'm pretty sure I could muster the strength to run if it meant getting away from you."

So sassy. My cock twitches at the mouth on her. I'd fuck that naughty streak right out of her. "Give me your hand."

Maisy shakes her head, planting her ass on the lush lawn. "Just go. I'll be fine."

"I'm not leaving you here in the middle of Central Park with a possibly sprained ankle so some psychopath can come by and take advantage of you."

"You're the only psychopath in the vicinity, Nico Rossi." She crosses her arms over her chest, and her breasts spill over the neckline of her fitted black dress. It's meant to be a demure thing with a polka dot cardigan covering her arms, but on her, it looks sinful as hell. I close my eyes for an instant and envision ripping off the sweater, shoving that dress up to her waist and fucking her atop the mountain of rocks.

Blinking away the much too vivid images, I glance over my shoulder. Not a soul in sight. No one to stop me. I might have done some fucked up things in my lifetime, but I've never forced myself on a woman. As painfully hard as my cock is, I won't start now.

"You're not wrong you know," I whisper.

"About what?" She glares up at me as I kneel in front of her.

"I am the most dangerous thing in this park."

CHAPTER 5
A LAMB & A LION

Nico

A shudder races up Maisy's spine, and her entire body trembles.

"But not to you, never to you." Before she can stop me, I snake my arm beneath her thighs and the other around her shoulder blades. I lift her easily and cradle her against my chest, despite her protestations.

"Let go of me, you son of a biscuit!"

My entire torso rumbles as she kicks and jerks in my arms. Luckily, the park is quiet today, and her shouts of annoyance go unheard. Which is exactly why I never would've left her out here wounded and vulnerable.

"I'm taking you somewhere safe, relax, little fox."

"Don't call me that!" she hisses.

"Then don't call me son of a biscuit." I can't help but chuckle around the last word. "If you're going to curse, say it like you mean it. Call me a motherfucker and own it."

"No!" She struggles some more, and I'm impressed by her will. I'm over a foot taller than her and easily have a hundred pounds on the little thing. "Mrs. Gloria Vanderbilt would have my hide!"

"Who?"

"Oh, fudge, me and my big mouth." She presses her lips together and makes a big show of running a zipper over them.

"Maisy, you certainly are one in a million."

Her eyes meet mine, and for an instant, I'm lost in the brilliant abyss. The fear is gone, and something unnamable remains. Is she flattered by my words? Surely, someone at some point in her life has told this woman how remarkable she is, right?

We remain in an oddly comfortable silence as I carry her across the winding pathway. Her eyes trail every bright flower, each butterfly that zips past. She drinks it all in as if it were her first time.

We finally reach the end of the park, the intersection where she spilled her salad just the other day only a few yards away. She presses her palm to my chest, and it looks so small against my torso. "Put me down, I need to try to walk."

"You're only going to hurt yourself if you put weight on it too soon."

Her lively eyes taper at the edges. "Did you just call me fat?"

"Of course not." I huff out an exasperated breath. This woman is beyond perfect, how could she ever think otherwise? "A sprain needs to be cared for or it'll swell, and you'll never be able to walk on it."

"Just let me try, please."

With a grunt, I gently release her legs. She slides down my body, and her eyes jolt open when my erection grazes her belly. Once she's on the ground, my hands close around her hips, holding her steady. Her gaze remains pinned to mine, my cock wedged between us. With our drastic difference in heights, it reaches her bellybutton.

To my surprise, she doesn't move for an impossibly long moment, those mossy green orbs locked on mine. Lust pulses through those blown-out pupils, and I'm so shocked by what I see in her gaze I tell myself I must be imagining it.

Could little Miss Maisy actually want me? Could the prim and proper lady be hiding a naughty side?

A scooter whizzes past us, blasting a bell and our gazes unlock. She clears her throat and takes a measured step back, but I keep my hold on her waist. It wasn't only an excuse, she shouldn't be putting weight on that ankle.

She shifts in front of me and winces as she tests out her wounded leg. "Oh, fudgescicles," she mutters. "I don't think I can walk on it."

"Come, I'll take you home."

"No!" she cries out and nearly wiggles free of my grasp.

"Why not? You can't very well walk there, and I have a car waiting just around the corner."

"I don't want you anywhere near my house."

I shrug and press a finger beneath her chin, forcing her eyes to mine. "In case you've forgotten, I already know where you live. I know your security code, zero nine twenty-three, you should know better than to use your birthday, and I'm intimately familiar with the layout of your three-story townhome. Your mailman steals the coupons from the weekly mailer and your pest control provider takes a nap on your couch each visit."

Her light brows jump up to meet her hairline. "Mother trucker..." she rasps out. "You really are stalking me?"

My shoulders lift again slowly as I ascertain her likeliness to bolt. "I was merely concerned with your safety."

"My safety?" she shrieks. "You're the only one who scares the bejesus out of me."

"I don't think that's true at all. What about Jasper?"

All the blood in her face leeches out, darkening the appearance of her faint freckles. I was right, she is scared of that sneaky son of a bitch. In the weeks I kept her ex as my captive and errand boy, he often spoke of his beautiful, loyal ex-wife. That was likely when I became enamored by the idea of her.

He never did admit what he'd done to her. At the time, it wasn't important, but now, the fear streaking across her face warrants answers. "What did he do to you, Maisy?"

She shakes her head, her lower lip beginning to tremble. "He's gone; it doesn't matter anymore. Jasper wouldn't dare show his face around here. Dante would tear him apart for what he did to Rose."

I grunt and roll my eyes at mention of my half-brother. The crazed, more than slightly unhinged, Dante Valentino is nothing compared to me. You don't know pain until you've walked through fire and lived through the excruciating torture.

Both Dante and Luca are weak. Marco and I were wrought in fire, molded and branded in hell while they lived a life of luxury.

"Why did you let Jasper get away?" Her question draws me from the dark musings.

"He served his purpose, and I had no further use for him." I shrug again.

"He's a rapist and a stalk—well, I guess now I understand why you felt an affinity toward my ex."

A wave of anger rushes my chest, and I wrap my hand around Maisy's throat. It's funny how in a city of millions, everyone's so consumed in their own life no one gives two shits about anyone else. My thumb strokes the indentation in her neck. "Let's get something clear, little fox, I am nothing like that *pezzo di merda*, Jasper. Nothing," I snarl.

"Then prove it and let go of me," she spits.

I loosen my grip on her throat only to lift her in my arms once again.

"What are you doing?" she cries.

"I already told you, I'm taking you home to rest that ankle." Despite her slaps, I march down Central Park West and find Max and the BMW waiting for me. I crawl in the back, cradling Maisy against my chest. "We're going to Miss Jordan's house, Max."

"Got it, boss."

"He knows where I live?" she blurts.

"Of course he does, he's my driver."

Her face pales, and I'm certain she's gone back to the day I took Rose and her hostage. I decide to let it go for now. There's no point in dwelling in the past. I've already apologized multiple times.

As I settle into the backseat, a few blank canvases catch my eye. Shit, I left my work in progress at the park. Reaching for my phone, I shoot off a quick text message to Jimmy to go fetch it. He's meeting with Qian Guo of the Four Seas on the other side of the park as we speak. If the Red Dragons have chosen to back the Kings, I'll make sure the other notorious gang of the Triad supports the Geminis. If the Valentino brothers want a war, they'll get one.

Maisy wriggles in my lap, reminding me of her presence. She's been surprisingly silent for all of five minutes. "Please take me straight home."

"Well, I certainly wasn't going to take you to the shipping yard if that was your worry."

A chill skitters up her spine, and I can feel her convulsing in my lap. The fact that she still fears me brings an odd tangle of emotions. Normally, I would like it, but with Maisy it's different. Her ex was an abusive asshole, and I hate that she thinks we're anything alike.

"What do I have to do to convince you I'm not going to hurt you?"

Her fiery eyes lance into me. "Not kidnapping me for one would be a good start."

"This is not a kidnapping. I'm merely offering you a ride home."

"No, you forced me into your car. I obviously said no."

"You're not thinking clearly. The pain must have gone to your head."

"I'm going to punch you in your head in a second," she mutters under her breath, and a fit of laughter loosens my hold around her waist.

"You really are something else, Maisy."

She scrambles off my lap and settles into the seat beside me, bringing the seatbelt across her shoulder.

I glance down at her ankle, and it's already beginning to swell. "You see? I told you not to walk on it." I point at the bruised joint.

"This is all your fault, you know. I was trying to get away from you when I tripped."

"It sounds like it's your fault then. You should know better than to try to run from fate."

Her jaw drops, eyes wide as she regards me. A long minute later, she swallows hard and shoots me a steely glare. "You are out of your mind, Nico Rossi, if you think fate had anything to do with bringing us together."

I cluck my tongue. "Maybe, or maybe not, Miss Maisy. But I am a man who makes my own fate."

Max pulls up in front of her brownstone a few minutes later, her home a short drive from Central Park on a pristine, tree-lined street. Despite residing in a very desirable area, I hate the idea of her living alone in that enormous townhouse.

Jasper is a twisted fuck, and though I doubt he'd return with the authorities and the Kings on his ass, one never can be sure.

Before Maisy can argue, I scoop her into my arms and carry her out of the backseat. Jimmy is already at her door when I make it up the red brick stairs. I know she hides a spare key under the potted plant on her windowsill, but I decide to keep that tidbit of knowledge to myself for now and wait for her to rifle through her purse for the keys.

She finally finds them and hands them to Max begrudgingly.

"Stay outside," I bark at my driver once the door is opened.

"Sure thing, boss."

"You can stay outside too," Maisy hisses as I walk her through the threshold.

"Not until I get you settled. Where do you prefer, couch or bed?"

"Well, I don't want you anywhere near my bedroom so definitely the couch."

A smirk pulls at my lips. "Oh, Maisy, I can't wait for the day you beg me to fuck you on your fancy four-poster bed."

Her lips curve into an O, and her cheeks burn a tempting deep crimson. "How do you know what my bed looks like?"

I drop her onto the couch and ignore her question. She doesn't need to know I had my tech guy hack into her home security system a few days ago. Instead, I march into the kitchen and take out the container of ibuprofen from the cabinet, then fill a glass with water and bring it to her.

She watches me, lips parted. God, I want to see my cock between those luscious lips. I offer her the pills and the water, and she downs it all in one go like a good girl.

I settle down beside her on the floral sofa. The scent of orchids fills the air; she has at least three of them in this room alone. "Can I get you anything else before I go?"

"No, thank you." She eyes me, like a lamb watches a lion.

"If you need anything else, call me. I've already programmed my number in your phone."

"What? How?" She searches her purse for her cell.

"I have a guy who's very adept with technology."

She gulps and eyes the camera perched atop her bookshelf. "Please go, Nico."

"Fine. For now." I dip my head and offer her a wicked grin. "I'll see you again soon, little fox."

CHAPTER 6
IN LUST

M*aisy*

A faint click draws me from a fitful sleep, and my heavy lids snap wide open. My living room coalesces, and I draw in a breath. I'm home and safe. The grand room is a blend of historic charm with modern comforts and had taken me months to achieve. Back when I was so intent on being the perfect wife to Jasper Whitaker. Now it only reminds me of our failed marriage. And that's putting it lightly. Was the whole thing a sham?

Shaking my head, I focus on the warm glow of natural light as it spills across hardwood floors, enhancing the richness of the room. I love this house, and my disastrous marriage shouldn't take away from that. I glance up at the high ceilings, accentuating the sense of space and elaborate molding adorning the walls, adding a touch of classic elegance.

Then my gaze travels to the fireplace with the ornate

marble mantelpiece. It's my favorite part of the house, providing both warmth and a nod to the brownstone's historic roots. My heart kicks against my ribcage as I focus on the portrait sitting next to the orchid atop the mantel.

Of me.

At Central Park, sitting on a bench, my auburn locks cascading down my shoulders.

I shoot up off the couch and mutter a curse, as a pang streaks across my ankle. Dang it. I'd totally forgotten about it. Limping over to the hearth, my pulse is like a battering ram. With a shaky hand, I reach for the painting and my eyes lock on the initials slashed across the bottom righthand corner.

N.R.

Nico Rossi.

Son of a biscuit! That man was in my house… but how?

I squeeze my eyes closed and force my racing thoughts to quiet. Nico brought me home yesterday afternoon and left. I clearly remembered locking the door after he'd departed. So how did this portrait find its way into my living room?

I want to hate the painting, but I can't seem to tear my eyes away from it. The way Nico captured the sunlight dappled across my hair brings it to life in a fiery riot of colors. I look beautiful, like a hundred times more exquisite than I have any right to be. Even my annoying freckles are toned down, nearly disappearing within the warmth of my perfect skin tones. Is that really how he sees me?

My stupid heart flutters around in my chest like a lost butterfly.

What is wrong with me?

I should be terrified… This man broke into my home, invaded my privacy and—and left me a present? *Oh, H, E, double hockey sticks.*

I finally force my gaze away from the stunning painting and place it back up on the mantel because clearly, I've lost my mind. I should throw it in the dumpster. But I can't bear the thought of destroying the masterpiece.

I should call the police and get the arrogant Nico Rossi arrested. That would teach the smug a-hole some manners. Surely, he was caught on my security camera. I march-slash-limp, because my ankle still hurts like a mother, over to my phone which I left on the coffee table and open the security app. I toggle through last night's images and find… nothing.

Not a trace of the sneaky stalker.

How is that possible? I flip through the footage again and again, but the only person I see all night is me sprawled across the couch. My legs spread-eagle, nonetheless. *Great…* Not only did Nico get his run of my house last night, but he probably also got a front row view of my lady bits.

With an exasperated sigh, I vow to call the security company when I get to work. There must have been a glitch in the system. And if Nico could get in—my thoughts jump to a dark place. No. Jasper's gone. There's no reason he'd ever come back.

Shaking my head to dispel the dismal thoughts, I scan my messages for a distraction.

Jack Dawson. Bingo.

I still hadn't texted or called him back like I'd promised myself. I stare at the blue text bubbles and put on my big girl panties. *Just move your fingers across the keyboard, Maisy.* It's easy, even four-year-olds can do it.

Me: *Hi, sorry for the late reply. I twisted my ankle and have been kind of out of it. It's a long story… I'll tell you about it if you still want to grab that coffee.*

Too rambling? TMI? I stare at the message, delete and rewrite it again for a full five minutes before forcing my finger to jab the send button. Within seconds, the little blue dots appear.

Jack: *No worries, I'm just glad to hear from you. Let's meet up tomorrow at* Joe Coffee *on Columbus at 9?*

Me: *Sounds perfect.*

I slip my phone into my pocket, all dresses should have pockets by the way, and stagger toward the stairs. I stare up the winding staircase and let out a super unlady-like grunt that would have my mother tsking with the best of them. Nothing worse than an ungrateful rich kid, but today with my throbbing ankle, I'm cursing my three-story townhouse.

Slowly, I ascend the white-washed wooden staircase, regretting each and every decision I've made since meeting Jasper Whitaker. At least it's Friday, and I can take it easy over the weekend.

I finally make it to my bedroom and release a long sigh. The room is my personal oasis, a peaceful escape of pale blues and airy whites. A light canopy hangs atop the four-poster bed, reminding me of the princess one I had as a child. The new king-sized bed was a gift to myself after the divorce. I couldn't stand the thought of sleeping in the same bed I'd shared with Jasper for all those years.

Stumbling to the closet, I peel off the dress I've been wearing since yesterday. I'd never admit it, especially not to a certain mob boss with stalker tendencies, but I probably should have gotten my ankle looked at. There was no way I would've made it up the stairs yesterday, and even now I'm not certain I'll make it to the bus stop by foot. Darn, dang it.

If that creepy butthead hadn't been following me, none of this would have happened.

I take a quick shower, all the while balancing most of my weight on one foot and hurry to get dressed for work. At this rate, I'm going to be late.

When I finally get back downstairs, I jerk out my phone and search for the Uber app. There's no way I'll make it to the bus. Every step is growing more painful. Whipping the front door open with my eyes pinned to my phone, I slam into a hard body.

My heart leaps up my throat, and I scream as a familiar spicy, charred scent fills my nostrils. "Holy smokes!" I cry out as piercing sapphire eyes lock on mine.

"Sorry I frightened you, little fox."

"What are you doing here, Nico?" I rasp out, my hand clapped against my chest.

"I assumed you'd need a ride." He glances down at my foot, which I hold slightly off the ground.

I wriggle free of his grasp and glare up at the towering butthead. "You assumed wrong. I'm perfectly fine and capable of getting to work by myself."

He lifts a dark brow. "Really?"

"Yes."

"Then let's see you walk down the steps." He pauses as I reach for the railing. "Without holding the bannister."

"I will not. There's a reason it's there. Safety first and all that."

He chuckles, and the warm sound is more lethal than a heated caress. He holds out a hand, which I ignore. "By all means then."

I take a step and wince. Then another and another. I refuse to be coerced into anything by this man ever again. I'm gritting my teeth so hard by the time I reach the sidewalk, I'm scared they'll crack.

But I make it.

A black BMW sedan is parked by the curb, and I recognize Nico's driver through the windshield. Spinning on my heel, or at least trying my best to, I glare up at the infuriating mob boss. "See? Totally fine."

I take a step and trip over the uneven sidewalk and go flailing into a brick wall of a man. Nico's arms come around me as I let out a string of colorful curses. Mother father, that hurt.

"Just let Max drive you to work. If you don't want me to come, I won't."

My brows nearly jump up to my hairline. "Seriously?"

"Yes, seriously. With your innately disastrous tendencies, I'm worried you'll do even more damage than what's already been done. And I can't have you laid up in bed for weeks. Well... not with an injury anyway." A sinful smirk parts his lips, drawing my eye to that scar, and heat races below my belly button. "Did you like my gift by the way?"

I swallow hard and force myself to take a step back. I need to breathe some air not polluted with his enticing scent. It's like my brain short circuits when I'm around him, tossing all rational thoughts to the farthest corners of my mind.

"I don't know what you're talking about," I finally force out.

"No?"

I shake my head.

"Hmm." His lips twist, and a strand of dark hair comes free from the tie at the back. I'm filled with the most inappropriate urge to twirl it between my fingers before tucking it behind his ear. I bet it's soft and silky and smells like—*ugh, stop it*!

It's a darned good thing I have that date with Jack tomorrow. I'm about a second away from rubbing up against a tree. Would it be completely inappropriate to invite a stranger back to my house after coffee? I'm starting to think it's going to be the only way to get over this ridiculous infatuation.

"Next time, I'll have to make sure you're well aware when I drop by." His lips slide into a devious smirk.

I should be terrified. He's basically just admitted to breaking into my home and has now promised to return. Only, I'm not. Instead, embarrassing dampness coats my fresh panties.

"Have a good day at work, Maisy. And I urge you to get that ankle looked at. Unless you'd like to make these drives to work a daily occurrence." He winks and whirls around, sauntering down the sidewalk toward Central Park.

My traitorous gaze follows his dark form, those broad

shoulders that taper down to a narrow waist and slim hips. And that perfect butt, like two ripe apples hidden beneath sleek slacks.

Oh, golly, the worst has happened: I'm in lust with Nico Rossi.

CHAPTER 7
PSYCHOS

N *ico*

The fact that Maisy refused my offer for a ride only fuels my anger as I stalk down the quiet alleyway in the Lower East Side. I should be happy she accepted a lift from Max at least, but her riding with my driver doesn't improve my odds at winning her over. And I must have her.

I've never felt the desire to possess a woman like I do with her.

I close my eyes and envision her splayed across the couch when I snuck into her home last night. It took every ounce of willpower not to shove the hem of that little black dress up to her waist, rip her panties off and dive into that warm pussy.

Because despite her protestations, I know she'd be wet and eager for my cock. That little Miss Maisy has a naughty side, I'm certain of it. And I can't wait to drag it out of her.

A door creaks open at the end of the alley, drawing my attention from thoughts of Maisy to the matter at hand. My meeting with Qian Guo, the third leg of the infamous Triad, and the head of the Four Seas. They've been making strategic moves into the Lower East Side for the past few months, pushing their way into Red Dragon territory. The three gangs that make up the Chinese Triad are no more stable than the Italian families who rule Manhattan.

Each alliance is as tenuous as a spider's silk, delicately woven to maintain a fragile balance between power, distrust, and the ever-present threat of betrayal in the ruthless underworld we navigate.

And I'm moments away from annihilating that delicate balance.

The guy at the door wears navy blue from head to toe, only a tiny slit showing his dark eyes, and a cowl covering his head. He motions for me to enter, and I follow him into the old brick building.

Qian Guo sits atop a velvet settee in the center of the sprawling warehouse with three scantily clad women draped over his broad form. House music blares in the background, and I'm not sure if I've walked into an underground night club or a business meeting. Qian's bald head glistens beneath the dim light, a long, black braid plaited down his shoulder. The sight is so at odds with what I'd expected, my mask of composure must slip.

A slow smile crawls across his thin lips as he regards me. "You must have been expecting my father." He slaps one of the females on the ass, mutters something in Mandarin, and the three of them scamper away.

I counter his bemused expression with a tight grin of my own. "I was."

"Be assured my word is as good as my sire's. He's long been waiting to retire, and the time is now upon us."

"I would love to hear it from his own lips."

Qian nods into a dark corner, and a form peels away from the shadows. Another male in all navy marches into the light holding an ornate silver box. The metal glimmers beneath the hanging pendant as he hands it over to the big male.

Qian pulls a necklace from underneath his muscle shirt and reveals a small silver key. Sliding it into the slot in the box, a hidden door opens. He slowly turns the metal container toward me, and it takes every ounce of that carefully honed control to keep my expression neutral.

The elder Qian Guo stares back at me, eyes vacant, and mouth twisted into a look of pure horror.

Mother fucker. The Triad psycho is keeping his dead father's head in a box?

I clear my throat and tug at my collar. I've seen a lot of fucked up things in my day, but to murder your own father? I can't say I never thought of it, or even dreamt of it more than once. To see the great Umberto Valentino begging for mercy as I press a knife to his throat while I force him to confess all his dirty secrets... God that would have been so satisfying. But even I wasn't capable of patricide.

"As you can see, Nico, my word is as good as my father's." Qian's voice draws me back to the present.

"Your word might be, but clearly your manners are not, Mr. Guo."

He nods slowly. "My apologies, *Mr.* Rossi. I meant no disrespect. I'm simply trying to modernize this ancient organization I now find myself at the head of."

No wonder there's been rumors of the Four Seas taking over Red Dragon turf. This new power has gone to Qian's head. I'm not sure I want to be involved with a loose cannon novice. Then again, the guy's got balls.

"Now, shall we get down to business, Mr. Rossi?"

I chew on the inside of my cheek, contemplating my options. The Kings have allied themselves with the Red Dragons and together, they could challenge all the headway I've made in lower Manhattan. An alliance with the weakest members of the Triad, Hao Wei's Golden Star, wouldn't help me at all. Their hold on the outer boroughs is tenuous at best, and the mainland is all that truly matters anyway.

Qian is my best option at finally destroying the Kings.

Gritting my teeth, I mutter, "That's what we're here for, right?"

I stand outside the urgent care center, waiting like a fucking fool. Normally, I would barge right in there and check on Maisy, but with patient confidentiality and all that bullshit, I can't risk it. Sullying the Gemini Corp CEO's name is not something I can afford right now. Not when I've come so far.

Marco and I have investors to please, a shit ton of loans to repay and our entire future riding on the success of the company. We built it from the ground up, hoarding away every last penny. I lucked out in college when I discovered I had a thing for coding. I developed a high-tech security app with a simple cell phone interface. It was cheap and easy to use, and the average Joe ate it up. With Marco's smooth-talking charm, he sold the shit out of it. A year later, one of the big players in the security industry bought it and suddenly, we went from working two part time jobs to scrounge our way through college to a substantial nest egg.

We used that money to start Gemini Corp, in an industry I purposely picked to compete against the Kings. I lied earlier, Maisy technically wasn't the first person I'd stalked. I'd spent countless years in the shadows collecting intel on my half-brothers.

My father, I barely knew.

When Mamma sent us here from Italy, we were only kids. She'd banked on the deluded assumption that Papà would welcome us into his family. Spoiler alert: it never happened. Instead, we spent a year with my Ma's second cousin and when she died, we ended up in foster care. It took me years to find the asshole who'd abandoned us. Mamma had never given us a name, nothing. By the time I figured it out, Umberto Valentino was dead and gone.

But I did find Dante and Luca.

At twenty-two, I made it my mission to destroy them.

It was painful as all hell watching my half-brother Luca rise to meteoric success. But I bided my time, and now here we are... a few more calculated moves and we'll surpass King Industry's holdings.

A smile curls my lip as I imagine the look on Luca's face when I rip away his precious company our Papà built all those years ago.

A flash of crimson jerks my attention across the street. Maisy staggers through the front door of the urgent care center on crutches.

Fuck. A swirl of unexpected guilt carves into my insides. It's my fault she's hurt. She twisted that ankle running away from me.

I sprint across the street, my feet moving before I can stop them. A taxi blares his horn as I dart in front of the yellow cab and narrowly miss getting nailed by the front end of his bumper.

Maisy's eyes widen as I jump in front of her, her pretty pink lips curving into a capital O. She stumbles back and the crutches go flying. I barely get my arm around her waist in time to keep her from hitting the ground. Dragging her toward me to steady her flailing arms, I tuck her into my chest.

My heart jackhammers against my ribs at her proximity. Her sweet vanilla scent mingles with the ever-present orchid.

"What are you doing here?" she sputters. Her lips are so close I can almost taste the cherries from her lip balm. Fuck, I *need* to taste her.

"Giving you a ride home." *Merda*, a rough edge laces my tone, and I can already feel myself hardening against her pinstriped pencil skirt. I glance at the minute space between us and with my height over her, my cock is nearly pinned against her blouse.

"You can't keep doing this." Maisy's palms press against my black button-down, but the rapid rise and fall of her chest gives her away. She's as affected by me as I am by her.

"Saving you?" The hint of a smirk curls the corner of my lip.

"No, stalking me like a psycho! Dang it, Nico, you're everywhere. I blink and you appear. When I'm at home or at work, I'm constantly looking over my shoulder. You're driving me crazy…"

"In a good way?"

"No!" She huffs out a breath.

"How were you planning on getting home?"

She shrugs. "Oh, I don't know, an Uber like a normal person?"

"You are not a normal person."

"No?"

"You are a goddess, and you should be treated as one."

Her eyes grow so wide, they're more luminescent than the most brilliant emeralds. Crimson coats her cheeks, and God, she's stunning. I can only imagine what she'll look like splayed across my bed as I fuck her from here to kingdom come.

She swallows hard, her throat bobbing.

"Just let me take you home. Then I swear I'll go." *For now.*

Her head dips, and she drags her tongue across her bottom lip. "Fine."

A growl vibrates my throat with the effort to keep from capturing her mouth and making those pouty lips mine. Instead, I reach into my pocket, while keeping one arm locked around her waist and shoot off a quick message to Max.

Her crutches are still strewn across the sidewalk, but I don't move. I'm too enraptured by the feel of her in my arms, and the unexpected rush of emotion it brings. I'm entirely unprepared.

I finally force myself to release her and take a step back, keeping one hand on her waist to keep her steady. "Hold still, I'll get your crutches and Max will be here in a moment."

She nods again, and I can practically feel her holding her tongue.

What is she thinking? I'd give anything to know.

Do I still frighten her?

I'm certain there's something more in that hypnotic gaze. Or maybe I'm completely delusional.

The rumble of an approaching engine jerks my attention to the approaching BMW. Max jumps out and rounds the car, opening the back door. I hand him the crutches and scoop Maisy into my arms.

She lets out a squeal but shockingly doesn't resist.

"Let's go home, little fox."

CHAPTER 8
HAPPY PILLS

M*aisy*

Nico glides across the living room, a glass of water clutched in his hand, with a fluidity of motion that should be impossible for a man his size. The familiarity that he has with my home is terrifying, while in the same vein oddly comforting. He looks good here. Dang good.

Oh, golly, I've clearly lost my mind. It must be the pain meds they gave me at the urgent care. It might only be a sprain, but my ankle hurts like a mother trucker. I close my eyes, and my world goes topsy turvy. A giggle escapes as I reopen them and find Nico watching me from across the kitchen island.

He cocks a dark brow, and darn dang it, he looks yummy enough to eat. Oh my gosh, what is in this bottle? I reach for the pain pills and stare at the white label. *Take with food.*

Yup, that's definitely the problem. I left in such a rush this morning, I didn't make my lunch and then I'd remained holed up in my office in a futile attempt at avoiding said mobster staring me down from across the room.

"Are you okay, little fox?"

"Shh-shure thing…" Oh lordy, am I slurring?

He stalks toward me, the faint crease between his dark brows deepening. "Then why are you looking at me like that?"

"Like what?" *A tasty burger I want to sink my teeth into.* Another burst of laughter explodes despite my best efforts to keep my big mouth shut.

Nico is hovering over me a second later, then folds down beside me, his dark slacks nearly brushing my skirt. An electric current surges between our thighs, and every nerve in my body is acutely aware of his proximity. What sorcery is this? His eyes remain locked on mine as he continues his lethal scrutiny. "Like you've become the stalker and I, your prey."

"Ah, ha, so you admit it! You are stalking me?" I jab a finger into his chest and regret it immediately. Man, those sessions at Palestra sure are working out for him.

He shakes his head, an unfairly attractive smile parting his perfect lips. "I prefer the term keeping an eye on you for your own safety."

It's the second time he's mentioned my safety. The first time, I blew it off as bull honky but now, I can't help but worry. I spin around to face him and crisscross my legs. "Why wouldn't I be safe?" My voice rises an embarrassing few notches.

"It's nothing," he mutters.

"Liar, liar pants on fire." I slap my hand over my mouth once the singsong is out. Oh, shitzu, what is wrong with me? All the words just keep spilling out without my control.

A real smile slashes across Nico's face, and it's the most beautiful thing I've ever seen. I'm about a second away from running to the mirror to make sure I don't have hearts bursting from my eyes. Yup, I've completely lost it.

"Tell me," I whine.

His lips purse as he regards me. "Not yet, little fox, but maybe one day if you're good."

"Good?" I squeak. "What does that mean?"

A wicked grin brightens those crystalline orbs, and my mouth goes dry in anticipation. His gaze flickers to the portrait he painted on my mantel. "Let me paint you… nude."

Fiery heat rises up my neck, diffuses across my cheeks and surges to the tips of my ears until I'm certain my face must match the deep red of my hair. "Are you out of your effing mind?" There aren't enough happy pills in this entire bottle to make me agree to that.

"Absolutely not. On the contrary, I've never been thinking so clearly in my life. And, I'm quite certain you'd enjoy it."

I snort on a laugh. The horrifying sound has my cheeks burning, and now I'm probably the shade of a tomato. "Not happening, buddy."

He smirks and leans back on the couch, stretching his arm behind my shoulders. "We'll see about that."

I eye him as he gets comfy on my sofa. I may not be operating at full capacity, but my brain isn't muddled enough to actually let him stay with me. Despite how good he looks sprawled across the floral pattern. His dark suit, his entire dark demeanor, is in such contrast to the light, colorful feel of my living room.

"Um, you can go now," I blurt.

"Why would I do that?"

"Well, you can't stay here."

"You're clearly not well, little fox. I won't leave you in such a vulnerable position."

"I'm not completely inept, and I have a security system." Which Nico apparently trampled right past last night. "And a gun." Dang it! Stupid loose lips.

"Good, I hope you know how to use it."

I don't. But I'm not admitting that to my stalker. Dante

gave it to me before he and Rose left for their pre-wedding honeymoon as a precaution. It sits in my nightstand, but the idea of using it makes my skin crawl.

"I can teach you if you'd like."

My head whips back and forth so quickly my head spins. Uh, oh, bad idea. Really bad. A wave of nausea unfurls, and my gut clenches. I jump up in an attempt to make a mad dash to the bathroom, but my ankle gives out despite the supportive bandage, and I stumble.

An iron band clamps around my belly, keeping me upright, but also forcing the roiling contents of my stomach up my throat. I keel over and spew the paltry insides of my gut all over the gleaming wood floor.

Since I'd barely eaten today, it's mostly liquid and the splatter has some range. I glance down, completely mortified, at Nico's black dress shoes covered in vomit. Oh, kill me now.

"Easy, little fox, I've got you." Nico's warm breath tickles the shell of my ear as he stands over me, still holding me upright. He holds my hair back, fisting it in one hand while his arm remains tight around my waist.

I want to die. I shoot up a quick prayer to any god willing to listen for the ground to open up and swallow me whole. My stomach heaves one last time before I attempt to straighten and wipe the saliva from my chin.

"You shouldn't have taken those pain pills on an empty stomach."

"Now you tell me," I mumble.

"Come on, let's get you cleaned up." He scoops me into his arms like I weigh nothing, and it occurs to me I'm getting way too comfortable with this move. I don't even fight him this time.

He carries me toward the spiral staircase, and I point to the second floor. "My bathroom is that way."

"I know."

A chill skitters up my spine. Of course, he knows, because he's a freaking stalker and I've willingly let him into my home this time. I am such an idiot. But with my head spinning like this, I'm not sure I'd make it up by myself without breaking another bone.

Nico marches through my townhouse like he's intimately familiar with each nook and cranny. He opens the double doors to my bedroom with one hand and walks straight to the attached bath.

I should be scared. Any normal person would be. How many times has he been here? Has he watched me sleep? Another tremor rolls up my spine.

"Are you cold?" He dips his eyes to mine, and our noses nearly touch.

"Yup," I lie. I must show no fear. Isn't that a thing with wild animals? And Nico Rossi is as wild and unpredictable as they come.

"Then let's get you out of these clothes and into a warm bath."

"Out of my *clothes*?" I squeal as he walks us into the master bathroom.

A teasing grin curls his lips. "It is generally how one bathes, isn't it?"

"Don't even think you're going to paint me while I take a bath, you crazy stalker."

A deep chuckle rumbles his chest, shaking me along with it. "No, not today, little fox, but soon." He lowers me onto the edge of the marble tub and spins on the faucet, then he turns to me, his gaze predatory. "Shall I help you out of that blouse?"

"In your dreams."

"You're right." He smirks again, and I wish that arrogant lift of his lips wasn't so darned attractive. "I spend most nights lately pleasuring myself as I picture your pussy wrapped tight around my cock."

A gasp explodes from my lips, and fiery heat races across my cheeks then doubles back to my lower half and settles between my legs. Good golly, I've never heard anyone with such a mouth. Nor have I ever been so turned on.

A sinful chuckle echoes over the rushing water as he stands. "As much as I would like to stay and watch you strip down into your lace lingerie, I can see you're not ready. But I promise, you will be soon. Before long, I'll have you splayed across that bed, bare before me. You'll beg me for another orgasm, and another and another. And if you're a good girl, I'll give it to you, again and again."

I stare up at him, my jaw practically unhinged. First of all, how does he know about my lace lingerie? All the moisture evaporates from my mouth and travels to my lusty cooter. Because somehow, I believe him. I'm quite certain Nico Rossi would be capable of giving me the one thing no other man has.

He crouches down beside me, and my ragged breaths catch in my throat. "Get some rest, little fox. I'll be back soon." Brilliant irises pierce mine as he cups my cheek and runs a calloused thumb across my skin. Before I can muster a word, let alone a sentence, he whirls around and stalks out.

The minute he's gone, my entire body deflates. I run through the last few hours, my mind reeling. I puked on Nico Rossi's shoes. An insane fit of the giggles has me buckling over, and I'm so distracted the water in the tub nearly spills over.

"Oh, crap!" I slide to the opposite end of the basin and turn off the faucet just in time.

As I start to unbutton my blouse, a pair of mesmerizing sapphire eyes fill my vision. Instead of my own fingers, I imagine his peeling off my clothes. That heat burns low in my belly, and I blink quickly, chasing away the completely inappropriate thoughts. If I could walk, I'd unwrap that present Rose ordered for me. I still hadn't taken that bad boy for a spin.

I'm delirious, clearly. I need rest and tomorrow, I'll be as good as new. I just have to find a way to stay far away from Nico Rossi.

CHAPTER 9
THE BEST DREAM

N*ico*

Shards of moonlight creep through the sliver between the heavy velvet curtains and lance across Maisy's milky white flesh. The thick, oppressive drapes are so at odds with the rest of her bedroom and the light, airy feel. The reason is so heartbreakingly clear it stabs at my cold heart, jerking it to life and forcing it to pump again. She's trying to keep someone out.

And as arrogant as I often am, I'm fairly certain it isn't me.

No, it's her abusive, asshole ex, Jasper.

Those weeks I kept him captive were quite enlightening. He used to brag about all the passive-aggressive, devious ways he tortured his wife, keeping her bound to him. Abuse comes in all forms, not always physical. Bit by bit, he'd destroyed her self-confidence and made her feel weak and useless.

After only a few hours with my little fox, I realize how wrong he was. How he could undervalue such an incredible creature is beyond me. I stalk closer, inching toward her bed. My heart kicks at my ribs with each step, the predator inside me pulsing to life at the thrill of my prey sprawled across the soft linen.

Her pale pink negligée is scandalous, soft silk caressing porcelain flesh and peaked nipples that barely extends to her upper thigh. A woman who sleeps in a nightgown like that wants to be fucked. She may not know it yet, but she's ready to move on from that bastard. And I will be that man for her.

I kneel at the side of her bed, right in front of her nightstand where I've left another gift - an orchid this time, an extremely rare one. The ghost orchid with its stark white color seems to float in the darkness. But no flower no matter the fragrance compares to her. My nostrils flare at her enticing scent. That sweet perfume of the flowers that fill her home mingle with her naturally tempting aroma and seep from each and every fine pore. I lean closer and sweep back a lock of auburn hair, pinning it behind her delicate ears.

A breathy sigh parts her lips at my gentle touch.

That faint sound has me instantly hard. *Cazzo*, this woman. I've always had a thing for redheads, but this obsession is unnatural. I allow my hand to linger along her cheek, running my thumb across her satin skin.

Even asleep, she leans into my touch. *Dio*, how I crave her, how I long to possess her. She shifts and the thin strap of her negligée falls down her shoulder revealing the perfect swell of her breast. For such a petite woman, her breasts are exquisite, full and curvy and just made for my palms.

My cock strains against my slacks, and I regret not going home to change into something more comfortable before coming here. Had I known I was to spend all night watching Maisy sleep, I would have put on some sweatpants. At least this way my erection wouldn't be so damned painful.

Too late now.

I chase the pointless thought away and focus on the beautiful woman before me. Next time, I'll bring my paints and a canvas. The way the light spills over her perfect form is truly breathtaking. My fingers twitch, the sight of her just begging to be captured in a portrait. Instead, I quell my artistic cravings by running a finger down her throat, then across her collarbone. Lingering just above her breasts, I'm practically salivating as I imagine my tongue replacing that finger.

I'm certain Maisy will taste like sweet cherries and sweeter redemption.

The quiet ones are always the most sinful, and the most satisfying to break. Once she gives into me, there will be no return. Descending into the depths of hell is a one-way trip for most. I crawled and clawed my way back from the inferno, and I have no intentions of ever going back.

Burying the dismal thoughts to the dark corners of my psyche, I focus on my little fox, on the gentle rise and fall of her chest. I run my finger between her breasts, repressing every carnal urge to graze her peaked nipples and blaze a path down her silk nightie.

As I reach the indecent hemline, her breaths quicken. I hazard a quick look up, but her eyes remain closed. I toy with the soft negligée then my fingers dance past the material to her bare leg.

Another faint sigh steals between her pink lips. It only urges me on.

I trace a path toward her inner thigh, running my fingertip oh so lightly across her sensitive skin. Goose bumps ripple across her flesh and she squirms beneath my touch, trapping my finger between her legs. Her hips begin to rock against my finger, and I barely repress a groan as her wet panties brush my skin.

My eyes lift to meet hers, but still, they're closed. Fuck. An instant of indecision keeps my finger still. I've crossed many lines in my lifetime, but I've never finger-fucked a woman in her sleep. But shit, do I want to.

"Mmm, Nico..." Maisy's breathy moan sends my gaze shooting up. Her bottom lip is snagged between her teeth as her hips continue to move, but still her eyes remain shut. Damn, those pain pills were strong enough to put down an elephant. I've never seen anything like this. Is she dreaming about me? Imagining my cock buried deep in that beautiful pussy? "Nico..."

My name on her lips once again serves as confirmation. My finger inches across her panties, stroking her center and she lets out another soft moan. *Dio*, that sound has a direct link to my cock. A few more of those sexy noises, and I'll come without even touching myself.

But why deny myself the pleasure?

As she rubs her pussy against my fingers, I unbuckle my pants with my free hand and slide my palm over my cock. I imagine Maisy's dainty fingers stroking my shaft, and a dribble of cum moistens my fingers. I stroke faster and my own hips begin to move as I picture my cock thrusting into that tight little pussy hidden beneath the lace.

She's so wet my fingers glide across her panties as if she were bare. Damn, this is a true test of my willpower. I'm fairly certain I could rip that scrap of lace right off and plow into her and not only would she allow it, she'd fucking love it.

"Mmm..." Another one of her groans has me so close to release I feel like a teenager again. God, what I wouldn't give to know what she's dreaming about right now. And will she remember any of this?

Her hips thrust to meet my fingers, her movements growing more agitated much like my own. She's close. Focusing on her, I slide my finger to her clit, easy enough to find even over her panties and circle the swollen nub. She lets out a moan, perfect lips curved into a capital O, and her cheeks a tantalizing cherry red that match her silky locks. Her cries spill out, eyes still closed as she comes on my fingers.

The feel of her, along with those tantalizing sounds, are all it takes to push me over the edge. I throttle my cock as warm cum streams into my hand, and all the air rips from my lungs. I ride the wave of ecstasy with my fingers still clenched between Maisy's thighs.

When I finally come down from the thrilling high, I gently untangle my hand from her limbs and reach for a tissue on the nightstand. After I've cleaned myself off, I toss the paper in the trash and zip up my pants. I still can't take my eyes off her. That rosy hue still lingers on her cheeks, and I can only imagine how incredible she'll look when I coax an orgasm out of her when she's awake.

Soon...

Her body's reaction to mine is primal, even unconscious. That sort of attraction cannot be contained. Maisy may not want to admit there's something between us, but her hungry pussy can't lie.

I bring my finger to my nose and breathe her in. Musky and sweet just like I'd imagined her. Then I pop that finger into my mouth and swirl my tongue around it. Mmm, heaven.

"Nico?" A soft, raspy voice sends my heart shooting up my throat.

With my finger still in my mouth, I meet those curious eyes. Some of the liveliness is gone, a sleepy glaze over the bright emerald. Releasing my finger, I drop down beside her on the bed. "Shh, it's okay, little fox, go back to sleep."

"I just had the *best* dream..." A silly grin curls the corners of her lips. "And you were in it." She snorts on a laugh as I tuck the comforter up to her chin. "Obviously, it was a dream. I would *never* let you touch me like that." Her eyes meet mine again, but they're glossy and unfocused. "Or let you into my bedroom."

"Of course not, little fox."

I run my hand through her soft hair and unexpected emotion tightens my chest as her eyes close.

"You are a bad man, Nico Rossi, and I should not be having

naughty dreams about you." She buries her head into the pillow, still smiling. "Especially not when I have a date tomorrow morning with another man," she mumbles.

Raw fury surges through my veins and spreads through my chest. "Another man?" I growl.

"With Jack from the park of course…" Her words fall away, and her eyes slide closed despite my nudging.

That motherfucker.

I jerk my phone from my pants pocket and type out a message to my tech guy, Riley. I need access to Maisy's phone to find out everything about this date. I could do it myself, but he'll be faster. Glancing at the clock on the nightstand, I let out a curse. It's nearly dawn. That doesn't give me much time to find out everything about this Jack Dawson man before I gut him like a fish.

No one gets to play with *my* toy and live.

CHAPTER 10
YOU AGAIN?

M*aisy*

A trickle of sunlight seeps through the heavy curtain and pries my eyes open. I wake up with an unexpected smile on my face. Hmm, I had the *best* night of sleep. Inspecting the French windows just a few feet from my bed, I make a mental note to shut them all the way tonight, so the early-morning sun doesn't wake me tomorrow. Plus, with so many high rises in Manhattan the last thing I need is a peeping Tom. After Rose's drama with a stalker and now my own issues with Nico, I should just have hurricane shutters installed all around the brownstone.

No, I refuse to spend my life in a cage.

I shove the comforter back and scoot to the edge of the bed, and unexpected dampness lingers between my thighs. *What the…?* A swirl of heat kindles low in my belly and the dream—no nightmare—from last night flits to the forefront of my mind.

Oh, my gosh... Another wave of heat flares as vivid images of Nico's fingers between my legs consume my thoughts. Good lordy, what was in those pain meds? It felt so real. I tug on the waistband of my panties and check out my cooter. Yup, she definitely thought it was real.

Wow, I really need to get laid.

Sliding off the mattress, I hobble to the crutches perched at the foot of my bed. Wait a second... I don't remember those being there last night. Shoving away the lusty dream, I try to focus. I vaguely recall Nico carrying me up the stairs and depositing me into the tub. Everything else is a big blur.

No way he came back. There is no possible way that dream was real, right?

Leaning on one of the crutches, I drag my hands over my face and let out a huff. No pain meds for me today. The last thing I need is to make a bad impression on my first date in a decade. With Jack. A perfectly nice guy and the complete opposite of the obsessive mafioso.

Today is going to be great. A fresh start is exactly what I need. Goodbye clumsy, beaten-down Maisy Whitaker and hello, single bombshell Maisy Jordan. Not only had I dropped my married name, but I'd freed myself from the oppressive binds of my illustrious parents' last name, Vanderbilt, and assumed my middle name, Jordan, as my official surname. Now, if I can only figure out how to use these things.

I stuff a crutch under each of my armpits and wobble toward the bathroom.

You can do this, Maisy.

Jack sits across the table from me, his silky blonde hair perfectly gelled to soft waves. A warm smile spreads his lips as he gazes down at me from over the rim of his coffee mug. "So you said you work at a gym?"

"Umhmm." I place my cup down, and my elbow hits one of the crutches propped against my chair. "Oh, sugar!" I cry as it falls on top of the table beside us and knocks over an older gentleman's coffee. "I'm so sorry!" I try to stand, but my bad ankle wobbles, and I fall back on my butt.

"Hold on, I've got this." Jack shoots up, grabs some napkins, and starts to wipe down the man's table. He's grumbling and looks pissed as all heck.

"I'm so sorry," I mumble again. "Let me get you another one."

"Maisy, sit, relax. I'll take care of it." Jack flashes the grumpy man a beaming smile and the tight set of his jaw softens a fraction. "What can I get you, sir?"

"Decaf with cream," he grumbles.

Ugh. What a boring coffee. And he's freaking out about that? What's the point of even drinking the stuff without the caffeine?

My gaze trails after Jack's tall, lean form as he marches to the counter and orders the man another coffee. I can practically feel Mr. Grumpy's hateful glare searing into the side of my face.

After Jack hands the new mug of piping hot liquid gold to Mr. Grumpy, his hatred seems to simmer. My date folds into the chair across from me once again, and his easy smile returns. "Now, where were we?"

"Um, I was about to tell you about my amazing job at Palestra."

"Oh, I've heard of that health club. Super elite. That must be a fun place to work."

My thoughts flicker to Nico, unbidden, to the stolen glimpses I've gotten of the bare-chested, tattooed Italian god working out on the weight floor. "Yup, tons of fun." I take a careful sip of my latte, careful not to knock anything over and cause another disaster. "What do you do?"

"I'm a teacher. I've been imparting my words of wisdom to

the lucky kindergarteners over at The Anderson School in the Upper West Side for the last five years."

My heart actually melts a little. A super hot guy who loves kids? This man must have fallen straight from heaven right into my lap.

"It's really rewarding work—"

"I bet it is." A familiar deep timbre sends my fluttering heart into freefall.

I spin around and piercing azure orbs meet mine. The easy-going, flirty man who carried me up to my bedroom yesterday afternoon is gone, replaced by a snarling devil. His nostrils flare as he glares down at Jack, those blazing eyes shooting daggers.

"You again?" Jack slowly lowers his mug, like any sudden movements might startle the massive beast looming over our table.

"Funny, I was about to say the same thing." Nico steals a chair from Mr. Grumpy and drags it beside me. His thigh brushes mine and even through the dark slacks, I can feel the tremor of rage coursing through his body. His teeth are clenched, a tendon in his jaw vibrating beneath the scruff. Iron fingers latch around my knee, and I jump, barely suppressing a squeal. "My apologies," he growls, eyes intent on my date, who I'm fairly certain has started to tremble. "Perhaps I wasn't clear when we met last time, that was my mistake."

"Clear about?" Jack asks.

Nico's glare pivots, those eyes lancing across my cheek. "About Maisy. She's *mine*." He turns that searing gaze to Jack and pulls a knife from his pocket. Then he drags it across the scruff of his cheek. The slow, deliberate scrape sends goose bumps rippling down my arms. "If I see you near her again, I'll carve your eyes out for daring to look at what's mine."

A gasp escapes, but I'm too shocked to string together a sentence.

Jack's eyes widen until they're bulging out of his head. "Are you insane?"

"Maybe." Nico shoots my horrified date a wink.

I should be appalled. This man just threatened a stranger's life for looking at me. Instead, the possessive edge to his tone has my inner vixen purring. What the blazes is wrong with me?

Finally gathering my wits from the puddle on the floor, I jab my elbow into Nico's side. "I'm sorry, Jack, you'll have to excuse my friend. He was dropped on his head a lot as a child and thinks he's funny." I glare at the psychopath beside me. "What are you doing?" I hiss in his ear.

"I told you not to go out with him."

Wrapping my fingers around Nico's big hand, I haul him up to his feet. "Excuse me, Jack, I need a minute with my friend." I plaster on what I'm sure must look like a slightly unhinged smile.

"Um, okay."

The poor man must think I'm insane too.

Wobbling on one crutch, I drag Nico to the narrow corridor that leads to the restrooms, which is no easy feat by the way since I'm five feet soaking wet, have a sprained ankle, and the man is a beast. Once we're out of sight, I pin the mobster to the wall and jab my finger into his ridiculously firm chest. "What do you think you're doing?"

"Friend? Is that what I am, little fox?" he answers, completely ignoring my question. A feral grin curls his lip. "Because there was nothing friendly about the sounds I coaxed out of you last night when you came all over my fingers."

The air punches from my ribs, and I let out a sharp gasp. My crutch falls to the floor with an obnoxiously loud crash. "What?"

Nico clucks his tongue. "Don't tell me you don't remember?" His hands close around my shoulders, and he spins us around so now I'm the one trapped against the wall.

I swallow hard, panic's claws lacing around my chest. No. It can't be. It was a dream.

He inches closer, his warm breath spilling across the shell of my ear. "You were so wet you soaked your panties for me." He slips his index finger into his mouth, and his cheeks hollow. "Mmm, I can still taste you, little fox. Just like sweet summer cherries."

"Oh, my lordy," I rasp out. This can't be happening. I should be mortified, no, I should have him arrested for assault. Instead, fire shoots through my core as muddled memories rise to the surface. My hips rocking against his palm, those piercing blue eyes scorching through me... *Sugar*! I *wanted* him.

His hands flatten against the wall, so I'm caged between two powerful, tattooed biceps. The full length of his body is flush against mine, a stiff erection prodding at my belly. "And before you panic, little fox, rest assured I was a perfect gentleman." A wicked smirk lights up his mesmerizing irises. "Well, almost. I couldn't resist fucking my own palm as I watched you find your release. But at least I kept my hands to myself. Mostly."

Good golly that was the best orgasm I'd ever had, and I thought it was a dream. And he'd managed all that *over* my panties?

"Now, back to the matter at hand." His nose nudges mine, warm breath inches from my lips. "You disobeyed me. I told you not to see Jack and here you are. I'm going to have to punish you now."

My breath hitches. "P-punish?"

"That's right, little fox."

Genuine fear punches my ribcage until my breaths come in ragged pants. He must notice the change from the false bravado because the hard line of his jaw softens.

"You know what? I changed my mind. I'll be lenient

because you're new to this game, and I'll allow Jack to take your punishment on your behalf."

"What are you going to do to him?" I squeal.

"You'll see." He finally releases me and takes a step back. My entire body sags forward at the sudden loss of his. "Now, go say goodbye to Jack and tell him that you will not be seeing him again."

Some unknown force snaps my spine straight, and I glare up at the psycho, palms slapped against my hips. "And if I don't?"

"I'll gift you his cock in a box."

I inhale sharply at the gruesome image. "You wouldn't…"

"Try me." Nico flashes me a sinful smirk. "One less douchebag on the streets of Manhattan, and I'd be doing every single woman a favor."

"What does that mean?"

His lips twist in disgust. "You should really do your research before agreeing to a date with a stranger, little fox. One would think you would've learned your lesson after Jasper but—" Nico shakes his head. "Luckily, you have me." He spins on his heel and marches toward the front of the café. I stand there, numb, feet rooted to the spot.

Mother trucker, what had I gotten myself into?

CHAPTER 11
TOYING WITH MY PREY

N*ico*

Screams echo behind me as I stalk out of the small studio in the Upper West Side, my gloved hands slick with blood. I'd spent nearly twenty-four hours toying with my prey, but now I had somewhere else to be. As soon as the door slams behind me, I scan the hallway for the trash chute. Anger still pounds through my veins, but now that I've slaked my thirst for revenge the monster begins to recede. Finally finding the garbage drop, I rip the latex gloves off, carefully holding the Ziploc bag with my prize.

Despite Maisy agreeing not to see Jack again, I decided a piece of shit like him deserved the full force of my wrath. I never promised I wouldn't hurt him after all...

Jack will never have the chance to ogle my girl again.

Or any other woman for that matter.

I pat the thumb drive in my pocket, confirming it's still there before I jab my finger at the elevator call button. I'm late for a meeting with the commissioner, and Marco's going to be pissed, but this couldn't wait.

The fury that scorched through my system at the sight of Maisy with another man was like nothing I'd ever felt before. *Cazzo*, what was this woman doing to me? I hadn't even fucked her yet and already I was out of my mind for her.

My nostrils flare at the vivid memories of Maisy sprawled across her bed, writhing for me. Coming *for me*. I'll have to pay her another visit tonight after I drop off my little gift. I lift up the clear bag, and a pair of vacant eyeballs stare back at me.

Twisted fucker.

To think he was going to film himself with my Maisy and spread it across the internet. If he would've succeeded there would've been nothing left but his eyes. Instead, I granted him a mercy. Or maybe I only rewarded him with a lifetime of torture. The ultimate punishment for a sick voyeur. Some of the girls on the videos I found were barely teenagers.

Scum like that deserves to rot in hell. But let good old Jack suffer for a bit first.

When I reach the ground floor, Max is already waiting at the curb. I slide into the backseat and find a box with a bright red bow on the seat beside me. "Thanks for grabbing this, Max."

"No problem, boss." He cants his head back and shoots me a lopsided grin. "Did you buy your girl a present?"

"Something like that."

Turning back around, my driver makes his way across the quiet avenue to the West Side highway. I have to get back to Gemini Tower before the end of the meeting. Though if I'm being honest, Marco is more than equipped to handle the commissioner. He's always been better at managing people than I have.

I crack my knuckles and sit back, leaning my head against the soft leather headrest. Keeping an eye on Maisy is proving more taxing than I'd imagined, but I can't shake the feeling that her ex, Jasper, isn't quite done with her. The numerous sleepless nights are getting to me. My heavy lids slide closed with the steady motion of the car, and I'm pulled into the darkness.

I shoot straight up in bed. The air is thick with acrid smoke, and the crackling flames roar like an enraged beast. "Marco?" *Panic claws at my chest as I push myself out of bed and stumble through the billowing darkness, my throat tightening with each labored breath. The heat presses in on all sides, an oppressive force that wraps around me, threatening to engulf everything in its path.*

Flames dance along the walls of the bedroom I share with my brother, casting eerie shadows that flicker and contort, creating a nightmarish ballet. The once-familiar surroundings blur into a disorienting haze, and the heat intensifies with every passing second. Orange and red tongues of fire lick at the edges of my vision, leaving a searing imprint on my consciousness.

"Marco, where are you?" I choke and cough around the words.

My heart pounds in my ears, a relentless drumbeat of fear. Panic sets in as the smoke obscures my path, and the crackling inferno devours everything around me. The air becomes a toxic blend of burning debris and desperation, and my eyes sting with unshed tears.

Every step feels like an eternity as I fumble through the choking darkness into the hallway, guided only by the distant glow of the front door that seems both tantalizingly close and impossibly far. The heat, the smoke, the deafening roar—it's a sensory overload that threatens to overwhelm my mind.

Where is everyone? Where are the Fosters?

A desperate sense of survival propels me forward, the instinct to find Marco and escape this fiery nightmare consuming my thoughts. In the midst of chaos, time loses its meaning, and the urgency to break free becomes the only reality. As I approach the door, a surge of cool air offers a momentary reprieve from the suffocating heat, fueling a fleeting glimmer of hope.

A familiar form catches my eye in the living room, and I abandon my trek to safety. "Marco!" I cry out. He doesn't move. "Get up!"

Flames engulf the room, the smoke so thick I'm shocked I found him at all. Dropping to the floor, I crawl across the peeling linoleum, my chest so tight every breath is a desperate struggle. I keep moving, never stop, despite the flames licking at my pajamas.

When I finally reach him, his eyes are closed, face covered in soot. That panic rears up again, strangling my heart. "Marco!" He's the only one I have left. "Wake up, cazzo!*" I wrap my arm around his motionless form and drag him back toward the front door.*

A sharp crack echoes overhead and instinct drives my movements. I splay my body across my brother's an instant before scorching pain razes across my back. A soundless scream tears from my mouth, and I descend into eternal night.

The sharp blare of a horn jolts me from the vivid nightmare, and my eyes snap open. My chest is heaving, sweat beading along my brow and pooling above my upper lip. *Fuck.* I haven't had a nightmare like that in months. I thought the endless years of therapy had finally paid off.

Ghostly flames flicker across my back, and my spine snaps straight. I shrug out of my jacket and toss it to the floor. Some scars would never heal. Despite how many tattoos cover them.

Max slows the car to a halt, and I glance out the tinted window. Shit, how long had I been asleep for? Gemini Tower looms over the BMW, dwarfing the surrounding skyscrapers. Heaving in a deep breath, I search for the calm. This building means everything to me, countless years of perseverance, a symbol of the epic phoenix rising from the ashes.

I jerk the back door open, not waiting for Max to get out. I'm so late I'll be lucky if I catch the tail-end of the meeting. Darting into the lobby, I speed past the reception desk and shoot the woman a smile.

"Happy Monday, boss," she calls out.

"You too, Amber."

Melanie's head pops out from around the corner a second later as I approach the elevator bank, holding the door open.

"Thanks," I mutter as I slip in beside my executive assistant.

"Of course. Marco told me to keep an eye out for you."

"How mad is he?" I toss the assistant my brother and I share a grin.

She shrugs as the elevator zips up to the penthouse. "You know Marco. Nothing really ever gets to him."

From the outside. On the surface, my brother is as charismatic and easy going as they come. All smiles and winks, he can charm any woman into bed, but like me, a monster lies below the surface just waiting to be let loose.

We all have our demons, what differentiates me from my sibling is the way we handle them. I like to let mine loose on joy rides whereas Marco keeps his on a tight leash. One day, it's going to come back and bite him in the ass.

I only hope I'm far away from the fallout zone.

The elevator doors glide open, and I jump out through the crack, heading straight for the conference room. My hand is on the modern black handle when it jerks open, and I nearly barrel into Commissioner Gordon.

I leap back, placing a hand on my chest. "My apologies, commissioner, both for my tardiness and nearly running you down." My lips slide into a practiced smile.

"Nothing to worry about, Nico." The silver-haired snake who's involved in more underhanded dealings than the Kings and Geminis combined turns to my brother behind him. "Marco has handled everything."

I shoot my sibling an appreciative smile, and he counters with a stiff nod. He's pissed, and I don't blame him. I'm the numbers guy, he's the sales guy, but clearly, he's pulled it off.

"Please, excuse me, commissioner, I have a call. It was a pleasure as always." Marco dips his head and disappears down the hallway.

"I said you can't go in there!" Melanie's shriek jerks my attention over my shoulder.

My other recurring nightmare stalks across the foyer. Fucking Dante.

"Commissioner Gordon, what a happy coincidence." My half-brother barrels by my assistant and thrusts his hand at Gordon.

The man flushes bright crimson. For weeks, he's been ruthlessly pursued by Gemini Corp and King Industries for the lucrative new docks project. He'd been under contract with my half-brother's company before all his equipment mysteriously vanished. Conveniently, we were able to swoop in and pinch the deal.

But Dante wasn't giving up that easily.

The commissioner clears his throat as Dante's hold on his hand lingers longer than appropriate. "Ah, *scusi*. Sometimes I forget how fragile the tiny bones of the hand are. So easy to break..." His lips curl into an ominous smile. "Commissioner, I certainly hope you aren't planning to renege on our deal."

"Dante—"

"*Signor* Valentino," he corrects.

I'll give my half-brother one thing, he's got fucking huge balls to threaten one of the most powerful men in New York City.

"Yes, *Signor* Valentino, I'm afraid I cannot wait any longer. Per the original terms of our deal, ground should have been broken by now."

"And it will be. I guarantee the docks project will be completed as scheduled in the original contract."

"I find that highly doubtful given the delays." Gordon shakes his head.

"I concur," I interject.

Dante turns his snarl on me, erasing the distance between us. "No one asked you, *coglione*."

With my younger brother's attention on me, the commissioner makes a run for the elevator. I don't blame the man. Dante can be intimidating as fuck. He's a wild card, a guy that I still haven't quite figured out. He tries to get past me, but I plant my palms on his chest and hold him back until the elevator doors slide closed behind Gordon.

"*Figlio di puttana,*" he mutters through clenched teeth.

Son of a whore? My mother may have abandoned us in this godforsaken country, but she did it to give us a better life. No one talks about my *mamma* like that and lives.

I wrap my fingers around Dante's collar and jerk him closer so our noses nearly touch. "What did you just fucking say, *pezzo di merda?*"

"It's an expression, relax, bro." Dante's dark eyes taper at the edges, and his fingers curl around my jacket's lapel. A glint of gold catches my eye on his ring finger. "Get your fucking hands off me if you want to keep them."

I release him and take a step back, running my hand down my tussled shirt. "I see congratulations are in order. You and that feisty Rose finally tied the knot?"

"Don't you dare say her name," he growls, rage streaking across the dark abyss. I recognize the look well, I've seen its reflection in my own eyes.

"Now who needs to relax, *fratellino*? I have no intention of hurting your precious Rose. Keep your wife, I just want the King's empire."

"Over my fucking dead body."

I shrug. "If you insist. Though I'd hate to make a widow out of Rose so soon."

A dark chuckle erupts from Dante's lips. "Try it and you'll find out I'm a pretty tough bastard to kill." He leans closer, the sharp notes of his cologne burning my nostrils. "And you'll only get one shot." He spins on his heel and stalks toward the elevator, jabbing his finger in the call button. The doors finally slide open, and he jerks his head over his shoulder. "Say hello to this mysterious brother of yours. I'm looking forward to meeting him sooner rather than later."

A faint smile curls the corner of my lip. I'm looking forward to it too. But I'd rather extend the anticipation. It's more fun that way.

CHAPTER 12
A VILE PRESENT

M*aisy*

I hate working from home.

Staring out the window at the brackish waves of the Hudson, I release an exasperated sigh and attempt to refocus on my laptop. With my stupid ankle still healing, I'm stuck at home for at least a week.

Who knew I'd even miss the stench of my fellow commuters on the morning bus ride?

It was exactly for this reason I'd gotten the job at Palestra in the first place. I couldn't just sit around at home all day, despite my generous divorce settlement. And I'd hoped I'd meet new friends, maybe even a guy someday…

My thoughts flicker back to the disastrous date with Jack on Saturday. I'd texted him all day yesterday and hadn't heard a word. Not that I blamed him. Any normal man would run away screaming after how Nico acted.

Stupid, possessive, psychopathic a-hole.

Who gave me the best orgasm of my life.

Just at the thought, warmth floods my traitorous hoo-ha. "Nope, not happening ever again, girl. Get that insane mobster out of your mind."

Yup, I really need to get out of the house. Now I'm talking to my private parts.

The doorbell rings, yanking me from my internal musings. I grab the crutches and stagger to the door. A long minute later, I finally make it and peer through the peephole. A delivery man fills the small circle, flashing a smile. Unlocking the deadbolt, I open the door a crack.

After being kidnapped all those months ago, I never open it all the way anymore.

"Delivery for Ms. Maisy Jordan?"

"Yup, that's me."

The guy hands me a small white box with a big red bow across the top. *Huh*. Well, that's unexpected.

"Thanks," I mutter as I sign the handheld device and tuck the box under my armpit, wobbling on my crutches.

"You got it?" The delivery guy shoots me a smile.

God, these crutches will surely be the death of me. Given my blundering tendencies, they've only heightened my probabilities of disaster a hundred-fold. "Yeah, I'm fine, thanks."

Closing the door, I hobble back into the living room with my present. Maybe it's from Jack... I refuse to acknowledge the more likely candidate because I've promised myself to completely remove the stalking mobster from my mind.

Too bad the same can't be said for my lusty cooter.

Even barely conscious she remembers every sinful touch.

Plopping back down on the couch, I tug on the end of the ribbon. A whisper of excitement quickens my pulse as the bright red bow sloughs off. Inching my finger beneath the tape holding the lid closed, I finally pry it open.

Confetti shoots out, and a faint gasp slips out. With a chuckle, I brush off the colorful dots covering my legs and the floral couch, then dig through the crimson filler paper. My fingers close around a small notecard. Ripping it open, I focus on the elegant handwriting.

I told you not to go out with him, little fox.

A tremor rolls up my spine, and goose bumps cascade across my arms. I grab the crinkly paper by the handfuls until I reach the bottom of the box. A pair of pale blue glassy eyes stare up at me through a small clear container.

I let out a shriek and drop the box. The container pops open, and the eyeballs roll out amidst a sea of crimson shreds of paper. Oh, my God. I clap my hand over my mouth as nausea claws its way up my throat.

It can't be...

Nico wouldn't have...

Would he?

I stare at the mess on my floor, my heart kicking at my ribcage. I try to force in a breath, then another, but my lungs have all but quit on me.

A glint of silver catches my eye within the crimson mess. Summoning my last remaining shards of courage, I crouch down, avoiding the bloody eyeballs and dig through the scraps. My fingers close around a silver thumb drive.

"What in all the world?"

My first impulse should be to call the police. Nico's depraved games must stop. He murdered a man for taking me for coffee! What kind of sick effer does something like that?

But that thumb drive burns in my hand. I need to know what's on it. I can deal with the eyeballs and the man who stole them later.

Hobbling over to my desk, I insert it into my laptop and hold my breath as it fires up. An array of files populates each with a female name and a date. There are literally hundreds of them.

A sickening feeling churns in my gut as I hover the mouse

over the first one. Inhaling a deep breath, I click on the folder, then on one of the mp3 files within. A dark image of two bodies coalesces on the screen and moans fill my living room. *Oh, shitzu*! I frantically jab at the volume button on my laptop until the sounds are nothing more than faint murmurs. Then, squinting, I take a closer look at the male screwing a young girl from behind.

Sugar, honey, iced tea! It's Jack...

I click on another file and another. Each one is worse than the last. Some girls look like teenagers. It's clear from the way he positions each woman, he's posing them for the camera, and from the looks of it, they're completely unaware they're being filmed.

That dirty, no-good, rotten douchebag.

Nico's words from the other morning at the café flit to the forefront of my mind. *You should really do your research before agreeing to a date with a stranger, little fox. One would think you would've learned your lesson after Jasper but luckily, you have me.*

Oh, lordy, he knew. Nico knew exactly what kind of man I was going out with. Why didn't he just warn me? A swell of anger fills my chest, chasing away the fear from a second ago. I was tired of being a pawn in sick men's lives.

Reaching for my phone next to my laptop, I pull up Nico's last message. My fingers fly over the keys as I punch out a scathing text.

Me: You are disgusting. I got your little present and if your intent was to scare me off for good, mission accomplished. You're no better than Jack, Nico Rossi. And if you ever come near me again, I will call the police and have you arrested.

I stare at the screen, my blood boiling, as I await the telltale blue dots.

Only they never come.

That jerk left me on read.

I toss my phone onto the couch and slump back in my chair with a huff. This can't be my life right now. How did I run away from the arms of one psycho only to fall into the clutches of another?

I stare at my computer screen for another few seconds, at the dozens of unanswered emails. Nope. I can't do it. Slamming the laptop closed, I reach for my crutches. I need to get out of this house.

"Thank you so much for coming to meet me." I squeeze Rose's hand on the bench.

"Oh, my gawd, Mais of course. I can't believe you didn't tell me about your ankle sooner. I could've come over to help." She brings her favorite Macha latte to her lips and sucks down a big gulp. "You know my workload has been pretty low since Dante forced me to cut back on my hours at Dr. Winchester's. Overbearing asshole…" she murmurs, but her lips curve into a goofy smile all the same.

She's so insanely happy with Dante it's crazy.

I wave a nonchalant hand. "It's really not necessary, I swear I'm fine." Then I swallow the lie down along with a mouthful of my cappuccino. I wish I could tell my friend about Nico, and Jack, all of it. But she's been through so much herself, I hate to drag her into my drama.

"Wait, so did you get to go on the date with Central Park guy?"

My lips pucker, and I want to smack myself for splattering my emotions across my face.

"What?" Rose's eyes widen. "Tell me everything."

Only I couldn't. How could I tell her that my stalker gouged out the eyes of the first man who'd taken an interest in me since Jasper. Oh, and that my admirer was a slimy pedophile who made videos of every woman he screwed.

Freaking, heck. How did this become my life?

"Maisy?" Rose flashes her hand an inch from my nose. "What's going on?"

"Oh, nothing. Jack was a dud."

"Not a problem, Maisy. You've always got to date a few frogs before you find your prince."

I nearly choke on a laugh.

She reaches for my phone, opens the Love Roulette dating app and starts to scroll. "But no worries, I'll find you someone."

"No!" I blurt and snatch the cell from her hands. Good lordy, the last thing I need is to get another man killed, innocent or not.

"Come on, girl, you can't give up just because of one bad date."

"Maybe she's learned her lesson." A deep voice from over my shoulder raises the hair on the back of my neck.

Rose's head twists around as fast as mine, her eyes bulging as they land on the monster coalescing from the shadows. "What the fuck are you doing here, Rossi?" she spits.

He lets out a chuckle and stalks closer. Every nerve-ending in my body snaps at attention at his looming presence. "Always lovely to see you too, Rose." His dark gaze lances over me, capturing me for an impossibly long moment before I tear my eyes away. "How lucky am I? Not only did I get to see my half-brother today, but now my new sister-in-law. I heard congratulations are in order."

"What did you do to Dante?" Rose reaches for her phone and types out a quick message.

"Relax, your charming husband is just fine. Call him if you don't believe me." He creeps closer, rounds the bench and settles in beside me.

"Stay away from her," Rose hisses with the phone pressed to her ear.

As she confirms Dante's well-being, Nico inches closer, his

thigh brushing against mine. "I see you received my latest gift?" he whispers.

"You're sick," I snarl. The image of Jack's eyeballs rolling across my floor make me want to rip my own eyes out.

"And I thought you'd be thanking me. Do you have any idea the shitstorm that would've rolled in if you'd actually gone home with that sick fuck?"

Another wave of nausea claws its way up my throat. Just the idea of me, naked, across the internet is enough to make my stomach bottom out. "You didn't have to kill him," I whisper-hiss. "You could have just warned me."

He shoots me an innocent smile. "I didn't *kill* him."

A shade of hope creeps through the darkness. "You didn't? You mean those eyeballs weren't real?" Because they sure as sugar looked real to me.

"Oh no, they most definitely were real. I just didn't kill him. I decided letting him live would be a much better punishment for daring to look at what's mine." His expression seems carved into stone, a gorgeous icy mask concealing the monster within.

"I'm not yours!" I hiss.

"Maybe not yet, but soon. Just remember, I'm the only one that can keep you safe."

My heart stammers out a ragged beat as those piercing irises drill into me.

"When your friend gets off the phone, tell her I will be the one to accompany you home."

"No." I glare up at the bossy a-hole. Who does he think he is telling me what to do?

"You will do as I say or your friend will suffer the consequences of your disobedience."

"Ugh, thank gawd, he's okay," Rose mutters, jerking me away from Nico's penetrating gaze. Her hand curls around mine, and she jerks me off the bench. "Come on, Dante's sending a car to get us. Aldo will be here in a few minutes."

Nico's hand clamps around my upper arm. "I'm afraid not, Rose. I'll accompany Maisy home."

Rose's expression morphs into disbelief, and a sarcastic chuckle tumbles out. She rises to her tiptoes and sears him with a fiery glare. "I don't think so, asshole. Why would she ever go with you?"

"Only the fact that I've brought her home every day since she twisted her ankle." His gaze narrows on my friend. "This little accident happened under my watch and therefore, I feel responsible."

Oh, shitzu.

Rose's eyes dart to mine, a mixture of shock and betrayal streaking across the bright blue. "What?"

"Not every day," I mutter lamely. "It's complicated."

"You've been hanging out with Nico Rossi? How is that complicated, Maisy? That's completely insane. Did you forget what he did to us? What Gemini Corp is doing to King Industries?"

"I know, I'm sorry. It's not like I wanted this…"

"Is he threatening you?"

My lips thin out into a tight line, and I shake my head. Kind of a lie. I can't even explain it myself. Despite everything, I feel safe with Nico. Even after the disgusting gift. If he hadn't intervened, my naked butt would've been plastered across the internet.

"Then why are you doing this?"

Nico's curious gaze lifts to meet mine, and that magnetic attraction zips between us. It's unlike anything I've ever felt in my life. Am I going to give into it? Heck, no. But do I need to understand it for my own sanity? Yes.

"He won't hurt me," I finally mutter.

"How do you know that?"

"Because he's had every chance to…"

Rose shakes her head, the hurt written across her face worse than a slap. "I hope you know what you're doing."

"Did you? With Dante?"

"That's so not the same," she cries. "Dante never kidnapped me—" Her mouth slams shut, and I know exactly where her thoughts went. To her best friend, Stella. Dante's brother, Luca, held her hostage in his penthouse before they fell in love. With one last heart-stabbing look, she spins on her heel and marches across the lawn. "Just be careful," she calls out over her shoulder before she gets far.

I follow her tall, slender form for an agonizing few seconds longer. But she's too fast and I'm on freaking crutches.

Nico's body folds around mine without ever laying a finger on me. It's insane how acutely aware of him I am. His warm breath skates over the shell of my ear as he dips closer. "Smart choice, little fox."

"Would you really have hurt Rose if I hadn't agreed to go with you?"

"I suppose it's a good thing you didn't have to find out." He moves beside me and offers his arm. "Let's go home."

"I'm only letting you escort me back so that you can clean up your vile present. I dropped the box and the *eyeballs* tumbled out."

A deep chuckle vibrates that massive barrel chest hidden beneath the fine suit. "Why am I not surprised?"

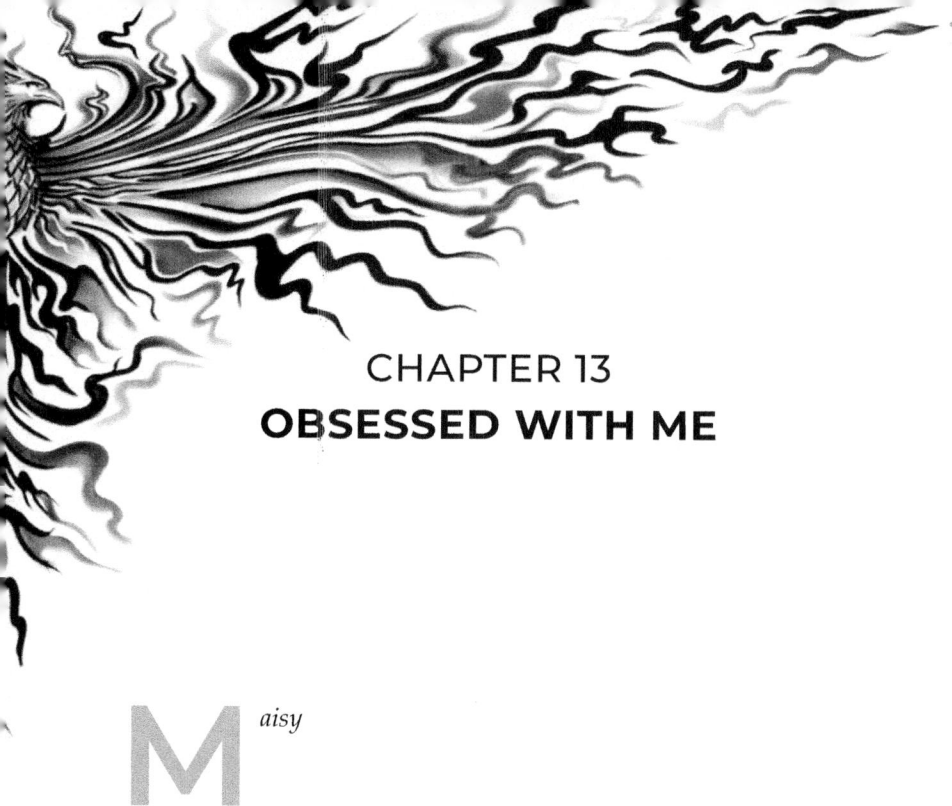

CHAPTER 13
OBSESSED WITH ME

Maisy

Strong fingers wrap around my throat, and crushing pressure squeezes my windpipe. My eyes snap open, and I gasp as all the air is torn from my lungs. I attempt to scream, but my failing organs are only able to squeeze out a faint squeak. A masked man hovers over me, powerful thighs pinning me to the mattress.

Even through the narrow slit, I recognize those pale blue eyes.

They're the same ones I woke up to every morning for years.

This can't be happening. Jasper is gone.

My ex-husband would have to be insane to come back here with the police, not to mention, Dante, searching for him.

This has to be a nightmare. My vision grows hazy, every breath becoming more difficult as my attacker's fingers tighten. I struggle beneath his iron grip, kicking and flailing my legs. This isn't real. This isn't real.

I jolt straight up in bed, my heart hammering against my ribs. Sweat slickens my nightie, wild tumbles of hair streaking across my face. Sweeping the auburn locks aside, I scan the familiar surroundings. Darkness blankets my bedroom, and I heave out a haggard breath. I'm safe. It was just a dream.

"Are you all right, little fox?" A deep voice echoes from the corner of my room, and my heart leaps up my throat once again. "I'll never let him hurt you again. You know that, right?"

A towering figure emerges from the shadows, peeling away from the endless black. Blazing azure eyes lock on mine, the deep hue so different than the one plaguing my sleep.

Nico.

"What are you doing in my house?" I shriek and tug the comforter up to my chin. Even as I utter the words, heated memories of the last time he was in my bedroom flood my mind.

"I was worried…" he murmurs. His eyes catch mine, and I'm drawn into that mesmerizing gaze. He moves closer, gliding over the old wooden floors like a wraith.

So much for my promise of staying away from him after he dropped me off yesterday. "Why?"

Nico folds his big form onto the corner of my bed, brilliant eyes intent on mine.

"Tell me the truth." I sit up straighter, forcing courage into my shaking limbs. "What is your deal with me? I just don't understand it."

"I don't quite understand it myself." For an instant, the arrogant smirk is gone, replaced by something genuine, and alarmingly beautiful. "You know I kept Jasper prisoner for some time… the man is a master manipulator. He's truly impressive actually. The way he spoke of you, it was mesmerizing. And then when I had the pleasure of meeting you in person—well, you've completely captivated me, little fox."

I snort on a laugh, the completely unladylike sound making me cringe the moment it's out. Why I even care is beyond me. I shouldn't give two shitzus what this maniac thinks of me or my embarrassing noises. But I do, which clearly means my months of therapy have been a waste.

"You're obsessed with me, that's all it is. It's sick."

His gaze drops to the floor for an instant before it pivots back, trapping me once again. "I've never experienced anything like it."

Samesies, buddy. Somehow, I manage to keep that completely inappropriate comment to myself. "Well, you need to get over it. I meant what I said the other day when you sent that little *present*." Crossing my arms over my chest, I squeeze my eyes shut. The vivid nightmare still lingers too close, those pale blue irises invading my vision.

"I don't think I can." The weight shifts on the mattress, and my eyes snap open. "You've done something to me, little fox. You've awoken feelings in me I was certain were long dead."

"Maybe you should shove them back where they came from, lock them up tight and throw away the key." *That's what I'm trying to do.* I mask my unease with a sweet smile. The truth is that his mere proximity has every nerve in my body lit up like the Fourth of July.

"I wish it were that easy." Nico smirks, and his hand moves beneath the covers to my injured foot. He dances his fingers across the bandage, and his gentle touch sends goose bumps scattering up my leg. I barely suppress a giggle. Then his fingers creep to my toes, and I'm totally squirming now.

"Stop, that tickles!" I squeal.

Nico dips his head beneath the comforter, and his warm breath skates over my toes. "Does it?"

"Yes!" I try to jerk my leg back but his hand clamps around my calf, holding it in place. He shoves the thick blanket back, exposing my bare legs.

A pair of wicked sapphire orbs lift to mine beneath a shock of dark hair as his tongue slides between his lips.

"What are you doing?" I cry out.

He runs his tongue over my big toe, and fiery heat rages from my foot straight up between my legs.

Mother trucker.

"Mmm," he murmurs as his mouth closes over my toe.

Oh, sugar, when was the last time I took a shower? Do my feet stink? This is sooo embarrassing.

"Nico, stop!" I try to wriggle free, but his hand only tightens around my calf.

His tongue swirls around my toe for another endless moment before he finally releases it, only to move onto the next.

"Nico!"

"What?" he mumbles around my pinky. Lifting his head, that lusty gaze sears into me. "Do you really want me to stop?"

"Yes!" I hiss.

"You're not enjoying this?"

"Not one bit."

His hand moves from my calf and slowly crawls up my inner thigh. "How about this, little fox, if you're not dripping wet for me, I'll stop."

I clamp my legs together, trapping his hand between my thighs. His sinful smirk only grows wider. Dang it. That was not what I was trying to do.

"If you prefer a replay of the other night, I'm fine with that as well."

"Absolutely not!" My knees fall apart, releasing him, but also completely baring my panties. Oh, my golly, I'm such an idiot. Before I can cover myself, Nico crawls up the mattress and kneels between my thighs. He drops down, muscled arms suspending his body over mine. Only inches of space exist between our forms.

"Get off!" Even as I say the words, I can hear how weak they sound.

Electricity crackles in the minute space as he watches me, an unreadable expression across that brutally handsome face.

Fiery anticipation rushes my body from the tips of my toes to the top of my head. I should shove him off. Any normal person would. This man kidnapped me only a few months ago and has been stalking me for just as long. He gouged out a guy's eyes for taking me out for coffee. I should be repulsed, and I'm clearly insane to allow him to put me in such a vulnerable position.

But only raging desire pulses through every inch of me.

He wasn't wrong before. Embarrassing moisture coats my panties, and if he keeps this up, I'll be soaked before long.

"Mmm, little fox, the things I want to do to you." His lips inch closer.

Those words streak straight down to my lusty cooter, and I'm clenching with need. "Don't..." I murmur, summoning every shred of willpower.

"Why not?" He drops his body down another inch, and his stiff erection brushes my belly. "One night with me and you'll forget Jasper ever existed."

A thrill races up my spine, and I don't deny it. I'm certain sex with this man would erase every horrible memory of my ex. But how could I run from one monster only to dive into bed with another?

"It's not right," I whisper.

"Oh, it's right, little fox. Maybe just not right now." He heaves out a breath and straightens, still kneeling between my legs. "But I promise you this, Miss Maisy, I will fuck you soon, and you will like it. You'll come on my cock again and again, until your pussy weeps for only me. And once I make you mine, you'll never crave anyone else."

My breath hitches, the intensity in his tone only stoking the blazing fires.

With one last panty-melting gaze, he crawls off the bed and turns for the door. "Don't worry, I'll lock the door on my way out."

"How?" I somehow manage to squeak out.

"I had an extra key made, silly little fox."

"What?" I shriek.

The cocky a-hole ignores me and stalks out of my bedroom like he owns it. I can't help my traitorous gaze from trailing his tall, muscled form or lingering on the clear outline of his erection.

Gosh darn it, what is wrong with me?

A dark, messed up part of me wanted him to screw the daylights out of me.

But he backed off when I said no. I'm shocked. And disappointed.

Muttering a curse, I roll over and bury my head in my pillow. Nico's musky, spicy scent floods my nostrils. How is that possible? He'd barely even touched my pillow, and now he's everywhere, including creeping into my vulnerable, lonely heart.

CHAPTER 14
I'M COMING FOR YOU

N*ico*

I stare out the floor-to-ceiling window, taking in the chaos of Park Avenue just below. The frenetic scene mirrors the chaos in my mind. Maisy. Maisy. Maisy. She's all I can think about. Not having her is what's killing me.

That defiant little fox has gotten under my skin.

I've never had it as easy as Marco with the ladies, but I've also never had to work *this* hard. Despite the nightly visits, the endless orchid deliveries, and my every attempt to make up for my past sins, Maisy wants nothing to do with me.

Or at least those are the lies her lips whisper.

Her body's reaction to mine speaks a different story.

Take her she's yours. A sinister voice echoes through my mind. The one that's been through hell and back, the one who took the reins years ago.

The door to my office whips open, and Marco struts in.

"You don't even knock?" I hiss, burying the dark thoughts.

My brother's lips slide into an easy smile. "Why should I? Are you jacking off to mental images of your new little pet?"

I pat my jacket pocket, and my own smile slips into place. "Why settle on mental images when I have them in full color?"

"Oh, let me see." Marco barrels toward me, and red-hot fury lashes through my veins at the idea of him seeing her in one of those scandalous nighties. He reaches for my phone tucked into my inner pocket, but I swat him away. "Are you serious? You're not going to let me have a peek?"

"Absolutely not." I cross my arms over my chest as a mix of rage and jealousy fight it out in my gut.

"Holy shit, Nico." My brother perches on the edge of the desk. "You actually like this girl? Is that why you've been so distracted?"

"I have *not* been distracted."

"Oh, yeah? So you know the commissioner still hasn't signed the final contract Mel sent over?"

My brows shoot up to my hairline. "He hasn't?"

Marco clucks his tongue, a smug grin stretching across his face. "It's not like you not to notice."

"Fuck... it's Dante, it must be."

He shrugs, and his shoulders lift a lazy inch. "Most likely. And his damned lawyer. Our half-brother is probably trying to force Gordon to stick to their original deal."

"*Merda.*"

"You sure you don't want me to send one of the guys to visit Dante's new wife?"

As tempting as that sounds, Rose is Maisy's best friend, despite their little argument a few days ago. If I have any hope of ever winning over my little fox, I must stay far away from Rose Valentino. "No," I growl. Besides that, I have no doubt Dante would retaliate, and I'm not certain he'd respect his wife's friendship with my Maisy. And if he came after her... my ribcage suddenly feels too tight. The idea of something happening to my little fox because of me sends my heart on a tailspin. "I mean it, Marco, stay away from Rose."

"Fine," he mutters. "So what's the plan then? We can't lose this deal. It's the final nail in the coffin for King Industries."

I heave out a breath and spin my chair toward Park Avenue. The King's skyscraper juts out over the other surrounding buildings. *Dio*, how I wish I could burn it to the ground. My nose twitches as smoke fills my nostrils, and goose bumps ripple across my flesh. No... I'd never submit anyone to that hell.

"Nico?"

My gaze pivots back to my brother. "I'm on it. I'll talk to Qian Guo of the Four Seas. It's time to test our newly wrought alliance."

"I thought you said he was a psychopath."

"He is. So who better to deal with Dante?"

Marco grins and slides off my desk. "Good luck." He whirls toward the door and hitches his thumb over his shoulder. "I'm going to grab lunch with Mel. We'll be back soon."

"Marco, you better stop fucking our assistant."

His eyes narrow, and a devious grin twitches at the corner of his lip. "I don't know what you're talking about."

I tick my head toward the wall we share between our offices. "At least cover her mouth next time. Her damn moans were making me hard. How am I supposed to get any fucking work done around here?"

"Will do, bro." He turns toward the door.

"And Marco, make sure you have her sign one of those workplace relationship consent forms. The last thing we need is Melanie suing us when you inevitably move onto the next thing with a skirt."

"I'm insulted, Nico. How do you know she's not the one?"

"Only because you're a complete man-whore, and I heard you fucking Laney from the reception desk two days ago."

He mutters a curse, but that damned smile only grows wider. "I can't help it. They just throw themselves at me."

"Yeah, I bet."

"You want me to grab you anything for lunch?" he asks with one hand on the door handle.

"You're really going to eat?"

"Sure, after we fuck. The bathroom at Serafina is surprisingly roomy."

"You're disgusting." Shaking my head, I roll my eyes at my brother. When we were young, I used to envy his ease with the ladies. Maybe I still do, a little.

"Is that a no, then?"

My stomach is already rumbling. With all these late-night visits to Maisy's, I've forgotten to eat dinner on a few occasions, last night included. "Grab me a pizza and just make sure you wash your hands before you touch my food."

"I'll try to remember." He chuckles and shoots me a wink before he darts out of my office.

Coglione.

My phone rings, drawing my attention away from my philandering brother to the familiar face on the screen. I stare at the haunted look in her eyes for a long moment before I finally slide my finger across the call answer button.

"*Ciao, Mamma,*" I mutter.

"Nico, *perché non rispondi alle mie telefonate?*"

"I'm sorry I haven't called you back."

"*E perché non parli in italiano?*"

"It's just easier for me to speak in English, Ma."

She sighs dramatically, but continues in English, nonetheless. Despite her thick accent, she speaks it as well as I do. Vague memories of her drilling my brother and me on vocabulary as we waited at the airport in Rome zip to the forefront of my mind. "I sent you and your brother to America to have a better life, not to forsake your blood."

"That's funny, Ma. I'm pretty sure my blood forsook us the moment our father rejected Marco and me."

"Your father did what he could."

"Right…" A ding lifts my gaze to the computer screen, to the new email from a name I was certain I'd never see again. I click on the unread message as Mamma chatters on defending the man who'd deserted us. If I wasn't so distracted by the email, I would've been furious. I still couldn't understand how she could stand up for Umberto Valentino even after all these years.

I scan the message, and ice ripples down my spine.

She's even more beautiful than I remembered. Thank you for reuniting us, Nico. I'll be forever in your debt.

Jasper

I double click on the attached image, and Maisy's face fills the screen. Her eyes are closed, and soft light illuminates her perfect features. Waves of auburn hair are splayed out like a halo across the now-familiar floral cushion of her living room couch.

"Fuck."

Panic frosts my veins as I fully digest the picture. It's much too close and the image too sharp to have been taken from anywhere other than *inside* Maisy's house. Reaching for my phone, I flip to the security app I'd hacked into which allows me unfettered access to her home.

Swiping through the video feeds with my heart rammed up my throat, I stop on the direct shot of Maisy's living room. She's sprawled across the couch with her laptop propped on her thighs. Her eyes are closed, and that fear claws at my insides, shredding me to bits. I zoom in until the camera focuses on the faint rise and fall of her chest.

She's okay.

The panic recedes, replaced by something far more powerful. I scan the rest of the townhouse, and once I confirm it's empty, I grab my jacket and jump out of my chair. That asshole got into Maisy's house right under my nose.

How?

As I race out of the office, I shoot a message to Max to meet me downstairs. My thumb hovers over Maisy's number as I contemplate a text. Before I compose the dreaded message, I shove the phone back in my pocket. I hate the idea of scaring her, especially now when she's in such a vulnerable state.

I'm coming for you, little fox.

CHAPTER 15
STAY

M*aisy*

My cell phone buzzes beneath my arm, drawing me from an uneasy sleep. I let out a yawn and force myself to sit up. My laptop is still perched haphazardly across my legs, and my sleepy gaze chases to the dozens of unanswered emails on the screen. Ugh. How did I fall asleep when I was supposed to be working?

Those dang nightmares are killing me.

Grabbing my phone, I recognize Palestra's phone number and send it to voicemail. The last thing I need is my boss hearing my raspy, I-just-woke-up voice. Forcing myself off the couch, I hobble to the kitchen with my crutches, turn on the faucet and splash some water on my face. A dozen orchids fill the space, the riot of colors brightening every corner of the room.

Normally, I'd be thrilled with the assortment, but every beautiful flower is tainted. I can't even look at them without seeing Nico. And the gorgeous mobster is the last person I should be thinking about right now. Or ever.

I flip through my text messages and scowl when I land on the dozens of unanswered ones I'd sent to my best friend. I'd never seen Rose so mad. I would give anything to go back in time. I never should have gone home with Nico that day, or any day for that matter.

Rose had offered Dante's men's protection countless times, but I never felt as safe as when Nico's looming presence filled my home.

I shoot off one more message apologizing, filled with emojis, and wait.

No response.

With a huff, I lift the phone to my ear and call my boss back. "Hey, Karen, sorry I missed your call, I was in the bathroom."

"No worries, Maisy. I was just checking in before I head out for the day. How's your ankle?"

Leaning the crutches against the counter, I set my foot on the floor and place some weight on it. "It's feeling better, thanks." Just a few more days and I'll finally be able to go back to work. I never thought I'd be so happy to be stuck in my tiny office.

"Great, glad to hear it. I miss having you around to give the new client tours."

"I miss them too." Nothing else gives me a better excuse to check out the hot, sweaty men working out. Mesmerizing blue eyes cocked over a bare tattooed shoulder fill my vision, and my pulse escalates. Ogling Nico Rossi had become my dirty little secret and favorite pastime. Long before he ever spoke to me at the park, I'd been watching him too. Purely as eye candy, of course. I'd never intended for it to go any further than that.

The click of the front door opening sends my head whipping over my shoulder. The devil himself fills the entryway, and I suck in a breath as I take him in. He's in a dark suit, midnight hair pulled neatly into a tie at the base of his neck. But it isn't his unfairly handsome face that has my breath hitching today, but rather the uncharacteristic, wild look in his eye.

"You okay?" Karen's voice jerks my attention to the call I totally forgot I'm still on.

"Yeah, sorry. One of those annoying door-to-door salesmen just showed up."

She laughs. "Okay, I'll let you take care of that. Have a good evening, Maisy, and we'll talk tomorrow."

"Thanks, bye, Karen." I press the call hang up button and slam my phone on the counter. "What are you doing here?" I dart toward him, completely forgetting that though my ankle is getting better, I can't be throwing all my weight on it, and I stumble forward.

Nico lurches toward me, catching me before my knees hit the floor.

That musky, tantalizing scent fills my nostrils as he crushes me to his chest. My nose gets buried in his crisp, white button-down, and I get a lungful of the tasty mob boss. Oh, sugar, tasty? *Really?*

Get it together, Maisy! Pressing my palms to his chest, I try to take a much-needed step back, but Nico's hold only tightens the more I squirm. "Let go of me," I hiss.

"No." His eyes sear into mine, and the remaining air in my lungs evaporates. "I need to make sure you're all right."

"Of course, I'm all right. I just tripped. It only happens about three times a day. It's par for the course when you're born with two left feet."

The harsh lines of his face soften, and the hint of a smile flashes across his scruffy jaw.

"Also, you need to give me my key back. You can't just come in and out of my house as you please."

"Why not? I've been doing it all week, and you haven't seemed to mind one bit."

My jaw drops, and I stare horrified. "All week?" I squeal.

"Mmm. I find watching you sleep very relaxing."

"Nico!" I swat at him and regret it instantly. It's like smacking a brick wall. "You know I could have you arrested for breaking and entering?"

"But I didn't break, I have a key." He jingles the key ring an inch from my nose. "And as far as entering... I hope you'll allow me entrance into that sweet little pussy soon."

Heat surges up my neck, coating my cheeks in fire.

Nico steps closer, and I stagger back. "Today would work," he purrs. "The rest of my calendar just opened up."

"In your dreams," I murmur as the heat across my face dives further south.

"Fine, then I suppose we could find something boring to do." He plops down onto the couch and crosses his legs.

"Uh, uh, buddy, you're not staying here." I waggle a finger at him.

"Why not?" Those brilliant blue eyes latch onto me, and my stupid, stupid heart flip-flops.

"Because we're not dating, we're not friends, and I didn't even invite you over."

"Not yet."

"Not ever," I hiss.

His hand snaps out and wraps around mine, tugging me forward. I fall into his lap, and a wicked chuckle echoes in the air. "You're so easy, little fox."

I glare up at him as he cradles me in his lap, one arm across my middle like a steel lap belt.

"Why do you fight this when I know it's what you want." His fingers dance down my arm, and goose bumps ripple in their wake.

"You know nothing." I try to get up, but his hold only tightens.

His free hand drifts from my arm to the top button of my blouse. My breath hitches as he toys with the silver fastener. "Tell me to stop."

"Stop."

"Say it like you mean it. Without your chest heaving, your pulse accelerating, or your pupils dilated."

"Eff you, Nico." I clench my teeth and force my traitorous heart to stop pounding.

"That's all I want, little fox." He smirks and darn dang it, that seductive look is so unfair. "I just want to make you come, while your conscious this time. Why won't you let me?" He pauses, eyes intent on mine. "There don't have to be any strings attached."

"There are always strings," I mutter. I clap my hand over my mouth as soon as the words spill out. Why am I even considering this insane offer?

"Let me stay tonight, and I promise you an evening like you've never had before. I'll make you come so hard that little kidnapping faux pas will be nothing but a faded memory. And if after that, you want me to stay away, I will."

"You will?"

He smirks and crosses his finger over his heart. "I swear."

This could be just what I need to finally get the obsessive mob boss out of my life. "You're that convinced that you're so irresistible one night is all it'll take?"

Nico nods. "I won't even use my cock if that's what you want. No pleasure for me, only for you."

"Well, I've never actually had an uh, org...orgasm from sex." Sugar, what is wrong with me? Why would I admit that?

His eyes go impossibly wide, the deep blue more fathomless than the Caribbean Sea. "You're kidding?" He continues to watch me, his stare so intense I'm not sure if I want to hide from it or dive in and get swallowed up in the shimmering depths. "Actually, on second thought, I'm not all that surprised, given my brief acquaintance with your ex. The arrogant sociopath seems like he would be a selfish lover. But no one else?"

I shake my head, holding my tongue before I spill the embarrassing truth that I've only ever been with one man.

"And yet, I made you come in your sleep without even truly touching you." A cocky smirk flashes across his face.

"Takes an arrogant butthead to know one."

A deep chuckle erupts from his lips and geez, the sound is like melted butter. His arm loosens from my middle so I'm able to sit up. He doesn't let me go any farther than that. His mouth inches toward mine, so close I can make out the scar across his upper lip. "Let me make up for what I did to you the only way I know how. Please, little fox."

All the air rushes from my lungs as those eyes pierce into mine. They're like scavengers searching and pillaging, until they find the cracks in my carefully constructed armor. Because the hold this man has on my body is much less frightening than what he's doing to my soul.

My head slowly dips, the movement so faint I'm not certain I had any control over it at all.

"I need you to say it, Maisy. Tell me you want me to stay."

I swallow hard, my heart like a battering ram against my ribs. The truth is that there's nothing I want more than for him to stay. Not only because of his promises of an epic night of passion, but because I feel safe when he's around. I convince myself that's the real reason I agree to this madness. "Stay."

CHAPTER 16
ALL ABOUT YOU

N*ico*

Stay.

That one word echoes in the silence, carrying with it the weight of a thousand unspoken emotions. My dull, lifeless heart kicks to life, sending heated blood rushing through my veins, and my cock hardens in anticipation.

Maisy must feel my excitement because she shifts in my lap, her cheeks turning a delightful shade of crimson. "You can stay for now, but I'm not promising anything," she amends.

"I didn't ask you for anything. I plan on doing all the giving."

Her shoulders tremble, a shudder racing up her spine and goosebumps swell across her bare arms. "I don't want you anywhere near my hoo-ha unless I say, got it?"

A cackle erupts from my lips despite my best efforts to contain it. "*Dio*, woman, can you not say the word pussy?"

"No!" she shrieks.

"Pussssy."

She shakes her head and claps her hands over her ears.

"Pussy. Pussy. Pussy."

"Stop!" She squirms in my lap, her cheeks growing brighter red by the second.

I chuckle again, her reaction so unexpectedly refreshing I can't stop grinning. "Maisy, by the time I'm done with you, you'll be begging for me to fuck your fine pussy with my cock."

She gasps. "I would never use such vile language."

My brow arches, and she instantly realizes her mistake. She didn't deny the fact that she wouldn't let me fuck her.

"I mean, I'd never ask you to do those things to me in the first place."

"Right... whatever you say, little fox."

She springs up out of my lap and hobbles to the kitchen. "I need wine, lots of wine," she mutters as she goes.

"I'll take a glass as well," I call out after her.

"Come get it yourself! I only have one working leg, for Christmas's sake."

I follow her into the kitchen, my gaze intent on hers as she pours half the bottle in the glass. "You're not taking the pain medicine anymore, are you?"

"No." She snorts on a laugh. "Never again." Then she hands me the wine, a vintage selection from Bordeaux that likely cost more than my first car. With Maisy's bungling charm, it's easy to forget her upper class upbringing. It was something Jasper frequently spoke of during our time together.

Once I've poured my glass, she points toward the door at the back of the kitchen. "Do you want to sit outside? The weather's been so nice lately. This winter was awful, I mean snow, cold, rain; man, I thought it would never end and I just can't pass up the chance--"

I raise my hand, cutting off her nervous rambling. "I'd

rather stay inside. We don't want your neighbors watching when I coax that first orgasm from your trembling lips."

She gapes at me, pretty pink mouth curved into a capital O. Then she swallows down half of her wine in one long pull.

I'd rather her believe my motives are selfish than mention the threat of Jasper. The last thing I want to do is frighten her.

"I didn't agree to all that…" She gulps down the remainder of her wine and refills her glass.

"Maisy, relax." I step closer and she takes a step back, then another until she hits the door that leads to the patio.

"Maybe this was a mistake—"

Closing the distance between us, I press my finger to her lips. "It wasn't. You and I belong together."

"Nico, when you say stuff like that, it makes me want to run away screaming. Can you just not be so intense?"

A flicker of amusement tugs at the corner of my lip. I love how honest and genuine she is. Every woman I've come across since the success of Gemini Corp has been nothing but plastic smiles and forced flattery. Their only interest lies in my bank account or my new connections to Manhattan's elite. Maisy doesn't care about any of that, and I'm certain of this because I've watched her for months.

"I suppose I can try," I finally mutter.

"Okay." She looses a breath and leans against the back door.

A red dot dances across her hair, nearly invisible within the deep auburn strands. Fuck! "Maisy!" I drop my glass and lunge before I have time to process what's happening. My arms wrap around her body, slamming her onto the floor. Her glass of wine crashes down along with us, spilling deep crimson liquid across the marble. My hand covers her head as I wait for the gunshot, my heart lodged in my throat.

"Nico, what the heck?" Maisy grumbles beneath me.

"Stay down." My entire body is tense, my muscles

straining as I blanket her petite form. Endless seconds pass, and then nothing.

"Can you please get off me, you big beast? I can't breathe."

"No, not until I'm sure it's safe."

"Safe from what?" she cries.

Cazzo. Had I imagined it? I know what I saw, or does my little fox have me so twisted up I'm seeing things now?

Straightening my arms, I slowly push up off the floor. "Stay down," I growl as Maisy starts to move with me.

"Bossy butthead," she mumbles under her breath.

I kneel by the door staying just under the glass pane that makes up the top half of the door and push aside the sheer curtain. Scanning the neighboring brownstones, I search for the muzzle of a rifle peeking through one of the windows facing into the patio. Then I survey the rooftops.

Nothing.

Fuck. I heave out a breath and press my back against the door. Raking my hands across my face, I squeeze my eyes closed. These sleepless nights are starting to get to me.

"Are you going to tell me what's going on?"

Rubbing my eyes to force the haze away, I focus on the woman splayed out across the marble floor. "I thought I saw something."

"Like what?" She props her elbow on the pristine marble and leans her chin on her palm staring up at me.

A sniper's mark. But I can't force the words out because they sound too insane. And if it were true, she'd be terrified.

"A shadow or something, walking by the door," I blurt.

"In my backyard?" She lifts her gaze to the window, eyes wide.

"I must have imagined it because there's no one there."

"Are you sure?" That flash of fear across the lively emerald is like a punch to the gut.

"You're safe, Maisy. I swear." Bending down, I offer my

hand. She eyes it for a long moment as if a simple touch could destroy her. She's not wrong.

When she's finally on her feet, she glances down at the mess of broken glass and puddle of wine. Her dress is splattered in crimson, and I blink quickly, forcing away the dark images that rise to the surface. Blood covering her from head to toe, not wine.

If anything had happened to her…

The momentary fear vanishes, replaced by pounding fury. If I'm not hallucinating, and that was Jasper, I'm going to ring his fucking scrawny neck. How dare he threaten what's mine?

Maisy's soft footsteps jerk me from the downward spiral of rage. She stands in front of me with a mop in one hand and a dustbuster in the other.

I reach for both, shaking my head. "I'll do it. I don't want you to cut yourself." With her luck, she'll bleed out in the kitchen from an errant shard of glass.

She watches me, curious eyes intent on mine. "Are you sure you're okay?" The fear in her gaze has diminished, a glossy sheen curtaining the deep green. She's probably already tipsy after inhaling nearly two glasses of wine in seconds.

"Yes, I'm fine. Are you?"

Maisy glances down at her floral-print dress and scowls. "I'm just peachy, but my dress on the other hand looks like wardrobe from a slasher flick."

I swallow hard, the grisly visual hitting much too close to home. Dropping the mop and the dustbuster, I scoop her into my arms, sidestepping the mess.

"What are you doing?" she squeals.

"I'm taking you upstairs to get cleaned up."

"I can walk, you know." But she doesn't make a move to push out of my hold. I'm wearing her down, finally.

"I know, but I can't help but feel a little responsible for your ankle, and now your dress."

"A little?" Her voice rises a few notches.

Ignoring her quip, I march to the living room and as we pass the kitchen island, Maisy reaches for the bottle of wine. Wrapping her fingers tight around the neck, she cradles it against her chest. "I think I'm going to need more of this."

"Whatever you want, little fox. Tonight is all about you."

CHAPTER 17
THIS WAS A BAD IDEA

M*aisy*

Nico gently lowers me onto the edge of the bathtub and spins on the faucet then pours in a cupful of lavender bath oil, much like he did the first time he brought me to bathe. How has this man weaseled his way into not only my bathroom but my life so easily? Not even Rose has ever been up here.

He stares down at me expectantly, and unlike last time, he doesn't move.

"You can go now," I whisper.

His jaw clenches tight, an unreadable emotion flashing across those profound blue orbs. "Not this time, little fox. I'm not letting you out of my sight this evening."

My breath hitches at his foreboding timbre, and a whisper of fear snakes up my spine. "Because of the shadow?" Could someone really have been out there? I was fairly certain my only stalker was looming over me as we speak.

"That and other things." A sinful smirk curls the corners of his lips and just like that the fear vanishes, replaced by something I should be much more terrified of. "I promised to make you come tonight, and I don't see any reason to prolong the inevitable."

Heat races between my legs, and I squeeze my thighs together to extinguish the burning flames.

Nico crouches down and twists the faucet, and with the absence of rushing water, a thick silence descends over us. His gaze moves from the splotches of wine at the hem of my dress up my torso, leaving a scorching trail in its wake.

For fork's sake, how does he do that with just one look?

His lips twist as they regard the wine splatters. "Let's get that off you."

A rebuttal sits on the tip of my tongue, but instead of letting it free, I reach for the bottle of wine and drown it with the pungent alcohol. I agreed to let him stay, right? If I'm going to hell, I might as well enjoy the ride.

As if he's read my thoughts, his long fingers clamp around the hem of my dress. A shudder races up my spine as he drags the soft material up my thighs.

"Wait!" I blurt when he reaches my panty line.

He releases a frustrated sigh, and those wary eyes lock on mine. "Yes?"

I slowly stand and hobble toward the vanity, then dig through the top drawer. Pulling out a cute navy-blue bandana I wear on bad hair days, which happens a lot with my wild, ginger locks, I stagger back to the tub where Nico eyes me suspiciously. "Sit, please."

He cocks a dark brow and crosses his arms over his chest.

"Just do it, you stubborn butthole."

A glimmer of a smile lights up his eyes, tipping up the corners of his lips, and gawd, it's unfair for such a bad man to be so beautiful.

Nico drops down to the ledge of the basin, and I move

between his thighs. His hands instantly latch onto my waist, and a gasp slides through my teeth. Even through the dress, his touch makes my blood sing. Steadying my racing pulse with a quick breath, I place the bandana over his eyes and tie it at the back of his head.

"Mmm, little fox, I didn't know you liked to play games..." The rough edge to his tone has my thighs clenching again.

"It's not a game," I finally manage. "It's a condition."

"So shy." A smile glides across his strong jaw. "But I'll accept it for now, since I promised this night was all about you."

I release the breath I hadn't realized I'd been holding and flash my hand in front of his covered eyes. "Can you see me? How many fingers am I holding up?"

He throws his hand out, skimming my breast. I let out a whimper, and a dark chuckle vibrates the air between us. "No, I can't see a thing, little fox."

"Mother father," I mumble.

Nico cracks another smile and his hands skate down the outside of my thigh, until his fingers find the hem of my dress once again. He cocks his head to the side, a sinful grin on his lips. "Now, may I?"

"Yes," I whisper on an exhale.

He draws the dress over my head devastatingly slowly, the soft silk on my heated skin igniting my sensitive nerves. The ruined outfit lands in a heap at my bare feet, and then his hands are on me again, blindly searching for my bra.

Sugar, maybe this was a bad idea.

His hand grazes the swell of my breast, and an embarrassing groan escapes. "Hmm, found it." His fingers make quick work of the clasp in the back, then they dance down my spine until they settle at the waistband of my panties right above my cooter. He dips a finger beneath the lace, grazing my soft curls and my heart leaps up my throat.

"Mmm, little fox, this is going to be pure torture. I can only imagine what that beautiful pussy covered in those red curls must look like."

Heat flares across my cheeks, and I internally curse myself for not shaving earlier. It's been forever since anyone has touched me down there, and I hadn't exactly been keeping up in the maintenance department.

Nico drags my panties down my legs jerking me from my spiraling thoughts. I stand bare before him, and though I know he can't see me through the makeshift blindfold, a wave of embarrassment still rolls through me. For someone who works at a gym, I could certainly afford to spend more time perfecting my body. After being married for so long, I'd let myself go a little. Okay, maybe more than a little. A soft pooch juts out from where tight abs once were, and my thighs had gotten flabby—

"Stop." Nico's command is so sharp, my eyes widen. "Don't do that."

"Don't do what?" I squeal.

"I can feel you squirming beneath my touch. You're perfect, exquisite in every single way."

"How do you know? You can't even see me."

His head bobs slowly. "I don't have to be looking at you, to *see* you, Maisy. If anyone ever made you feel less than perfect, they were the ones who were too blind to see the beauty that radiates from the very core of your being."

My heart clenches, my insides liquifying at the sincerity I feel in his words. Heaving in a steadying breath, I hold onto his shoulder and step into the bath. The warm water envelops me, and I sink into the fragrant bubbles.

Dipping my head underwater, I allow the warmth to wash off the day, to drown the fear, the uncertainty. I remain there for as long as I can hold my breath, soaking in the peace. When I finally resurface, Nico stands over me, still blindfolded and completely naked.

A gasp and a squeal tumble out of my mouth as I take him in. Good gracious, he is absolute perfection. Carved abs ripple across his torso for days and intricate black ink paints the flawless canvas, descending to a deep V which directs my bulging eyes to his bulging—Oh, lordy. He's huge.

"What are you doing?" I finally cry out.

Feeling his way with his hands, he steps into the tub and settles in across from me.

"Nico!" I shriek again.

"What? I'm following your rules. I'm still blindfolded. What's the problem?"

I bring my knees into my chest and lace my arms tight around my legs. "The problem is that you're naked in my tub!"

His hands move under the water, and his fingers find my toes. I let out another squeak.

"That tickles!"

A devious grin parts his lips, and his hold tightens around my foot. His fingers exert more pressure as he massages the soles of my feet and the giggles vanish, giving way to an embarrassing moan.

"That's right, little fox, give in to me." He tugs on my leg until I finally straighten it. "Relax. For once, don't think and just enjoy it."

Oh, hells bells, I've definitely lost my mind. I reach for the bottle of wine and take a long pull. He must hear the clinking of the glass on the marble because a smug grin curls his lips. "I wish I could see your mouth wrapped around the tip of the bottle so I could imagine just what it will look like when those perfect lips take my cock."

I gasp again, not because I'm insulted by his dirty words but because I'm so dang turned on by them. Heat pools in my core, and I'm certain if I wasn't already wet, I'd be well, soaked.

"Good, I'm glad you aren't denying the eventuality of it happening." His arrogant tone raises the hackles along the back of my neck.

"Oh, I'm denying it, all right," I announce, "I just needed a minute to compose my thoughts after the shock of your vile mouth. I will never suck your... you know." Even as the words are out, I can taste the lie. My gaze drops between his legs to his massive erection. I don't think I could even take him all in one go if I wanted to. Which I don't.

"Cock." He smirks.

"Whatever," I grumble.

Nico inches closer, his free hand blindly searching again. My traitorous body nearly leans into his touch before I can knock some sense into it. Instead, I reach for the wine again. As I take another big gulp, his hand finds my upper thigh. His thumb skims dangerously close to my hoo-ha, and my entire body lights up.

"Come closer," he growls.

I freeze, a tangle of fear and excitement rocketing through my chest.

"How can I make good on my promise, if you won't even let me touch you?"

"Yeah, about that, I'm starting to think I may have jumped into this without thinking—" His thumb brushes across my center, and my entire body convulses. "Oh, gawd," I moan.

Nico's wicked chuckle fills the air and while I'm still reeling from that faint touch, his hands grip my hips and jerk me toward him, spinning me around so that my back is pressed against his unyielding chest.

His rock-hard erection fits squarely between my butt cheeks, and I nearly yelp again from the unexpected invasion. His arm locks around my waist, pinning me against a wall of pure muscle, and his free hand dives beneath the water.

Nico's warm breath spills across the shell of my ear as he exhales slowly. "I'm going to dip my finger inside your pussy now, little fox, and you're going to tell me truthfully if you like it."

I suck in a breath, torn between telling him not to and screaming at him to hurry up already. My lower half is on fire, just the feel of his body blanketing mine has every nerve-ending ablaze.

His fingers dance along my inner seam before he dips one long finger inside me as his thumb starts to circle my clit. My hips buck from the jolt of pleasure. He slides deeper inside then pulls out, and I'm writhing against him, desperate for more.

"Did you like that, little fox?" His jagged tenor only intensifies the swirling heat below. He nips at my earlobe when I don't answer for a long moment, and goose bumps race down my arm. "Answer me."

"Yes," I finally blurt.

"Do you want more?"

"Oh, fudge, yes."

His hold tightens around my waist, so his erection presses firmly against my butt, then his finger glides across my center once again. A groan tumbles free as my hips start to move in rhythm with his touch.

Oh, my goodness, he's barely been inside me and already I can feel myself so close to an orgasm. I've never found a release so quickly in my life, not even with the new toy Rose bought me.

His thumb circles that taut bundle of nerves faster, and my hips buck, straining against his palm. He dips a second finger inside me, and a squeak erupts from my clenched lips.

"Do you like it when I'm inside you, little fox?"

I press my lips into a hard line as I continue to grind against his devastating fingers.

"Answer me, or I'll stop." He pulls out, and an exasperated groan falls from my lips.

"Don't stop," I murmur.

"Why? Tell me why I shouldn't stop?"

"Because I like it," I hiss out, squirming with need.

"Mmm, that's a good girl." His finger finds its way back to my center, and I rub up against its length. "Tell me exactly what you want. Tell me you want me to fuck you with my finger until you come so hard you're screaming my name."

"Nico," I whine. Yes, it actually comes out as a whiny plea.

"Say it, little fox, or I stop now." His finger slows its maddening circles around my clit, and I grunt in irritation. I'm so close.

"Fine," I hiss as my fingers wrap around his wrist, keeping his hand between my legs. "I want you to eff me with your finger until I fall so hard I'm screaming your name."

A satisfied smile splays across his handsome face, and two fingers thrust inside me. I nearly scream from the pleasure. He drives deeper then pulls out excruciatingly slowly. His thumb exerts more pressure against my clit, and fiery heat courses up my spine. I'm about a second away from exploding.

"Say my name when you come," he orders.

My head bobs up and down, unbidden, too wrapped up in the pleasure to deny him anything in this moment. Electrifying desire surges through every corner of my body, and a sensation like I've never experienced in my life slams into me.

With one final thrust, I'm thrown over the edge, a wave of scorching pleasure consuming every inch of my body. "Nico, oh, Nico," I moan again and again.

He doesn't stop, his finger sinking deeper and harder until he's wrung out every ounce of pleasure, and I sag against him completely boneless. My chest heaves, my ragged breaths the only sound between us for an endless moment.

Finally, his iron grip around my waist relaxes but never quite falls away. His warm breath skates across the shell of my ear and another wave of goosebumps spirals down my arm, the echoes of the orgasm still reverberating through my body.

"Judging by the sounds I just coaxed out of you," he whispers ever so softly, "I suppose I won't be forced to stay away from you anytime soon."

CHAPTER 18
ENOUGH TO BREAK ME

N*ico*

Maisy tightens the tie around her silk robe as she staggers from the bathroom. With my blindfold now removed, she insisted I wait out here while she dressed. Those few minutes apart had been pure torture. Irrational, I'm fully aware. There is no way Jasper could get into the bathroom undetected. Despite the large French windows, that side of the townhouse is completely unscalable. The man would've had to sprout wings to get to her.

A rifle though… that is another story.

My mind still reels from the possibility. Had I imagined it? Or was Jasper that insane? What would he gain by murdering his ex-wife? The man is wealthy already, though his family doesn't have the money Maisy's does. Old money versus newly acquired wealth. I felt the stigma from loathing eyes every time Marco and me attended one of those hoity-toity Manhattan balls.

The creak of the mattress draws me from my dark musings and back to the alluring woman perched at the end of the bed. I slide onto the edge of the chair, balancing on the balls of my feet. It takes all my self-control not to lunge at her. After that bath, I'm hard as hell and horny as fuck. There's something about robbing one of sight to intensify every other sensation. I'd tied up and blindfolded a woman or two in my day, but I'd never been on the other end.

I'd enjoyed it much more than I'd imagined.

"Stop staring at me like that," Maisy squeals. "Or I'll blindfold you again." She fidgets with her robe covering more of her milky-white skin.

"Don't mistake my willingness to play along with your little game with weakness, little fox. If I wanted, I could have you on your back, ravaging every inch of you."

Her breath catches, and a whisper of fear darts across those expressive orbs.

I don't want her to be frightened of me, but I need her to understand how this dynamic will work.

"You wouldn't..." she mutters, but her eyes flit to the doorway. She's likely calculating her chances of escape. There are none.

"No, I wouldn't," I say matter-of-factly. I've never forced myself on a woman, nor would I ever. There are some sins too depraved even for me. "That doesn't mean I wouldn't push your limits."

She swallows hard, the elegant slope of her neck bobbing.

"I told you this night was all about you, and we are far from finished." I teeter on the edge of my seat, eyes locked to hers.

Crimson coats her cheeks, and she crosses her legs. "I think I'm good."

"One orgasm?" A chuckle squeezes through my clenched teeth. "You think I'm an amateur?"

"Nico..."

"Maisy..." I echo her wary tone. "You deserve this. After what you've been through, you've earned a night of pampering, of limitless pleasure. Just think of it as a long overdue apology for the warehouse incident."

"I think you've done enough." She eyes her freshly bandaged ankle.

I spring to my feet and stalk toward her. She scrambles back on the bed, her eyes wide. Her robe parts as she crawls backward exposing her bare beneath. A growl vibrates my entire chest at the sneak peek of her pussy and those auburn curls. *Merda.* I've always been a sucker for redheads, but just one look at Maisy and I'm on fire.

I crawl up her body, cursing every shred of clothing that stands between our bodies. Perhaps I was too hasty earlier. Promising not to use my cock was a mistake. A big one I'd be paying for all night.

Her legs part for me without even having to ask. *Dio,* she wants this. As fucked up as this thing between us is, she craves me as much as I desire her. I fix my eyes to hers, scrutinizing the deep emerald and the tiny flecks of gold that blaze like the sun.

"Are you scared of me, little fox?" I whisper as I drop some of my weight on her. She's tiny, fragile, and wounded right now. I could crush her beneath my body alone.

"No." She grits her teeth and glares up at me.

"Mmm, so feisty. Good answer." I lick my lips, and her eyes trace the movement of my tongue. "Are you ready to come again?"

Her thighs clamp around my hips even as she shakes her head.

"Liar," I whisper. "I bet your pussy is still drenched." Lifting up an inch, I run my hand between our bodies and down the inside of her thigh. "Shall I check?"

Her head whips back and forth. "No, don't."

"Because you're afraid I'm right? Or because you truly

don't want another orgasm?" I whisper the words, my mouth hovering over hers. *Dio,* how I want to claim those full lips. The desire is almost greater than my need to taste that sweet pussy. But I know she'd never let me. For some odd reason, for women a kiss is so much more intimate. It's absurd really.

Her eyes squeeze closed, and she breathes out a soft exhale. "Both."

"I think you're lying, Maisy. I think you're simply embarrassed to admit the truth. You hate the fact that your body reacts to me, to my touch, to my fingers. I'd wager no one has ever made you come like that in your life and you're dying for me to do it again." I pause, my fingers dancing toward her seam. "Am I right?"

"No." It's nothing more than a whimper, and her weak denial alone betrays her.

I slide my finger through her wet folds, and a moan fills the mere inches between our lips. "Liar," I hiss out again. "So you don't like this?"

Her back arches as my finger inches toward that sensitive nub. "No," she utters weakly.

"So you want me to stop?" I pause my finger's wicked dance.

Her head slowly dips, but her lips press into a tight line.

"You want me to leave?"

A flash of fear darkens the brilliant luster of those emerald orbs. Her hands find their way to my lower back, and that simple touch has my entire body aflame.

She doesn't have to say another word. I crawl down her body and spread her legs, fitting myself between her thighs. She's so wet her arousal glistens on her curls. I inhale a deep breath, scenting her natural perfume then hazard a glance up to meet her eyes.

They're wide, pupils blown out as she watches me.

"Mmm, little fox, you smell like the sweetest sin and the promise of pure salvation."

A giggle bubbles from her pretty pink lips. "Oh my gosh, that mouth."

"You haven't seen anything yet." My tongue dives across that slick heat and her head falls back, a moan replacing the laughter from a second ago. "Mmm, I was right."

I drag my tongue through her wet folds, relishing in her exquisite taste, the sweetest summer cherries. Her pussy tightens around my tongue, sucking me in. I devour every inch of her, circling her clit then plunging my tongue deep inside her. I'm completely ravenous, mad with desire. I've never wanted to claim anyone more than this woman.

"I'm going to lay claim on every delicious inch of you, little fox."

She wriggles beneath me, hips bucking with each stroke of my tongue. Her hands find my hair and that touch only magnifies my arousal. She tugs at the roots, moving her way to the tie that keeps my long hair neatly tethered. She rips it off, unchaining all my control along with it as the dark tendrils fall across my face.

My hands move around to cup her ass, driving that sweetness into my face. She gasps as my fingers dig into her backside. The monster I strive so hard to keep buried surges to the surface. I drag my teeth across her sensitive flesh, and she lets out a cry. Then I drive two fingers inside her, and she squeals, tensing beneath me as she pulls my hair. "Nico!" Unshed tears glisten in her eyes. The monster craves pain, desires darkness.

This woman is nothing but light.

I want to drag her into the depths of my depravity, to ruin her...

Fuck.

I draw in a deep breath and chain the beast, forcing him down to the dark recesses of my fucked-up psyche. *Merda.* I will not ruin her. For the first time in my life, I don't want to.

"I'm sorry," I mumble against her, slowly withdrawing my

fingers. I gently run my tongue across her center, soothing the sensitive flesh. "I'm sorry I hurt you."

"It's okay," she murmurs. "Just be more gentle."

Gentle? Ha. I barely repress the wild laugh. I don't know how to do gentle. I don't know how to make love. I can fuck and claim and bring women to their knees. But this? I'm fucking lost.

"Like this." She runs her fingers through my hair, sweeping the wild tangles behind my ears. Then her hand cups my cheek, and she draws her soft thumb across the prickly stubble. "And this."

My eyes find hers, and my black, battered heart staggers on a beat. Those walls I've forged so desperately for so many years start to crumble. *Shit.* This wasn't how it was supposed to go.

I drop my head between her thighs, ripping free of her hopeful gaze. Because the loathing I could stand, but that look, that glimmer in her eyes is enough to break me.

CHAPTER 19
HE'S BACK

M*aisy*

My lids flutter open, a ray of early morning sunlight seeping through the curtains. A delicious soreness vibrates through the muscles in my lower half. Despite the sting, I feel more rested than I have in weeks. Rolling over, I focus my bleary eyes on the Roman god sprawled on the chair beside my bed. And that's the reason why. Nico is shirtless and asleep, the first time I've ever caught him in such a vulnerable position.

With those piercing blue eyes closed, he's much less intimidating even with that scar across his upper lip. And possibly more gorgeous. The harsh lines that generally cut across his handsome face have vanished, replaced by a softness I've never seen before.

My heart lets out an embarrassing stutter as I take him in. Nico wasn't wrong last night. I am a liar. I've been lying to myself for a while now. I want this man, despite knowing how wrong that is, and yesterday evening was proof. My body has never lit up for anyone like that before. Four orgasms in one night are a world record for me.

And he wasn't even done. After he'd spent hours with his face buried between my thighs, coaxing out orgasm after orgasm, he went downstairs for some water and came back for more. I was so spent I'd fallen asleep while he was gone.

He'd attempted to wake me for another round, but muscles I didn't even know I had down there were so sore I didn't think I'd survive anything more. I already couldn't walk because of my ankle, I didn't need to make it worse with a sore cooter.

Speaking of, I really have to pee.

I push myself off the bed, moving silently so as not to wake the slumbering beast. I am not ready to face him, to discuss what happened last night and what it meant. Because I was so not going there. Not yet. Maybe not ever.

In the light of day, everything seems more real, so much more terrifying. I tell myself it was a one-time thing to ease away the guilt, and I plan to keep it that way. One wine-fueled night of incredibly bad judgement and unbelievable orgasms.

As I hobble to the bathroom, I can't keep my eyes away from Nico's perfect form. To the swathes of black ink that paint the hard planes of his body and transform it into a brutally beautiful work of art.

I round the chair and catch a glimpse of puckered flesh on his shoulder. Pausing, I inch closer and examine the patch of angry red skin between the tattoos. A scar. A bad one by the look of it. It expands across his shoulder disappearing down his back, but I can't make out anything more because it's hidden by the high-backed chair he leans against.

What happened to you, Nico?

My countless therapy appointments with Dr. Winchester surge to the surface. What terrible trauma had shaped this brutal mobster?

A prickle of fear races up my spine as memories from last

night resurface. For a moment, I *had* been afraid. Another thing I'd lied about. Most of the time, Nico didn't frighten me, which clearly proves I belong in those therapy sessions, but last night, something dark had flashed across those brilliant sapphire orbs. And it had vanished nearly as quickly as it had appeared.

I stand there still staring as Nico begins to stir.

Sugar!

I whirl around to hide in the safety of the bathroom, but a steel grip closes around my upper arm before I can get away.

"Good morning, little fox." That rough voice immediately escalates my pulse, and my bare feet freeze in place.

"Morning," I mutter without looking at him. If I don't meet his gaze, he won't be able to see what's lingering just below the surface, right?

"Look at me, Maisy."

I know he's serious when he uses my real name instead of the annoying pet one. His hold tightens around my arm, but he doesn't force me to turn. Slowly, I pivot my gaze. The fire I find in those eyes rips the remaining air from my lungs.

"Don't do this," he whispers, eyes fixed to mine.

"Do what?" I can barely hold his gaze, the burning intensity making my stomach cramp. Instead, I glance down his body to the tight boxer briefs and the thick outline of his growing erection. *Oh, heck.*

"Try to pretend that last night didn't happen."

Heat flares in my lower half and rises to smother my cheeks. Like I could ever forget. "Why not?" I finally mumble.

"Because it was real, Maisy. It was more real than anything I've ever felt, more than the danger that constantly surrounds me, and more powerful than the secrets we guard in the depths of our hearts."

My breath hitches as his thumb gently strokes my arm.

"And it was *everything*."

My heart catapults up my throat, his confession too much after the raw intensity of last night.

"Nico..." I murmur. I don't even know what to say so I let his name hang in the air between us. I can't give into this, no matter how much I may want to. I can't forget who this man is and what he's done.

I refuse to fall for another monster. And despite the beautiful packaging, Nico *is* a monster. He's never even bothered to hide it, not like Jasper.

A loud crash echoes up the stairs and jerks my attention from my spiraling thoughts. Nico is on his feet, his gun drawn, before I even turn toward the door.

My eyes nearly pop out of my head as I scan the sleek black weapon. "Where did that come from?" I squeal.

He ignores my question and drags me behind his back. "Stay behind me and don't say a word."

Like I could. For once in my life, I'm completely speechless, my throat tied in knots and fear strangling my lungs. It takes me a second to realize why. It's Nico. The murderous gaze, the strained set of his jaw, the tense posture, all of that I've seen before, but behind it, there's a hint of fear.

For me?

He creeps toward the stairwell, and I trail behind, practically glued to his back. His back. My mind whirls back to a few moments ago, and I search for the trace of puckered skin on his shoulder. I follow the scar down his shoulder blade where it practically disappears beneath the massive phoenix tattoo I'd been ogling at Palestra. No wonder I'd never noticed the scars before.

Nico's hand tightens around my arm as we descend. The panic returns, drawing my thoughts away from the scar and what may have caused it. I really know nothing about this man, other than the obvious. He is a ruthless killer, completely unhinged, and a total stalker.

And I never feel safer than when he is by my side.

The front door slams closed, and I jump back, but Nico's unyielding hold keeps me steady. He mutters a curse and quickens his pace, racing down the final few steps. I struggle to keep up as he drags me along with him.

When we finally reach the front door, Nico opens it a crack and peers out onto Riverside Drive. I rise to my tiptoes to see over his broad shoulder and can just make out a hooded figure already nearly a block away. My heart punches at my ribcage. Nico trains his gun at the fleeing intruder before a little boy and his dog emerge from a building right between the man and us. He lowers the weapon and mutters a curse in Italian.

I release the breath I've been holding and sag against his powerful form.

"Fuck!" he grits out.

"Who was that?" I finally manage, "and why were they in my home?"

"I don't know but when I find out, I'll string the *bastardo* up by his toes and bleed the life out of him." He still stares down the street as if he could somehow shoot bullets from that terrifying glare.

A chill races up my spine at the venom in his tone. But what's more disturbing is the pleasure I derive from the promise. If anyone can protect me, it's Nico Rossi.

What if he hadn't been here? What if I'd been all alone asleep upstairs?

That panic rises anew, and ice crystalizes through my veins. A shudder sends a tremor coursing through my entire body, and it's so violent Nico must feel it. He spins toward me and yanks me against his chest. Despite the hard planes, I sink into his embrace and revel in the security of his muscled arms. "I promise no one will ever hurt you again. You're mine, little fox, and no one touches what's mine and continues to draw breath."

I should be insulted because I am a strong, independent woman and I don't *belong* to anyone. But my feminist streak is currently in hiding because gosh darn it, someone just broke into my house and scared the bejesus out of me!

A long moment later, he releases me, and I hate how my body reacts to the absence of his.

"Come, sit down over here where I can see you. I need to check the rest of the house." His hand wraps around mine, and he tows me to the living room sofa. I perch on the edge of the cushion, ready to leap up if a shadowy figure emerges from a closet. With gun cocked at the ready, Nico searches the rest of the first floor, every creak of the old wooden planks elevating my racing pulse.

When he disappears behind the staircase, my gaze bounces between the area he vanished behind and the front door. A flash of yellow beneath the entrance table catches my eye. An envelope?

Slowly, I stand, gathering my nerves as I creep toward the note as if any sudden movement could set it off. Crouching down on the floor, I reach for the envelope with trembling fingers. I draw in a deep breath before yanking the flap open.

A picture slides out, one I know so well it has bile oozing up my throat. Jasper and I on our wedding day. He's drawn a heart around our heads in black marker and across the bottom in his typically eligible scrawling just one word. *Soon.*

"Maisy?" Nico appears around the corner, and the picture slips through my fingertips. "What is it?"

I shake my head, tears welling in my eyes. I thought it was over. I thought I was finally rid of the man who'd ruined my life. But I was stupid to think he'd give up so easily.

Nico snatches the picture from the floor and releases another string of Italian curses.

"It's Jasper," I murmur. "He's back and he wants *me*."

CHAPTER 20
AN IMPOSSIBLE ULTIMATUM

N *ico*

Fuck. Why had I let that *pezzo di merda* escape? I'd had him in my grasp for weeks, using him to scare my half-brother's girl and to keep Dante so busy he wouldn't notice as Gemini Corp stepped in and stole everything away from the King's. It had worked perfectly.

Now the same *bastardo* had turned on me? Talk about fucking irony.

I tear the picture of Maisy and Jasper in half then rip his half into tiny pieces. Much like I'll do with his body when I find him. "Pack a bag," I bark at Maisy.

"Wh—what?"

"You're not staying here by yourself with your ex on the loose."

She eyes me warily. "So where am I staying?"

"With me, of course."

"Ha, I don't think so." She plants her hands on her hips and glares up at me.

"This is not a discussion, and I was *not* asking."

"You aren't the boss of me!"

A smirk curves the corner of my lip despite the irritation. "Little fox, if I have to, I will throw you over my shoulder and stuff you into the trunk of my car, but I can tell you one thing for certain, I am not leaving this house without you."

"You wouldn't dare," she hisses.

"Try me." I throw her a glare that would have my men scrambling for cover, but the feisty little thing just stares back at me defiantly.

What happened here? When did I lose my edge over this woman? Oh right, it was likely at some point last night when she had me on my knees worshipping at the altar between her thighs.

I take a step toward her, and panic flares across those expressive emerald orbs.

Now that's more like it.

She staggers back a step, and I lunge.

"No!" she squeals as I wrap my arms around her torso and toss her over my shoulder. She kicks and squirms despite that wrapped ankle, and I'm proud of her. At least I know she wouldn't go down without a fight should the worst happen.

The mere thought sends my heart into a panic. What if I hadn't been here? Would Jasper have taken her? In the month the man spent as my captive, he frequently spoke of his ex-wife longingly. He was obsessed with her that was clear, but to what lengths would he go to get her back?

As she fights against me, I pull out my phone and shoot a quick message to Max. He must be nearby, he always is, which is exactly why I hired him.

"You can't just kidnap me again," she shrieks.

"This is different, it's for your safety."

"Why do you care anyway?"

I smack her on the ass, and she lets out an enticing squeal. "You know why."

"No, I don't." Her tiny fists batter my back. It's a good thing the burns I suffered all those years ago deadened most of my nerve endings. My little fox is a spirited thing.

"This is your last chance to pack a bag, or you'll have to make do with what's on your back."

"But I'm in my nightgown!"

"Exactly." A wicked grin tips up the corners of my lips. My little fox in nothing but a nightie for the next few days sounds heavenly. Even better, I'm fairly certain she's not even wearing panties unless she snuck them on when I wasn't looking. The idea of unfettered access to that sweet pussy has my cock hardening, despite the traumatic start to the day.

"Fine, you infuriating beast," she hisses out. "Put me down so I can pack."

"Don't even try to run. You know you'll only end up hurting yourself, and I'll catch you anyway."

"Blah, blah, blah."

I gently place her down on the floor, and she shoots me the three-finger salute. I nearly die of shock.

"Read between the lines," she grits out.

A chuckle parts my lips, releasing the tight set of my jaw. "You really are something else, little fox."

"Fork you," she mutters as she marches up the steps.

I watch her take the steps gingerly, but I'm pleased to see she's finally able to put more weight on her ankle. I need her in fighting form for what's to come next.

"Why didn't you tell me you lived at the Waldorf Astoria?" Maisy stares up at the iconic hotel as Max unloads the car. Towering columns frame the entrance, adorned with intricate detailing, creating a sense of timeless elegance. The exterior architecture, a blend of art deco and neoclassical styles, exudes a regal charm, exactly what I need when entertaining the cream of Manhattan's crop.

I shrug in response to her question as Max passes by, struggling with Maisy's luggage. When I'd said to pack a bag, she'd filled two suitcases worth of clothing and a carry-on brimming with toiletries.

Cazzo, perhaps I'd been too hasty with this arrangement.

Not to mention the fact I'd never okayed any of it with Marco. Fortunately, my brother was out of town for the week, and with any luck, I'd have Jasper six feet under by the time he returned.

"Come, follow me." I motion toward the red-carpeted entrance. I lead Maisy through a set of imposing glass doors, which are flanked by impeccably uniformed doormen, ready to welcome guests into Manhattan old world luxury.

With Maisy's upbringing I'm certain she's quite used to the pomp and circumstance but perhaps she didn't expect it from me.

The lobby unfolds in a breathtaking display of grandeur. A sparkling chandelier hangs from the ornate ceiling, casting a warm glow over the marble floors. Unlike Maisy, I wasn't raised in such luxury. Once I was able to afford it, I leapt at the chance. Not only was the Waldorf only a few blocks away from Gemini Towers, but it also offered short term rentals. Until this standoff with the Kings was settled, I couldn't risk retaliation to a more permanent home.

I escort Maisy past the luxurious furnishings, from plush velvet sofas to gilded accents that create an ambiance of refined sophistication. Even better, the residences are all furnished in the same style. Exactly what I need given my current time constraints. What I need right now is a hundred percent focus on taking down my half-brothers' business.

The female draped at my side as we wait for the elevator reminds me my efforts haven't been where they should be since I forced my way into her life. Now that she is staying with me and her safety is ensured, it should be easier to focus.

Surely.

The elevator doors glide open, and we step inside. Maisy leans against the gilded walls and tips her head back, closing her eyes. With her brilliant auburn hair cascading down her shoulders, she looks absolutely exquisite. We're finally alone after the adrenaline rush of this morning. I inch closer, unable to stop myself. I'd hoped for another round this morning, one in which she finally allowed my cock entrance. After all, the night all about her had come to a satisfying end, and my needs are burning to be sated.

There is only so much selflessness and control even I can exert.

I cage her against the wall and her eyes snap open, a gasp tumbling from her lips. "What are you doing?" She slaps her palms against my chest.

"Fucking that pretty little pussy in the elevator?"

She lets out another gasp, her eyes growing impossibly wide. "No," she rasps. But her hips tilt toward me all the same.

I eye the emergency stop button as I harden against her. With our height difference, my cock rubs against her belly. There's no way she can't feel it.

"It was only one night, Nico," she blurts.

"I don't remember that ever being discussed."

"It's an addendum, one I added after the fact." Her hands still press against my chest, but the determination in her eyes is lackluster.

"Why?"

"You know why." She hurls back my earlier comment like an insult.

I take a step back, a bucket of ice water dousing the building flames. "If it's time you need, I'll give it to you."

"Nico, it would take me until the end of time to allow

anything to happen between us again. It was a moment of weakness and wine. Lots of wine."

"I have wine in my apartment." I cock a challenging brow.

"I can't." A battle surges across those expressive irises, one between her head and her most innate desires.

"What would I have to do to convince you that we are perfect for each other?"

Her brows knit, my impromptu confession clearly surprising her. She isn't the only one. When I'm around this woman I can barely control my mouth.

A rueful chuckle escapes as she shakes her head. "Give up your war against my best friend's husband."

A kick in the groin would've hurt less. I stare at her unbelieving. Of all the things she could ask for. I've spent my entire life working toward this day. To see Dante and Luca's business crumble, to burn it to the ground and finally exact my revenge.

"I can't…" I mutter, the words painful to force out. "Why would you ask for the one thing I can never give you? Anything else, absolutely anything—"

She shakes her head, the glimmer of hope in her eye vanishing. She's serious about this…

I find it completely absurd that she can get past the murder, the torture, the kidnapping, all the countless illicit activities, but this, this is where she draws the line? For a friend who won't even speak to her?

The elevator doors open, and Maisy rushes out. I don't even have the energy to stop her. Though she clearly has no idea where to go, her only desire is to get away from me.

CHAPTER 21
INESCAPABLE

M*aisy*

Come on, Rose.

I stare at my phone, willing those dang blue bubbles to pop up. *Answer me.* The first real friend I've had for years hasn't responded to a single text message for days. And it's completely my fault. I never should've left with Nico that day.

I lean back against the cushioned footboard of the bed and heave out a sigh. I'm ninety-nine percent sure in my mad escape from the elevator yesterday, I'd commandeered Nico's bedroom. I'd slammed the door shut upon my arrival and had refused to emerge since. My stomach is growling, and I wish I had a change of clothes, but surely, my suitcases are in some other room in this sprawling penthouse.

Eyeing the elaborate décor, I scan the room for a hint of the mobster who resides here, but the only tell-tale sign is the musky scent smothering the sheets. I may have never actually slept with Nico, but his essence wrapped around me all night.

It had been a fitful sleep plagued with visions of Jasper *and* Nico. I tossed and turned running away from one monster only to fall in the arms of another.

I'm totally hopeless.

Snagging my bottom lip between my teeth, I glance back down at my phone and type out one last message. One I really didn't want to resort to, but here we are.

Me: *Nico's keeping me captive in his penthouse.*

Guilt eats at my insides as I jab the send button. It's kind of true. I mean he coerced me into coming here and hasn't left my door since I arrived yesterday.

Those blessed little blue bubbles appear, and my heart bounces with joy.

Rose: OMG, Maisy. Why didn't you tell me sooner?

Rose: I'll have Dante and his men there ASAP.

Rose: Where are you?

As panicked message after message rolls in that guilt squeezes tighter around my lungs, and I punch out a quick reply.

Me: *No, don't. It'll start a war.*

One I'd be completely responsible for.

Me: *I may have exaggerated the truth a little bit in hopes of getting you to answer. Sorry.*

Rose: ...

Those darn dots crawl across the screen.

Me: *I just wanted to apologize for the other day and try to explain myself. But I know there's nothing I can say to make it right, other than I've clearly lost my mind. I'm staying with Nico, but I'm safe. Kind of. Please, call me so we can talk. It's important.*

The dots disappear, and my heart sinks right along with them. She's never going to forgive me.

I have to tell her about Jasper's reappearance, but it's not something I want to do over text. Dante could help track him down, and all of this could be over. Too bad Nico is too dang proud to ever ask his half-brother for help.

"Little fox..." Nico's rough voice seeps through the door. "Not that I mind you in my bedroom, but I'd hoped when the time came, I could be in there with you." His fingers slide beneath the door, and he reaches for me.

Dang it. I was right. This *is* his room.

Why couldn't I have run into a random guestroom instead?

I should have known as soon as I walked in. My fingers dig into the plush carpet beneath the massive king size bed. The entire space looks like it was plucked out of a Restoration Hardware show room. Not a single personal item litters the room. Only dark navy walls and lofty windows with views of downtown Manhattan and towering skyscrapers.

"Maisy, please talk to me."

I grind my teeth together to keep from spilling all the curses poised at the tip of my tongue. My mother would have my hide if she heard a single awful one.

The door creaks, and every muscle in my body tenses.

"If you don't let me in, I will break down the door. I've been more than patient, but enough is enough."

"I'll never talk to you again if you do," I hiss.

I can almost feel his eyes roll from the other side of the dark mahogany.

"We are at an impasse, little fox. You've asked me for the one thing I can never give you. I cannot, and I will not stop until my half-brothers' empire crumbles. Luca and Dante ruined my life, and I will never be at peace until I ruin them."

"Then you'll never have me."

He huffs out a breath, and judging by the thud against the door, he's either hitting his head against it or some other part of his body. A long minute later, it finally stops. "You're clearly not thinking rationally right now. And that's understandable given the traumatic return of your ex. I will allow you to stew in my bedroom for only a short time longer."

"Allow!" I grit out. That son of a gun has a lot of nerve. I should just march out of here and run to his enemy's open arms. Dante was my friend, okay maybe acquaintance, long before this jerk strolled into my life, and Rose may be pissed, but she'd never leave me to deal with Jasper alone. Would Nico let me walk out of here?

"If you refuse to come out, can you at least toss out a change of clothes? I have a meeting in forty-five minutes."

"But it's Saturday." I cringe at my whiney tone. Good golly, what is wrong with me? It's not like I expected the mob boss to spend the day with me, a walk in the park, brunch, maybe? *Gawd, you're an idiot, Mais.*

"I'll be back as soon as I can, and I'll have guards stationed both inside and outside of the penthouse. You'll be perfectly safe."

"Whatever," I mumble.

"Maisy?"

"What?"

"Don't even think about trying to escape while I'm gone. You'll only succeed in angering me, and when I return, you *will* be punished."

My cheeks heat as completely inappropriate images of me sprawled across Nico's lap with my bare butt exposed flit to the forefront of my mind. Where the heck did that come from? I've never been spanked in my life, and I do *not* think I'd enjoy it.

"I'm not some child you can punish, you arrogant douchebag. And if I want to leave, I will. I'm not your prisoner, despite your twisted convictions. I appreciate you trying to look out for me, but clearly, it was a mistake coming here."

"No," he snarls. "I will not have you alone and unprotected while that psycho ex of yours is on the loose."

"Then find him so I can get the heck out of here."

"I'm working on it." He looses a frustrated breath, and I realize I've hit a nerve. The great Nico Rossi hasn't been able to find one sneaky, stalking, two-timing, run of the mill surgeon.

"So the clothes..." he mutters.

I force myself off the floor and trudge over to the massive walk-in closet. The only good thing about the last twenty-four hours is that my ankle feels surprisingly sturdy. Maybe I'll finally be able to go back to work on Monday.

Peering inside the custom built-ins, I search the sea of black suits. "Do you want black or black?" I shout over my shoulder. A smirk flashes across my face despite my irritation with the stubborn son of a biscuit.

"Funny, little fox," he yells back. "I'll let you choose."

Running my hand over the fine fabric of the myriad of suits, my fingers close around one at random. Much like the bed, the entire closet reeks of the man. That musky, charred scent fills my nostrils and drags me back to the other night. Instantly, heat races between my legs. Squeezing my thighs together to ease the burning ache, I remind my lusty hoo-ha that those earth-shattering multiple orgasms aren't in our future anytime soon. Or ever again, frankly.

Grabbing a button-down black shirt and suit, I haul them out of the closet and march toward the door. With each step, my ankle feels less unsteady, too bad I can't say the same about my heart.

My hand closes around the ornate gilded knob, and I draw in a steadying breath. *Just throw the clothes out the door and slam it shut.* Painfully slowly I twist and open the door a crack.

A hand snakes through the opening and wraps around my throat. All the air catches in my lungs as piercing irises bore into me. Heat floods my cheeks then streaks down my center. Jiminy crickets, what is wrong with me?

Do not look at him. Do not engage. I repeat, do not engage.

"Open your eyes, little fox."

Crapsicles, when had I closed them?

"Look at me."

My lids slowly flutter open as his thumb moves slow circles across my throat. His nose nearly brushes mine, his breath mingling with my own ragged exhales.

"I will find a way to convince you that we are inevitable, so it would make things easier for both of us if you simply gave in now."

I narrow my eyes at the cocky mother trucker and press my lips into a firm line. "Never," I grit out.

He releases a grunt, and his hold on my neck tightens for an instant. "This is nowhere near over, little fox. We are unavoidable, as inescapable as the ocean's tides or the inexorable march of time. We are only just beginning."

A shudder surges up my spine at the intensity of his words. Because as much as I'd like to deny it, I can't refute the truth I feel in his statement any more than I can deny the pull of gravity under my feet.

Nico Rossi has drawn me into his massive, looming orbit, and I'm helpless to withstand that unstoppable force. Worse, I don't want to.

CHAPTER 22
A SURPRISE PROPOSAL

Nico

My mind is a jumbled mess as Max speeds down the highway to the Lower East Side. That woman has my insides tied in knots. Maisy is out of her mind if she thinks I'll abandon my quest for revenge against Luca and Dante. I may be dying to bury my cock in that sweet pussy, but that is too steep of a price.

My fingers curl into fists at my side. I force them to straighten and reach for my phone. Still nothing from Jimmy. How has no one set eyes on Jasper yet? It's been over twenty-four hours and none of my men have anything to show for it? It's fucking impossible. Jabbing my finger at the screen, I call my right-hand man, and he answers on the first ring.

"What's up, boss?"

"Where the fuck is Jasper Whitaker?"

"Good morning to you too."

I can practically hear the smile from across the line, but I'm too pissed for jokes today. I slide to the end of the seat, rage simmering just below the surface. "Don't fuck around today, Jimmy, I'm not in the mood."

"Noted."

"So if you haven't found him yet what are you doing to ensure success in the next twenty-four hours?"

"Is that the timeline?"

"No shithead, the timeline was five minutes ago."

"Relax, Nico, damn I've never seen you so uptight. We're on it."

"Work faster."

"Done."

The call drops, and I shove my cell back into my jacket pocket. A faint scent lingers on my lapel, and I sniff at the material like a fucking mangy dog. Maisy. I never should've let her touch my suit. Now her perfume, much like her entire being, is engraved into every corner of my life.

Fuck. Why did I bring her to my penthouse?

That fiery redhead distraction is the last thing I need right now. Not when I'm so close to getting everything I've ever wanted. I have Dante by the balls and Luca is in hiding like the enormous coward he's become. Love has ruined both powerful men, and I vow never to follow in their misguided footsteps.

The sooner I find Jasper the quicker all of this will be over. It's the irrational fear for Maisy's life that's robbing me of logical thought. Once she's safe, I can move past this unhealthy obsession. If she won't let me fuck her, then I'll simply have to move on. There are countless women in this city begging for my cock.

There's nothing that special about her pussy.

Liar. A dark voice wriggles through my subconscious calling me out on the bullshit. At some point in the last few months, Maisy has become so much more than a warm hole to bury my cock into. She's an unattainable conquest, the focus of every waking thought.

Cazzo.

It can't be. I cannot be falling for her. I'm fairly certain I don't even know how to love. Everything I touch I conquer, then I ruin and destroy. Maisy doesn't deserve a fate like that with all the pain she's already endured.

The car screeches to a halt outside the familiar warehouse, and I shove all the tumultuous thoughts to the furthest recesses of my mind. I must focus. Qian Guo is the key to destroying the Kings, he's the final nail in the coffin, and I can't wait to drop that fucking hammer.

Max opens the door a moment later, and I step out, game face on. Qian is a shady fuck, and I can't afford to be unfocused around him. What kind of *bastardo* kills his own damned father to ascend a throne?

"You ready, boss?" Max asks as he pats the gun hidden in the interior pocket of his jacket.

"I'm always ready, Max, but this should be a friendly visit so follow my lead."

"Will do."

We march up the dim alleyway, dark shadows crisscrossing our path even in broad daylight. *Dio*, I hate the Lower East Side. If it were up to me, I'd put an end to all our shady dealings and dabble only in the shiny high rises of the legitimate side of Gemini Corp.

One day...

A male at the end of the alleyway offers us a stiff nod and opens the rusted metal door. "Qian Guo is waiting for you." Dark eyes peer through the small slit in the cowl of his navy uniform.

"Great," I mutter.

Like last time, the head of the Four Seas sits in the middle of the cavernous chamber. Only this time, he sits atop a gaudy gilded throne with a woman riding his cock. Her head spins toward us, eyes widening. She attempts to flee but Qian's hand closes around her throat and forces her back down. "I'm not done," he hisses at the blonde. "Hurry up."

I slant a look at Max who stares unabashedly at the naked, writhing female. Her ass bounces on Qian's lap as he forces her up and down by the throat. Crossing my arms over my chest, I try to block out the sounds of flesh slapping against flesh, the faint groans. I almost wish that dreaded house music was on, anything to block out the moans.

"Qian," I growl. "If you needed more time, you could have simply said so, instead of wasting my own. Watching you get off isn't how I'd prefer to spend my precious time." I'd rather be convincing a certain redhead to allow me balls deep inside her. And every moan has me hardening, imagining her straddling *my* cock.

His head falls back, and a dramatic moan fills the echoey chamber. He shoves the woman off, and she scrambles, landing on the cement floor with a whimper. "Go," he hisses as he zips up his pants. She leaps to her feet and darts toward the darkness, the soft footfalls disappearing an agonizing moment later.

I grit my teeth to contain the building rage, reminding myself it's none of my business how he treats his women. This ruthlessness is exactly what I need to secure the rest of the Lower East Side from the Kings. He can get his hands dirty where I, the CEO of Gemini Corp, cannot.

Qian stands and claps his hands, his dark gaze focusing on me. Two males in navy appear from the shadows and place two chairs across from Qian's self-appointed throne. "My apologies for keeping you waiting, Mr. Rossi. Sometimes, a need arises that simply cannot be quelled."

I grunt and stalk closer. "This relationship has been created to ensure a mutually beneficial arrangement. If and when I no longer find that to be the case, it will end." I flash him a sneer. If this shithead thinks he can fuck with me, he's got another thing coming. Sliding into the seat, I glare up at him until he folds into his garish throne. "Have you made any advances in King or Red Dragon territory?"

He nods slowly, his bald head glistening beneath the dim

lighting. "Of course, we have. The Four Seas have burned down three more Dragon warehouses since we last met."

My nostrils flare, and the acrid scent of smoke burns my lungs. My heart stamps out a rapid beat, desperate to escape its skeletal confines. Darkness blurs the edges of my vision and all the voices muffle, as if they're underwater, or maybe I am. I'm drowning. Drowning in an inferno.

A dull pain in my side centers me, and the scene rushes back in full speed.

"Boss," Max hisses, his elbow grinding into my ribs. "You okay?"

I blink quickly, and Qian's curious gaze coalesces across the murky space. Fuck. Shoving back the dark memories, I clear my throat and don the mask, the cool, icy one that shields everyone from the truth.

"Excuse me," I mumble. "I lost my train of thought."

"The warehouses," Qian repeats.

"Ah, yes. Three you say?"

"Yup." He pops the P, the irritating sound sharpening my focus. "They're nothing more than ashes. It'll be a big hit to the Red Dragons coke supply."

"Good." I squeeze my eyes closed as screams ricochet through my skull. The other foster kids that didn't make it out that day. I heave in a breath and force the memories into that ever-expanding vault in the back of my mind. "And what about the Kings' warehouses along the docks?"

His arrogant smile falters. "That's a bit more complicated. Given the recent attacks, the Kings have doubled their security. They've even got cops on their payroll. I can't risk my men getting caught."

"That's bullshit," I snarl.

"No, it's smart business." Qian eyes the males who have emerged from the darkness. Two stand on either side of his throne. He barks something in Mandarin, and they all dip their heads, then one skulks off toward a doorway. "If you're so dead set on destroying the Kings, why don't you send your own men?"

"I've already told you why I can't. Dante is on high alert when it comes to the Geminis. He knows what I'm up to. Not to mention my corporation's legitimate dealings. I cannot under any circumstances compromise what we've built. I'd hoped that you and your men could handle this side of the business with the necessary discretion, but it seems I was mistaken." I start to rise, but Qian lowers his hand.

"Wait."

I drop back down on the edge of the chair and tap my foot on the cement. "I'm a busy man, Qian. You already wasted my time forcing me to watch you fuck that girl, for what? Some sort of power play? You want to measure my cock against yours? It won't even be a competition."

The corner of his lip curls as he regards me. "I would like to see your cock, I'm sure it would be quite impressive. I don't discriminate, Mr. Rossi—males, females, they're all the same in the end, nothing but a warm hole to sink my dick into."

A wave of fury rolls through me, and I leap up. Is this guy for fucking real? Max is at my side, gun drawn before the Four Seas asshole can blink.

Qian smirks and holds up his hands innocently. "Relax, Nico, no disrespect intended. I'm only letting you know the option exists. You seem strung a little tight." His gaze drops to my crotch and my hard-on straining against the zipper.

"I'm. Not. Interested," I grit out.

"Suit yourself." He shrugs, turning his attention to approaching footsteps. One of the males in a navy hood appears escorting a dark-haired woman.

Unlike the last one, she's fully clothed in a form-fitting silk gown and completely breathtaking. With creamy porcelain skin and jet-black hair pulled into a flawless bun, the woman is the picture of a dainty, demure, Asian beauty.

"Perhaps she'd be more to your liking." Qian follows my gaze, lifting a dark brow.

He would probably be right if I wasn't so damned obsessed with a certain redhead waiting for me at my penthouse.

"Mr. Rossi, I'd like to present my sister, Jia."

The girl offers me a tight smile and a bow, and I return the gesture despite the surprise rattling my insides. How that beautiful creature could be related to the beast in front of me is beyond my rational thought.

"A pleasure," I mutter.

Qian clears his throat and slides to the end of the crushed velvet cushion. "You see, I was thinking, if I'm to put my men in such risk, perhaps there's something you could do in exchange." His gaze flits between his sister and me. "Perhaps we could bind our families in marriage."

CHAPTER 23
READ BETWEEN THE LINES

M*aisy*

An hour my butt. Where was that infuriating mobster? I stare out the French windows off the living room that face an enormous silver skyscraper. I'm surrounded by them, stuck in the concrete jungle of midtown Manhattan. It's only been twenty-four hours and already, I miss the peaceful solitude of the Upper West Side. Give me the green of Riverside Park over these towering office buildings any day.

If I wasn't truly terrified of Jasper, I would've marched my butt right back to my townhouse. That and the burly Italian stationed at the door.

I cast a quick glance over my shoulder and offer a smile. The big male with a barrel chest grits his teeth, his lips sliding into more of a sneer than something friendly.

"Housekeeping!" A quick knock sends my heart into a tailspin, and I draw in a steadying breath as I creep to the door.

"I've got this," the big guy interjects, holding his arm out to block me before I reach the entrance. He peers through the peephole for a long minute before finally twisting the knob.

"*Hola*, Pepe." A young woman rushes in, a messy bun propped on the top of her head, with dark tendrils of hair spilling down her heart-shaped face.

"It's Giuseppe," he grumbles.

"Ah, *si*, that's right." She offers him a smirk and already I love this girl. She stops in front of me, looks me up and down, and her dark brows furrow. "And who might you be, you pretty little thing? I've never seen a woman in this place since the Rossi brothers moved in." She lowers her voice to a whisper. "To be honest before I actually saw Marco, I thought they were lovers but then—"

"*Zitta*," Giuseppe barks. "Clean the house and keep your mouth shut like you're paid to do."

She lifts a nonchalant shoulder like the scary beast didn't just scare the living daylights out of her like he did me. "Don't be so grumpy, Pepe." Rolling her eyes, she drops her bags by the door and starts tidying up the space.

Which is nearly an impossible task since the place is already immaculate.

I follow her around for a bit, her fiery energy contagious. That and I'm just so dang bored. I notice there's one door she purposely avoids which piques my curiosity. I'll have to come back and explore when I'm alone later.

"I'm Maisy," I finally say once we're tucked away in a guestroom at the far corner of the penthouse. The walls are a pale pink, and a beautiful orchid sits atop the ornate dresser, its sweet scent lingering in the air.

"Nice to meet you, Miss Maisy, I'm Blanca from the beautiful island of Puerto Rico, housekeeper by day and aspiring actress extraordinaire by night." She sings the last few words, and a giggle tumbles out.

"You're really good!"

She dips into a dramatic bow, holding up her duster with

an elaborate flourish. "Thank you, thank you very much. I've been in two off-Broadway productions since I moved to the city from Florida last year. I had to get a side gig at the hotel to cover rent and other expenses, but this is my year, baby, I'm going to Broadway!" She sings the last word again, and my sullen mood instantly lifts. Without Rose around and being forced to work from home, I hadn't realized how much I'd missed people. And not just moody, brooding mob bosses.

"That's amazing. I wish I had a passion like that." I slump down onto the bed as she flits around the bedroom like a fairy with wings.

She stops her manic dusting and swings a questioning gaze in my direction. "What are you doing here, *chica*? You're not dating one of the brothers, are you?" Her lips pucker like the thought is the most revolting thing in the world. Either we've got really different taste in men, or she knows about the Rossi's illicit dealings. "And what happened to your foot?" Her gaze traces down my bare leg to my wrapped ankle.

"I—I'm..." My words trail off because I can't seem to find a logical answer. Nico and I certainly aren't dating, and we're far from friends. But somehow, I can't seem to force out the true nature of our relationship. He kidnapped me, stalked me, and somehow became my savior all in a matter of months. And the other stuff... well, there's no way I'm going into my twisted desire for the man. "I'm staying here temporarily while I heal," I finally blurt.

Her dark brow lifts into an incredulous arc. She holds her stare for an excruciatingly long moment before she shrugs. "Okay."

The slam of the front door has Blanca rushing into the adjoining bathroom. "The boss is home so back to work, *chica*. We'll chat later."

A mixture of anxiety and excitement tangle in my chest as heavy footfalls resonate across the marble floor of the penthouse. I'm filled with the most insane urge to hide.

"Maisy, where are you?" Nico's voice echoes across the hallway.

My flight or fight instincts kick in and good golly, it's nearly impossible to keep my feet still despite the faint ache in my ankle. I should've run back to my room or followed Blanca into the bathroom, but now I'm stuck.

"There you are." A deep voice fills the room, seeping into every corner of my being.

Don't turn around. I keep my gaze fixed to the colorful painting on the wall, a landscape of the quaint towns of Cinque Terre if memory serves me. Every year, my parents would drag my sister and me along with a troupe of nannies on whirlwind European tours. It would've been lovely if I'd only gotten to spend time with them instead of the au pair.

Soft footsteps pad across the plush carpet, and every nerve ending lights up at Nico's approach. Warm breath spills across the back of my neck, and a shiver darts down my spine. "It's beautiful, isn't it?"

It takes me a second to realize he's speaking of the painting since my body is thrown into overdrive just at his mere presence, and I'm having trouble focusing. "Yes," I finally answer.

"Do you like this room? It was the one I'd originally imagined you could stay in." He inches closer, and my bare shoulder blades brush the fine fabric of his suit. "But I'd be more than happy to allow you to remain with me in my bedroom."

I snort on a laugh. "Not happening."

"Why do you have to be so difficult, little fox?"

"If by difficult you mean smart, geez, I don't know." I wrap my arms around myself to keep my fidgety fingers from reaching out to touch him. His hands close around my shoulders and spin me around to face him.

His dark brows are pinched, and fine lines furrow his brow.

"What's wrong?"

The carefully constructed mask slips back into place, and an arrogant grin replaces the hint of worry. "Nothing," he mumbles. "But I'm pleased that you care."

"I don't," I bite out.

"Liar." He snaps at my earlobe, just grazing the sensitive flesh, and I let out a squeal. Taking a step back, his dark gaze razes over me, pausing at my ankle. "How does it feel? Can you put all your weight on it?"

"Almost healed, I think. I'll be back to work in no time."

A growl rumbles in the back of his throat, the sound more beast than man. "I don't think that's a good idea given the Jasper situation."

"Speaking of, how was your meeting? Did it have anything to do with finding him? Because I was thinking, I could talk to Rose and I'm sure Dante—"

Nico's hand lifts so fast I jump back, certain he's about to strike me. Anger carves into his strong jaw, but he doesn't make a move toward me. "Stop," he grits out. "The day I ask my half-brother for help is my last day on this earth." He grinds his jaw, teeth gnashing. "No, I take it back. I'd rather die a million times over than ask him to lift a finger for me."

"It's not for you, it's for me."

Nico closes the space between us, and I stagger back, hitting the fancy armoire. His hand wraps around my neck and jerks me toward him. "You're mine, you come with the package. Anything relating to you directly impacts me. Don't you see that?"

Narrowing my eyes at the possessive psycho, I grit out, "I. Am. Not. Yours."

"Just keep lying to yourself, little fox. One day it'll grow tiresome. I know it has for me." He spins on his heel and marches out of the bedroom.

My entire body lurches forward, and I draw in a steadying breath the moment he's gone.

I finally emerge from my new bedroom a few hours later because judging by the sounds coming from my stomach, my insides are eating themselves. Tiptoeing down the hall, I'm ecstatic with myself for being able to put all my weight on my toes without wincing. If all goes well, by Monday I should be back at Palestra.

And not a moment too soon.

I need some space from the suffocating mob boss.

Speaking of… a familiar deep tenor echoes from the kitchen. I halt at the end of the hallway and peer around the wall. Nico sits at the marble island with a cell phone pressed to his ear.

"I told Qian I needed to think about it," he growls at whoever's on the other line. Another lengthy pause. "It's not that simple, Marco."

Ah, the elusive brother. As terrifying as it is to consider living with two Rossi's I can't help but be curious about Nico's sibling. My stalker has been hanging around for weeks and still, I've never met his brother. It is weird.

"Yes, I understand what it could mean for us. I'm not stupid. I'm also not going to jump into an arrangement that would be extremely difficult to extricate myself from."

What arrangement? I inch closer trying to put together a discussion from only half the conversation. My stomach lets out an embarrassing rumble, and Nico's dark gaze spins in my direction.

"I have to go," he mutters. "You're not back until next week, right?" Nico's brother must say yes because a relieved smile slips over the tense set of his jaw. "Good, see you then." He pockets the phone and beckons me out of the shadows with one long finger. My thoughts instantly snap back in time to that wicked digit, and the multiple orgasms it persuaded out of me. "Come here, little fox, you sound hungry." The rough edge to his tone speaks of a hunger I'm very familiar with. One in which I absolutely, positively refuse to satiate unless my Dante demands are agreed to.

I cross the distance between us slowly.

"I take it you met Blanca today?"

I nod.

"She picked up some food from *Serafina's* before she left. It's in the oven." He ticks his head at the stainless-steel double oven which I'm certain was spotless even before Blanca walked in the door.

I will my lips to say I'm not hungry, but my stomach growls the instant he opens the oven door and the scent of garlic and fresh tomato sauce finds its way to my nostrils.

"Mmm, pizza," I groan.

A chuckle parts his lips, bringing light to those deep azure irises. "I knew I'd wear you down eventually, little fox. I just never thought it would be pizza making you moan again."

Heat flushes my cheeks and I tuck back my thumb and pinkie, holding up my three remaining fingers. "Read between the lines."

"I can't wait until you tell me to fuck off one day." He hands me a plate and drops a slice of pizza on top. The mozzarella is still melty and gooey, and I'm practically salivating now.

"It'll never happen." I slide onto the barstool and take a big bite.

"We'll see about that." He inches his chair closer to mine so that his muscled thigh brushes my bare one. Even through his sweatpants, his heat permeates right through to my skin. Sweatpants? I glance down, completely unnerved by the sight.

I've never seen the great Nico Rossi in anything so casual. My gaze rakes down the soft gray pants and the clear outline of his—

I jerk my eyes up as another flash of heat races up my neck

and blossoms across my cheeks. Good lordy, living with this man will be the death of me.

"What was that call about?" I ask around another heaping mouthful.

"Nothing important." His expression shutters, and I can practically see the icy mask slide back on.

There's nothing I hate more. The few glimpses of the mobster's true self he allows to slip through is what gets me every time. If he only let me in more often, I'd break. So maybe that mask isn't just for him, maybe it's best for both of us.

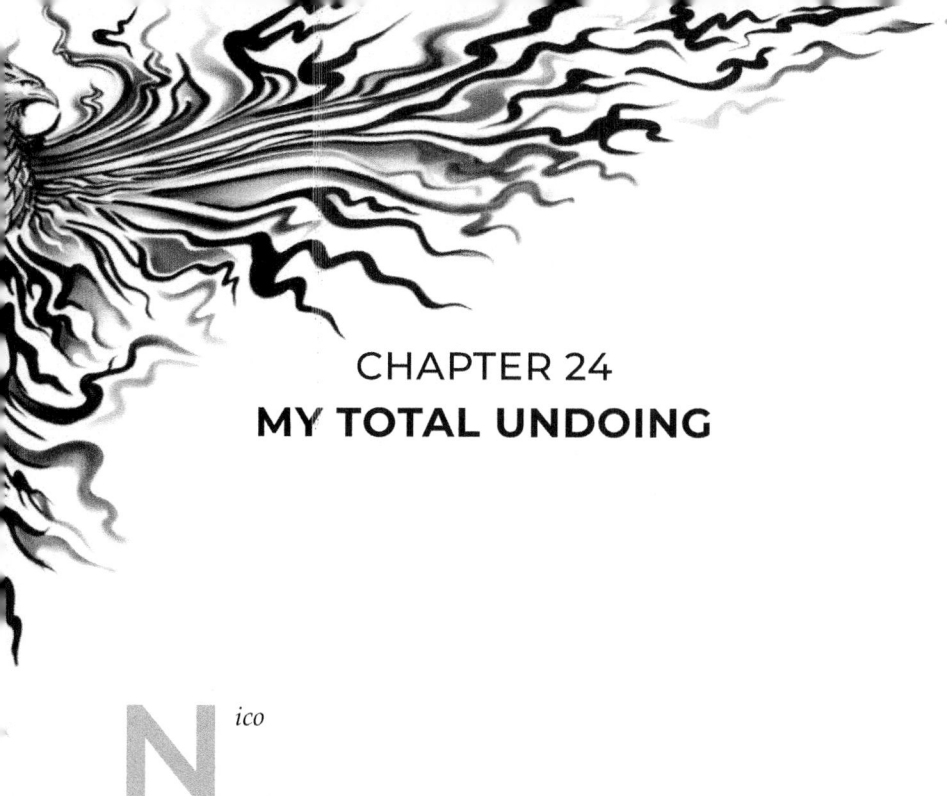

CHAPTER 24
MY TOTAL UNDOING

N *ico*

Rolling over, I reach for my phone and open the home security app. Before the grainy image appears, I slam my cell back onto the nightstand face down. *Stop it*. Instead, I stare at the clock beside it willing the minutes to tick by faster. I've been awake for hours, tossing and turning, unable to get my mind to stop churning. Marco is right, taking the deal Qian offered would cement the Gemini's supremacy throughout the five boroughs, then why can't I stomach the thought?

A pair of lively emerald eyes flash across my vision, answering my unspoken question. Maisy. She consumes every waking thought, and even the idea of an arranged marriage with another woman is completely unacceptable.

Because the terrible truth is that I want *her* and no one else.

But if I admitted that to my brother, he'd lose his shit.

After years of plotting how to destroy Dante and Luca, the answer is now at our fingertips but I'm too obsessed with this woman to reach out and grab it. She would never accept any sort of relationship with me if I were married, even if it was just a business arrangement.

I heave out a breath and drag my hand through my hair.

You're an absolute fucking idiot, Nico. No one says she'd accept a relationship with you anyway. I'm risking my half-brothers' certain demise for flimsy wisps of a chance with a woman who despises me.

My hand moves to my phone unbidden. This time I allow myself a quick glance at a peacefully sleeping Maisy. I watched her sleep for half the night like a complete *pazzo*. I'd gotten so used to the routine that even now that she's under my roof I can't seem to stop myself.

There's something so comforting about watching the gentle rise and fall of her chest, the faint flutter of her lids and listening for any slight sound that tumbles from her perfect lips. My finger traces the wild locks of red hair framing her face, and my cock hardens as I imagine her soft skin, my lips kissing that milky white flesh, my tongue tasting every inch of her. Fuck. This is getting completely out of control.

Tossing my phone on the bed, I shove the comforter back and slide off the mattress. Maisy is only a few yards away from me. Why should I force myself to settle for a shitty video image when the real thing is only down the hall?

I stalk toward the guestroom, my pulse escalating with each step closer. The door is ajar, the heavy blackout curtains sucking every ounce of light from the room. Irrational fear pummels my insides until I can make out her familiar form curled beneath the blanket. What if she tried to escape? Worse, what if Jasper found her?

This little fox has burrowed her way into my cold, black heart and has sunk her cute claws into my dark soul. I stand there in the doorway, staring like a complete fool. Normally, I would simply take what I want. I want to fuck her so I would. But this woman has me paralyzed and completely out of sorts.

I'm scared to step inside the room and wake her. I'm not the only one not sleeping well. She's plagued with nightmares of the asshole that abused her both physically and mentally. No physical scars remain, but I'm fully aware it's the ones that cannot be seen that carry the most weight, that carve deepest into your soul.

Maisy rolls over, a whimper escaping her puckered lips. *"No…please."*

The faint cry pierces my heart, and my feet move of their own accord. I creep across the room and perch on the edge of the mattress. "Maisy," I whisper.

"*No!*" she cries again, and her eyes snap open.

"Shh, it's okay, little fox. I'm here."

"Nico?" Her voice is jagged, laced with fear.

A mix of fury and anguish twist in my gut. I hate that Jasper has caused her so much pain, and I'm furious at myself for not having found the fucker yet. I caress her cheek, running my thumb across her supple skin like I'd imagined doing only a few moments ago.

"Stay with me," she whispers as she settles her head back down on the pillow.

My heart riots against my ribs.

All the nights I've watched her sleep, I've never dared lie next to her. I've been so damned tempted, but there's something so intimate about the act of sleeping beside someone. To be completely vulnerable and at their mercy.

In my thirty years on this earth, I've never slept with another soul beside my mother and brother when I was young. The sinister side of foster care doesn't exactly instill a man with trust in humanity.

Another whimper and my heart kicks at my ribs. "Nico…"

That's it. My name on her lips does me in. I crawl under the covers beside her and she immediately rolls toward me, burying her face in the crook of my shoulder.

My entire body tenses for a never-ending moment. I remain

that way, every muscle frozen until she lets out a contented sigh. Her arm slips around my bare waist and holds me flush against her. She's so soft, so warm against the hard, cruel planes of my body. She couldn't possibly be more different than me, more different than any woman I've ever been with.

I haven't even fucked her yet and in that moment, I'm certain that the instant I sink my cock into this woman's warmth, I'll be ruined. Because she's too good, too kind, too sweet to be anywhere near a monster like me. But that's the thing about monsters, we're too fucked up to care who we drag down with us along the road to damnation.

And this woman right here will be my total undoing.

Movement jerks me from a deep sleep, and my eyes pop open as I instinctively reach for my gun in the nightstand. Only it's empty. I blink quickly and the dim room coalesces, the darkness illuminated by slivers of light seeping through the curtains. The guest room, not my bedroom. And the movement was the tantalizing redhead sprawled across me.

Bright auburn hair spills across my bare chest, the sight pinching my ribcage and forcing my lungs to work a little harder. Her arm and leg are both slung across my torso, pinning me to the spot. I don't think I could move even if I wanted to.

Slowly, I lift my hand attached to the arm buried beneath her neck to make out the time on my watch. Shit. It's almost ten in the morning. I can't remember the last time I slept this late.

The slight movement must jar Maisy's head because she begins to stir, stretching out the leg hooked across my lower abdomen. Her knee brushes my raging erection, and fire licks up my spine at the faint touch.

Her head suddenly shoots up and she twists toward me, green eyes bright and wide awake. "Nico?" she squeals.

"Mmm, good morning, little fox."

She yanks the comforter up to her neck and rolls off me, curling into a ball. "What are you doing in my bed?"

A hint of irritation flares at the insinuation. "You asked me to sleep with you last night."

"I did *not*."

"I'd be happy to replay you the footage if you don't believe me." I reach for my phone on the nightstand and again come up empty-handed. Damn it, I'd left it in my room last night.

"Footage?" And I thought her eyes were wide before.

"I have cameras across the penthouse. Surely, you've noticed?"

She shakes her head, horror streaking across her expressive features. "Everywhere?"

"Not in the bathroom, if that's your concern."

She snags her bottom lip between her teeth and gives it a tug as her cheeks go awash in crimson.

Well, this is unexpected. "You naughty little fox. Have you been doing wicked things in the privacy of the bathroom?"

"No!" she cries, but the rosy hue only deepens.

"Dare I ask who you were thinking about as you stroked that precious pussy?"

"Not you!" she blurts. "I mean, I wasn't doing *that*. But if I were, it definitely wouldn't be you."

"Such a little liar." I tsk, waggling a finger at her. Sitting up, I crawl closer, and she inches back until she hits the headboard. I loom over her, my arms pinning her against the cushioned bedframe. I'm painfully hard after spending all night with Maisy wrapped around me and my cock tents the boxer briefs, like an arrow pointing straight toward the pussy I can't stop dreaming about. Her gaze drops to my arousal, and a faint gasp purses her lips. "You'll have to excuse my lack of self-control but sleeping beside you has exacerbated the situation."

Her tongue slides between her lips, and she runs it across her full bottom one before she swallows hard. *Dio*, am I reading this wrong, or does she want to touch me? Fuck it. I reach for her hand and bring it to my cock, closing her fingers around my boxers.

She gasps again but doesn't let go. A slight tremble vibrates across her clenched hand, and I lift my gaze to meet hers. "Take it," I whisper, "every part of me is yours."

A hiss parts her lips, and she drops her gaze as she starts to stroke my cock over the boxers. I kneel to give her better access and plant my palms on either side of the bed board, trapping her against it and my heaving chest.

Cazzo, just a few pumps and this woman has me on my knees.

I watch her, those emerald eyes pinned to my cock as her hand moves up and down. "Do you like this, little fox? Do you take pleasure from the power you hold over me with that one little hand?"

She smirks, and her eyes finally lift to meet mine. "Yes," she murmurs.

"Good." My fingers close around her wrist and draw her hand beneath the waistband. Her breath catches as our flesh collides. I mutter a curse when her fingers wrap around my length. Her touch is so gentle, too gentle, as if she's worried I'll break.

Maybe she's not as wrong as I thought.

As her hand slowly strokes my cock, all the walls I've built around my battered heart begin to crumble. "Mmm, Maisy," I murmur, my lids heavy, "you're going to be my utter devastation."

The ghost of a smile curls the corners of her lips.

CHAPTER 25
SCARS

Maisy

I'm doing this. I can't believe I'm fudging doing this. And oh my gosh, do I love it. I love the feel of his silky skin against my palm, I love the power that it gives me, but most of all I can't get enough of the look of utter devastation in his eyes.

"*Dio*, little fox, do you have any idea what you're doing to me?"

I barely keep the giggle from bursting free. Holy crapsicles, this is amazing. To have the great Nico Rossi coming undone in the palm of my hand is a rush like no other. After being treated like shit-zu for most of my adult life by the man that was supposed to love me unconditionally, this, this feeling is— beyond my wildest dreams.

I don't even know what came over me when I saw him in my bed this morning. Once I'd gotten over the immediate fear, a weird sense of calm had descended over me. For the first time in as long as I could remember, I'd slept like a baby and woke up feeling like a brand new woman.

There's no way that was Nico, right? How is it even possible?

Fuzzy images of a tanned, muscled chest and strong arms wrapping me against an unyielding form fill my mind. Not only had we slept together, but I'd also practically slept on top of him. And gosh darn it, it was the best sleep of my life.

Then when I saw the overwhelming physical proof of his desire for me, I just couldn't stop my twitchy fingers from reaching out and—. Let's be honest, I'd been dying to touch him since that day in the bathtub. And now, it's happening.

Maybe I was too quick to make that stupid ultimatum about Dante.

I internally chastise myself and my lusty inner vixen. No, ending the war with Dante and his brother is what's best for everyone. Besides, I said Nico would never *have* me if he didn't give up the war. *Have* has a very broad interpretation, right?

Semantics, I know, but I just can't seem to think logically with this man's huge erection in my hand.

Nico's hips start to pump against my palm and all spiraling musings halt. My focus is solely on his hard length and the beads of moisture glistening on his enormous head. Mother trucker, this cannot be normal. I always assumed Jasper was on the smaller end of the spectrum but without a basis for comparison my guesses were purely based on speculation and smutty romance novels, of course.

Nico is huge. Like it's a good thing we're never having sex huge because I'm fairly certain he'd break me.

He lets out a groan and thrusts faster. I can barely keep up with his manic pace. My fist glides up and down his length, the increasing moisture dribbling down my fingers easing the hurried tempo.

"Mmm, little fox, I'm so close. Your hand is incredible,

those fingers like magic. I'm going to come faster than when I was a horny teenager."

A totally inappropriate cackle bursts out as I imagine a young Nico fondling himself in a dark closet.

A feral grin flashes across the sharp planes of his jaw. "You laugh now but wait until my warm cum spurts across those pouty little lips."

I gasp, which only broadens that mischievous smile. His dirty words go straight to my lower half, and now I'm aching for his wicked tongue. Nope, not happening again. Clenching my thighs together, I attempt to extinguish the building flames as Nico reaches the point of combustion.

I'm not sure how I can tell as I've never seen the man on the precipice of an orgasm, but there's something about the softening of his jaw, the slight crinkle at the corners of his eyes and the flash of excitement in his darkening sapphire eyes.

"Get ready," he rasps out.

"Ready for what?" What does he expect me to do with it?

"Give me your nightgown."

"No!" I screech.

"I'm going to come all over this bed in a second if you don't. Unless you'd prefer to use your mouth?" A sinful smirk has his eyes sparkling with mirth. "Because trust me, little fox, there's nothing I'd like better than that pretty little mouth wrapped around my cock."

"What about the sheet?" I reach for the silky material.

"The housekeeper isn't back until tomorrow and this is the only clean set."

Somehow, I'm pretty sure he's a big fat liar. Still, caught up in the heat of the moment, I rip the nightie over my head with one hand, toss it at him, and my breasts tumble free. Nico's eyes zero in on my peaked nipples and with one last pump, he throws his head back and the orgasm rips free. "Oh, fuck, Maisy..." His eyes practically roll back in his head before he sags against me, his arm encircling my very naked body.

Tossing my nightie on the floor, he presses his forehead to mine and rests his hands on my thighs. My nipples graze the hard contours of his chest, sending sparks of electricity through my veins.

His thumbs are only inches away from my throbbing center. Oh, fudge do I want him to touch me there. Like so bad! His warm breath ghosts across my face, his lips only a heartbeat away.

Nico's forehead rests against my own, a glimmer of sweat on his brow. I press my mouth into a thin line to keep from capturing those lips. One kiss and I'd be done for. Despite my ultimatum, after seeing this tiny break in Nico's defenses and having him on his knees for me, I'm not sure how much longer I can hold out.

The feeling is completely and utterly addictive. Just one taste and now I'm certain it'll never be enough.

His ragged pants finally begin to subside, and he straightens, looming over me once again. "That was a hundred times better than I ever could've imagined, little fox."

Embarrassment coats my cheeks as I cross my arms over my bare chest. The truth is that I'd gotten so good at hand jobs because by the end of our marriage, I absolutely loathed Jasper touching me. It was the quickest way to get him off and off of me.

"May I return the favor?" A glint of mischief ignites those piercing azure orbs.

It takes every ounce of willpower to shake my head.

"Are you sure?" His heated gaze drops to my panties and an arrogant grin flashes. I follow his line of sight to a wet spot on the light pink silk.

Oh, sugar, kill me now.

The heat from my lusty hoo-ha flares all the way up my neck and deepens the flush across my cheeks. So embarrassing.

"I can ease the ache, little fox. It'll only take a minute judging by how wet you already are."

"It's not that," I blurt, "I just have to pee."

Oh, fricking heck! Did I just tell this man I peed myself?

A dark chuckle fills the minute air between us, and Nico sits back, that stupid grin etched into his unfairly handsome face. "Why do you continue to deny this thing between us?"

"Because it's nothing more than misplaced lust," I snap and tug the sheet around my bare breasts. "And loneliness." Fudge, what is wrong with my tongue? Why do I have constant verbal diarrhea around this man?

"So what's wrong with a little lust?" He eyes my cleavage barely concealed by the silk covers.

I grit my teeth to keep from saying something completely inappropriate. I've already developed an unhealthy attachment to this psycho and sex would only intensify the absurd feelings. "What's wrong with giving up a ridiculous vendetta against a half-brother you don't even know?"

Fury carves into his features, and the teasing man from a second ago vanishes beneath the dark surface. "I don't want to talk about Dante…"

"He's a good man, you know." *Kind of.*

"A good man?" He snorts on a laugh. "Clearly, your dear friend Rose hasn't let you in on my brother's numerous past sins. Don't be fooled, little fox, none of the Valentinos are good men. It all started with our bastard father—"

His shoulders twitch, calling my attention to the scar along the top of his shoulder. The one that's so carefully hidden beneath a canvas of dark ink.

"Did he do that to you?"

That scowl deepens, and a hint of fear snaps my spine straighter. Nico has never attempted to hurt me, but something about the wild look in his eye has the tiny hairs at the back of my neck prickling. "Not directly," he finally grinds out.

"What happened?" I'm not sure where I acquire the courage to continue in this line of questioning, especially since I'm butt naked, but my loose lips seem to have taken over for my brain.

He remains silent for a never-ending minute, and I'm certain he won't respond when his jaw ticks. "It was a fire, when I was young." His voice comes out so quiet, so frail, that I would've never recognized it as Nico's had I not been sitting right in front of him.

Tucking the sheet tighter beneath my underarms, I crawl around him, moving slowly so that he has the chance to stop me. Only he doesn't. When I'm finally kneeling behind him, I search beneath the massive phoenix inked across his shoulder blades. It's beautiful with fiery, flaming wings, a long, elegant neck and eyes that seem to stare right into your very soul. It spans the width of his broad shoulders and descends down his spine until the dark whorls and spirals disappear beneath the waistband of his boxers.

My fingers find his shoulder, and he releases a sharp hiss. I nearly jerk my hand back, but he remains still, and it urges me on. I trace the magnificent, mythical creature with my fingertips, following a path over the scarred skin.

I can't imagine how bad the damage must have been to leave this sort of scar. And as a child? Hot tears burn the corners of my eyes, and I blink quickly to keep them from spilling over. *Do not cry.*

"I'm sorry," I finally murmur once I'm certain I won't start balling.

"It was a long time ago."

"And still, you bear the scars."

His hand finds mine on his shoulder, and he gives it a surprisingly tender squeeze. "Not all scars are on the surface, Maisy. I've learned long ago to deal with mine."

"By covering them up?"

Nico huffs out a breath. "By doing whatever I had to in order to survive."

CHAPTER 26
WHAT DID HE DO TO YOU?

N *ico*

Maisy marches into the kitchen in a conservative but chic pale gray skirt suit and a soft pink blouse. I instantly drop my iPad and the article from the Wall Street Journal to gawk. With her hair in a prim updo that exposes her long, delicate neck, she has that naughty librarian look down pat. All she needs is a pair of cat-eye glasses to complete the ensemble and bring me to my knees.

I'm momentarily too distracted by her sexy outfit to put the pieces together. "Where do you think you're going?" I finally manage.

"To work. It's Monday morning." She lifts her leg and twists her ankle from side to side. "See? All better."

I wrinkle my nose at the sneakers which are completely at odds with my hot librarian fantasy then refocus on the matter at hand. "I didn't say you could go into the office today, little fox."

"Oh, you didn't say?" She slaps her hands on her hips and glares up at me. "Let's get something straight, Nico Rossi, I am staying here of my own free will. I am not your prisoner, and you do not get to control my entire life."

I stalk toward her, my teasing smile morphing into a scowl. She doesn't even budge as I approach her. The little fox is getting too brazen for my liking. She's not even scared of me anymore. When I'm standing in front of her toe-to-toe, I loom over her petite form and glare down. "Let me be clear, Maisy. You. Are. Mine. Mine to protect, mine to keep, mine to torture and before long, mine to fuck."

She snorts on a laugh and the little firecracker squares off with me. "I'm sensing a pattern to your delusions." She tosses me a sweet smile, flashing her teeth. "I've already done this before with Jasper, and I refuse to do it again. I'm thankful for your help with my ex, but I won't be some princess locked away in an ivory tower, despite your best intentions."

"You misunderstand me, little fox, I never said anything about best intentions." I flash her a smirk. "My only intentions at this point are purely selfish."

"Don't do that," she hisses then jabs a manicured finger into my chest. "Don't pretend that all you want is to claim me, to use me as some sort of toy. You're full of it, Nico Rossi. You hide behind this monster's mask, but I've seen glimpses of the real you. It's the only reason I'm still standing here today. You may want everyone else to fear you, to believe you're a sociopath, but I know real evil, real depravity. I slept beside it for four years."

I stare at her, jaw slack, as she finishes her monologue. Just when I think I know this woman, she surprises me.

"I'm going to work now, and I'll see you this evening when I come ho—back." She spins toward the door, and I'm so shocked it takes me a minute to chase after her.

"Wait," I shout. Reaching for her, I wrap my hand around her upper arm and jerk her toward me. "I'm coming with you."

She rolls her eyes dramatically. "You can't babysit me all day, Nico."

"It's not always all about you, little fox. I'm simply going to accompany you so that I can get my workout in for the day." I certainly need something to ease the sexual frustration, and I've been so busy with Maisy I haven't gotten a moment to paint. My studio has sat vacant since this woman whirled into my life.

Maisy lifts a skeptical brow, but she finally releases a lengthy exhale when I don't relent. "Fine, you can drop me off and pick me up."

"How kind of you." I offer her a smirk. "Max will be thrilled to be allowed the honor."

"Oh, shut it." With a satisfied grin, she marches toward the door, and I trail behind her like a whipped dog.

What the hell is happening right now?

"Fuck," I yell, earning a glare from the woman manning the front desk at Palestra. In spite of my promises to Maisy, I'd spent the entire day at the gym. I'd maintained a low profile hiding out in the men's locker room while I attempted to work until a second ago when that email came through my inbox.

I scan the text from my assistant, Mel, for the tenth time muttering curses. The fucking commissioner didn't take the deal we've been working on for months. Which means he must have gone back to the damned Kings.

Fucking Dante.

He must have threatened the man or his family to get him to comply. *Good man*, my ass. Maisy's words still echo across my mind, the irritation at her believing my crazy half-brother is a good man writhing beneath my skin like a venomous snake.

How could she be okay with her best friend with that monster and have qualms about me?

My phone vibrates in my jacket pocket, and I jerk it out,

nearly ripping the delicate stitching of the bespoke suit. "What?" I grind out.

"Did you see Mel's email?" Marco growls.

"I'm not fucking blind, brother."

"What the hell happened? I go away for a few days, and everything goes to shit?"

"It's not like it was a done deal when you left. The commissioner has been on the fence about it for months. Clearly, Dante did something to shove him over to his side."

"How are we going to fix this?" he snarls.

"I'll figure it out. You keep your head on the task at hand."

"I've got a handle on the Puerto Ricans. It's not my head I'm worried about, it's yours. You're too obsessed with that damned girl. If she wasn't in the picture, there's no way this deal would've fallen through."

"Fuck you, Marco, you have no idea what you're talking about." My free hand curls into a fist at my side.

"If I'm so wrong, where are you right now?" I can practically hear my brother's shit-eating grin over the phone.

"You're probably tracking me with that stupid friends and family app. I'm disconnecting you from the service immediately so you stop stalking me."

He snorts. "Right... because *I'm* the stalker. End this thing with the redhead and sign the damned agreement with Qian. It's the only happily ever after we'll get, brother."

Soft footsteps resound across the tile and before Maisy turns the corner, I already know it's her. I don't even know how it's possible, but every part of this woman is already ingrained in my mind. "I'll take care of my business, you take care of yours." Jabbing the call end button, I slip my phone back into my pocket as my little fox rounds the corner.

A few tendrils of red hair have come loose, framing her face in that cute, frazzled way. I haven't seen her all day, and my childish heart comes alive at the sight of her. I'm smiling like an idiot.

Cazzo. What if Marco is right? Have I lost sight of what's truly important because of my crazed obsession with this woman?

"You're early," she says as she approaches.

My phone vibrates again in my jacket, but I ignore it. I've had enough of Marco for now. "I had a meeting nearby," I mutter lamely.

The receptionist glances up at my blatant lie, but she doesn't utter a word, dropping her gaze to the computer screen. Smart girl.

"Come on, Max is waiting outside." My hand instinctively falls to the small of her back, and perhaps I'm imagining it because I truly am delusional when it comes to my little fox, but I could swear she leans into my touch.

By the time we reach the BMW parked outside on Central Park West, I'm breathing easier, my entire body more relaxed simply because of her presence. Which is insane. I'm not certain at what point the tables flipped in this dynamic.

Max jumps out of the car as we approach. He runs his hand through his shaved hair, a nervous twitch making his brow jump.

"What's wrong?" I hold the door open for Maisy as she slides into the backseat.

"I just heard from Jimmy, boss. I got bad news."

"What now?" I reach for my phone again, remembering I'd ignored an incoming call only a few seconds ago.

"The Red Dragons broke into two of Qian's warehouses. They got away with hundreds of thousands in blow. Jimmy thinks they're retaliating for the shit the Four Seas burned down last week."

"*Merda,*" I snarl.

"Qian wants to know what we're going to do. He lost a shit ton of money, and he's pissed. He's threatening to pull out of our agreement."

Damn it. If we lose the Four Seas, everything else will crumble.

"Where is Qian now?" I bark.

"He's at the warehouse on Grand Street assessing his losses."

I eye Maisy who sits in the car, scrolling through her cell phone. I hate bringing her to this meeting, but I need to handle this ASAP.

"Take me there now." I slide into the backseat beside her, a lethal mixture of rage and irrational fear twisting my gut.

Max guns the engine, and we weave between the traffic deadlock of rush hour.

Maisy glances out the window, and the faint line between her brows puckers. "Where are we going?"

Perceptive little thing.

"I need to make a quick stop to see a business associate. I'll be in and out."

She eyes the murky waters of the Hudson as it speeds by. "You could have just let me walk ho—to your place."

It's the second time she's almost called my penthouse home, and the pleasure it brings me is absurd. Once I hit thirty a few months ago, I'd convinced myself I would be happy living out my life as an eternal bachelor. Then this woman appears in my life and everything changes.

"I'd rather have my eye on you at all times until Jasper is six feet under."

Her mouth curves into a capital O, and *cazzo*, my thoughts instantly go back to a similar expression when my tongue was buried between her legs.

"Do you *not* want me to kill him, little fox?" I watch her carefully, eager to make out any subtle tell.

"No," she finally murmurs. "I want to."

Just when I think there's nothing this woman can say that would surprise me, she does it again. The calm, icy tone reminds me of... of me. It makes me wonder if Jasper hadn't been completely honest as to the extent of torture he put his ex-wife through.

I pivot my body toward her, my thigh brushing her bare one. Even with the slacks between us, that faint touch has me hardening. "What did he do to you?" I growl, low and deadly.

She shakes her head slowly, tears glistening in her eyes. "I just want him dead, okay?"

I nod. "Your wish is my command, little fox."

The remainder of the ride to the Lower East Side flies by in a weighty silence. I will find out exactly what Jasper did to her so that when I find him, I can repay the kindness. I know my little fox, and despite her brazen talk, she would never be able to kill him. More than that, I wouldn't want that eternal stain on her conscience.

Max pulls the BMW up in front of the sleek, modern warehouse along Grand Street. It seems completely out of place beside the dilapidated, graffiti-covered ones surrounding it. I reach for the door handle, then spin back to Maisy. "Stay here with Max. I'll be right back."

She eyes the structure, and a tremor shakes her slim shoulders.

Shit, I never should have brought her here. It's likely dredging up old memories of when I held her and Rose captive at that old shipping yard. Fucking idiot.

"Who's in there?" she asks as I open the back door.

"Just an associate, like I said."

"Is it Dante?"

"No," I hiss.

Her brows knit as if she doesn't believe me, and my irritation rises. I've never lied to her about anything. I've been as honest as possible given the nature of my business. I rush out of the car and slam the door behind me before I get more wrapped up in this nonsense. I need a clear head to deal with this shit.

Exhaling a frustrated breath, I march toward the entrance.

A prickle of unease raises the hair on the back of my neck as I approach the double stainless-steel doors. I slow, my feet dragging.

The sharp slam of a door closing spins my head over my shoulder. Maisy stalks toward me with her hands on her hips and a slight hitch to her step.

I spin around and glare at the obstinate woman. "Get back in the car," I snarl.

An explosion vibrates the air behind me, the heat from the blast razing across my jacket. I leap forward, wrapping my arms around Maisy, and we fall.

CHAPTER 27
SLEEP NOW, FIGHT LATER

M*aisy*

I blink slowly, my ears ringing so badly I can't focus on anything else. A jackhammer pounds at my skull and an immoveable weight pins me to the concrete sidewalk.

"Oh, shit! Boss, are you okay?" Max appears over Nico's shoulder, dragging his body off me. The moment he's gone, my lungs begin to function again. Until I scan his face laying on the concrete beside me, searching for those blazing blue eyes and find them closed.

"Nico?"

A trickle of blood seeps from his earlobe, and panic strips me of all senses. I try to sit up, but my head spins and nausea crawls up my throat. *Oh, no, please not now.* I buckle over despite my pleas, and my measly lunch spews out.

Wiping the saliva from my chin with the back of my palm, I lean against the car as sirens start to wail in the background.

"Shit, we have to get out of here." Max's voice echoes

somewhere behind me, but I'm too out of it to turn my head in the right direction. "Boss, wake up, boss!"

I hold my breath, praying to every single deity there ever was that Nico answers. *Please be okay, please be okay.* This time someone answers my prayers.

"Maisy..." His voice is faint, but it's there. He's okay. My head falls back against the cold metal of the car. "Get Maisy first." It's a little stronger this time, a hint of the domineering mob boss flitting to the surface, and a rueful smile parts my lips.

Max appears in front of me and hauls me up, his big arms curling under my armpits. Man, I hope I don't smell bad. After all day at work, I can't be as fresh as a daisy. An insane giggle tumbles out, and now I'm worried I hit my head harder than I thought. My hand moves to the back of my skull and my fingers come back wet and sticky.

"Oh, shit, boss," Max hisses when his darting eyes lock on my bloody fingers as he carries me to the back seat.

I catch a quick glance at Nico sprawled across the dark leather before the edges of my vision grow blurry.

"Maisy, you're going to be all right. Just hold on."

My head dips slowly but even that faint movement turns the backseat of the car topsy turvy.

"Call Dr. Pacetti and tell him to meet us at the penthouse immediately," Nico barks. Or at least I think that's how it's supposed to sound like. To me it sounds all slow and muffled, like I'm at the fun house of an amusement park.

A strong arm wraps around my shoulders, and I sink into a familiar scent. I'm so sleepy. My lids droop, and it takes everything I have to keep them open. I'm vaguely certain I'm not supposed to sleep.

"Maisy, you must stay awake." Nico slaps my cheek, a bit harder than necessary if you ask me.

"Ow!" I squeal. "I just want to close my eyes for a second."

"You can't!" The fear in his voice momentarily snaps my lids wide open.

"Okay, I'll try."

"You can do it, little fox. Just stay with me." Warm breath spills across my hair, and soft lips press against my forehead. I must be severely concussed because why else would the brutal Nico Rossi be gently kissing me?

The back seat begins to blur, the black of the leather upholstery melding with the darkness creeping in.

"Maisy!"

That deep voice anchors me to the present for an instant longer before the tide of oblivion washes over me, and I'm lost.

"Why the fuck isn't she awake yet?" That familiar furious tone seeps through the thick haze clouding my mind.

"I already told you, Mr. Rossi, head injuries are tricky." A male voice, one I've never heard before. "The girl should be in the hospital. I did what I could here but without an MRI there is no telling how substantial her injuries are."

I try to fight my way back to consciousness, but waves of exhaustion drag me under again and again. A minute passes or maybe an hour. I'm in and out, amidst a confusion of frantic voices and vague consciousness.

"*Cazzo.*" That familiar growl summons me to the surface. Heavy footfalls echo around me as if a lion with designer loafers is prowling around my bed. Another inappropriate giggle bubbles to the surface at the visual. Yup, I definitely have a traumatic brain injury. "Fuck it, I'll take her to the hospital."

"Are you out of your mind?" Another male voice I don't recognize. "You can't do that, boss. They'll ask questions, and they'll end up placing you at the blast site. It won't be good for business."

"You think I haven't thought of that shit, Jimmy?" Nico hisses.

"Then why would you risk it?"

Another string of Italian I can't make out muddled with curses I do recognize pours out, and now I wish I would've paid more attention in Latin class back in high school. Mother always said it would be invaluable. How could a dead language be worth anything? Now I know.

"I can take her back to the hospital with me." The first voice who I'm assuming is a doctor of some sort. A chilly hand presses against my forehead, drawing me closer to the surface, then it curls under my neck.

"Don't touch her," Nico snarls. "No one touches her but me. I'll take her to the hospital."

"But boss—"

"Shut the fuck up, Jimmy, before I lose my shit. If you'd been able to handle Qian none of this would've happened."

Nico's comforting, musky scent envelops me even before he's touched me. I breathe him in, my nostrils flaring, and my lids flutter open. The big bad mob boss hovers over me, dark circles beneath his eyes, a bloodied scrape and a deep purple bruise forming on his cheek. A look I'm certain I've never seen before is carved into his features.

"Maisy," he breathes. He takes me in, devouring me with just one look, like a starving man who's stumbled upon a feast after days lost in the wilderness—desperate, ravenous, and utterly consumed by hunger for something he never knew he needed. "Are you okay?"

I nod slowly, and my head only spins a little this time. "I think so." I reach for the back of my head and find a soft, gauzy bandage.

An older man with glasses peers over Nico's broad shoulder, and I immediately recognize the light blue scrubs. "Let me take a look at her now that she's awake."

Nico doesn't budge, his eyes stubbornly locked on mine like if he blinks I might disappear.

"Mr. Rossi," the doctor grates out. "Step aside, please."

He finally does, but his gaze never falters, never deviates. Which makes me suddenly feel awkward as all heck when the doctor starts examining me.

"Do you have a headache?" he asks.

"Yes."

"How bad on a scale from one to ten?"

"Maybe like a six."

"Good." He flashes a light in my eye and asks me to follow it, then resumes his examination, taking all my vitals. A few long minutes later, he takes a step back from the bed. "She seems fine. It appears to be only a mild concussion but again, I recommend an MRI to be certain. She needs to rest and take it easy for the next few days, avoid screen time and any strenuous physical activity."

"I'm fine," I mumble. "I don't need to go to the hospital." The last thing I want is to be stuck in the emergency room all day.

"Are you certain?" Nico is in my face again, the line between his dark brows furrowed. His concern is so unexpected it has my chest tightening. But still, I refuse to admit I'm familiar with a mild concussion and its aftereffects. I experienced two at the hands of Jasper...

Chasing away the dark memories, I force my tongue to loosen. "Yes, I'm sure." I also don't want to be associated with whatever happened down at the warehouse either. Which reminds me... "What the heck happened anyway?"

Nico grits his teeth, and the fear from a second ago morphs into rage. "It was probably my asshole half-brother. You know, the one you want me to make amends with. He almost got you killed."

I shake my head a little too quickly this time, and the room spins with it. "No way Dante would do that," I somehow manage despite the wave of nausea.

"You have no idea what he's capable of or the lengths he'd go to destroy me." Nico clucks his tongue and pivots to the doctor and this Jimmy guy. "We're done here, you can both go." The man in scrubs marches out the door without a second glance but Jimmy lingers, his mouth set in a hard line.

I recognize the name, but this is the first time I've met Nico's right-hand man. He's young with dirty-blonde hair, around the same age as him I'd guess but covered in tattoos from his neck down to his fingertips. He eyes me, and I immediately drop my gaze. The guy is scary and intimidating as all heck, nothing like the security guards that patrol the penthouse who try to look mean but, in the end, let me do whatever I want. Jimmy looks like he'd murder me in my sleep. A chill skirts up my spine, and Nico's head swings in my direction as if he's felt the shudder himself.

"Are you cold?" His anxious gaze rakes over me.

"A little." I'd rather lie than admit the truth that his colleague has me freaked out.

Nico tugs the blanket out from under me and pulls it up over my legs. "I'll be right back." Then he practically shoves Jimmy out the room. It's only when they're both gone that I finally take in my surroundings, the navy walls, the scent of spicy cologne, the silky sheets. I'm in Nico's bedroom, not mine—I mean the guest room.

Muffled voices echo from the corridor and from the sounds of it, both males are pissed. My temples start to throb, and I rub small circles with my fingers to dull the pain. Good golly, twenty-four hours back at work, and it looks like I'll be out again for another few days, trapped in this penthouse on bedrest.

I lean my head back against the pillow, and my lids begin to droop. I must have fallen asleep for a few seconds because

Nico's sharp gasp jerks me from the peaceful void. My eyes snap open, and the flash of relief in his gaze is palpable.

"*Merda*, little fox, you scared me." He sinks onto the edge of the mattress and drags his hands through his wild hair. Dried blood sticks to his face, and the bruise on his cheek is darkening. I have the most overwhelming urge to touch him, to wipe away the blood and press my lips to his discolored skin.

"You scared me too," I whisper. "You know, if I hadn't insisted on chasing after you, you would have been inside when—" Unexpected emotion cuts off the remaining words. The great, indestructible Nico Rossi would've been no more. The man I've come to solely depend upon and trust wholeheartedly could have died today. A rumble of nausea cramps my belly at the thought of a world without him in it. I blink quickly as tears burn my eyes, and a sob builds in my throat.

His eyes meet mine and the depth of emotion hidden beneath those piercing sapphire orbs threaten to pull me under. He crawls up the bed and settles on top of the comforter beside me, his front pressed against my back. His arm latches around my waist, and all the air flees my lungs. "Let's sleep now and fight later," he whispers against the back of my neck.

There are about a million things I want to say, but the feel of his warmth against my body quiets my racing thoughts, and I drift off to sleep with the steady beats of Nico's heart beating in time with my own.

CHAPTER 28
INTO SUBMISSION

N *ico*

This is the second time I've slept with my little fox without getting anything out of it. I'm not sure I like the precedents I'm establishing. And still, when I crawled into bed with her last night, holding her was all I wanted. I hadn't even had time to process the fact that if she hadn't been so disobedient I'd be dead right now.

I'd been so damned terrified at seeing her hurt again because of me I couldn't fucking think straight. I was a second away from risking it all just to take her to the hospital. Marco would've ripped my head off, and rightfully so. All the years we'd struggled, everything we'd achieved so far, I could have lost in one moment of weakness.

No. I couldn't do this anymore. This obsession with Maisy has gotten completely out of hand.

Untangling my arm from around her waist, I force myself off the bed. She stirs beside me, and a sigh of irritation parts her lips. That faint sound has my morning wood straining against my slacks. I never even bothered to remove my clothes last night, and I hadn't even noticed it. I slept like a damned baby with Maisy in my arms.

But that was it.

The next time I find myself in bed with this woman it will be with her on her back and my cock thrusting in that sweet pussy or nothing. I can't afford this distraction anymore. She isn't worth it, no one was. *Liar.* I ignore that irritating voice in the back of my mind.

I stalk to my closet and peel my clothes off before traversing the room to the master bath. Before I disappear into the bathroom, my traitorous gaze pivots to Maisy. Her eyes are open, peeking from beneath the comforter tucked up to her nose. Her heated gaze rakes over my bare form, and fuck, if I wasn't hard before, now, my cock is pure steel.

Gritting my teeth to compose myself, I don the cold mask and arrogant smirk. "See something you like, little fox?"

She squeezes her eyes closed and lets out a forced yawn. "No... I was just wondering why there was a naked man dancing around my room." A shit-eating grin curls the corners of her lips.

"You mean *my* room." I stalk toward her, my rash feet moving of their own accord. *Cazzo,* what is wrong with me when it comes to this woman? My whole life is about control, but one word from those tantalizing lips and all my resolve shatters.

Heat floods her cheeks turning them a tempting rosy hue that matches that wild hair. "Well, you shouldn't have dropped me off in your bed last night then. I wasn't exactly in my right mind. If I had been, I would've insisted you bring me to my—the guest room."

My legs eat up the remaining distance between us, and I stop at the edge of the mattress, my cock standing only a few inches from Maisy's mouth. She lets out a gasp, her eyes fixed to my erection despite her vain efforts to look away.

"I've decided the price for a night in my bed is those perfect lips wrapped around my cock."

"Excuse me?" she rasps out.

"You heard me." This is what I should have done weeks ago. I've gone soft, letting her set the pace for this arrangement. That's completely unlike me.

"If I'd known the price was so high, I would've gladly slept on the floor." Her brows knit, but a hint of mischief flashes across those emerald irises. She wants this, I can feel it. She needs this as bad as I do after yesterday's trauma.

"Please, little fox, I know you want it. Tell me you've never thought about the feel of my full cock in your mouth, the warm salty spray of my cum on your tongue…" I inch closer and her hot breath ghosts over my dick. "Because it's all I can think about."

She lets out another faint whimper, but she doesn't move. Her eyes are still fixed to my throbbing head.

"Come on, just a tiny taste. Let me see that naughty side, little fox. I know it's in there, hiding just beneath the surface. Take my cock in your mouth and bring me to my knees."

Her hand snakes out from beneath the covers, and her slender fingers wrap around my thick length. A hiss parts my lips at the faint touch, and a satisfied grin stretches across her face. "Now use your mouth like a good girl."

Maisy glares up at me defiantly, flashing her teeth, as she starts to stroke my cock. Beads of cum seep from the tip, and her gaze falls to the glistening moisture. She licks her lips.

"I know you want to taste me…"

"Close your eyes," she whispers.

A growl vibrates my throat as my lids slide closed. There's nothing I want more than to see that mouth gliding up and down my cock, but baby steps, I suppose.

After the longest minute of my life, her warm tongue

circles the crown, and I instantly drop to my knees on the edge of the mattress. "Fuck," I purr. I fucking *purr* like a damned cat. I didn't think I'd ever made a sound like it in my entire existence.

Her mouth closes over me and her hand starts to pump faster, moving in tandem with that wicked tongue. Fucking hell, how did this innocent, clumsy woman learn to give head like that?

She sucks and licks, swirling her tongue around every inch of me. With my eyes closed, I can really imagine my cock in her pussy, thrusting deeper, harder until I'm so far inside her we're one. *Dio*, what is this romantic bullshit? Then a hand curls around my balls, and I nearly explode on the spot. My head falls back, and a moan slips free despite my best efforts.

This woman literally has me by the balls, and I'm not certain I like it.

In an attempt to level the playing field, I reach out blindly and snag a fistful of her hair. She lets out a whimper as my fingers tangle in thick locks and guide her head up and down more forcefully. Now that I have a general idea of her position, I reach out with my free hand and find her breast, instinctively. Her nipple is already hard through the silk blouse she slept in, and I want it in my mouth. I want to devour every inch of her soft, supple form but *cazzo*, this woman is so damned stubborn.

Blindly, I find my way into her top, and my palm closes around her silky flesh. She releases a sexy moan, and the sound vibrates through my cock. Fire surges across my veins, pleasure building with each stroke. "If you keep making those sounds, I'm going to come, little fox."

I can practically feel her looking up at me as her mouth slides to my head.

"Is that what you want? Do you want me to come in that pretty little mouth?"

She mutters something I can't quite make out, but the vibrations alone have me skirting the point of no return.

"I'd rather come inside your pussy, but I suppose beggars can't be choosers."

She laughs, and the sound carries through every inch of me. I guide her head up and down, faster now, my hips bucking so that the tip of my cock reaches the back of her throat. She only sucks harder as if the naughty little vixen is truly enjoying this.

I roll her nipple between my fingers, and she lets out a squeal of pleasure.

"You're wasting a perfectly good opportunity here, little fox. We could both be enjoying this more if you'd only give in."

She releases my cock, and I growl my disapproval. "I'm not giving in until you promise to give up this war with the Kings."

My eyes snap open, fury bleeding into the burgeoning pleasure. "Never," I snarl. "You're asking for the one thing I can never give you."

Her eyes narrow, and she sits up, shooting me a scathing glare. Still kneeling on the edge of the mattress, I tower over her but she's not the least bit intimidated.

"Then I guess we're done here." She scoots to the end of the bed, and I watch her, jaw hanging open with my fucking dick in my hand.

"That's what this was?" I roar. "You thought you could suck me off into submission?" Rage pounds through my veins, all the pleasure from a second ago ebbing away.

Maisy spins at me, those emerald irises blazing. "Eff off, you mother trucker!"

"I'm trying, little fox. I'm really trying to *fuck* off. Damn it, just say the word! What are you twelve?"

"I hate you, Nico Rossi! I never should've agreed to come here. This was a mistake, a ridiculously huge mistake." She wraps her arms tight across her chest as she glares at me. "I'd rather let Jasper have me than spend another second here with you." She storms out of the room, and I race after her, still naked.

For someone with a sprained ankle, Maisy's moving pretty damned fast. She darts down the corridor and disappears into the guest room. A lethal mixture of anger, frustration and disappointment battle it out in my chest as I round the corner behind her.

When I reach the guestroom, she's in the closet throwing clothes into her suitcase. I stalk toward her and block the doorway.

"What the fuck do you think you're doing?" I snarl.

"I'm leaving." A tear trails down her face, but she sweeps it away, angrily.

"The fuck you are."

I stare unbelieving as she attempts to zip up the suitcase with clothes still spilling out. Somehow, she finally manages to close it and even gets it to stand upright. "Move," she hisses.

I brace myself in the doorway, glaring down at her. "No."

"I swear to God, Nico, if you don't get out of my way, I'll scream bloody murder."

"No one will hear you. The penthouse is soundproof."

She grinds her teeth, eyes shooting daggers. "If you can't give me what I want, what I need, then you have to let me go." Tears well in her eyes, and a storm of unfamiliar sensations tighten my chest. Fear. Panic. Pain.

The last few months flash across my mind in a spinning carousel of brightly colored images and powerful emotions. Before Maisy, my existence was meaningless, utterly devoid of life. Everything changed the moment her glaring light illuminated the bleak shadows in which I existed.

I can't lose my little fox.

"Fuck it." I close the distance between us in one long stride and fisting Maisy's hair, I force her mouth to mine.

CHAPTER 29
INSIDE ME

M aisy

Nico's tongue pushes past my clenched teeth, his entire body blanketing mine in a blur of hard planes and black ink. My brain tells me to stop, to push him off, but my stupid heart tells it to shut up. Because Nico is *kissing* me. Of all the tempting things this man has done since he forced himself into my life, nothing prepared me for this.

Despite his tongue being inside me only days ago, there's nothing more intimate than this kiss. The way his hand tangles in my hair, the way his lips perfectly mold to mine. It's not sweet or gentle, it's rough and desperate but dang it, it's got my heart in a chokehold.

He takes a step forward, pushing me against the closet wall, and his tattooed arms cage me in. "You will never say no to me again," he hisses against my swollen lips.

I open my mouth to reply, but he cuts me off with another fiery kiss.

Clearly my brain is severely concussed because the neurons aren't firing as they should. Maybe I should have gone to the hospital. I can't even put together a complete sentence with his tongue tangling with mine and his arousal digging into my belly. He's hard again, moisture dripping from the tip and seeping into my silk blouse.

That'll be an embarrassing stain to explain at the dry cleaners.

I allow my hands to wander the unyielding planes of his back, moving slowly over the puckered flesh. Squeezing my eyes closed, I picture the giant phoenix tattoo and the dark, tortured past it conceals.

I'm so swept up in the moment that I nearly forget my ultimatum. The errant thought is like ice through my scorching veins. Smacking my palms to his chest, I push free of his overpowering hold.

"Wait," I mutter. "I can't do this, Nico. Nothing has changed..."

His eyes lock on mine, the blue so profound I just want to get lost in it forever. "I'll try," he murmurs.

"Excuse me?" I blurt because I'm certain I'm hearing things.

His lips thin before he releases an exasperated breath. "I'll try to do what you want."

"To give up your plot to destroy Dante and Luca?"

His head slowly dips, but his eyes never leave mine.

"For real?"

The hint of a smile curves his lips. "I will agree not to purposely set out to ruin King Industries, but that doesn't mean I'll let them step all over the Geminis either. If they start something, I will retaliate."

I swallow hard, considering. If I can just get Rose to speak to me, I know we can find a way to make this work. She can keep Dante in check, and hopefully I can bribe Nico with sexual favors. The brothers are family after all. Okay, so I don't see cute double dates in our future, but at least they could be civil to each other. A hint of hope kindles in my chest.

"And of course your sweet little pussy will be my prize." A beaming smile flashes across Nico's handsome face, and I'm sure it's the biggest grin I've ever seen on the moody mob boss.

"We'll see about that."

He leans closer, pressing his palms on either side of my head against the wall. His lips are only a heartbeat from my own. "That part is non-negotiable, little fox." That smile turns feral as he glances between our bodies. The top two buttons of my blouse have come undone, revealing the swell of my breasts. He lets out an appreciative growl and his hand slides off the wall, down my shoulder, over my hip and finds the hem of my skirt. He jerks it up to my waist, and all the air catches in my throat.

"Swear to me, Nico," I rasp out.

"I swear I'll back off the Kings." His hand glides down to the apex of my thighs, and an embarrassing whimper escapes. "Mmm, that's my good girl, you're already soaked and ready for me." He tugs my thong to the side and runs his finger across my throbbing center.

Freaking heck do I want this. I want this so badly, but I'm terrified what will happen once I give into him.

His finger finds that aching bundle of nerves, and he begins to circle. "*Cazzo*, little fox, I've been dreaming about this moment since the day I saw those pouty lips and big green eyes staring up at me in that dark container. I remember thinking that asshole Jasper never deserved you. And if I ever had a woman like you, I'd show her what it felt like to be worshipped."

My head falls back as his thumb takes over my clit, and he dips a long finger inside me. He thrusts long and slow, and my hips begin to move to the rhythm.

"You're already drenched but you're so tight I want to

make sure you're ready for my cock, baby. I don't want to hurt you."

Hot tears threaten to surface, but I blink quickly shoving them back. *It's just sex, Maisy, chill out.* Sure, he's only the second person I've ever had sex with but still... It doesn't make it important or anything.

A second finger joins the first, and I groan at the intense sensations rolling through me.

"When was the last time you were fucked, little fox? Your pussy feels amazing, as tight as a virgin's."

Those dang tears threaten to resurface so I look away, staring at the sea of black suits over his shoulder.

Nico pauses, something like terror racing across those expressive orbs, and his free hand grips my chin, forcing my eyes to his. "You're not a virgin, are you?"

"Practically." A rueful laugh bubbles out.

"What does that mean?"

I try to look down, but his hold only tightens keeping my eyes level with his. Releasing a sigh, I compel the words out. "I've only ever been with Jasper, and I told you I never orgasmed, so sex was never really something I enjoyed."

There it is. The embarrassing truth.

Which is exactly why I'm so scared. A part of me truly believed Nico would never give up on his revenge quest against his half-brothers. That ultimatum was my easy out. But now...

"Well, get ready, little fox because all of that is about to change." He drops to his knees and drags my panties to the floor. "Are you on the pill?"

"IUD," I mutter. Jasper was adamant the moment we got married. I thank God everyday I'd listened despite how disappointed I'd been when he first brought it up. I couldn't wait to have kids.

Then Nico runs his hands up the back of my thighs and cups my bare behind and all thoughts of Jasper and babies flee. Finding the zipper to my skirt, Nico makes quick work of it, and the stiff gray fabric lands in a heap on the plush carpet. "I'm going to fuck you right here right now, little fox. I can't wait another second to sink my cock inside you. Then I'll take you on the bed, on the dining room table, in my studio, on every surface of this damned penthouse until you've come on my cock so many times you won't be able to see straight."

A thrill of excitement snakes up my spine as his fingers move to the buttons of my blouse. I'm so wet I can feel the moisture sticking between my thighs. No one has ever done that to me before. My luck it'll dribble to the floor, and I'll slip and fall from the wetness.

Oh, goodness, that would be absolutely mortifying.

Once my blouse and bra have joined the other articles of clothing on the floor, Nico stands. Those piercing eyes raze over me, blazing a scorching trail across every inch of skin. I've never felt so exposed. My arms instinctively move to cover myself, but he clucks his tongue, wagging a long finger covered in my arousal.

"Don't do that. Don't hide in front of me. You're the most magnificent creature I've ever seen. Let me look at you for a second."

That heated gaze gets my blood pumping more rapidly than when his face was buried between my thighs. Good golly, I don't think I'm going to be able to stand for much longer. An impossibly endless moment later, he stalks toward me and lifts me off the ground. Wrapping my legs around his hips, he props me up against the wall. The tip of his thick erection presses against my entrance, and I freeze.

Instantly, my mind scrambles. I'm too heavy. How can he carry me like this? I'm going to fall, then he's going to fall and we're going to end up in a tangle of legs on the floor, then I'll probably break something—

"Maisy, stop."

I blink quickly, focusing my frazzled thoughts. Brilliant blue eyes meet mine, and I'm caught in their lethal sights.

"Whatever has you all flustered, stop it." His mouth captures mine, hard and rough before releasing me again.

Somehow, he always knows what I need, sometimes before I do. It's an uncanny ability. One that I find terribly frightening and comforting all at the same time. "How do you always know what's going on in here?" I point to my temple.

An unreadable expression flashes across that ruggedly handsome face. "Maybe we're not so different you and I, little fox."

I find that hard to believe but I nod anyway.

He claims my mouth once more and everything else falls away, the incessant voices of doubt finally go silent. All I feel is Nico, his tongue dancing with mine, his hands palming my backside and keeping me pressed firmly against him, his warm, spicy scent infiltrating the air between us.

Nico slips his hand between our bodies, and I watch as he guides his erection toward my entrance. He glides it across my center, and I groan at the silky feel of his hardness.

"Do it, Nico," I breathe. "I want you inside me."

CHAPTER 30
NEVER BEEN TAUGHT

Nico

I want you inside me.

That pleading tone pierces my chest, each word like a bullet straight to the heart. Finally. After months of waiting, stalking, lurking, my little fox has given in. And it has only cost me *everything*.

But fuck it, I'll figure out a way to ensure Gemini supremacy while keeping my word to Maisy because I'm so crazy about this woman I *would* give it all up for her. I can't even start to process what that means. The word *love* is too vast a concept to wrap my head around in this moment.

There's no denying it though. I've fallen for Maisy, completely and utterly, at the cost of what I'd spent my entire life working toward.

Maisy wriggles against me, her hips rubbing her slick heat against my cock. Closing my eyes, I savor the moment, the feel of her legs tight around my waist, her wet pussy gliding across my length. Then my eyes snap open, and I thrust.

Maisy's head falls back, and a sexy moan erupts from those pouty lips. I can't help but echo the sound. She's so tight, so hungry for my cock.

"*Dio*, you're heaven, little fox." I fix my gaze to hers, on those blown-out pupils, on the brilliant shimmer of her jewel-toned irises, and I realize I want to spend the rest of my life looking into those eyes, with my cock buried in her sweetness.

I've never felt this way about anyone. I've never connected with another soul in any significant way before. It's alarming and amazing all in the same breath.

I slowly withdraw then drive in deeper this time. She's so tight I really am worried I'll hurt her. And with Maisy's tendencies to get injured the last thing I need is something to happen to that precious pussy.

"Oh, Nico," she groans as I pick up the pace, lifting her in time with my thrusts. My muscles burn from the strain, but I live for the tangle of pleasure and pain.

At this angle, the crown of my cock rubs against her clit, and I can already feel her tightening around me. I'll have her coming in seconds. And it's all I want. To show her the pleasure she's been deprived with that bastard and shower her in nothing but the best until the end of her days.

"You are mine, little fox. Do you understand that?"

"Mmhmm," she murmurs against my lips.

Harsh pounding echoes across the penthouse, and I slow my ravenous pace, muttering a curse.

"Is that the door?" Maisy rasps out.

"Ignore it." I drop my lips to her neck and suck hard, marking her as mine as I pound into her. Faster, harder, she takes it all.

The knocking grows louder.

Maisy tenses, and her eyes lift to mine. "Maybe you should see what's going on."

"No," I growl and plunge deeper inside her. "I'm not going anywhere until I make you come."

She lets out another satisfying groan, only urging me on. *Cazzo*, if this is just a quickie in the closet, I can't wait to hear the noises I'll coax out of her when I have her splayed out on my bed with all the time in the world.

"Uh, Mr. Rossi, sorry to barge in but—" Giuseppe's gruff voice echoes down the corridor.

"Fuck," I hiss and pull out, dropping Maisy back to the floor. "I'm so sorry." She wobbles as I release her, and I just barely get my arm around her in time to keep her standing.

Her cheeks are flushed and *Dio*, she looks beautiful with her auburn locks wild, draped across her bare shoulders. "No, I'm totally fine."

"This better be fucking important," I shout out the closet door.

"It is, boss. Marco's in trouble."

I want to fucking strangle someone as my knee bounces impatiently in the cabin of my private jet. We're landing in Puerto Rico in minutes, and I've spent the entire flight cursing my damned luck and most of all my brother. Meanwhile, Jimmy is sound asleep in the seat behind me, snoring like a baby.

Leaving Maisy on the brink of orgasm was one of the hardest things I've ever had to do in my life. I promised to be the first to make her come by fucking her into sweet oblivion, and I went back on my word for the first time since we met.

She begged me to bring her along, but I have no idea what I'm walking into, and I won't risk her life again after the Four Seas' warehouse incident. According to Jimmy, Marco went radio silent, and his last communication had been a distress call.

I never should've sent my brother to deal with the Puerto Rican mob alone.

The flight attendant appears from the front of the plane, swinging her hips in that tight navy skirt. I glance up at her again, and I recognize the full pouty lips and flashy red hair pulled into a tight bun. I'd fucked her on a particularly long flight when she first joined the crew a few months ago. Any redhead used to do it for me, but now, I feel nothing.

"Good afternoon, Mr. Rossi, we'll be landing momentarily." She leans in and drops her hand to my thigh. "Is there *anything* I can do for you during our final descent?" Her gaze flickers to my crotch, and I wait for the burst of heat, but my cock doesn't even stir.

Fuck, my little fox has broken my dick.

"No, thank you." I shove her hand off and cross my legs. "Tell the captain I need all the paperwork cleared before we hit the ground. The moment we touch soil I need off this jet."

The flight attendant dips her head, the disappointment evident in the flash of her dark eyes. "Of course, Mr. Rossi."

I watch her as she sashays to the cockpit, willing my cock to spring to life at the sight of her curvy ass, but nothing.

Shit. I'm in love with Maisy. It's the only possible answer. But how? I don't even know how to love someone. Only a dark hole exists where that organ should reside. My father never wanted anything to do with us, my mother abandoned us, and Marco has been the only constant in my life. Do I love my brother? I suppose, I must. But certainly not well.

How can you love when you've never been taught?

The jet lands on the tarmac, and I slide to the edge of the leather chair. Once the wheels stop spinning, I unbuckle my seatbelt and reach for my briefcase in the overhead bin. Securing my gun in the waistband of my slacks, I prepare to disembark.

"Wake up, Jimmy, we're here."

My righthand man rubs his eyes, lets out a yawn and pushes himself out of his seat. "I'm ready, boss."

The only reason I'd sent Marco to make a deal with the Puerto Rican mob was to gain a stronger foothold in their territory in Manhattan. It was all part of my grand scheme to ruin the Kings. Now it seems this entire venture would prove fruitless at best and put my brother in the crosshairs at worst.

Fuck. This is exactly why men in my line of business avoid any meaningful connections at all costs. They're nothing but complications.

And yet, the idea of cutting out Maisy from my life is already unbearable.

The flight attendant appears again and without sparing me a glance this time, marches to the cabin door and unlocks it. My entire body twitches as she takes her damned sweet time. Every second away from Maisy has my anxiety reaching new levels, and the concern for my brother's safety isn't helping either. It's not like him to just disappear.

The door finally glides open, and the darkness beyond momentarily scrambles my senses. When my pupils grow accustomed to the night beyond, I can just make out a few figures surrounding a suped-up Hummer on the private airfield.

Narrowing my eyes, I step onto the tarmac and focus on the familiar form taking shape. Marco stands between two large males, bound and gagged while a woman twirls a gun around her middle finger.

Inhaling a steadying breath, I march toward them with my own hand on my gun. Jimmy trails beside me, his pistol already cocked.

"Welcome to San Juan, Mr. Rossi."

CHAPTER 31
IT WAS LOVE

Nico

The cool mask slips on, and I offer the head of the Puerto Rican cartel a seductive smile. "A pleasure as always, Esmeralda."

The dark-haired beauty saunters closer, full, pouty lips smeared in crimson puckered. Her leather pantsuit molds to every curve of her lethal figure as she approaches. "Your brother fucked me, poorly at that, then tried to force me into a deal that was not only blatantly disrespectful but was also utter bullshit. I know exactly what is going on in Manhattan right now, and it's a complete shitshow. I have no desire to become embroiled in a family feud. The Kings and *La Sombra Boricua* have long had a mutual respect and understanding, and I plan to keep it that way."

Marco struggles against his captors and mutters something that sounds like a curse, but with the gag I can't quite make it out. Fucking idiot. What was he thinking screwing around with her?

"I fully understand your concerns and I apologize if my brother was less than tactful when he approached you. Can we at least untie him so that I may get to the bottom of this?" I flash her my best smile. "For me, Esmeralda. I believe that we too have always had a sort of understanding."

With a grunt, Esmeralda ticks her head at the two men holding Marco. "*Desátalo.*" As her men begin to loosen the binds, she turns to me once more. "Get your brother out of my sight. I'll give you the opportunity to clear this up, but if I don't like what I hear, Marco will be returning to New York an only child."

Jimmy tenses beside me, and I can feel him move a step closer. We're surrounded by her men, far away from our turf. I'll be forced to play nice for now.

"Fair enough." I keep my voice level and cast my right-hand man a side-long glance. I've got this. With Maisy in the mix, the situation has changed anyway. If I can keep things status quo with *La Sombra,* I'll only have to deal with Qian. "Will you allow me a minute to escort my brother to the jet?"

She nods. "*Cierto.*"

One of her men removes Marco's gag, and he mutters a curse as he stalks toward me. "About fucking time you got here," he grumbles.

"You're lucky I came to save your ass at all," I whisper-hiss as I turn him toward the jet and shove him forward. "What the hell were you thinking fucking around with her?"

"Please, she wanted it as bad as I did, and she's a liar if she claims otherwise. You know I've never had to beg for pussy. And she must be the best actress on this goddamned earth because I had her moaning my name all night."

"*Cazzo,* Marco, you know the rules, business before pleasure, you *coglione.*"

He spins at me as we reach the steps to the jet. "I'm sorry, okay? I was all riled up with the commissioner shit, and I ran my mouth when I shouldn't have."

And he hasn't even heard about Qian. My brother's really going to lose his shit when he finds out about that. "What does she know exactly?"

He shrugs. "I offered her the deal we'd discussed, ten percent of our take on all future development projects in Lower Manhattan in exchange for cutting all ties with the Kings. Then she found out we lost the commissioner's bid. That's when things turned ugly."

"Fine. I'll tell her the truth and walk away."

"What? Why? Just offer her a better deal. We need *La Sombra*—"

I lift my hand cutting him off. "I'm done here, Marco. We're taking a step back. We've made significant gains in Lower Manhattan, Gemini Corp has more projects in the books than we can handle, and once I straighten things out with Qian, I'm hitting pause on this trajectory of mutual destruction."

Marco's brows slam together, his mouth twisting. "What the fuck are you talking about, Nico? We're nowhere near done. Dante and Luca still rule Manhattan, the Kings reign supreme. What happened to bringing them to their knees? To stealing King Industries out from under their stuck-up noses?"

"Things have changed," I roar, frustration gnawing at my insides.

"Holy shit. This is about that redhead, isn't it?" His mismatched eyes lock on mine, fury raging below the crystalline surface. "What the fuck happened?"

"I don't answer to you, brother. I don't have to explain myself after the mess you've made with *La Sombra*."

He jabs his finger in my chest, digging the button of my shirt into my skin. "The mess I made? You haven't been right in the head since the moment you kidnapped that girl. Who the hell cares about Jasper? You've got all our men trying to hunt down that rapist, and everything else is crumbling around us. This isn't over, not by a long shot. Go to Qian, marry his fucking sister and fix this."

"No," I growl.

Marco rakes his hands over his face and lets out another string of curses. "I can't believe you're doing this for a piece of ass."

My hand juts out and wraps around my brother's throat. "Don't fucking talk about Maisy like that. Ever."

His eyes widen, the brilliant blue one and dark brown both turning murderous. "*Cazzo*, Nico, you're going to completely fuck us over for this girl? Everything we've worked so hard for?"

"It's not just about her," I snarl. The lie tastes bitter in my mouth, but I continue all the same. "I'm tired of this bullshit, Marco. You're right, we've fought our whole lives to achieve this success, and now I just want to enjoy it. We have everything we need. Can't it be enough?"

His head whips back and forth, jaw clenched tight. "It'll never be enough. Not until Dante and Luca are on the streets without a penny to their names. Just like we were when we came to this godforsaken country and our father rejected us. Or did you forget about that? Did that fiery pussy erase all the shit Umberto Valentino did to us?"

"He didn't do shit, Marco," I shout. "He just didn't want us."

A rueful grin tips up the corners of his lips into a chilling smile. "Oh, I get it now. So now Maisy wants you, so that's it? You're wanted and loved by the perfect woman, and now everything that was so important to you before doesn't matter? *I* don't matter?"

"It's not like that, damn it."

"Fuck you, Nico." He whirls on his heel and marches up the steps to the jet.

I grit my teeth, searching for something to say, but anything I can think of sounds hollow. Because he's right in a way. All this time, I sought to fill the void in my chest, and I thought revenge was the only way to satisfy it.

But I was wrong.

It was love.

"I'm pleased we were able to come to a mutually beneficial agreement." I offer Esmeralda my hand across the pale teak table. Jimmy stands ever at attention beside the sliding glass doors off the veranda. The relaxing sound of waves crashing along the shore behind Esmeralda's house has done wonders for my mood in the past few hours. Allowing Marco to return to New York on the jet first was a stroke of genius. The two-hour plane ride would've been unbearable together. Now, I can already feel a sense of calm soaking through my body.

"Yes, me too, Nico. I hope that the stability you desire in Manhattan will soon come to be." She crosses her long legs and loosens the tie of her sarong. The head of the cartel wears a skimpy bikini beneath, accentuating hazardous curves. "Would you like to join me for a celebratory swim?" She ticks her head toward the azure waves and white sand beach rolling up to her back yard.

I slowly shake my head. "Unfortunately, I must return home as soon as possible. The jet should be arriving at the airport shortly."

She tsks. "That's a shame. I would have loved to give you a tour of my beautiful island."

"Maybe next time." I rise, and she leaps up beside me.

"Should you ever change your mind, you are always welcome in my home." A mischievous glint sharpens her dark eyes. "And in my bed."

Clearing my throat, I take a measured step back. "As tempting as that sounds, I make it a practice not to sleep with women my brother has already fucked."

"That is also quite a shame."

"Maybe, but I find it prevents potentially awkward situations."

Her head dips, and she motions toward the glass doors that lead into the modern house. "Come then, and I'll have my driver bring you and your man to the private landing strip."

"Thank you, I appreciate it." Now that our affairs have been settled, the urge to get home to Maisy is overwhelming. I purposely let slip to Esmeralda about the waning feud with my half-brothers in hopes it reaches Dante's ears.

I have no intention of reaching out to him myself, but perhaps, it'll be enough to smother the powder keg in Lower Manhattan. The final issue I must contend with is Qian, and then I can solely focus my efforts on finding Jasper and making Maisy mine forever.

CHAPTER 32
A NIGHT YOU'LL NEVER FORGET

M*aisy*

Sprawled out across Nico's bed I stare at my phone, at the message I typed out over a half hour ago, and still no response.

Me: Rose, I need to talk to you it's important. It's about Nico and Dante.

Jabbing my finger at the call button, it rings and rings but no answer. *Come on, Rose!* The voicemail comes on, and this time I leave a message. "Rose, it's me. I know you're angry and you have every right to be. I never should have lied to you about Nico, but I know how to fix this. Please, call me back, it's super important."

With a huff, I hang up and toss my phone at the foot of the bed. Laying back, I bury my face in Nico's pillow, allowing his familiar scent to smother the unease. Good golly, when had I become addicted to the mob boss?

I squeeze my thighs together, reveling in the ache still

thrumming through every inch of me. It just wasn't fair Nico leaving like that. I couldn't believe how close I'd been to my first actual orgasm from sex. It had been incredible, mind-blowing and my gosh, I can't wait for Nico to get back so we can try it again.

A silly grin splits my lips, and I can't even hide it. Cheese and rice, I'm falling for my stalker. Who the heck am I kidding? I can try to deny it all I want, but I've fallen. I'm totally, butt-crazy in love with this possessive, psychotic, beautifully brutal man.

Oh, geez, what am I going to do now?

I groan into the pillow and think back on the choices that led me here today. Somehow, Nico was right. We were inevitable.

The creak of the front door opening sends me shooting straight up. "Nico, is that you?" I call out.

"Mmhmm." His muffled response echoes through the large penthouse.

Oh, heck, the last thing I need is for Nico to find me moping around in his bed waiting for him. Which is exactly what I've been doing. I'm even back in a sexy, lace negligée. I'm about a second away from springing out of his bed to hide when my inner vixen takes the wheel.

She wants this. No, *I* want this.

Forcing myself to still, I attempt a seductive pose, propping myself up against the upholstered headboard. The slap of approaching footfalls on marble thumps in time with my raging heartbeat. I run my hand through my wild locks, in a last-ditch effort to tame the tousled auburn strands and hold my breath.

I blink, and Nico's dark form appears in the doorway. He's wearing sunglasses and a t-shirt and jeans, which is so at odds with his typical black suit. It's late though, so maybe he changed on the jet on the way home. There's something different about the way he looms at the threshold, darkness carving into his chiseled features.

"Your hair!" I blurt. The long, midnight strands are gone, replaced by a short, spikey do.

He clears his throat and runs his hand through the bristling spikes. "Yeah, it was time for a cut."

My mouth twists into a frown. I'd spent more nights than I care to admit dreaming about running my fingers through those silky locks. I'm a little disappointed now that I finally can, they're gone.

"You're sleeping in my bed?" he mutters.

A prickle of unease skates up my spine, and I shrink beneath the covers. "Not exactly sleeping," I whisper lamely. "I was waiting for you to get back."

"Mmm. I see." He steps through the threshold and stalks toward me.

That ache between my legs ratchets up as he looms dangerously at the edge of the bed.

"Why are you wearing sunglasses at night?"

"One of the Puerto Ricans roughed me up, and my eyes are a little swollen. I didn't want to scare you…"

My brows twist as I regard him. "Are you okay?"

His head dips. "I'm fine."

"What about Marco?"

"Yeah, my asshole brother is just fine. He's about to get what's coming to him though."

I inch back at the sinister edge to his tone. "What does that mean?"

"Nothing, don't worry about it." He crawls onto the bed, the mattress dipping beneath his weight. His hand snakes around the back of my neck, and he jerks my mouth an inch from his. "Now I want you to make all this shit worth my while. Show me exactly what I'm getting in exchange for everything I gave up."

I swallow hard, something about his tone, his very

demeanor not right. All Nico's wanted since the first day was to give me pleasure. He's never once been selfish about his needs.

His mouth captures mine, tongue pushing its way between my teeth. The pungent scent of whiskey lingers on his breath, a taste I've never associated with him. I try to settle into the familiar groove, but everything is all wrong. He settles over me, the kiss becoming more punishing as he presses me into the mattress. His muscled abs are nearly crushing as he spreads my legs and fits himself between my thighs.

"Nico, slow down," I murmur against his teeth.

"Why? I thought you liked it rough, Red."

Red? My entire body goes rigid.

The front door whips open, and the slam of thick timber against the wall vibrates across the penthouse. "Marco, where the fuck are you?" A familiar voice echoes down the hallway as rushed footsteps pound closer.

"Marco?" I glance up at the man pawing at me, and ice rushes my veins. No, no, no. It can't be.

Nico bursts into the room, and I can just make out his murderous glare from over his brother's shoulder. His mother trucking *twin* brother. How could Nico not share that rather important detail?

"Oh, my gawd!" I try to wriggle out from beneath Marco, a swirl of embarrassment and anger pummeling my insides.

"You motherfucker!" Nico lunges and rips his brother off me, easily tossing him to the floor. "How dare you touch her?"

"I had to see what all the fuss was about, *fratello*. Maybe if I had a taste, I wouldn't care about revenge anymore either."

"Are you drunk?" he roars.

"I may have stopped at a bar for a few hours after you sent me home like a disobedient child." A wicked grin parts his lips, and rage erupts across Nico's face.

He drops to the floor, and the crack of bones smashing into each other sends me scrambling to the foot of the bed. He has

Marco pinned to the carpet, throwing punches again and again. The dark sunglasses sit broken across the room.

"Nico!" I shout. "Stop!"

"How could you, you *bastardo*?" He throws another punch, and Marco's head bounces against the rug.

Marco tries to open his mouth, but he just gets another fistful of Nico's knuckles.

"Stop!" I cry again. Sure, the guy is a total dickwad for tricking me, but he doesn't deserve to die for it. And more importantly, I don't want Nico in jail for it.

"You're going to pay for this, you fucking asshole." Another punch.

"Enough!" Marco spits.

"It'll never be enough. You just tried to fuck the woman I love, you *pezzo di merda*!"

Marco's eyes go wide, his mouth curving into a capital O. The exact expression I imagine I must be wearing.

"Love?" I blurt out because I have no self-control.

"Oh, fuck me, Nico, you love her?" He spits out a wad of saliva mixed with blood.

Nico straightens and drags his hand through his wild hair, his eyes settling on me. The tie at the back has come undone, and with the rage streaking through those brilliant orbs, he looks like an avenging dark angel ascended straight from the bowels of hell. "I love you, Maisy." He stands and walks toward me, his head hanging low. "You've done something to me, something far more powerful than my relentless desire for revenge or power. I'd do anything for you. I'd be anyone to make you happy. I'm completely mad, obsessed and in love with you."

My fragile heart shatters into a million pieces as I meet those tortured, tormented eyes. "I—I..." I want to say those three little words back, but fear lodges them in my throat.

Marco pushes himself off the ground, wiping at his split, bloodied lip. "I'll, uh, give you guys some privacy." He turns to me, and I can't help but stare at Nico's exact duplicate. The brothers are nearly identical with the exception of Marco's eyes – one blue and one brown. "I'm sorry. I shouldn't have fucked with you like that, Maisy. I was just messing around. I didn't realize things were so serious between you two—"

"Leave the penthouse," Nico interrupts. "But don't go far, *coglione*. I'm not done with you yet."

Marco dips his head and trudges out.

A long minute of silence lingers after he's gone. "I'm so sorry he pulled that stunt on you, little fox," he finally mutters. "*Dio*, he's such a child, pulling shit he used to do when we were kids. He's angry at me and—it doesn't at all make up for what he did, but fuck, I just don't know what to say other than I'll make him pay for it."

I slump onto the mattress and tug the comforter up to my chin. "Why wouldn't you tell me you had a *twin* brother?"

"It's not something I typically share with anyone. Over the years, we've found our likeness can come in handy, especially when it comes to keeping our enemies off guard."

"Because you've been pulling these switcheroos?"

He nods. "As much as I want to kill my brother for what he did, it's a game we've been playing our whole lives. It's a tactic that has gotten us out of many challenging situations."

"You should have trusted me..." The fact that he didn't is almost worse than what happened.

"I know."

Nico stands in the exact same spot he's been glued to since his brother left. His eyes are cast down, dark brows furrowed, and his lips are pinched. The typical proud set of his broad shoulders is gone, despite the fine suit he still wears.

He finally exhales a long breath and turns to face me. "I'm so sorry, Maisy, about all of this. And obviously, that's not exactly how I pictured this rather pivotal moment going."

I cross my arms over my chest and inject steel into my tone. "Which part? Your brother pretending to be you, or you blurting the first thing that came to your head in the heat of the fight?"

He shakes his head, his expression turning like stone. "It wasn't the first stupid thing that came to my head, baby." A rueful laugh escapes his thinned lips. "I wish it were that simple, but the God's honest truth is that I am in love with you." He drops to his knees and places his strong hands on my thighs, but his eyes lift to meet mine. "I don't expect you to say it back just yet. I know this has come as a shock—to both of us. I'm not certain I understood it myself until I almost lost you in that explosion. But I promise you this, Maisy, you *will* be mine."

I nod slowly, taking in the depth of emotion burning through his mesmerizing gaze. I'm not exactly certain Nico Rossi knows what real love is, but I believe he feels whatever this is with every piece of his dark soul.

"I don't want to talk about Marco anymore or his deplorable behavior. This isn't about him, it's about us." His eyes lock to mine, the brilliant depths teeming with emotion. "Now spread your legs for me, little fox, because I owe you a night you'll never forget."

CHAPTER 33
I'M NOT GOING ANYWHERE

N*ico*

Maisy lifts a challenging brow as my hands move up her thighs and crawl beneath her negligée. She was waiting for me in this sexy little number. Before my asshole brother showed up and nearly ruined everything. Anger still throbs through my veins at the thought of his hands on *my* little fox.

Merda, if he'd sullied her with his filthy cock, I would've ripped it clean off and shoved it down his throat. I didn't give a shit if he was my brother. And his punishment was far from over. If I wasn't so hellbent on giving Maisy a night she'd never forget, I'd still be beating him bloody.

My fingers latch around the lacy waistband of her thong and draw her panties down her thighs. She tries to clench them together to hide her beautiful pussy from me, but I pry her legs apart and draw my tongue through the light smattering of auburn curls.

I'm just getting started, and I can already taste her arousal.

She squirms beneath me, but I tighten my hands around her thighs holding her steady as I dip my tongue inside her pussy.

"Mmm, little fox, you taste like candy."

A breathy squeal echoes over my head.

"Have you ever tasted yourself?"

"No!" she blurts.

"You will tonight." I draw my tongue across her slick heat and devour her musky sweetness. My hands move around to her ass, cupping her cheeks and drawing her closer so my nose is buried in her curls. Her taste coupled with her tantalizing scent has me rock hard. I can't wait to fuck her across every inch of this penthouse. After the bed, I'll try something a little more exciting. Knowing my little fox, we'll have to start slow.

My tongue moves to her clit, drawing quick circles as I run my finger across her center. Dipping a finger inside that tight pussy, she pulls me in, so hungry. Her moans ring out over my head, and I can feel her clenching around my finger as I thrust faster.

Maisy's hand tangles in my hair, and her hips buck against my face. "Nico," she groans.

I glance up, my finger still working her in and out. "Hold on, little fox, I want you to come on my cock. Can you do that for me?"

Her head bobs, lids heavy with desire, and I release her only long enough to unbuckle my pants. Her eyes open, and her tongue glides across her lower lip as she reaches for me. Her fingers make quick work of my slacks, then she latches onto the waistband of my boxers. A look of pure giddiness lights up her eyes as she drags them down my thighs.

My cock springs free, and desire pulses through those deep green orbs. *Cazzo*, she's gorgeous when she looks at me like that. Her hand closes around my cock, her thumb circling my thick head. Beads of moisture trickle out, and she sticks her tongue out to lick the tip. My little fox is becoming quite bold.

A groan tears through my clenched jaw at the feel of her lapping me up.

She looks up at me with a mischievous smirk as if she knows exactly what she's doing to me.

"I'm going to fuck that naughty expression right off your face, little fox."

She flashes me her teeth as she moves down my shaft.

"Don't you dare."

Her devious laugh vibrates through my hard length, and fire surges through my veins. If she keeps that up, I'll be the one coming.

"As much as I hate to say this, you're going to have to stop with that tongue or I'll come all over that pretty little mouth."

Her lips come off my cock, and my insides riot at the sudden absence of her warmth. To make up for the disappointment, I reach for her nighty and draw it up over her head. She's perched on the edge of the mattress bare before me, and pulsing desire sears through my dick. I want to claim every inch of this woman, erase every memory of any man before me.

"*Dio*, you're gorgeous, little fox." I can't even restrain the reverent quality in my tone. She's a fiery angel fallen from heaven to save my dark, broken soul.

She squirms beneath my heated gaze, but she doesn't hide this time. Progress, at least. My hands wrap around her hips, and I lift her off the bed, twirl us around so I'm sitting on the mattress now and lower her across my lap. She lets out a gasp as my cock rubs across her center. It stands thick and erect between us. Her gaze chases down to the minute space between our bodies.

"I want you to ride my cock until that orgasm rips out of you. You're in control, little fox. As much as you are mine, I am yours."

She squeezes her eyes closed, and a single tear seeps from the corner of her eye. Fuck. I don't want her to cry. There's nothing that makes me feel more powerless. My thumb sweeps across her cheek, erasing the tear, then I pop it into my mouth. I taste her saltiness then run my thumb across her bottom lip.

"I'm here, Maisy, and I'm not going anywhere. You'll never be alone again, I swear it."

Her head dips slowly then her hand wraps around my own, and she draws my thumb into her mouth. She sucks hard, and my cock twitches. She must feel it because she starts to rub her wetness against my length, and now I'm all fired up again. Wrapping my hands around her ass, I press her against me so my crown rubs her clit. Her head falls back, and she lets out a satisfying groan.

"Are you ready for me, baby?"

She snags her bottom lip between her teeth and murmurs a yes.

I scoot us both back on the bed until the upholstered headboard is against my back. Then my hands find her waist, fingers digging into the soft flesh at her hips, and I lift her up over my cock. Arousal glistens across her pussy, and heady anticipation rolls through me.

I drop her down onto my erection, and moans fill the air between us, as I sink in and in and in. Her pussy stretches to accommodate my thick length then tightens, pulling me in.

"Mmm, you feel so good, little fox." I've fucked more than my fair share of women, but nothing has ever felt like this. *Cazzo*, maybe there is something about this making love shit.

"Umhmm," she murmurs above me as her hips begin to move.

I lift her up and down, up and down, that slick heat wetting my cock with each thrust. Her hands wrap around my shoulders as I pick up the pace. She's panting, her head tipped back, and I can already feel her constricting around my dick. Another few thrusts, and she'll be mine.

"You look incredible riding my cock, little fox. The flush of your cheeks, the sparkle in your eyes, that silky hair draped across your shoulders. My God, you're absolute perfection."

Running my hands up her spine, I pull her closer and wrap my lips around her nipple. Twirling my tongue around the peaked bud, her back arches. "Oh, mother--," she groans.

"Say it, little fox. Tell me how much you love fucking my cock."

She shakes her head, pupils blown out with lust as she grinds against me.

"Say it, Maisy, or I won't let you come."

Her eyes widen, lips screwing into a pout. "You wouldn't..." she breathes.

A devious grin stretches across my face. "I would. I'm fairly certain the word cock out of your mouth would be enough to push me right over the edge." I thrust deeper, earning another breathy moan.

"Come on, little fox, just one time, for me."

Her eyes snap open, emerald eyes shooting daggers. "I love riding your penis."

A chuckle snakes out despite my best efforts, but I release her hip with one hand and waggle a finger an inch from her nose. "That's not what I said."

"It's close enough," she whimpers, bucking against me.

I hold her down, forcing her hips to still.

"Nico!" she growls. "I'm so close..."

"I know, baby. So just tell me how much you love to fuck my cock like a good girl, and I'll let you come."

"I hate you," she grits out.

My grin only grows wider. "And I *love* you."

"You don't love me," she whines. "If you did, you wouldn't make me say it."

I capture her lips, my tongue tangling with hers until we're both breathless. "I don't know much about this love thing," I whisper against her lips, "but I know I've never felt this way about anyone. All my life an enormous gaping hole has resided in my chest, and I thought that was normal." My shoulders lift then fall slowly. "Then I saw you that day in the shipping container all those months ago, and something snapped inside me. I may not know how to love you the right way yet, but I vow to spend the rest of my days learning how."

She releases a sigh, her chest heaving, and those perfect nipples brush my chest, inciting another wave of desire. "I love fucking your cock," she whispers against my lips.

The remaining walls around my heart crumble at those ridiculous words rushing from her mouth. An unstoppable smile claims my lips, and I crush her body against mine as I start to thrust with renewed vigor.

We pick up a perfect rhythm, each thrust sending liquid lightning coursing through my veins. Maisy's lips curve into a capital O and I plunge deeper, our bodies moving in flawless synchrony. My heart kicks at my ribs as it struggles to keep up with the ragged tempo of my lungs.

"Nico, I'm going to come," she pants. "Don't stop. Oh, my, gawd, I'm going to come so hard."

"That's right, baby." I take over, guiding her up and down the length of my cock as she contracts around me. I'm about a second away myself, barely holding onto my sanity. "Come for me, little fox."

With one final thrust, her head falls back and a ragged moan parts her lips. "Nico, oh, Nico…"

As she collapses on top of me, I hurtle over the edge, spilling inside her. "Fuck, Maisy, you're amazing," I growl as an earth-shattering orgasm rolls through me.

We sit there for a long moment, foreheads pressed against each other as the final tremors echo through our bodies. I could feel her release as clearly as I felt my own. Her heart pounds against my chest, and my own battered organ rushes to keep up the manic tempo.

Dio, this woman owns me body and soul.

CHAPTER 34
ALL OURS

M*aisy*

My legs feel like jelly, my cooter still throbbing from the last mind-blowing orgasm as I follow Nico out into the foyer, completely naked. A ridiculous smile is plastered across my face as heated memories of the last few hours assault my mind. They'll live there rent-free for the rest of my life. A giggle tumbles from my lips as I see the same giddy expression on the hardened mob boss's face.

I don't think I've ever seen Nico so happy. It looks good on him, makes him seem younger. There are so many things I don't know about his life, so many secrets he hasn't divulged. I can't imagine what sort of upbringing forces a man to become a monster just to survive. Promising myself I would find out everything about him before I fall harder, I squeeze my fingers around his and push away the dark thoughts for now.

Nico stops at the sliding doors of the balcony, and the pale moonlight illuminates the hard lines of his cheeks and jaw. He looks terrifyingly beautiful. A feral smile spreads his lips as he takes me in, lingering over every inch of my body, that careful scrutiny almost painful.

He slides the door open with his free hand, and a rush of cool night air sends goose bumps rippling across my skin. My nipples pebble, and Nico's gaze turns ravenous.

"Come with me, little fox." He tugs me closer until I reach the threshold of the balcony.

I plant my heels into the marble floor and stare up at him. "What in the world are you doing?"

"I promised a night to remember, didn't I?" A mischievous glint streaks across those brilliant blue eyes.

"And that means being naked on the balcony?"

"No, that means you fucking me on the balcony as we take in the sprawling city below us and watching you come above the greatest city on earth."

A naughty streak that I'm certain I caught from Nico sends heat shooting down to my hoo-ha. "Are you serious?"

Nico tugs me outside, and the crisp breeze washes over my heated skin. Darkness looms above but the constant flicker of lights reigns supreme in the city that never sleeps. The majority of skyscrapers around us are office buildings and it's nearly two in the morning, but still, what if someone sees us? The urge to cover my exposed breasts is overwhelming. At least my bottom half is covered by the wall of marble pillars that make up the elegant railing.

Nico walks me to the edge of the veranda and envelops me in his arms. With his muscled form draping over me, I feel much less exposed. His chin rests on my shoulder, and his erection is already rubbing up against my butt. The man is a beast. I'm not even sure how it's physically possible to still be aroused. We peer over the barrier, forty floors down. I have the most overwhelming urge to shout, "I'm king of the world!" but somehow, I smother the embarrassing line before it bursts free.

"It's all ours for the taking, little fox," he whispers against my ear, igniting another swell of goosebumps.

Ours. That word shouldn't hold as much weight as it does. I'd grown up with everything, and then I married into more, but nothing truly felt mine. I was only Gloria Vanderbilt's daughter, or Jasper Whitaker's wife. With Nico, I feel more like myself than I have my entire life.

I spin around and find hypnotic eyes waiting. "I want to start a foundation for abused women," I blurt. It had been something on my mind for a while now, but I'd never had the courage to admit it.

The hint of a smile tugs at the corner of his lip, and I swear something like pride glimmers across the shimmering blue. "I think that's a wonderful idea, little fox, and you're just the woman to spearhead the venture. And Gemini Corp will be the first to fund the non-profit with a significant donation."

My chest inflates, my heart taking off like it actually grew wings. Jasper had laughed when I'd suggested establishing a charity years ago. My arms tangle around the back of Nico's neck, and I press my lips to his. "I'm desperately close to falling for you, Nico Rossi," I whisper against his mouth. "And I'm terrified."

Those piercing orbs lock on mine, and his smile morphs into something darker. "You should be, little fox. But please don't stop." His mouth claims mine, and fiery heat rages through my core. He whirls me around, his mouth still fixed to my own and his hand slides down to the apex of my thighs.

Arousal still slickens my center from the countless orgasms he's given me over the course of the night, and his finger easily glides through my wet folds to find my clit. He begins to circle, and my hips instantly react to his touch, echoing his movements. Speaking of not physically possible, I don't know how I'm still ready to go.

He releases my mouth to nibble at my earlobe, and my back arches against him at the spine-tingling sensations. His free hand wraps around my chin, forcing my gaze to the skyline. "Take it all in, baby. The entire city is it our fingertips. I want to give it all to you."

And I want to take it all from him. I want *him* utterly and completely.

I reach around behind my back and stroke his hard length. A ripple of excitement surges up my spine. I can't believe I'm about to do this. I'm going to let Nico Rossi bang me on his balcony in the middle of the night. I bend forward slightly so my breasts brush the smooth marble railing and direct his arousal toward my throbbing center.

From this angle, I have no idea what I'm doing, but I'm just hoping Nico gets the idea. The image of him taking me from behind as we look out onto the city is oddly thrilling.

"Mmm, little fox, you drive me crazy when you take control," he whispers against the sensitive shell of my ear. "Do you want me to fuck you right here for all of Manhattan to see, baby? To pretend that all of these uptight businessmen in suits are watching and will now understand without a doubt that you belong to me?"

"Yes," I pant as his finger starts to move faster.

His thick head glides across my drenched core, and tiny sparks of electricity light up each and every nerve ending. They've already been conditioned to his touch, and they know exactly what tantalizing pleasure comes next.

He slides the tip in, and a groan tears from my lips. "Is that what you want, little fox?"

"More," I practically mewl.

"You want my cock balls deep inside you?"

"Yes, Nico, gawd, yes, I want your cock." I snap my jaw shut the moment the dirty word is out.

A dark chuckle echoes behind me an instant before he thrusts inside me, filling me to the hilt. I'm so overcome with pleasure I can't focus on that little slip of the tongue. Mother father, Nico Rossi really is getting to me.

He thrusts deeper still, pressing my breasts against the chilly marble. The icy stone against my heated skin intensifies every thrilling sensation. I hated it when Jasper took me from behind. I felt like a dog being humped. But with Nico, it's different. His lips run across my back and shoulders, worshipping every inch of me with his tongue and mouth. His fingers work my clit in rhythm with his thrusts, and freaking heck, it's incredible. I can already feel another powerful orgasm building.

His mouth closes around the back of my neck and he sucks hard, teeth grazing my delicate flesh. "Mine," he growls.

"Are you giving me a hickey?" I squeal.

"No, that's what teenagers do. I'm marking you as mine. Very different."

"Clearly." I snort on a laugh as he lavishes my skin with his warm tongue.

His free hand moves from my hip to my neck again, and he forces my gaze to the sprawling city. "I want you to look at it, little fox, and memorize it, every single detail. I never want you to forget this night."

"I don't think I ever could." It isn't every day one gets railed on a balcony in the middle of Manhattan. There's something about his tone that chases away the snark and compels me to turn my head to face him. "Is everything okay?"

He nods slowly, but an unreadable gaze darkens the luminescent blue. "I haven't had many of these perfect moments in my life, Maisy. I simply want us both to remember this one. You never know how quickly happiness can be snatched away from you."

A hint of fear cuts through the rush of sensations. He doesn't think there will be more? I push the stupid thought aside and try to focus on the heat pulsing below as he slowly glides in and out, savoring each thrust.

"I'll always remember," I whisper.

"Good." His hand closes around my hip, gripping my flesh

possessively. He plunges harder, deeper, until I'm practically thrown against the marble barrier. I'm so enraptured by the sensations I don't feel anything but pleasure as his finger circles the taut bundle of nerves at my apex, and I tighten around his hard length.

I'm so close. "Nico," I groan. "Don't stop."

"I'll never stop, baby." His hips slam against my butt, over and over again as fire surges through my lower half.

I didn't think it was possible to have a single orgasm from sex, and now Nico is close to managing five in one night. With one final thrust, I careen over the edge as wave after wave of pleasure laps over me. Thank goodness for the wall keeping me upright because without it, I'd be a puddle on the floor.

Nico falls an instant later, his orgasm vibrating through every corner as his warmth spills inside me. I'm suddenly extremely relieved I never had that IUD taken out. I just hope it's up to the task. This man is relentless, and I can't get enough. Of his cock. *Hehe.*

CHAPTER 35
AIN'T LOVE GRAND?

N*ico*

"This is your fault," Qian snarls from his throne in the cavernous warehouse. "I've lost millions because of you and now you're backing out?"

The man is lucky I just had the most incredible night of my life, or he'd be clawing his way out of a shallow grave before nightfall. I maintain the mask of calm, despite the leader of the Four Seas' threats.

"I'm not backing out," I say calmly, enunciating every syllable. "My focus has changed, that is all."

"Well, I don't accept that. My father spent years positioning the Four Seas to take over Red Dragon territory, and you swore you'd make that happen."

"I will." I simply must find a way to do that without inadvertently destroying the Kings at the same time. Damn my little fox and her ultimatums.

"How?"

Repressing a growl, I ignore the disrespectful piss ant and attempt my most congenial smile. "Gemini Corp will cover the losses incurred by the fire." Marco will kill me, but after his blunder with the Puerto Ricans he doesn't have much room to talk.

Qian slides off his throne and stalks toward me. Jimmy and Max are by the door and from the corner of my eye, both visibly stiffen. I'm not scared of this asshole. I'd have him on the ground before he could blink if he makes a move against me. "How does that make sense, Rossi?" he snarls.

"Let's just say I'm willing to incur certain losses in order to be compensated in other ways." His dark brows furrow as he regards me like I've clearly lost my mind. Which in a way I have. I'm giving away millions for my little fox. Ain't love grand? "Just tell me where to send the money, and you'll have it by this evening."

He still eyes me with that incredulous gaze, his thin brows arching to meet that shiny bald scalp. Cocking his head over his shoulder, he barks something in Mandarin and one of his men peels away from the shadows. "Chao will coordinate the details."

"Perfect." I tick my head at Jimmy who relaxes a smidge and marches toward the navy-clad male Qian had indicated. Straightening my tie, I mentally prepare for the second, more distasteful discussion of this meeting. "Now that that's been handled, may we proceed? I would like to discuss how we can maintain the foothold we've acquired within the Lower East Side without specifically targeting the Kings."

"It's not possible," he hisses. "Our entire arrangement hinged on their annihilation and the Red Dragon's resulting downfall."

"I don't give a shit about the Dragons." I loom over Qian, nearly reaching the end of my patience. "Do whatever you want to them but stay away from the Kings from now on. I'll handle the Valentinos. Are we clear?" I grit out each word.

Qian shakes his head, anger pinching his brow. "This is bullshit, Rossi."

My arm snakes out, and my hand wraps around the piece of shit's throat. A dozen navy hoods coalesce from the shadows. His men move like a silent wave arcing around us. Jimmy and Max appear at my side, both with guns cocked. "I didn't ask your opinion on my decision." My fingers curl tighter. "I simply want to know if you will politely comply, or will I have to make my demands more forcefully?"

A raspy curse vibrates his throat as I dig my thumb into his windpipe.

"I can snap your neck with one little twist, Qian. You'll be dead before your best man can pull the trigger. Is this how you want to die?"

I loosen my grip a touch so he can inhale enough air to answer my question.

"No," he rasps.

"Good." Removing my thumb from his throat, but keeping hold of his neck, I tick my head at the circle of navy surrounding us. "Tell them to back down."

He mutters something in Mandarin, and his men lower their weapons, disappearing back into the shadows.

Releasing Qian, I take a step back and clear my throat. "Are we clear on the expectations now?"

"Crystal," he hisses. Straightening to his full height, he stalks toward his grand throne. The king of the Four Seas may have been taken down a notch today, but he still believes himself to be a god. Already, this alliance is turning out to be more trouble than it's worth.

I turn to leave, but his raspy voice freezes me to the spot.

"About the other arrangement..."

Merda. I hoped he'd forgotten about the marriage deal with his sister. "What about it?"

"Have you come to a decision?"

"I'm still considering." The truth is that holding this

arrangement over Qian's head might be the only way to keep this rabid dog at heel.

"What is there to consider? Do you not find my sister worthy?" He spits the last word, and I know I must tread lightly. The concept of honor is something sacred to the Chinese.

"Of course, I do. It's not a decision to take lightly, Qian. Surely, you understand. This arrangement would tie our families together forever, not just one generation but for countless to come."

He dips his head, lips twisting. "Which is why this pact would be so beneficial. After backing down on one agreement, I certainly hope you wouldn't renege on another."

I offer him a tight smile. "Of course not. You'll have my answer by the end of the week." Spinning on my heel, I whirl to the door, anxious to get out of here. Not only is Maisy waiting for me at home, but I must now also find a way to extricate myself from this predicament without causing an all-out war.

Damned Qian's theatrics cost me the peaceful evening at home with Maisy. By the time I return, she's asleep in my bed, which brings me all sorts of wicked delight. Since I'm loath to wake her, I tiptoe past my bedroom to my studio, a sanctuary I haven't visited in weeks. As much turmoil as my little fox's appearance into my life has caused, I can't deny the joy it's gifted in return. So much so that I haven't needed my painting as an escape.

But I do miss it, nonetheless.

Unlocking the door to my most private refuge, I flick on the light and the large room filled with canvases sparks to life in an array of colors. Shrugging off my jacket, I hang it from the hook on the wall, then do the same with my shirt and tie.

Normally I'd find an old shirt and shorts to work in, but I hate the idea of disturbing Maisy's sleep, so today I'll have to settle with painting in only boxers.

Plucking an empty canvas from the bin, I sit at the easel and attempt to banish the myriad of concerns stifling my creative thoughts. Qian, Jasper, Dante, Marco... so many issues to deal with. My brother has called and messaged me incessantly since I tossed him out of the penthouse the other night. I haven't responded because I'm not certain I'll be able to face him without wringing his neck. Maybe I'll send him to deal with Qian next time. Actually... my twin could be the answer to one of my biggest problems.

A smile flits to the surface as I dip the brush into the small pot of deep red. And this is exactly why I paint. The stillness, the quiet, it allows me the peace to solve the complex puzzles of the dark world to which I'm bound.

My brush strokes grow more fluid as I allow the image to come alive in my mind's eye. My little fox. I could paint her in a million different poses, a thousand varied angles. Perhaps now she'll finally let me paint her nude. It's just what she needs to boost her self-confidence, to see the magnificent woman I see every time I look at her.

If only I could divert more resources to finding Jasper. That man's been a thorn at my side for far too long. Perhaps now that things quiet down with the Kings, I'll finally be able to nail down the bastard. My fingers curl around the wooden handle of the brush as I imagine crushing that asshole's windpipe.

The vibration of my phone from across the room jolts me from the dark musings. My jacket hanging from the hook on the wall shakes from the steady pulsation. I contemplate ignoring it, but it continues incessantly. With a growl, I wipe my hands on an old rag and stomp toward the sound.

Yanking my phone from the pocket, I stare at the slew of messages on the screen.

Marco: *Answer me*, bastardo.
Marco: *I need to get back into the penthouse.*
Marco: *I don't have any clothes.*
Marco: *Come on.*
Marco: *At least send my stuff down. I'm in room 4563. I'm sorry I messed around with Maisy, okay? I had no idea you really felt something for her.*

I hiss out a curse as the texts continue to populate, one after another. His tone is getting more desperate with each one. Shaking my head, I punch out a response before he destroys my Zen for good.

Me: *I'll have Blanca drop something off to your room tomorrow. Now leave me alone or I'll make this living situation permanent.*
Marco: *You wouldn't.*
Me: *I most definitely would. As a matter of fact, I suggest you start looking for your own place as the penthouse will be a bit too crowded with three.*
Marco: *You're going to ask Maisy to live with you?*
Me: *I'm not some silly teenager asking her on a date. I want Maisy in my life forever.*
Marco: *Damn...*
Me: *Goodnight, brother.*

Turning off my phone, I slide it back into my jacket pocket and stalk back to my easel. Now I only hope my muse will resurface after the unforeseen irritation of my brother. At least, our exchange has made something clear: I want Maisy to stay here permanently. Something we'll have to discuss once she is fully healed from the concussion. Luckily for me, I have two weeks before she'll have to return to work in person.

I set my brush against the canvas, and the strokes return naturally as the paint brings Maisy's radiant form to life. *Cazzo*, how had I managed to capture the heart of this pure woman?

The click of the door handle turning sends my head spinning over my shoulder. It opens a crack, and Maisy peeks through the opening. My heart expands simply at the sight of her, dancing a happy jig.

"You're home," she murmurs, her voice raspy from sleep.

"I am."

She eyes my bare chest, then her hooded gaze lowers to my boxer briefs. "And painting practically naked?" The hint of a smile graces her lips.

"What can I say? When the muse strikes, she will not be denied."

She gently pushes the door open and creeps into the studio, her gaze traveling to every nook, every painting along the walls. "They're beautiful, Nico." She eyes them each, almost reverently. "Why is this the first I've seen of this room?"

"I like to keep my paintings private." Her lips pinch, and I realize I've said something wrong. "But not from you. Not anymore." I extend my hand, and an unexpected swirl of anxiety fills my chest. I've never allowed anyone unfettered access to my studio, my collection, my heart. "Come, sit with me."

CHAPTER 36
MY GREATEST WORK

Maisy

I settle into Nico's lap, still unable to tear my gaze from the magnificent canvases lining the space. Each one is beautiful and unique in its own right, some colorful, sprawling landscapes, other quiet, tense portraits and so many of *me*.

Me sleeping in my bed.

Me eating a sandwich at Central Park.

Me desperately holding onto the safety bar on the bus.

Despite the backdrop, I always look stunning, much more beautiful than I have any right to look at seven o'clock in the morning on a crowded bus ride across town. Is that really how Nico sees me?

Warmth floods my chest, and I finally turn to face this beautifully tortured, artistic soul. Blazing azure irises sear to mine, and an expression I'm too frightened to name lingers on his handsome face. "Your paintings are incredible," I whisper.

"Or maybe it's the subject."

An embarrassing giggle sputters out because there's something about his gaze that's much too raw and intense. "I don't think so," I blubber.

"You never give yourself enough credit, little fox."

I shrug and lean against the hard planes of his stomach. Despite the unrelenting rigidity, I never feel as comfortable anywhere than in Nico's embrace. His hands settle on my thighs, fingers playing distractedly with the lace hem of my nightie. The mere touch sends heat racing between my legs. "Are you coming to bed soon?" The breathy plea comes out so pathetically.

He chuckles behind me, the rumble of his broad chest vibrating through my entire body. "I have a better idea."

I cant my head over my shoulder to catch a mischievous smirk. "Oh, yeah, what's that?"

"Let me paint you." A sinful smile smolders across his perfect lips, sending waves of desire coursing through every inch of me.

I know exactly what he means, but I ask for further clarification only to buy myself some time. "You've already painted me many times before. Most of them clearly without my approval." I arch a teasing brow.

"This sort of painting would warrant your express approval, little fox. Unless I snuck a quick sketch in the darkness of my bedroom one of these evenings after fucking you from here to kingdom come."

A chill races up my spine at the rough edge to his tone.

His fingers tangle within the lacy hem, drawing it further up my thighs until my matching panties are exposed. "If you allow me this, I promise to make it worth your while."

"Oh, yeah?" I waggle my brows. "What will I get in return?"

"Whatever you want."

I pause and nibble on my lower lip. I've really been blessed in this life, despite all the more recent drama. Besides Jasper gone for good, I'm already so close to having everything I could ever desire. "Jasper," I murmur.

His expression turns savage, bright blue eyes darkening. "His head in a box wrapped in a pretty red bow?"

I swallow hard. "I just want him out of my life."

"Out of *our* lives."

I nod slowly.

"You'll have it by the end of the week, I swear." He cups my cheek, drawing my mouth to his and sealing the promise with a scorching kiss. As he kisses me senseless, his hands move beneath my nightie, drawing my panties down my legs. Then he releases my lips only long enough to tug the negligée over my head.

A hiss escapes through his bowed lips as his heated gaze rakes over my bare breasts then glides down my tummy and settles at the dash of auburn curls between my thighs. "You're absolutely perfect, little fox. I cannot wait to paint every curve of that exquisite form."

Hot tears prick at the back of my eyes, and I have no idea why. Maybe it's because no one has ever told me how beautiful I was. More than that, no one ever made me feel it.

I blink back the tears as I feel him stir beneath me.

"As much as I would love to paint you while sitting on my lap," he whispers at the shell of my ear, "I'm afraid it would prove rather impossible even for me."

"Oh, right." I scoot off his lap and follow his line of sight to a small chaise lounge by the window. I hadn't even noticed it when I first came in.

Nico ushers me toward it, his hand pressed to the soft dimples at my lower back. "Normally I'd prefer to do this in the daylight, but I'd never miss this incredible opportunity and risk you changing your mind by morning."

I throw him a smirk and an eyeroll for good measure. I can't believe I'm doing this either. This is so unbelievably unlike me. My pulse pounds with a mix of nerves and excitement as I fold onto the chaise, and Nico positions me to his liking.

He squints, snagging his bottom lip between his teeth as he adjusts the pillow, the chenille throw, then the tall floor lamp. He cradles my cheek, turning it just so, then arranges my wild hair across my shoulders. "There, perfect."

Nico rushes across the room, and I struggle to remain still as he hauls an easel, paints and a new canvas over. Once he's finally settled on the stool, he turns that mesmerizing gaze on me. "This will be my greatest work yet. I can feel it in the depths of my soul."

An embarrassing chuckle bursts free, the intensity of the moment too much. "You're so cheesy sometimes."

He grins. "You bring it out in me."

The fact that I bring any sort of light to this man's dark world brings me a swell of satisfaction. He brings the brush to the canvas, and the soft strokes fill the silence between us. I'm scared to move, scared to breathe. But I'm shockingly comfortable completely naked beneath my former stalker's scrutinizing gaze.

I've certainly come a long way from the insecure bundle of nerves Nico kidnapped all those months ago. I can't help but wonder how I've impacted his life. Despite the strides we've made, the king of Gemini Corp still remains tight-lipped about his past.

Maybe now that he's relaxed and doing what he loves would be a good time to delve a little deeper…

"Can I talk?" I murmur through clenched teeth, trying to keep my face perfectly still.

"Yes, just try not to move."

I heave out a breath and watch him for a minute longer before I summon the nerve for my first line of questioning. His brows are furrowed in concentration, his lips smashed tight together. I almost hate the idea of disturbing his focus, but how often do I have his full, undivided attention when we're not in bed naked?

Well, I'm naked, but still…

"So while we're here," I blurt before I lose my nerve. "I figured maybe we could play a game."

"A game?" His dark brows arch. "I'm kind of preoccupied, little fox."

"It's easy, it's called twenty questions."

He clenches the paintbrush between his teeth. "Mmm, I see."

"Is that a yes?"

"I suppose we can try it, as long as I don't find it too distracting."

"Great." I nearly jump up and clap my hands, until Nico's gaze cuts across the room. "Okay, right, I'm keeping still while asking questions."

"I'll go first," he interjects.

Well, that's unexpected. "Okay."

"Were you ever intimate with another man before Jasper?"

Embarrassment floods my cheeks, heat racing up my neck. My eyes nearly bulge out of my head, and it takes every ounce of restraint not to wrap my arms around my bare chest like flesh and blood armor.

"I—I…"

"Please don't misunderstand my intention, little fox. I'm not asking because I find you inexperienced or your abilities not up to par because trust me, you are the best I've ever had. I'm only curious to confirm that once Jasper no longer walks this earth, I will be the only man to lay claim on that beautiful pussy in any and all respects." A smug grin curls his perfect lips. "It only heightens the incentive to find and end the man."

"What if he wasn't? Would you go around killing all the men that have seen me naked?"

He cocks his head to the side, and the brush's strokes grow wilder and more rushed. "Maybe," he finally growls.

A chill skitters up my spine, and I can't hide the fine tremor this time. "Well, then I guess it's a good thing it's just you."

That smile grows wider, and my stupid heart beats faster for this monster of a man.

"I suppose so."

"Now it's my turn." I can barely restrain the excitement from my voice. Picking through the dozens of swirling questions in my mind, I finally latch onto one. "I've only ever heard of your family history from Rose. I'd love to hear your side of the story."

CHAPTER 37
YOU ARE A MASTERPIECE

N*ico*

Unearthing the dark memories of my past sounds as enticing as spearing a hot poker across my chest. Something I experienced with foster family number one, but I'd never share that with my gentle-hearted Maisy. It would destroy her rosy-colored view of the human race. Because what kind of man would do that to an eleven-year-old boy for the sin of walking into the house with muddy shoes?

I clench the paintbrush in my hand, the muse temporarily disappearing into the dark recesses of my fucked-up psyche. I glance up to find Maisy's expectant gaze heavy on me. I hate to dash her hope of getting to know me better, of finding some ounce of decency within the soulless man with whom she's found herself entangled.

"There's not much to tell, little fox," I finally manage.

"How did you end up in New York from Italy?"

I grind my molars as memories flit to the surface and drown me in visions of the past.

"Marco, Nico! Vieni qui!" *Mamma's voice fills the sun-soaked kitchen.*

My brother and I race inside from the patio, our little dog barking behind us. It's summer and we're at the beach house with our grandparents. Nonno *is famous in our small town. People from all over come to see him, and they bring him all kinds of gifts, even money.*

One day I want to be like him.

Mamma *stands by the stove, and the sharp scent of garlic clings to her apron. Our grandfather sits at the table, the big smile he reserves only for us gone today. I look between him and* Mamma, *and I already know something isn't right.*

"Come sit, my little ones." Our mother pulls out the two chairs on either side of our nonno. *"We have something important to tell you."*

Marco settles into the chair to the left of our grandfather, and I take the right. I glance up at Mamma *again, and this time I notice the light splotches around her eyes and the rosy tint on her nose.*

"You boys are going to America," Nonno declares.

Marco's mismatched eyes light up, but I steal another glance at Mamma, *taking in her reaction before I say a word. She doesn't look happy at all.*

"Is Mamma coming with us?" The question spills out.

"No, Nico. You are going to stay with your Papà.*"*

I could barely believe what I was hearing. At ten years old, Marco and I were the only kids in our class who'd never met their father. I'd dreamed of the day he'd show up to find us. Mamma *always said he was a very busy man who lived in America, and that one day, he'd come for us.*

I couldn't believe the day was finally here.

. . .

I never met Umberto Valentino. He never showed up at the airport to claim us like he was supposed to, and we never got our happily ever after.

The past disintegrates, and Maisy's hopeful gaze coalesces in its place. I hate to shatter her excitement because there are no happy endings in my story, unless somehow, I manage not to fuck up this incredible thing with her.

I heave in a steadying breath and murmur, "My grandfather sent us to New York to find our bastard father. According to *Nonno*, he and our mother were to be married, but he disappeared like a coward when he found out she was pregnant." My fingers curl into fists as I try my damnedest to keep the mounting rage at bay. "He never came to meet us at the airport, never visited when we spent a year with *Mamma*'s cousin before she passed away. And then we ended up in foster care." I shrug, praying to a God I knew didn't exist she wouldn't want more details.

"I'm so sorry..." she whispers. Her lips are pressed into a hard line as if she's trying to hold back a thousand questions and conceal a bevy of emotions. "Why didn't you just go back to Italy?"

"My *nonno* thought it would be a good experience for us, to toughen us up a bit. Besides, everyone knows America is the land of great opportunity, right?"

A long moment of silence passes, and I unclench my fingers from around the paintbrush I've been strangling.

"Did you ever try to reach out to your father?"

I shake my head. "When he didn't show up at JFK or the weeks following, *Mamma* refused to give us his name. It took me years to put the pieces together and figure it out myself. My grandfather had been a powerful man in our country, and he'd arranged the marriage between his daughter and Umberto Valentino, but apparently, he ran off with Dante and Luca's mother instead and reneged on the deal."

"But you and Dante are nearly the same age..."

I nod. That little detail hadn't gone unnoticed by me either. My bastard father must have been fucking both women at the same time. *Pezzo di merda.*

Maisy stands, abandoning my work-in-progress and crawls into my lap. Her soft hands frame my face, and she presses a gentle kiss to my lips. "I'm so sorry for what you suffered. All children deserve to grow up feeling loved, cared for and protected." Her thumb moves across my upper lip and traces the curve.

"What's this scar from?"

A smile comes unbidden. "This was just Marco... we were playing a little too rough along the shore in Italy one summer when we were kids, and I went headfirst into the rocks. He has a matching scar on his knee when he fell trying to help me up."

Maisy's eyes glisten as she regards me, some unreadable expression across her exquisite face. I brush my lips against hers, anxious to lessen the pain etched into her half-smile. I run my hands up her spine, leaving sticky fingerprints of mottled reds and pinks as she kisses me harder. I was so engrossed in the past I forgot to wipe my hands on the rag. My little fox doesn't seem to mind though.

Her mouth releases my lips, but her hands still cup my cheeks as she sits back and regards me, tears glistening in her eyes. "I love you, Nico Rossi. It may not be enough to erase the dark memories of the past or make up for the love you missed out on as a child, but you have it now."

My heart rushes headlong against my ribcage at those words. Words I never knew I needed to hear so badly. "You love me?" I mumble.

"I do. I love you more than what my psychologist would probably consider healthy." A rueful smile glides across her lips. "But what does she know, anyway, right?"

I don't think I've ever smiled so hard in my life. This angel of a woman loves me... She wants to be with me, even after everything I've put her through. "*Dio*, I love you, little fox, and I'll spend the rest of my life in an attempt to be worthy of your pure heart."

My mouth captures hers in a desperate attempt to seal this moment in time. She scrambles on my lap, trying to get her leg across my hips to straddle me and hits the easel. The canvas falls, crashes into the paint tins and a rainbow of colors splatter all over us.

Maisy lets out a squeal as paint coats her hair and dribbles across her naked form. Her cheeks heat as her wide eyes drop to mine. "Oops." She tries to stand, but I hold her firmly in place across my lap.

"You're not going anywhere, little fox." I press my finger to the splotch of red paint on her chest and draw it down between her breasts. Her entire body trembles at my touch.

"What are you doing?" she breathes.

"Something I've dreamt of doing since the moment I first painted you in Central Park." I lift her hips and slide my boxers down. My cock springs free, already hard with anticipation. "The paints are all natural, so don't worry."

I fist her long, auburn locks and draw her head back, exposing her elegant neck. My tongue runs down her soft skin as I knead the slick paint over her breasts. A moan rents the air between us, and now I'm hard as fuck and ready to sink my cock into the woman who loves me. Actually, fucking loves me.

Maisy's back arches as I slather the paint across her body and claim her lips with a driving force I have no control over. I not only want this woman, but I need her with every shred of my being. Her hips grind against my erection, wetting my length with her arousal. There's paint everywhere, and *cazzo*, mixing the two things I love more than anything in this world is so erotic.

"Are you ready for me, baby?" I whisper as I nibble on her ear.

"Mmm, yes." She lifts her hips without me having to ask, and I drop her down on my cock.

Her lips spread for me, stretching until I fill her so deep, I swear I can feel her spine.

"Oh, Nico," she moans, her head falling back. "Oh, effing heck, I love you."

A dark chuckle seeps out as I guide her hips up and down, slowly at first then faster as we fall into a more frenzied rhythm.

"You're so tight, so wet for me, baby." I thrust into her as she grinds against me. My hands are covered in paint, palming her ass. She's going to have handprints all over her body. I wish I could make them permanent, so everyone knows she's mine.

Maybe I'll tattoo my name across her forehead.

A sinister grin curls my lips as my mouth moves over hers. Or maybe something less obvious like an enormous diamond.

Lifting her up as I continue to drive into her, I stand and gently splay her out across the mess of paints and canvases on the floor. I thrust again, changing the angle and she lets out another satisfying groan. Bracing my arms on either side of her head, I move slowly, savoring every second. She glances up at me, eyes sparkling, and my heart feels so full I'm certain it'll burst.

"Better?" I ask against her swollen lips.

"So good, daddy." Crimson flushes her paint-splattered cheeks, and she snaps her mouth closed.

A roar of laughter tumbles out despite my best efforts at restraining the outburst. *Daddy?* That's new.

"Oh, my golly, can you just erase that from your memory, like forever? It was so cringe!"

My smile turns downright wicked as I pull nearly all the way out before sinking back into her warmth. "I'm not certain I ever could." I roll my hips earning another squeal of pleasure. "You can call me whatever you'd like, little fox, as long as you say my name when I make you come."

"I'm close," she rasps, her pussy tightening around my cock with each thrust.

"I know."

Her hands close around my ass and urge me deeper.

"Mmm, yes, baby, I love it when you take control. You want more of my cock, don't you?"

"Yes." Her eyes are glossy, lids heavy with desire. "I want you so bad."

"Are you ready to come all over my cock?"

"Yes, I'm *so* ready." She rubs her clit against my thick crown, desperate for the friction.

"I know exactly what you need, baby." I slide my hand between our bodies and find that engorged bundle of nerves at her apex. Two quick circles with my finger and her head falls back.

"Oh, Nico, I'm going to come..." Her pussy clenches around my cock, drawing my own orgasm to the surface.

Our haggard moans fill the air between us as heady pleasure sends tremors rippling through our joined bodies. My lungs falter, even my heart staggers as the spine-tingling desire roars through every inch. Just when I think the orgasms can't get any better, my little fox goes above and beyond. When the final tremor subsides, I collapse on top of a paint-splattered Maisy and drop my forehead to hers.

"You are a masterpiece," I whisper against her lips.

"I love you, too."

CHAPTER 38
A RELUCTANT APOLOGY

Maisy

"I can't believe you're making me do this." Nico's pout is worse than my little nephew's.

I shoot him a narrowed glare and press my finger to my lips. I fully expect him to meltdown into a tantrum as we stand in front of the looming giant in black in the foyer of the fancy Upper West Side condo. The guard's thick finger is pressed to the com at his ear and judging by the flustered look in his eye, his boss is about as pleased to discover that we're here as Nico is.

Finally, the big guy looks down at me, mustache quirking as he regards me. "The capo said you can go up, but *he* has to stay down here." He ticks his head at Nico and my mobster, stalker, boyfriend? I don't even know what to call him, goes feral.

"Maisy is not going anywhere without me," he snarls, those luminescent eyes shooting daggers.

Clasping my arm across Nico's chest, I keep the raging beast from lunging at the poor guard. "Can I please talk to Rose?"

The guy mutters something in Italian, then he digs through his pocket for his phone and hands it to me.

"For fuck's sake, Mais, what are you doing bringing Nico here?" Rose shouts the moment the phone is pressed to my ear.

"You left me no choice. You wouldn't answer any of my messages or calls, and well, he wouldn't let me come here alone so here we are."

"Oh, my gawd, please don't tell me you two are like together, together."

I cast a glance at the fuming mob boss and swallow hard. "We are. We're in love actually."

Nico groans beside me then lets out a string of curses. "Nothing like putting a bigger target on your back, little fox," he grumbles.

"Dante would never hurt me," I hiss.

"Who do you think set off that explosion that nearly got you killed?" he counters.

"We don't know that was him for sure and how would he have even known I was going to be there? Maybe he was just trying to kill *you!*"

"Oh, shit, Maisy, you're really in love with that monster, aren't you?" Rose's yelp of surprise turns my attention back to the call.

"Nico would never hurt me either, Rose."

"Well, yeah, sure because he's like obsessed with you." I can practically hear her eyeroll over the phone.

"Can you please just let us up? I'm sure you can find a way to convince Dante," I grit out.

"Fine, put Mickey back on."

I hand the beefy guard his phone and a moment later, we're riding the sleek elevator up to the penthouse.

Nico glares at me from across the lift, his back pressed against the smooth metal walls.

"You can stop giving me the evil eye, Nico Rossi." I slap my hands on my hips and glare right back at him. "It's time to end this feud once and for all. Unless you're backing out on our deal?"

"It's too fucking late for that," he growls. "I'm already hopelessly addicted to that sweet little pussy." The glimmer of a smile lights up his murderous gaze.

"Good." I creep closer and slide my hand down his slacks, closing my fingers around his crotch.

He lets out a satisfying groan and immediately hardens in my palm. "Mmm, little fox. Are you trying to make me come in this elevator?"

"Would it put you in a better mood?"

"Fuck yes."

I shoot him a wicked smirk as I run my hand up and down his length. "How about this? You play nice with Dante and Rose, and I'll let you do whatever you want to me on the ride home in the car."

His hand wraps around my throat, thumb gently stroking the indentation in my neck. A flicker of excitement has stars exploding across those deep azure orbs. "Anything?"

I lick my lips and nod as that excitement bleeds into me.

"You have a deal, Miss Maisy." His mouth captures mine, tongue lashing against my own in a heated kiss as his fingers tighten around my throat. As if his kiss didn't already make me breathless and weak in the knees.

The elevator doors glide open, and I extricate my hand from his pants. Nico groans his disapproval as I run my fingers through my hair in a vain effort to tame the wild locks. Another dark-suited guard stands in the hallway in front of Dante's door. He eyes me, then Nico, and his lips curl into a grimace. Still, his free hand, the one not holding a gun, wraps around the door handle, and he holds it open for us without a word.

Nico grabs my hand and jerks me to his side as we cross the threshold into the super modern penthouse. Dante and Rose stand by the kitchen island, mirroring our pose with Rose tucked into her intimidating husband's side. Now that I'm in the same room with the half-brothers, I start to see the family resemblance—the dark, wavy hair, the strong jaws, and high cheek bones. Even their piercing stares are similar except Dante's blazing irises are a bottomless midnight instead of the brilliant blue. Not to mention they're both dangerously gorgeous.

My friend eyes me, then snags her bottom lip between her teeth, and I can practically see the indecision warring along her brow. A long moment later, she digs her elbow into Dante's side, and he releases her with a grunt of annoyance.

Rose sprints toward me and I wrench myself out of Nico's hold, meeting her halfway. Her long, slender arms wrap around me, and I sink into her embrace. "I'm so sorry," she murmurs against my ear. "I've been a total bitch and a horrible friend."

"No, I'm sorry. I never should've lied to you about Nico. I was just so confused and embarrassed…"

"I would have been embarrassed too," Dante mutters under his breath, "to be associated with that man."

"Fuck you, Dante," Nico growls. "Like Rose hit the jackpot with you, psycho?"

"Enough." I release Rose and take a step back toward Nico before the two morons really start to go at it. "We came here to apologize."

Dante's eyes widen to the size of twin bottomless onyx moons. "Come again?"

Nico tenses beside me, every muscle in his body as taut as a bowstring. I tangle my fingers through his and give him a reassuring smile. "Please," I whisper.

He looses an exasperated breath and grits out through clenched teeth, "The Geminis are no longer at war with the Kings."

"Oh, how kind of you, brother. Sure, now that King Industries has secured the commissioner's deal you don't have a leg to stand on—"

"Dante," Rose hisses. "Just be quiet for once and hear him out."

I throw my friend an appreciative smile. If it weren't for us level-headed women, these insufferable beasts would throttle each other with their bare hands.

"Please, continue," Dante grouses.

"Why don't we sit?" Rose motions to the living room and the impeccable white leather couches. Behind them, sweeping views of Central Park shine through the sliding glass doors, and I'm filled with a sense of longing. I've missed my little townhouse on the Upper West Side. If Nico upholds his vow to deliver Jasper by the end of the week, I could be home by the following one.

My gaze flickers to Nico and anxiety crushes my insides at the idea of him not by my side twenty-four-seven. I heave in a breath and toss the unwanted sensations to the back of my mind for now. *Stay on target, Maisy!*

Nico and I fold onto the couch across Dante and Rose. Both men are still eyeing each other like a lion stalks a lamb. I dig my elbow into Nico's side, urging him onto the apology portion of today's visit.

He clears his throat and slides to the edge of the cushion, propping his elbows on his knees. "First, let's clear something up." He glances from me to Dante and back. "Did the Kings set off that explosion at the Four Seas' warehouse last week?"

Dante's dark brow quivers before he sits back and draws in a breath. "No, it wasn't us. It was Feng and the Red Dragons. I knew it was going down, but I had no idea Maisy would be down there. I could give two shits about your life, but I'd never hurt little Red."

"See!" I throw Nico my best I-told-you-so look then pivot to the other stubborn Italian. "Either way, Rose and I would never get caught in the crossfire if you just both agreed to stand down."

Nico clears his throat and heaves in a steadying breath. "As I was saying, I have decided to pursue other things in my life and destroying the Kings is no longer my primary objective."

"How magnanimous of you." Dante smirks.

I cut in before the wild Valentino says something snarky just to rattle his half-brother. "There's no reason the Kings and Geminis can't coexist peacefully."

"Yes!" Rose blurts. "I couldn't agree more. You are family after all."

Nico and Dante scoff in perfect unison. It's kind of freaky actually.

"His father abandoned my mother," Nico hisses.

"Because your grandfather was trying to force him to marry her," Dante interjects, "when he was already in love with *my* mother."

Nico's brows slam together as he regards his half-brother. "What do you mean?"

Dante rakes a hand through his dark hair. "If you weren't such an asshole I would've told you months ago. I found some letters..." He trails off as he stands and stalks down the corridor, disappearing around the corner.

"Finding out about Nico and Marco sent Dante into a deep dive into the Valentino family history," Rose whispers. "With Luca still gone and all the drama lately, he's been a bit out of whack."

Nico practically vibrates with anticipation beside me until Dante returns a long minute later with a small shoe box. At least a dozen envelopes fill the cardboard container. Even from this distance, I can make out the Return to Sender and No

Forwarding Address stamps on the correspondence. Dante slumps down onto the couch beside Rose, his shoulders rounding.

"Finding out about you and Marco was a huge fucking blow. Papà was our idol. Discovering he'd betrayed Mamma... It just didn't sit right. So I went through all his old stuff at Mamma's house and I found these." He tosses the box at Nico. "Our father, Umberto Valentino, was in love with my mother long before he met yours. Your grandfather tried to negotiate an arrangement between the Valentinos and Rossi's and from what I can gather, he pretty much forced my father and your mother together one time. He'd hoped it would cement the arrangement. Instead, you and your brother must have been spawned from the encounter." He shrugs. "Papà married my mother shortly after despite our grandfathers' wishes, and he had no idea about the two of you."

"It can't be," Nico growls. "*Nonno* said he sent word of our arrival. We lived in the city for years and never heard from him."

Dante ticks his head at the letters. "When Papà eventually found out about you two, he tried to contact you. All the letters are there, read them for yourself." His lips twist into frown. "I'm not sure what went down, but someone lied to you because Papà tried again and again. So whatever beef you have with him, drop it. If you hate us, fine, but our father was an upstanding man. He worked hard his whole life so that we could have a better one."

A thick silence descends over the living room as Nico's fingers run over the old envelopes. A glossy sheen brightens his eyes as he thumbs the faded black ink. He is so silent, so still, a prickle of unease lifts the hair on the back of my neck.

Nico suddenly leaps up, and my heart jumps along with him. Without a word, he marches to the door, and I scramble to race after him. "Thank you," I call out over my shoulder. "And let's do lunch soon, Rose!"

CHAPTER 39
FIND ME

N *ico*

I read the damned letters at least a hundred times overnight instead of sleeping or fucking Maisy which is what I should have been doing. Instead, my entire past is turned upside down. Umberto Valentino wasn't a *pezzo di merda*. My fucking half-brother was right. He'd been a decent man, trying his best to remedy a situation with no easy solution.

My entire life was built on a lie. I spent years hating a ghost, fostering vengeance with no basis in reality. *Merda...*

I run my finger over the dark text, reading the words over and over again. Papà tried to contact us so many times, attempted to arrange a meeting with *Mamma*'s cousin. Why would she keep that from us? *Dio*, if we'd only gotten these letters, we might have never ended up in foster care. The deadened nerves along my back twitch as invisible flames rage across my flesh. I grit my teeth and chase away the ghostly pangs. Our entire lives could have turned out differently. We could have grown up in a loving home with Dante, with Luca…

I squeeze my eyes closed and shove back the unfamiliar burn. Glancing over at a peacefully sleeping Maisy, my ribs tighten. If it wasn't for her ultimatum I would still be trapped in a lie. I never would have given Dante the chance to explain, and he never would've bothered to try.

I must tell Marco. At least it would lessen the sting of my decision.

The Kings weren't my enemies anymore. They never had been.

The sharp squeal of my phone on the nightstand sends me reaching for the cell before it wakes Maisy. She stirs beside me as I scan the screen. It's not even seven yet. Who is calling me at this hour?

The shriek of sirens wailing escalates my pulse, and I answer the unknown number.

"Naughty, naughty, Mr. Rossi." A familiar voice croons on the line. "All this time, I've wondered where my little Maisy had gone, and now I've found her in your bed."

"Jasper?" I hiss, unable to keep from blurting his name out loud. "Where the fuck are you?"

"None of your concern, traitor."

An incoming call diverts my attention as Max's name lights up the screen. I press the call ignore button as Maisy's lids flutter, and her sleepy gaze turns toward me.

"I suggest you turn yourself in to the authorities, Mr. Whitaker, because when I get my hands on you, I'm going to rip your lying tongue out and give it to Maisy as a present. You held this woman's heart, had the gift of her love and you squandered it. You warped it and abused it, until you made her believe your lies. You made her feel unworthy, and now, I will make you pay for that."

"If you can find me." The line goes dead.

Rage billows up in my gut, expanding as I take in the fear in Maisy's eyes.

I pull her into my chest and hold her tight against me. "You never have to be afraid again, little fox. I'm going to end this, I swear."

The steady howl of the sirens sounds closer, but I can barely hear them over the thundering frenzy of my pulse. My phone rings again, and I nearly send it to voicemail until I see Max's name once more.

"What?" I shout into the speaker.

"Uh, sorry to call so early boss, but there's been a fire in the garage. Your cars are scorched."

"*Merda*," I grit out. "That little mother fucker." My nose twitches, the thick scent of smoke cloying. Every remaining nerve ending across my back riots at the dark memories.

"What's going on?" Maisy cries.

"Fucking Jasper must have had Dante surveilled, and when we went over there today, he probably saw us. He must have followed us home and torched my cars."

A sharp gasp curves her mouth into a capital O.

"I need to go downstairs and deal with the authorities." Releasing her, I slide to the end of the bed.

"I'll go with you."

"No, I don't want you anywhere near this, Maisy." I spear my legs through a pair of sweatpants and tug a shirt over my head. "Jasper is probably nearby watching the whole thing. The last thing I need is him getting exactly what he wants. You."

A tremor races down her back, forcing her shoulders to shudder. *Dio*, I hate seeing her like this. I'm going to kill that motherfucker.

Tugging her into my chest once more, I press a kiss to her trembling lips. "I'll be right back. There's a guard at the door, so you'll be safe."

She nods and sits back on the bed, pulling the comforter up to her chin. "Hurry."

As I ride down to the garage on the elevator, I shoot a quick message to Marco. He's probably still asleep, but he needs to know what's going on with Jasper. The moment I settle this arson report with the cops, I'm heading out to find that asshole myself. Forget the end of the week. I'll have Jasper's head on a platter before morning.

No one fucks with my cars.

And to set them on fire? It's almost as if he were familiar with my dark history.

To my surprise, Marco answers my text immediately.

Marco: I'll meet you downstairs in a minute.

Perhaps, he is just getting in from an all-night bender. The elevator doors glide open, and the pungent odor of smoke assaults my nostrils. Flames dance across my subconscious and searing pain streaks across my back. My hand juts out, instinctively searching for something to hold on to. I find the rough stone wall and cling on for a moment as the darkness threatens to consume my vision.

Breathe, dammit, *coglione*.

You're not a kid anymore, and it's just smoke. There's no fire anymore.

Squeezing my eyes closed, I fight through the PTSD, the crushing weight on my lungs. I don't even register the ding of the elevator behind me until a firm hand settles on my shoulder.

"You okay, bro?" Marco's voice jerks me from the downward spiral.

I cant my head back to find my twin in an old t-shirt and pajama pants. His short hair sticks up at odd angles and sleep crusts his eyes. Of course, he came running when he heard about the fire. He knows it's the only thing that can bring me to my knees.

Except for Maisy, now.

Breathing through the panic, I force the darkness away and focus on the warmth spreading through my chest at my brother's appearance. Marco can be a dick, but he's my brother.

"I'm okay," I finally manage and peel my hand away from the wall.

"You ready to talk to the cops?" He ticks his head at the uniform-clad officers running around the garage like ants.

I nod and start to walk toward them with Marco at my side. From the looks of it, nearly a dozen cars were destroyed before the firemen got the blaze under control. Three were mine.

"Damn, it's a good thing I left my car at Mel's last night." Marco smirks because he just can't help bragging when he gets laid.

"How many times have I told you not to fuck my assistant?"

His smile only grows wider. "I can't help myself when *our* assistant throws herself at me."

"I find it hard to believe that *every* woman throws herself at you."

"What can I say I'm blessed."

I shake my head. My brother is a complete man-whore, but it's about time to put an end to that for everyone's good.

By the time I reach the cops, I've got my head on straight and I'm able to answer all their questions. If I didn't want to disembowel Jasper myself, I would have told them exactly who set fire to my cars, but the truth is that I want the pleasure myself.

Once the police and firemen leave, I grab Marco and usher him to the elevator. Jasper isn't the only story he needs to be caught up on. As soon we start the ascent, I turn to my brother. "I need you to watch Maisy while I go after that fucker."

"Are you sure you don't want me to go with you?"

My head whips back and forth. "I need you with Maisy. You're the only one I trust with her life now that I know Jasper's after her."

He nods slowly. "You're really in love with her, huh?"

A stupid grin stretches my lips as I think about my little fox. "I am. And the craziest part is that she loves me too."

"Who would've ever thought?" He smirks as he leans back against the elevator wall.

"Maybe it's time for you to settle down too."

"No fucking way. I'm never getting married. Love is for the weak." His grin grows wider. "No offense, of course."

"Of course."

The doors glide open, and I practically sprint out the elevator to see Maisy. When I walk into the penthouse first to make sure she's decent, I find her standing in the kitchen trying to reach for a mug from the upper cabinet.

Her bright green eyes dart to mine. "Is everything okay?"

"For now." I tick my head back over my shoulder. "Marco is here. Is it okay if he comes in?"

She shrugs, but I can't help but notice the twist of her lips. "It's his apartment, isn't it?"

"Not if you don't want him here."

"Hey…" Marco's grumble echoes through the entrance, and Maisy's frown softens.

She wraps her fuzzy pink robe tighter around her middle and waves a nonchalant hand. "It's fine, let him in."

"You can come in, asshole, but keep your distance," I shout over my shoulder.

Maisy's eyes round as they take in my brother. I always find it comical to see others' reactions when they see us together. My entire life I've been accustomed to having a trailing mirror-image of myself, but I suppose it could be startling at first.

"Morning, Maisy." Marco gives her a sheepish grin. "Sorry again for the other day…"

"Let's just forget about it." She wraps her hands around the mug, and I close the distance between us, filling it with the coffee from the fresh pot she's made.

"Good," I whisper as I press a kiss to her temple. "Because I want Marco to stay with you while I go hunt down Jasper."

"Right now?" she squeals.

"I promised you his head by the end of the week, did I not?"

"That was pretty overzealous," Marco mutters under his breath.

"It's Tuesday, I have plenty of time," I bark at my meddlesome brother.

Maisy wraps her arms around my middle and stands on her tiptoes to brush a kiss against my lips. "Can it wait just a little longer?"

"I thought this was what you wanted."

"It is," she whispers. A hint of that fear rises to the surface again. "I'm just worried is all."

"Don't be. I can handle your ex."

"I know…" A twinge of mischief eclipses the panic, and her lips curve into a naughty smile. She rises higher onto her tiptoes and whispers, "You never did get to claim your reward after ending the feud with Dante."

Her excitement is contagious, and a huge smile spreads across my face. "You naughty little fox, are you trying to seduce me so that I won't leave?"

Her head bounces up and down. "Is it working?"

"Of course it is." I lace my fingers through hers and drag her toward the hall to my bedroom. The sweet scent of orchids and warm vanilla fill my nose. Everything in this apartment is laced in Maisy's scent, she's invaded every dark corner of my life, and I couldn't be happier. "Maybe it can wait a few minutes…" Before

I get far, I double back and turn to Marco. "There's something you need to know about our father." I tick my head at the box on the coffee table. "Read the letters. We'll be done in an hour tops."

"Really?" Marco's lips twist in disgust.

"Okay, you're right, more like two." I shoot him a wicked grin. "Happy reading."

"Happy fucking," he calls out as I disappear with Maisy down the hall.

CHAPTER 40
WHEN YOU KNOW, YOU KNOW

M*aisy*

I heave out a breath as I stare at the blinking cursor on the screen. I've spent all morning filling out paperwork to set up my foundation. I've contacted former high society acquaintances and even called in a favor with my mother. She's already promised to help me host a charity ball to kick off the inauguration of the abused women's organization. Now, I just need to come up with the name. The cursor continues to blink, taunting me.

Throwing myself headfirst into this project has been the perfect distraction to keep my spiraling thoughts away from Nico and Jasper. Never in a million years did I think I'd feel afraid for the brutal mob boss. Nico always seemed untouchable; the flawless hunter, his entire body is honed to lethal perfection. He's a born weapon of destruction. And still, I can't shake this terrible feeling.

Maybe that's what real love does to someone.

"*Hola, chica!*" A bubbly voice pulls me from my inner musings. Blanca pops her head into Nico's office where I sit in his oversized desk.

"Morning, Blanca."

She whirls around the already impeccable room with a duster, shaking her hips as she goes. I'm actually thankful for the company. This is the second day Nico has been gone from sunup to sunset, and it's kind of embarrassing how much I miss him. Giuseppe is a permanent fixture at the door, but he doesn't talk much, and Marco has locked himself up in his bedroom with the box of envelopes Dante gifted Nico. I thought *my* Rossi twin had taken it badly until I saw what this revelation was doing to Marco. Not that I knew him well but based on everything I'd heard from Nico about the easy-go-lucky, eternal flirt and fun guy, he was not acting like himself at all.

Lifting my gaze from the computer screen, I turn my attention to our housekeeper-slash-actress. "How was your audition yesterday?"

She pops out her earbud and shuffles over, dark eyes brimming with contagious excitement. "It went ah-mazing!" She sings the final word in a high-pitched tune. "I already got a call back this morning."

"That's incredible!"

"It's an off-Broadway number, but it's a big part. This could be my lucky break, Miss Maisy. If all goes well, this may just be the last you see of me and my duster." She flutters the fluffy white feathers an inch from my nose, and a giggle tumbles out.

"Well, I'll certainly miss you, but you were definitely made for greater things, Blanca."

"*Gracias, chica.*" She blows a kiss my way as I finally pry myself away from the computer and head to the kitchen.

I need a coffee and a snack. Then back to work. With all the excitement about my new charity, I haven't exactly been the most dedicated Palestra employee. I'm lucky my boss is such a sweetheart. If all goes well with the foundation, I'll be saying goodbye to my assistant gig before long. A twinge of disappointment squirms its way across my chest. That job at Palestra was the first step in my life without Jasper. It had given me hope when I'd been drowning in pity and self-doubt. And the eye candy wasn't bad either.

Heated memories of my first glance at a bare-chested Nico Rossi spring to the forefront of my mind. Yup, we were completely inevitable. Speaking of my hot Italian, it's time for my hourly check in. I reach into my back pocket for my phone, but my fingers come up empty. Dang it, I must have left it on Nico's desk. Whirling around, I scamper back down the hall to his office.

Turning the corner, the click-clack of nails on a keyboard slow my pace. I tiptoe toward the door and peer around the opening. Blanca hovers over Nico's computer, her eyes intent on the screen. What the…?

Inching closer, I try to make out what's on the screen, but the angle is off, and I can't see a thing. Why would she be on Nico's computer? I take another step, but I ram my big toe against the baseboard and let out a squeal.

Blanca whirls toward me, her dark eyes wide. She clicks the mouse, and whatever she was looking at is gone.

"What are you doing?" I finally ask after bouncing on one foot like a moron as I cradle my injured toe.

She yanks out her phone from her pocket and flashes it in my direction. "No service and I was trying to check my email to see if the director sent me the audition script. Sorry, I hope you don't mind."

My brows furrow as I regard her, but that beaming smile sets the alarm bells at ease. Of course that's all it is. I've clearly been spending too much time in the dark, twisted world of the mafia. Now I'm getting paranoid too.

"Sure, no problem."

She dashes out the room as I march toward Nico's desk and

find my cell next to the mouse. "There you are." I sneak a quick peek at the screen and a message from Nico brings a cheesy smile to my face.

Nico: Miss you.

I type out a quick reply before pocketing the phone and turning for the door. But before I do, the screensaver pops up on Nico's computer, a picture of me while asleep. It was taken in my bedroom, and I'm fairly certain it was during his stalking days judging by the dark room. It should freak me out, but it only floods my chest in warmth. Even back then, he was already looking out for me.

The image fades, and the password and login prompts pop onto the screen. *Wait a second...* Nico had given me his login to use his computer, but how had Blanca gotten on? Had I forgotten to log out before I left?

"Miss Maisy!" Giuseppe's gruff bark sends my thoughts scattering. "You have a visitor."

Tossing the thoughts aside for now, I resolve to mention it to Nico later. The last thing I want is him distracted while he's out there hunting Jasper. Hurrying down the corridor, I find a scowling Giuseppe by the door.

"Who is it?"

"A Miss Rose Valentino is downstairs asking to see you."

"Oh, yes! Send her up." Only two days and Rose and I are back to texting on the regular. I hadn't realized how much I'd missed her until the messages started streaming in. She had a yoga class this afternoon and had promised to stop by on her way home. I'd been so absorbed by my work I'd nearly forgotten.

The shuffle of approaching footsteps spins my head down the hall. Marco trudges closer still wearing his pajamas and that box of letters firmly pressed to his chest. He's been a walking zombie for two whole days.

"Morning," he mutters as he passes and continues onto the kitchen.

"It's almost two in the afternoon," I reply.

"Oh, is it?" His mismatched eyes are bloodshot, a haunted look carved into his disturbingly familiar countenance. There's been something I've wanted to ask him since his babysitting duties began, but I just hadn't gathered the nerve. I should just get it out now. This way if it gets awkward, Rose's arrival will be a built-in distraction.

I creep closer to the kitchen island, summoning my nerves. Marco leans against the counter as the fancy schmancy coffee maker churns up an espresso.

"Can I ask you something?" I blurt.

He reaches for the small cup of coffee and takes a big gulp. "Shoot."

"The other day when you came back from Puerto Rico, and you kissed me and stuff…" I nibble on my bottom lip as heat swarms up my neck. "Would you have gone all the way if I'd allowed it?"

His eyes taper at the edges, full lips twisting into a pout. Flashes of those lips, or rather Nico's lips, an identical version, sail through my mind. A long moment of silence descends between us, and a part of me wishes Rose would just barge in already. "That's a no," he finally answers. "I was just trying to fuck around. I wouldn't have actually *fucked* you. When Nico and I were kids, we used to do that shit all the time. We'd drive our teachers nuts and our adoptive parents hated it when we tricked them." He shrugs. "I guess old habits die hard." He drops the tiny espresso cup on the counter and slides it toward the sink. "In retrospect, it probably wasn't the right thing to do."

"Ya think?" I exclaim.

He drags his palm over the back of his neck. "Like I said, I didn't realize you two were serious. When we were teens, we'd occasionally hook up with each other's girls, just for fun. We even had a threesome once—"

I lift my hand, nausea unfurling in my gut. "I really don't

want to hear about you and your twin gangbanging some girl."

A wicked chuckle parts his lips, and I get a glimpse of the man Nico had described. "If you ever change your mind, I can probably talk my brother into it—"

"No!" I squeal.

Another dark laugh. "I can see why he fell for you, Maisy. There's something sweet and innocent about you, something men like us don't often get the pleasure of indulging in."

I'm not sure if I should be insulted or flattered by that kind-of compliment. Luckily, I'm spared having to answer because Rose barrels into the apartment at that moment.

"Ooh, nice digs, Mais!" She wraps me into a hug, her eyes flitting over my shoulder as she takes in the sophisticated space. "At least your psycho stalker has good taste in décor."

Marco emerges from the kitchen, and Rose's eyes nearly fall out of her head.

"Holy shit," she hisses. "I know you told me they were identical but that is freaky."

"Hello to you too." Marco has another cup of coffee clenched in his fist as he scrutinizes his (half?) sister-in-law. "How did my psychotic half-brother manage to snag a girl like you?"

"I'm not as nice as I look." She tosses him a savage smile, and I can't help the laugh from bubbling out.

"I bet," he murmurs as he takes a sip of the coffee and turns for the hall. "You two behave, I'll be in my room."

"Will do."

"I thought you said he was the fun one?" Rose whisper-hisses the moment his footsteps fall away.

I lead Rose into the living room and plop down on the crushed velvet couch. "I guess he was until Dante dropped the daddy bombshell."

Hurried steps resound down the hall, and Blanca appears pushing the housekeeping cart. "*Adios, chica.* I'm done for the day. I'll see you the day after tomorrow, unless I don't, and then you'll know that means I got the part!"

"Good luck—er, I mean break a leg," I call out.

The moment the door slams behind her, I settle into the couch and turn to Rose. "I can't wait for Jasper to be out of my life for good so I can just nonchalantly walk out of my own apartment."

"My?" Rose waggles her brows. "So is this living situation with Nico permanent?" For once, she doesn't seem completely disgusted by the mere mention of his name.

Heat races across my cheeks. "We haven't exactly discussed it, but he's always alluding to the fact. He's even told Marco to find his own place."

"That does sound serious."

A stupid grin stretches across my face. "The last thing I wanted was to jump into another relationship, but I don't know… it just feels right."

Rose shrugs, a knowing smile creasing the corners of her lips. "When you know, you know."

"Speaking of knowing, does Dante know you're here?"

"Nope." She pops the P with a smirk. "He doesn't exactly buy Nico's story about giving up his quest for revenge against the Kings. He says no pussy can be that good." An evil laugh erupts from my friend's lips. "Besides, he's meeting with the Red Dragons for some business crap. I'll be back at the penthouse before he notices I'm gone."

I nibble on my bottom lip as I imagine a life with Nico. The constant worry, the attacks, the fear. "What's it like being married to a mobster?"

"Well, we've only been married for a few months, but so far so good." Her slender shoulders lift. "The fear never really goes away. Every time Dante comes home it's like a huge weight falls from my shoulders. But it also makes every moment so much more precious. And the sex…" She runs her tongue across her bottom lip. "It's sizzling."

Now that I can relate to.

My friend eyes me, her light brow lifted into a skeptical arch. "Do you really see a future with Nico?"

I nod. "Is that crazy?"

"Well, yes, but clearly I've got no room to talk." She squeezes my shoulder and offers a reassuring smile. "Just make sure you keep going to see Dr. Winchester."

I snort on a laugh. "Deal."

Rose's gaze flickers to the kitchen. "So do you have some bubbly or something? I feel like we need to celebrate. I've missed you so much, Mais!"

CHAPTER 41
FLAMES

N*ico*

A growl of frustration echoes across the back seat of the BMW loaner I've been forced to ride in since that piece of shit Jasper torched my car. It's already Thursday, and I'm nowhere closer to finding that asshole than I was when I began my search.

That surgeon is a slippery little fucker.

I have all my best men tracking a ghost, leaving my territory unprotected. If it wasn't for the stalemate with the Kings, we'd be taking on huge losses. I have one more stop to hit up today before I return home to Maisy.

I hate these endless days without her.

Most nights by the time I get home, she's been asleep but that doesn't keep her legs from parting as I crawl into bed. She's always drenched and ready for me like a good girl. Even half asleep she's incredible, and I simply can't get enough. I'm hard just thinking about sinking my cock into her slick heat right now.

I grab my phone and type out a quick text filled with dirty emojis. I've been forced to up our sexting game in the past few days since we've been apart.

She immediately responds with a blushing emoji, and I can practically see her flushed cheeks as I pound into her. For someone so prude, my little fox is becoming quite the little minx in bed. There's nothing she won't try, and everything I do has her coming on my cock like a porn star. *Dio*, I love her.

Max pulls the car over in front of a four-story walk up in the Upper West Side only a block away from Maisy's townhouse. The hair on the back of my neck prickles. According to one of my guys, Jasper was spotted here only two days ago. Is this where he's been hiding all this time? So close to my little fox?

Rage pounds through my veins and I whip the back door open, not waiting for Max to move his ass. I stalk up the steps to the front door and jimmy the crappy lock in seconds. Once I'm in the foyer, I pull out my gun and Max moves into step beside me as we ascend the old wooden staircase. There's one apartment on each floor and two have already been cleared. That leaves two possibilities which should be easy enough. I point at the apartment on the third floor and Max peels off as I continue upstairs.

The scuffle of footsteps emanating from the fourth-floor apartment stops me at the landing. I freeze, straining to make out a sound. Noiselessly, I tiptoe to the door and press my ear to the dark timber. Faint creaks seep through the doorway.

According to the landlord, this unit is supposed to be vacant. So either there's a rat in that apartment or an even bigger motherfucking rat. Counting to three, I ram my shoulder against the door and the wood splinters on contact. The hinges squeal and the door whips open, revealing a dark shadow racing across the murky space.

"Jasper!" I shout.

The figure turns for an instant before racing down a narrow

corridor. I sprint behind him, feeling my way through the darkness. He disappears into a room and slams the door. I nearly barrel right into it before jerking it open. The shadow huddles at the fire escape for an instant, and flicker of light illuminates a familiar face.

Jasper holds a lighter an inch from his nose. His blonde hair hangs in greasy strands across his face, and the prim and proper surgeon looks like he's lost at least twenty pounds since I last saw him.

"You're a dead man," I hiss.

"You have to survive the fire first. Or should I say again?" He tosses the lighter an instant before the scent of gasoline creeps up my nostrils.

Fuck.

I whirl toward the door as the lighter hits the floor, and the soaked carpet ignites. I blink and the entire room is engulfed in flames. The fire licks up the polyester curtains, climbing up the walls and devouring everything in its path. The entire damned room must be drenched in gasoline. My chest constricts, my ribs suddenly too tight to restrain my rioting heart.

Darkness seeps into the corners of my vision, and I freeze. I'm twelve years old again with a raging inferno surrounding me. The pungent smoke burns my throat, and each inhale is pure torture. The flames morph into horrific creatures, clawed fingers reaching for me, threatening to drag me down into the depths of hell, where I belong.

I attempt to draw in a breath, but the thickening smoke clogs my airway. The blossoming heat scorches my face, singeing the overgrown stubble on my cheek. The sudden sharp crack of wood sends my gaze up to a splintering rafter.

"Hey, boss! Nico, are you in here?" Max barrels into the room a moment later where I still stand, completely immobile.

A wooden beam crashes down, but somehow Max gets a hold of my arm and jerks me out of the way at the last second.

Heat licks up my spine, then my neck, and the scent of burned hair reaches my sensitive nostrils as he drags me out into the hallway.

"Oh, shit!" Max's eyes widen as he peels off his jacket and tosses it over my head. "I got you, boss."

Fuck, my hair. I've been meaning to get it cut. The errant thought bounces across my mind in some crazed delirium.

Max hauls me up and practically carries me down the steps.

By the time I reach the bottom floor, my senses start to return, and embarrassment floods my being. I just stood there like a complete idiot. I'd nearly let the entire apartment come down on top of me.

"Thanks," I mumble at Max.

"No problem, boss." He tugs me toward the BMW and shoves me into the backseat. "Let's get out of here before the fire department arrives."

I nod numbly as he slams the door behind me.

Quiet sobs echo through my subconscious and my lids flutter open, waking me from a fitful sleep. I roll over to find Maisy curled in a ball at the edge of the mattress.

"Little fox?" I murmur as I pull her into my arms. "Are you okay?"

"No, I'm not," she cries. Her eyes are bloodshot and swollen as she peers up at me. "God, Nico I was so scared… I don't think I'll ever get the image of Max carrying you into the penthouse out of my mind."

"I'm fine." I caress her cheek, reveling in her soft skin. "He was being overly dramatic."

"You could have been killed!"

"Unfortunately, it's part of the life I've chosen, baby."

"I don't like it. I hate it actually." Her lips twist into a pout, and I can't help myself from capturing them.

She only fights me for a second before giving into the kiss. I was so out of it when I returned earlier I barely remember crawling into bed with her. Now I'm fully awake, my cock straining against my boxers.

Rolling on top of my little fox, I fit my hips between her inner thighs. My erection brushes across her center over her panties, earning me a faint gasp.

"Nico, you can't sex your way out of this."

"Why not?" A wicked grin crosses my face as I shamelessly rub my cock against her. "I think I deserve some sort of reward after what I've been through today."

She shakes her head, but a faint smile erases the fear etched into her expression. "I love you, dang it, Nico, and you scared the bejesus out of me. I never want to feel that way again. It was all my fault you were out there searching for Jasper. I don't care about you finding him; I want you to forget that stupid promise you made me."

Hovering over her, I press a kiss to her forehead, then move down her jaw and settle on her lips once more. "It wasn't your fault at all. It's *never* your fault. And I will never not do my utmost to keep a promise to you. I wish I could say once this is over, I won't be in danger again, little fox," I whisper against her mouth, "but I refuse to lie to you. Getting involved with someone like me comes with inherent risks. If it wasn't Jasper, it would've been someone else."

"But I thought that now with this feud ending with the Kings you'd be safe..."

"I'll be safer that's for sure. And that's all because of *you*." I press another kiss to her pouty lips.

"You have to try to be more careful, Nico, please. I—I don't know what I'd do if I lost you." Her fingers tangle through the burned tips of my hair. Another sob builds in her throat, and I'm so overcome with emotion, hot tears sting my eyes.

I never cry. I can't remember the last time I shed a single tear.

"Of course I'll try, Maisy. I just found you. Do you think I'm going to let something like death tear me away from you?"

Her smile widens, the spark lighting up in those expressive orbs.

"Now, can I please fuck the woman I love? I think it's the least I deserve." My hands are tugging down her panties before she has a chance to respond.

Her head dips, those eyes shining brighter than the most brilliant sunrise. "I love you, Nico—" Maisy's words are swallowed up by a moan as I thrust inside her.

Her hips move with mine, falling into a perfect rhythm as her hungry pussy devours my cock.

"Mmm, Maisy, you're so perfect for me, and I'm going to spend the rest of my life proving it to you."

CHAPTER 42
A COFFEE AND A KIDNAPPING

M*aisy*

"Please don't go." I press a kiss to Nico's mouth, not even caring how needy and desperate I sound as Rose looks on from the kitchen. It's Friday, the self-imposed deadline for finding Jasper and despite my pleading, Nico is adamant about going out there to find my ex. Never mind that he was nearly barbecued alive yesterday and lost half of his beautiful long hair. One of the girls from the salon in the hotel had already been up this morning to trim the charred remains. I'm not sure I'll ever get used to it.

Nico even brought my best friend over as a distraction, but not even Rose's presence can suppress the fear blossoming in my gut. He cradles my cheek with his warm hand and deepens the kiss, stepping into me so I can feel the full length of his body against me. It's all I can do to keep from buckling over as his tongue ravages my mouth. When he pulls away, I'm all breathy and flustered.

"I promise I'll be back before dark with Jasper's head on a platter for you, little fox."

"Nico…" I whine.

"I want you to feel safe, and that will never happen until he's out of our lives for good."

"I do feel safe. I always feel safe with you." I run my hand through his shorn locks and hold him close against me. I just can't shake this overwhelming sense of dread.

His expression darkens, and he heaves in a breath. "Wait up for me, I have a surprise for you when I return."

"It better not be more eyeballs," I whisper.

A dark chuckle rumbles his chest. "No, I promise you'll like this present much more."

"All right, you two," Rose interjects and scoots between us. "Get out of here, Nico, or I'll be babysitting all day."

I toss my friend a scowl. "Hey!"

"I'm just kidding, Maisy, you know I love you." She turns to Nico and practically shoves him out the door. "Now, you, I could do without."

Nico snarls but allows his new sister-in-law to shoo him out all the same after one last quick kiss. Just a few days and Rose has all the brothers wrapped around her little finger. She's incredible.

The moment the door closes behind Nico, I elbow my friend in the side. "I want to be you when I grow up."

She lets out a cackle and throws her arm around me. "You already are, Mais. I never thought I'd see the day when Nico and Dante weren't at each other's throats. You did that."

I did, didn't I? A swirl of satisfaction momentarily stifles the impending sense of doom. I grab my mug off the island and wrap my fingers around it, allowing the warmth to soothe me.

Marco strolls into the foyer in nothing but low-slung sweatpants and drags his hand through his messy hair. In the short time I've come to know Nico's twin, I've discovered he lacks

Nico's penchant for suits. The less clothes the better for this Rossi brother.

Rose gives him an appreciative once over, and I can hardly blame her. Marco may like to show off his body, but it's well earned. Nothing but carved abs, tan skin and dark ink go on for miles.

"Ugh, I need a coffee," he grumbles.

"We're out, sorry, I just gave Rose the last cup." My friend shoots him a cheeky grin and holds up her mug.

"You're scavengers both of you." He shoots us a glare before a yawn parts his lips. "Do you know how late I was up last night? There's no way I'll be in full-functioning guard duty capacity without my caffeine."

"Where were you anyway?" I ask. I'd been up late myself, unable to tear my eyes away from Nico long after he fell asleep.

He waves a dismissive hand. "Not important."

"Oh, let me guess, you were with some girl?" Rose teases.

"Not just any girl," I interrupt. "You were with your executive assistant again, weren't you?"

Marco rolls his eyes, but a grin teases the corners of his mouth. "You know how much Nico frowns upon that… so of course, I wasn't with Mel."

"Liar," I hiss.

"Naughty Marco, fucking the admin." Rose's singsong has my second roommate scowling. "That's why I love Clara. She's like sixty and a little firecracker. She keeps the Valentino brothers in line without any funny business to worry about."

"Hmm, that's a good point. I should suggest a change of staff to Nico."

Marco drags his hands across his face and lets out a grunt. "You keep your opinions to yourself, Maisy. I don't need you ruining a good thing. And fuck, I will never survive all day in this apartment with the two of you without my coffee."

"So let's go get one." Rose tips her empty cup. "I could use a refill."

"And I would love out of this penthouse for an hour," I add.

"I don't think so." Marco shakes his head.

"There's a Starbucks literally across the street." I grab his forearm, rise to my tiptoes, and give him my best puppy dog eyes. "We can even bring Giuseppe."

"And you know Aldo goes everywhere I go." Rose ticks her head at the door where her guard stands. The tension may have defrosted between the half-brothers, but it didn't mean Dante ever let his wife out of his sight without a guard at all times.

"Or I could just send Giuseppe to get something for all of us," he replies.

"No, come on!" Rose and I whine in unison.

"I want to see what specials they have."

"There's an app for that," Marco retorts.

"Please!" I'm bouncing on my tiptoes like an over-eager puppy who has to pee now.

"Fine," he growls. "But we keep it quick."

"Yes!"

A few minutes later, the three of us, along with our two trailing bodyguards are crossing Park Avenue to the nearby Starbucks. Marco is on high alert, the joking, laidback twin I've come to know morphing into an exact replica of his brother.

Turning to Rose, I ignore his paranoia and enjoy the lovely spring day with my friend. As worried as I am for Nico, I can't deny the hint of excitement at the possibility that this will all be over soon. Once Jasper is gone, I can go back to some sense of normalcy. I can consider building a new life with Nico.

As we walk into the coffee shop, Rose lets out a groan, her nostrils flaring. "Mmm, it smells amazing in here."

"I never remember you being such a coffee fan. I thought you were all about the Macha lattes?"

"I was, but Dante's on my ass about transforming my body

into the perfect temple..." Her words fall away, and crimson coats her cheeks. "He's adamant about putting a baby in my belly."

I let out an embarrassing squeal that has every head inside Starbucks spinning in our direction. My own cheeks flush before I lower my voice and whisper, "Oh my gawd, Rose, that's amazing! So you guys are officially trying?"

Her head dips. "That's the understatement of the year. We've been fucking like rabbits." She flashes me a silly grin. "It's pretty fun, I'm not going to lie. But it's also slightly terrifying. I feel like Dante and I are barely responsible enough to take care of ourselves."

"You guys are going to be great parents, I know it."

"Thanks, Mais." She squeezes my hand and leads me up to the barista.

Once we've all ordered our beverages, Marco sits with our guards and lets Rose and me have a table to ourselves. He clearly wants nothing to do with the squealing from earlier. Thank goodness. I can't really catch up with my friend with Nico's brother hovering.

"So what else is going on with you?" I take a quick sip of my piping hot latte as I glance up at my friend.

"Don't tell Nico because Dante will probably kill me for spilling, but I think Luca and Stella might finally come home."

"No way..."

She nods. "If everything is really settled between the Kings and Geminis and the Red Dragons and etcetera, etcetera, then there's no reason for them to stay away anymore." She leans closer and lowers her voice. "You think Nico will really stick to his word?"

I pause for a moment, understanding how important the next few words are. I know how much Rose loves her best friend, and if I make a bad judgement call and Nico goes back on his word, it would be my fault. But I trust Nico... with all my heart. "I do."

"Good." A beaming smile flashes across her face, and she takes a big sip of her latte. "You are going to love Stella. She's the best. And who knows, maybe we'll all be sisters-in-law before long." Rose shoots me a wink.

Heat rushes up my neck and washes across my cheeks. "I just got divorced, Rose. I'm in no hurry to tie myself down just yet." Even as I say the words I can hear how hollow they sound. As insane as it is, I *can* see myself with Nico for the rest of my life. Not to mention the fact that I'm certain he'd *never* let me go.

"We'll see about that." Rose takes another sip and groans. "Mmm, this is so fucking good."

A laugh tumbles out as I watch my friend licking the whipped cream from her upper lip.

The sharp ring of Rose's phone has me nearly jumping out of my skin. I guess I am still a little on edge. Glancing over at the guys' table, luckily, no one notices my freak out.

Rose scans the screen and mutters a curse. "Dammit, it's like Dante knows I'm cheating on his healthy shit! He was supposed to be busy with the Red Dragons all morning." She takes another quick sip before answering. "Hey D, what's up?" Her gaze lifts to mine before falling to her coffee cup again. "Yeah, I'm with her."

I watch Rose's expression as it morphs, the corners of her lips falling, the sparkle in her eye dimming.

What the heck is going on?

"Mmhmm. Okay, thanks for letting me know, babe. I love you." Rose pockets the phone, and her weary eyes meet mine.

"What's going on?" I blurt.

She snags her bottom lip between her teeth, indecision warring in her gaze.

My pulse ratchets up, and a whisper of fear re-kindles in my gut. "What did Dante say? Did something happen to Nico?"

Rose shakes her head. "I—I just don't know what to say…"

"Is Nico okay?" Panic laces my tone as I stare at my friend, willing her to speak.

"Yeah, I mean, I think so." She eyes the table of guards over my shoulder and reaches for my hand. "Bathroom break?"

My head bounces up and down. I call out to Marco over my shoulder, and he nods, barely sparing me a glance as I follow Rose to the restrooms in the back.

Rose drags me into the ladies' room and locks the door behind us. Luckily, they're the single person private ones.

"What's going on?" I repeat, my voice nearly at the point of hysterics now.

"Okay, listen, before I tell you this, you need to promise not to freak out. It might not even be true…"

I grab Rose's hands and shake her. "Just tell me!"

"Dante was at a meeting with the Red Dragons and Feng told him he heard that Nico was engaged to the sister of the Four Seas' leader."

"What?" I shriek.

"Dante doesn't know if it's true or not, but he figured you'd want to know…"

"It can't be." My thoughts whirl back in time to whispered conversations, and panic unfurls. "What's his name?"

"Who?"

"The leader of the Four Seas or whatever?"

"Qian, I think."

I told Qian I needed to think about it. Nico's words echo in my mind from the phone conversation I overheard when I first moved into the penthouse. *I'm also not going to jump into an arrangement that would be extremely difficult to extricate myself from.*

No. It can't be… Nico wouldn't lie to me about this, would he? My heart kicks at my ribs, and all the air squeezes from my lungs.

"Maisy, are you okay?" Rose reaches for me, but I stagger back and hit the wall.

"It might not be true."

"It is." The confession bursts out. "I overheard him on the phone one night—I didn't know what he was talking about, but it all makes sense now." I lean against the wall, a crack racing across my stupid, stupid heart. "How could I have trusted him?"

"Mais, maybe there's some explanation."

I swallow hard to keep the sob down. Hot tears burn my eyes, and I need to get out of here immediately before I have a total meltdown. "I—I have to go," I stutter.

"Okay, let's get the guys and we'll go back—"

"No! I don't want them to see me like this." The dam breaks, tears streaming down my cheeks despite my best efforts.

"Okay, then we'll just go out the back." She opens the door a crack and ticks her head at the rear exit.

I nod quickly and follow her out. Rose weaves her arm around my shoulders and pushes through the door. The bright light streams into the dim hallway, temporarily blinding me. I squeeze my eyes closed and allow Rose to lead me outside. The back exit spills out into a narrow alleyway.

"It's going to be okay, Maisy," Rose whispers as she tugs me down the alley. "As fucked up as this sounds, Nico must love you, or else why would he have ever agreed to the stalemate with the Kings?"

It doesn't make any sense, none of it. I just need to talk to him and find out what the crap is going on.

A door whips open, and I stagger back just before the metal barrier nearly breaks my nose.

"Hey! Watch it!" Rose shouts.

Four hooded men spill out from the doorway and surround us.

CHAPTER 43
ANOTHER TROPHY

Nico

I'm going to string that piece of shit up by his toes. Not only did Jasper try to scare my little fox, but he also fucked with my cars. And now he's trying to flee the country? I stand outside the crappy hotel just a few miles from the airport. For a man who'd managed to remain untraceable for so many months, he'd made a piss poor decision booking a commercial flight out of JFK. He must have felt the noose tightening this past week to get this sloppy.

The moment his name popped up on the fly list, my tech guys had him by the balls. Then it was only a matter of finding the right hotel. Jimmy had been quick deploying the troops, I'd give him that but if he doesn't get his ass here soon, I'm going in by myself.

At least I've got Max to watch my back in case the asshole gets flame happy again.

My phone vibrates, and Jimmy's text comes through.

Jimmy: I'm five minutes out. Traffic is a shitshow.
It always is.
Me: Hurry the fuck up. I'm going in with or without you in five.

The last thing I need is this fucker getting away again. I promised Maisy his head on a platter, and I would deliver. I want a life with Maisy, with all the fucking bells and whistles. I want peace, and I want happiness, things I never thought I deserved. I'd made the difficult call to Qian this morning to break the news about the betrothal to his sister. There is only one woman I want in my life, and I'd have to deal with the consequences of backing out on the arrangement with the Four Seas later. With Qian and Jasper out of the way, we could finally start a life together.

I stare at my pocket watch and scowl. I can't wait any longer. Untucking my gun from my waistband, I tick my head at Max who stands across from me. His eyes are fixed on Jasper's room, just around the corner. It's time to end this.

With my back to the wall, I silently creep forward then pause a foot from the door. The curtains are drawn over the windows, but I can just make out a figure sprawled on the bed. I nod at Max, and he rams the worn timber with his broad shoulder. The wood splinters with a crash, and the hinges squeal open.

The form rolls off the floral bedspread, sinking between the beds.

"Come out now, Jasper," I hiss, "and I promise to cut out an hour of torture."

Max moves silently behind me with his gun trained at the hiding spot between the twin beds.

"Jasper? This is no way for this to end, after all we've been through. Are you going to go down like a coward, whimpering under the bed?"

"Fuck you, Rossi." The tip of his blonde head appears over the mattress, along with the muzzle of a gun. Max locks on it, but I wave him off. A shot to the head is too quick a death for this *pezzo di merda*. He put Maisy through years of suffering, and he deserves at least a few hours of torture. "Why'd you have to have *her*? Of all the women, why my Maisy?"

"Because you didn't deserve her," I bark. "You took her for granted, you verbally and physically abused her. She's an angel, and she sure as fuck didn't deserve a husband like you."

"Oh, and you're so much better?" His sinister laugh claws at my insides. "The brutal mob boss who stalked her for months?"

"I'm trying."

"That's comical."

"Come out here and face me like a man," I growl.

"Nope, I think I'm good down here. You start shooting and the security guard will be here in minutes."

"You overestimate the hotel security. You'll be nothing but broken bones, and I'll be long gone by the time they get here, *bastardo*."

"I'll take my chances." He has the balls to point the pistol in my direction.

I'm done with this asshole. I throw Max a barely perceptible nod, and I lunge.

A shot goes off, and Jasper lets out a curse. Max is my driver by choice; he used to be a sniper in another life. The bullet sails right through Jasper's hand, and he drops the pistol as I pummel into him.

With a bloodied hand and whimpering curses, he attempts to fight me off, but it's no use. Unadulterated rage flows through my system, feeding the monster I keep locked up tight. After months with this guy on the loose, I'll finally be able to breathe without worrying about Maisy's safety. I straddle the fucker and rain down a hailstorm of punches until blood pours from a dozen lacerations, and his eyes are swollen shut.

"I've already shown Maisy what it's like to be with a real

man, Jasper. I've had her coming on my cock all night long, something you could never do."

His eyes glaze over, but he still hisses a curse. "Fuck you, Rossi. Allowing you into my life all those months ago was the worst decision I'd ever made."

"Maybe, but it was the best thing you could've done for your ex-wife."

"Yeah ex, just remember whose cock filled her cunt first." A grin splits his bloodied lip, and rage rips through my soul. "I took her virginity. She'll *never* forget that."

"Oh, trust me, she already has." I pull a switchblade from my pocket, and his eyes widen in terror. "But just to be sure, let's cut off that cock for daring to defile what's mine."

"No…"

"You're not going to need it where you're going anyway." A wicked smile curls my lips as I drag the blade across the button of his jeans, and they fall open.

"No!" His shriek echoes across the room. "Please, don't."

"Did Maisy beg? How many times did you make her cry when you degraded her? Do you even have any idea?"

"I didn't!"

I drag the blade's lethal tip over his briefs and a line of blood coats the white cotton. "You're a fucking liar."

"Son of a bitch," he cries out. "I'm sorry, okay?" Sweat beads across his forehead. "Please! Don't do this! I never meant to hurt her; sometimes things got out of hand."

"It's not me you need to apologize to, it's Maisy."

"Okay, I'll do it. I'll apologize, I'll do whatever you want." He squirms beneath me like a little rat.

I squeeze my thighs harder around his hips to keep him from squirming. "First, I want you to confess your sins. Tell me everything you ever did to that woman."

He blanches, his chest rising and falling as the perspiration multiplies across his brow. "You can't be serious?"

"One-hundred-fucking-percent." I wrap my fingers around his throat and apply a little pressure. "Now start."

His eyes bulge as he watches me, and my fingers tighten. "Okay, okay," he chokes out. "I was a terrible husband. I ignored her, degraded her, I treated her more like a possession than a wife, sometimes I even hit her when I got angry… are you happy?"

On the contrary, I'm about a second away from snapping his scrawny neck. I draw in a deep breath, trying to maintain the mask of calm. I need to separate myself from the situation or his punishment will be over before it really begins.

Maybe I'll capture his confession along with his apology on video to send to Maisy later. She's a bit squeamish and might not enjoy all the blood though. I reach for my phone, deciding to film now and decide later.

Five missed calls.

And a video message.

Fuck. I glance at the number, and ice surges through my veins.

Maisy's face appears on the screen, and I press the playback button, my finger trembling.

Tears roll down her face, and a dark bruise mars her cheek. "Nico, please, come get me."

That fury ignites, blazing through every inch of me. "What the fuck?" I roar.

Max is at my side a moment later as the image of Maisy switches to that of a smiling Qian.

"I told you that you made the wrong decision, Rossi." The camera pans out revealing a hooded male with a knife pressed to Maisy's throat. Then the view switches to Qian. "Marry my sister or watch your whore die."

"*Merda!*" I growl and slam the phone to the floor. It bounces off the carpet and hits Jasper in the face.

A bitter laugh rasps out of his bloodied mouth. "Uh, oh, looks like you're the one that hurt Maisy this time."

Uncontrollable rage rushes my being, and the corners of my vision darken. My hand finds the knife at my side, and I plunge it into Jasper's crotch. His scream echoes around the room, the shriek only aggravating the monster I keep buried deep inside.

I rip the blade out and clean it on the carpet as blood pools between his legs. "Sorry, old friend, I wish I could stay longer, but this is the end of the road for you. I have to go save the woman I love."

"That's laughable—" A choked cry erupts through his lips as I drag the knife across his throat. I wait for only a few seconds, watching as the life drains from his pale blue eyes. I wish I could have tortured him for hours, so that he got what he truly deserved for hurting Maisy, but fucking Qian ruined everything. Now he'll pay too.

Inhaling a deep breath, I allow the icy calm to take over. I need a clear mind for what comes next.

The door to the hotel room squeaks open, and Jimmy fills the entrance. "Perfect timing," I snarl. "Cut off his head and meet me at Qian's warehouse. I've got another trophy to claim today."

CHAPTER 44
UNALIVE YOU

M*aisy*

"Let go of her, you asshole!" Rose's scream echoes through the dim alleyway.

My heart thunders in my chest, a mad pounding vibrating through every inch of my being. A masked man holds me down against the asphalt, while another flashes a phone a few inches from my face, videotaping the whole thing. A crack lances across my cheek, and a scream sneaks through my gritted teeth.

"That's enough," says the man with the phone. He shoves it into his pocket then drags me off the floor.

From the corner of my eye, I can just make out Rose being hauled into a car by two masked men at the end of the alley. A minute later, the males toss me into the backseat beside her, shove something into my mouth, and drop a hood over my head.

I'm trembling by the time I feel Rose next to me.

"It's okay, everything is going to be okay, Mais," Rose mumbles around the gag.

I lean into her as tears start to tumble free. God, I hate being so weak. I suck down the sobs and force my lower lip to stiffen.

"We have to stop getting into these messes," Rose utters.

Despite the fear lancing through my chest, I manage a rueful laugh. At least last time, it was Nico's hands we'd fallen into and even then, I'd felt a modicum of reassurance as I sat beside him in the backseat of the van. Now, I had no such protection.

My cheek stings from the jerk who roughed me up before he forced me to make that video for Nico. He must be terrified.

The car roars down the highway by the sound of other vehicles zipping by. But which highway or where we were headed, I have no idea. I draw in a breath through my nose, trying to still the mad pounding of my heart.

"Fucking Qian and the Four Seas," Rose mumbles. "The Kings are going to destroy them for this."

All this time, I was so worried about Jasper finding me that I'd never even considered another one of Nico's enemies getting to me first. Rose and I had fought like heck, but in the end, we'd been overpowered by the Four Seas masked a-holes.

Dang it, I needed to brush up on my knowledge of the city's seedy underground if I was to survive this relationship with Nico.

"See, I told you there had to be more to this engagement thing," Rose mutters. She squirms beside me and without being able to see, I know she's trying to get the ropes around her wrists untied.

"What do you mean?" I whisper, struggling with my own to no avail.

"Why would the Four Seas want us if they had brokered a successful deal between Nico and this guy's sister?"

"Hmm, true, I hadn't thought of that."

"Quiet!" A man hisses. The voice comes from what I think is the front of the car.

"Don't worry, Mais," Rose murmurs, "Dante and Nico will come for us."

My head dips before I realize she can't see the movement with the hood over her head. "I know." It's crazy really but in spite of the fear coursing through my veins, a certainty ices the panic. Nico will come for me, and he will tear these men apart for touching me. A weird sense of satisfaction fills my hollow chest.

The car slows, and my heart rams against my ribs as it rolls to a stop.

"Bring the redhead to Qian," a male voice barks.

"What do we do with the other one?"

"Just keep her out of the way."

"Should I kill her?"

"No, you fucking moron. The last thing we need is that psycho Dante Valentino coming after us for murdering his wife."

A wild cackle titters out of Rose. "That's right, assholes."

A hint of relief sets in at their whispered words. At least Rose will be safe. I guess it pays to be married to an infamously savage mob boss. The back door of the car swings open, and rough hands jerk me out.

"Rose!" I cry.

"It's okay, Maisy, you're going to be okay." Her voice grows more distant, and that fear ratchets up.

Be brave, dang it, Mais.

I'm jerked down a rough gravel road, and my feet get caught up under me. I nearly keel forward, but somehow, the guy holding my arm keeps me upright. I struggle with the binds around my wrists as he hauls me forward, but they're too tight.

The creak of another door swinging open sends my pulse skyrocketing. Where are we? And where is Nico? A terrifying thought squeezes the remaining air from my lungs. What if Jasper hurt him somehow? I mentally chastise myself, forcing away the dark thoughts. Nico can handle my sniveling ex. There's no way he'd get the drop on him again. Right?

The slam of a heavy metal door swinging closed forces my heart up my throat. I nearly jump out of my skin, but my escort's fingers digging into my arm keep me grounded.

"This is her?" A raspy voice cuts through the roar of my thundering pulse.

"Yeah, boss, this is the redhead who's been living with Nico Rossi."

"Where's the other one?" he barks.

"Chao's got her back there."

"Why the fuck you idiots nabbed Dante Valentino's wife is beyond me. I only needed her."

"The blonde got in the way. She's a wild one that girl, she was kicking, punching and biting. The bitch wouldn't let us take this one without her."

A faint smile curls my lips beneath the mask. Despite the last few turbulent months of our friendship, Rose had really been there for me today. She could have just run away, but instead, she fought our kidnappers with everything she had.

"I can't believe you couldn't take on a couple girls." The man hisses a curse.

"Sorry, boss."

"Take off her hood and gag."

A gasp peels out as the gag falls, and the cowl is torn from my head. The murky lights nearly blind me after the intense darkness. Blinking quickly, my pupils adjust to the dim surroundings and the man glaring down at me.

The man I assume is the leader of the Four Seas is built like an ox, with a thick barrel chest and a gleaming bald head with a dark braid jutting from the top. "So you're the one," he snarls. "You're the reason Nico Rossi has reneged on the deal to marry my sister..."

"He did?" The excitement in my tone is just embarrassing, but I can't keep the happiness from spilling over despite my current predicament. Nico chose me. He ended his war with the Kings for me, and now he possibly started a new one with the Four Seas *for me*.

My heart sputters out a giddy little dance. Which is just ridiculous because I'm probably about a second away from being tortured or worse.

Qian, or at least I'm assuming that's who looms over me, eyes my body from head to toe. "I refuse to accept Rossi's answer, so you see, I had to take matters into my own hands. Maybe, if you don't exist, he'll reconsider his position."

Oh, sugar, I'm so dead. I gulp and try to stagger back a step, but I hit a wall of muscle. I spin around to find the guy who, judging by his rather memorable stench, escorted me from the car. His meaty hands wrap around my upper arm and force me toward Qian.

"What do you want me to do with her?"

He ticks his head at a dark corner, and I can just make out a few chairs around a table. Beside it, a gaudy gold throne sits against the wall. "Tie her up. We're about to find out how much this girl really means to Mr. Rossi."

I swallow hard as the guy drags me toward the dark nook, and Qian stalks out. The moment he's gone, I spin at my captor. "Where's Rose?"

"Don't worry about it," he mutters before shoving me down on the chair.

I hiss out a curse as my tailbone smacks against the hard metal. "Shitzu!"

"Excuse me?" The Four Seas goon stares at me like I've hit my head or something.

"Nothing," I mumble. "You know, you should just let me go. When Nico gets here he's going to gouge your eyes out or something even more horrible. Trust me, I know. I went on a date with this guy and—"

The man stares at me, dark brows furrowed.

"Sorry, I ramble when I'm nervous, but seriously, if you don't want to die today, you should really just let me go."

A dark laugh spills from his drawn lips. "I'm not the one dying today, little girl. If Rossi doesn't agree to marry Jia, it'll be your blood all over the floor."

Jia? Bleh. The idea of Nico married to anyone else sends nausea crawling up my throat.

The slap of heavy footfalls jerks my attention across the room. Qian marches back in, a satisfied smile on his lips. "Your boyfriend is on his way."

"You're both so dead," I hiss. "My boyfriend is scary as fork, and he's going to unalive you both in the worst possible way."

A sinister grin flashes across Qian's face. "I guess we're about to find out exactly who the scarier mother fucker really is."

CHAPTER 45
A SHOT RINGS OUT

N*ico*

Rage hemorrhages through my veins as I jerk my arm back and smash my fist into the face of the guard at the door of the Four Seas' headquarters. The crack of bone against bone wakes the monster inside, and the need for violence rushes to the surface. I rip open the metal door with a resounding crash and barrel inside. Marco, Jimmy and Max flank me, each with guns cocked. My revolver is tucked into its holster for safekeeping because I'm about a second away from losing my shit and shooting up the entire Lower East Side.

That *pezzo di merda* Qian is going to die a slow and excruciating death for daring to touch Maisy. He thinks he can fuck with me and my girl? He'll understand what a gross error he's made when I gut him from spine to navel with my fingernails then dance on his entrails.

"Where the fuck are you, Qian?" I roar as I stalk through the dark warehouse.

That damned house music blasts in the background, grating on my last nerve.

"Come out here before I crush your entire empire, you sneaky piece of shit rat."

"Relax, bro," Marco whispers, and my hands curl into fists at my side.

"You relax. It's taking all I have to keep it together right now, *coglione*."

"Don't worry, we'll get her back." He slaps me on the back, and the tense set of my shoulder blades loosen a fraction.

"Damn right, we will." I swallow hard and drag my hand through my newly cut hair. It feels strange, like I'm someone else, but then again, this entire day has been a shitshow.

Qian emerges from the shadows with Maisy at his side. A wave of navy surrounds him, each of his men with guns drawn. Qian's arm snakes around her from behind, and he presses a blade to her throat.

"Let. Her. Go." Icy calm laces my words despite the storm of emotions battling in my chest. I've never known fear like this, never tasted it so viscerally.

A dark bruise mottles my little fox's cheek, and her eyes are red and puffy. My jaw ticks with barely restrained fury as I grind my teeth to keep from screaming.

"I won't let anyone hurt you," I mouth to Maisy.

Her head dips imperceptibly, and a mixture of rage and fear pummel it out in my gut. It's my fault she's in this mess. I was so concerned with Jasper I'd completely underestimated this Triad asshole.

"I'll release your little whore once you agree to marry my sister." Qian ticks his head and one of his hooded men appears from around a corridor, toting the attractive dark-haired woman I met weeks ago. Another male in a gray suit follows them, holding a few sheets of paper to his chest.

His sister looks about as happy about this as I do.

"Don't you dare call Maisy that," I growl once I have a minute to process the fact he called the woman I love a whore.

"My apologies, Mr. Rossi, what would you like me to call her? Your ex, perhaps?" A shit-eating grin curls his lips. "Because things are over between you."

"You won't be calling her anything when your body is decaying six feet underground for daring to touch what's mine."

He quirks a bemused brow. "Jia, come here," Qian barks.

The woman's ruby-stained lips press together, and she steps forward with the two men trailing her. Her arms are crossed tightly over her chest, and the fire brewing in her eyes nearly matches my own. She bites out something in Chinese, and her brother counters with a sneer.

"Zûfù has no say in this anymore, Jia. I'm in charge now."

"Grandfather will always be in charge," she hisses.

Ignoring his sister, the *bastardo* returns his attention to me. "This is how it's going to go, Rossi. You'll sign the marriage license, you and my sister will be officially bound, and I'll let your precious girl free. It's really for the best if you think about it. A high-society girl like Maisy Jordan Vanderbilt doesn't belong in our dark world."

"I don't want to hear her name from your vile lips," I hiss and take a step closer.

He shrugs nonchalantly then ticks his head at the man in the suit. "Is the paperwork ready?"

The man nods, a slight tremble to his hands as he holds out the papers.

"Sign, Rossi, or watch your sweet Maisy bleed out in front of you." He presses the knife against her throat, and she lets out a squeal.

My blood boils as a line of crimson streaks across her neck, and the beast within surges to the surface.

"I'm going to fucking rip your cock off and shove it down your throat, Qian."

"But will it be worth it if she's dead?" He runs his nose across Maisy's temple, and crimson creeps into the edges of my vision.

"The only one who's going to be dead is you." I draw my revolver and the click of a dozen triggers being cocked rings out across the silence. "I'll put this bullet through your head before your finger twitches," I snarl.

"Are you willing to risk her life on that bet, Rossi?"

My gaze flickers to Maisy's and indecision ravages my entire being. Her lips are clenched together, a look of pure defiance in her eyes. *Dio*, I love that woman. But I'm petrified of losing her, of being a fraction of a second too slow. A trickle of sweat dribbles down my spine. I never doubt, never falter, but now everything is different.

A shot rings out from behind my back, freezing the blood in my veins. The entire scene moves in slow motion. A bullet whirs over my head and sinks into Qian's skull. He drops the knife, and Maisy squirms out of his hold.

"No, but I am." A familiar thick accented voice jerks me from the haze an instant before the warehouse explodes into chaos.

A hailstorm of bullets rains out across the dim chamber, and I sprint toward Maisy. She runs toward me and slips in a pool of Qian's blood. I lunge just in time to catch her and clutch her trembling form against my own. "I got you, little fox."

A sob wrenches free, and she sinks into my embrace. "Nico…"

A tremor races through my body as I hold her tight, blanketing her against the pelting bullets. "I'm here. I told you I would always come for you, baby. You're safe now. I'll never let anyone near you again." I press a quick kiss to her forehead before I pull her low to the ground, shielding her with my body, and head toward the door to escape the raging firestorm.

A bullet grazes my arm, and I let out a curse.

"Nico!" Her eyes bulge as they land on the blood dripping from my forearm.

"It's fine. Just a flesh wound. We have to keep moving." I cover her head with my good arm and urge her forward.

"What about Rose?" she cries as I pull her toward the exit.

"She's fine. Who do you think called Dante?" I tick my head at the blonde standing by the door with a slew of Kings' bodyguards surrounding her.

My new sister-in-law is a force to be reckoned with. She's possibly deadlier than her own husband. To whom I now owed Maisy's life. *Fuck.* That's not a position I like to be in.

Dozens of Kings surround the warehouse, consuming the floundering wave of navy. With Qian dead, it won't be long for the remaining Four Seas to surrender. A part of me is loath to leave in the middle of the action and allow the Kings to take all the credit.

Also, I'm pissed as hell that Dante ended Qian's life so quickly. I wanted that fucker to pay for his blatant disrespect.

"Can we get out of here?" Maisy tugs me toward the door, and it's only then I realize I'd stopped moving. "You're bleeding..."

Marco, Jimmy and Max are still caught up in the gunfight and my craving for violence remains unquenched. Until my gaze dips to those brilliant emerald orbs and those pouty pink lips. The thirst for revenge is slaked by that face, those eyes searing into my own. The entire city could burn, and I'd let it if it meant having my little fox at my side.

"You're right, let's go." I sweep Maisy into my arms, despite the sting, and carry her the final steps to the door. Rose stands at the threshold, a satisfied smile on her lips.

"Tell your husband I'm a little irritated he stole all my fun," I growl.

"You mean thank him for saving the day?" She shoots me a smirk in return.

"Yes, that's exactly what he means," Maisy interjects. "Are

you okay, Rose?"

She waves a dismissive hand. "Those idiots didn't even take away my phone. Once I got the ropes loose, I called D and he had the cavalry here before they could lay a hand on me."

"You're so cool." Maisy rewards her friend with an adoring smile.

"You're not so bad yourself, Mais." She squeezes her hand as my arm begins to throb. "Now go on, get out of here, the Kings have this."

I let out a grunt of disapproval. I hate the idea of someone else cleaning up my mess and dread what it will cost me. Still, I find myself muttering, "Keep an eye on my brother, will you?"

"Which one?" Rose's smirk is downright evil.

"Marco."

"Oh, right, sure." She slants a glance in his direction. "I'll try to make sure he doesn't get himself killed."

"Thanks again, Rose," Maisy calls out over my shoulder as I march her through the threshold.

I need to get my little fox home. With all that pent up rage unspent, I need a different sort of release. I'm already hard just at the thought. And now with Jasper and Qian dead, I can finally focus on our future. And a few days locked in the penthouse with the woman I love and can't wait to fuck sounds like absolute heaven.

I capture her lips the moment we reach the alleyway, and she releases a satisfying moan against my mouth. "God, I needed that," I whisper against her pillowy lips.

Her tongue juts out and drags across her bottom lip. "Me too."

Cupping her cheek, I brush my thumb across the bruise. That anger bubbles up, and a snarl escapes my clenched teeth. "I was so scared, Maisy... I've never known fear like that in my life."

"It's called being in love." She smiles up at me, and the

raging darkness recedes.

"I'm not sure I like this part of it, little fox." My mouth crashes to hers once more, and I devour her lips, her tongue, every inch of her mouth. "But this, this I love."

"Samesies." Her hand cradles my cheek, and a smile lights up those jewel-toned orbs.

Those ridiculous phrases have me grinning like mad, and for a second, I forget about everything that happened in the past few hours, including the wound in my arm. "Jasper's dead," I mutter.

Her eyes widen, and an unreadable expression crosses her face. She remains quiet for an endless moment.

"I hope you're pleased?"

"Of course, I am. I'm so *relieved*." She releases a breath, her entire body relaxing against me. "I'm just so glad it's finally over, and I never have to see that mother trucker again."

A rueful chuckle vibrates my chest. "If you keep saying things like that, I'm not sure I'll be able to wait until we get home to fuck you."

A faint gasp parts her lips, and my cock is now rock hard. I don't think I'll ever get used to her little reactions to me.

"Who says we have to wait?" A mischievous grin spreads her lips. "As long as your arm is okay…"

"Well, for one, we don't have a driver." I tick my head back at the warehouse as I quicken my pace to get to the car.

"Is the new BMW bulletproof like the old one?" she asks.

My head dips.

"Then I see no reason why we'd have to wait when we have a perfectly good backseat."

Just when I don't think I could possibly love this woman anymore, she says something like that. "*Dio*, I love you, Maisy." I toss her over my shoulder as she squeals and practically sprint the last block to the car. Fuck the bullet wound. Nothing will make me feel better than sinking my cock into this beautiful, maddening woman.

CHAPTER 46
FINALLY PERFECT

M*aisy*

"We're going to have to get out of bed eventually. I can already hear Blanca out there, and it won't be long until she makes her way to the bedroom." I tug at the unfamiliar short strands atop Nico's head as he lays sprawled on top of me. They're not quite as close cut as Marco's, but Nico's new do makes the twins even more indecipherable.

"Let her wait." He presses a kiss between my breasts. "It's not even nine yet, and we deserve this after yesterday." His tongue slides out between his lips and lavishes my sensitive bare skin.

Nico made love to me all night, never letting go of me once. Even for the few hours we managed to sleep, his body remained pinned to mine, as if I'd somehow magically disappear if our skin wasn't touching. For once, it didn't feel like crazy hot forking. He took his time, sliding in and out of me, and we reveled in every minute. I'd never felt so loved, so cherished. Emotion burns my eyes at the heated memories, and I blink quickly to keep the tears at bay.

"You don't have to cry, little fox." Nico's inquisitive eyes find mine, and his mouth draws into a frown. "If you want to get out of bed that badly, I'll let you go."

I shake my head, a weak laugh tumbling out. "It's not that, silly." Framing his face with my hands, I tug his lips to mine. His scowl immediately falls away as he yields to the gentle kiss. "They were tears of happiness," I finally admit when he pulls back.

He scrutinizes me for a long moment, as if he doesn't quite believe what I'm saying. "So you're really all right?"

My head dips. "I'm happy. Last night was incredible, and now that Jasper and Qian are out of our lives—"

"We can move forward," he finishes.

A long moment of silence descends over us as we remain locked in each other's gazes.

"You know I never had any intention of going through with the engagement to Jia, right? That's why I never told you."

I swallow hard, that tightness in my chest returning. I'd doubted him for a few terrible hours yesterday.

"From the moment I saw you in that shipping container, I knew. You were it for me. I only kept up the charade with the betrothal to keep Qian in check. Obviously, those efforts proved futile once I informed him it wasn't happening." His thumb gently grazes my cheek. "I should've told you, but I never thought it would come to that."

"It's okay. It's over, and we're both alive. That's all that matters."

Nico presses a kiss to my forehead. "*Grazie a Dio.*" Thank God is right.

"Enough of all the dark and gloomy. I vaguely remember you mentioning something about a surprise yesterday?"

His brilliant blue eyes flicker with amusement. "Mmm, yes, I did say that, didn't I?"

"Please don't tell me it's Jasper's head in a box." A swirl of nausea crawls up my throat at the disgusting thought. He hadn't given me many details about my ex's demise, but knowing Nico's temper I'm sure it was horrible and violent. Just what the jerk deserved.

He pops up, giving me a front row view of his perfectly sculpted male form. I blatantly ogle him as he saunters to the walk-in closet. That beautiful phoenix stretched across his broad shoulders vibrates with life with every twitch of his carved muscles.

Nico disappears inside the closet, and a pathetic sigh seeps out. Goodness, I'm way too obsessed with this man. A second later, he re-emerges, holding a small white box with a big red bow strategically positioned in front of his male parts.

I can't help the laugh that bursts free as he stalks closer. "That's definitely too small for Jasper's head. It barely covers up your…stuff."

He grins wickedly. "My rock-hard cock?"

"Yes." Heat burns my cheeks as I take him in.

Nico sits on the edge of the mattress and places the gift box between his legs. "You know I love it when your cheeks get flushed like that. They turn the same enticing hue as when I'm buried deep inside that pussy, and you're seconds away from coming."

The heat intensifies and I swallow hard, focusing on the present instead of the warmth now pooling at my apex. I snatch the little box and eye it warily. "It's not his eyes, is it?"

"Well, open it and find out."

"If it's eyeballs, I'm not going to be amused."

"Just open it, little fox."

My stomach churns as I turn the box around in my hand, scanning all the corners. I shake it and something hard hits the sides. Definitely not eyeballs. Drawing in a breath, I tug on the ribbon and the four flaps of the box fall open.

A pink key sits in the center with the word HOME engraved across the top.

My now stinging eyes dart from the key to Nico and back, my throat tight with emotion.

"I need you to move in with me permanently, little fox. I want to make a home with you. I can't imagine a life where I don't wake up to you by my side every morning. Before you moved in, this penthouse, like my heart, was a dark, fathomless void. You've filled it with so much love, so much joy that the thought of losing that is completely unacceptable. I adore you, Maisy Jordan, and I want to spend the rest of my life showing you exactly how you deserve to be treated."

I clutch the little metal key in my palm as a tear spills over. As much as I've missed my townhouse, home is wherever Nico is.

"So what do you say?"

"You're actually giving me a choice?" I tease. "I thought you'd just keep me captive in the penthouse forever."

"I'm attempting to be a better man, little fox. Now will you just play along?"

I throw my arms around the back of his neck and pull him down on top of me. Smothering his lips with kisses, I murmur, "Of course, I will, you crazy stalker. If I said no, I'd just find you watching me in my bedroom at all hours of the night, wouldn't I?"

"You know me so well, love." His lips capture mine and I sink into the mattress, with his reassuring weight pressed against me.

"Love, I like that," I whisper against his mouth.

"Better than little fox?" He looks downright insulted.

"I've actually grown quite fond of that one too."

"Good. Because that one's never going away." He fits his hips between my thighs and his arousal brushes my center.

I groan at the heady feel of him prodding at my entrance. "Nico… I thought we were finally getting out of bed so Blanca can come in here and clean."

He pushes inside me, just the tip, and my back arches as the taut bundle of nerves lights up. "I'd rather live in filth than *not* fuck you right now." Those mischievous eyes find mine, and he thrusts all the way in.

A moan tumbles out at the utter feeling of fullness.

"Is that a yes, then?" His grin widens as he slowly pulls out then fills me to the hilt again.

"Fine, just be quick." There's something important I keep forgetting to tell him about Blanca, but with his strong arms caging me in and him doing *this*, I can't seem to keep my thoughts focused.

"Yes, ma'am. I'll have you screaming my name in no time, Miss Maisy." He thrusts again, and my head falls back as raw pleasure races through my veins.

A few hours later and we finally emerge from the bedroom, now fully bathed and clothed. Nico's fingers are tangled through mine as he leads me to the kitchen. I'm starved after the night and morning of earth-shattering orgasms.

"Morning, Blanca." Nico ticks his head at the housekeeper who's sitting on the couch playing with her phone. The entire penthouse is spotless, so she's clearly been waiting for us to get out of the master bedroom.

How embarrassing. I hope she didn't hear my mewling moans. I know I sound like a cat in heat despite how sexy Nico says they are.

My gaze flickers to hers and that memory flits to the surface. "Morning," I murmur.

She barely offers a nod before she scampers down the hall and disappears into the master. As soon as I'm certain she's out of earshot, I inch closer to Nico who's already started pouring the coffee.

"I forgot to tell you something weird that happened with Blanca the other day," I whisper.

He takes a sip from the mug and watches me over the rim. "What happened?"

"I found her sitting at the computer in your office. She said she was trying to check her email, but does she have a password to get on?"

Nico shakes his head, his dark brows furrowing. "You and Marco are the only two with that privilege."

"That's what I thought…" I chew on my bottom lip before adding, "I was on your computer right before it happened. Maybe I forgot to log you out."

His head dips, and he stares down the quiet hallway. "Maybe. Thank you for telling me. I'll have to keep an eye on her. I've had all the hotel staff that enters this apartment checked out, but one can never be too sure." He takes a measured sip, and I can practically see the gears grinding in his head. "You've become close with the girl, haven't you?"

I nod. "We've chatted a few times, but nothing crazy."

"She's from Puerto Rico, right?"

"Yup."

The line between his dark brows deepens. "You've become quite the cunning little fox, love." He presses a kiss to my forehead and draws me into his arms.

"Is there something wrong?"

He holds me tight against his chest, and I sink into his firm embrace. With Nico's arms around me, everything else melts away.

"No, nothing. Everything is finally perfect."

EPILOGUE

Marco – One Month Later

My brother is so whipped it's embarrassing really. I watch him flitter around the penthouse trailing after Maisy like a nervous bride. A chuckle vibrates my chest as I sip my whiskey relaxing on the couch. The couch that used to be mine until I was kicked out of the apartment so Maisy could move in.

Unbelievable.

Our entire lives it has been the two of us against the world. Now he has her, and I'm kicked out like a mangy mutt. It's a good thing I have more than a few female friends who've opened up their beds for me until I find a suitable new home. Living in a hotel room got tired fast.

Choosing an apartment on my own is a big commitment, one I'm not certain I'm ready to take on. Kicking my bare feet onto the coffee table, I take another long pull from the crystal tumbler, swirling the smoky, honeyed taste on my tongue.

"Get your feet off the table," Nico growls as he darts by

holding a vase filled with ruby red orchids. The entire penthouse is constantly filled with the colorful floral arrangements. So much for our bachelor pad...

Lowering my bare feet to the plush carpet, I glare up at my brother. "I don't understand why we're making such a big deal about this."

Maisy scrambles over and nearly trips over my discarded shoes. If it wasn't for Nico's arm snaking around her waist, she would've ended up headfirst in the coffee table. I quickly wipe away the smirk before she notices. As much as I want to hate my brother's girlfriend, I have to admit she's grown on me.

She's the type of girl you can't help but love. I actually understand why he's fallen so hard.

As she tugs on the hem of her dress and straightens, her gaze drops to mine. "We're making a big deal about this because Rose is my best friend, and Dante and Luca are your brothers."

"Half-brothers," Nico and I interject in perfect unison.

She raises a dismissive hand. "And Luca's return to the city should be celebrated since you've never officially met."

Officially is true. My brother and I had been skulking in the shadows learning everything we could about our half-brothers for years. Even when Dante finally met Nico, he was adamant about not revealing the fact that we were twins. Our identical faces had helped us pull off many a scam when we were younger. He'd hoped to keep that little tidbit a secret until the time was right, but then Maisy ruined that plan.

Okay, so maybe I did, but still.

A sharp knock at the door has my twin and Maisy whirling toward the entryway.

"They're here!" Maisy shouts. "Come say hi!"

"I'm not deaf." I roll my eyes and reluctantly lower my half-empty glass to the table.

Nico clings to Maisy as he ticks his head at Giuseppe to open the door. Nothing like a slew of guards to show how much trust exists between the Valentinos and Rossi's. I'm sure my half-siblings will have a dozen in tow.

The door swings open, and the Valentinos darken the entryway. Dante holds his wife tight against his side, while Luca remains a few steps behind with his arm around his fiancée.

The silence lingers between us for an excruciatingly long minute until Rose extricates herself from her husband's grasp and throws her arms around Maisy.

"Thanks so much for having us!" the blonde cries out and just like that, the tension dissipates.

Rose's bubbly nature has that effect on people. She's spent many an afternoon with Maisy here at the penthouse before I was kicked out, and I must admit, I like her too. Peering over Dante's broad shoulders, I catch my first glance at Stella. I don't know much about Luca's fiancée other than the fact that she is *amazing* per Rose's vivid description. She's an Italian beauty that's for sure, with long raven locks, full, pouty lips and curves that go on for miles.

"Come in, everyone!" Maisy ushers the happy couples into the pristine penthouse.

I offer my half-brothers tight smiles as they pass.

Rose helps herself to a flute of champagne perched on the kitchen island, then passes out the rest to the others. We'll need lots of alcohol for this awkward encounter to go well. Quiet murmurs echo across the space as the girls greet each other.

The four males, myself included, remain locked in a battle of deadly silence.

"Everyone, this is Stella, one of my oldest friends." Rose pulls Luca's fiancée into a hug. "I've missed her sooo much." The dark-haired beauty returns the smile.

"I've missed you, too, Rose. I've missed everything about Manhattan really, and I'm so glad we're finally back."

"And have a wedding to plan!" Rose squeals.

Luca grunts, and he exchanges a quick glance with his brother.

The great CEO of King Industries was forced into hiding for months with his fiancée after bounties were placed on their heads by the Red Dragons. According to the rumors, Dante had essentially kidnapped the newly engaged couple to compel them to leave the country.

"Sit, everyone, get comfortable," says Maisy, motioning to the living area.

I return to my spot on the couch and cradle my drink. Nico sits beside me before tugging Maisy into his lap. The two are nauseatingly in love. I suppose it's a good thing I moved out or I never would've been able to handle their constant fucking. Knowing my brother's obsessive tendencies, he's likely desperate to impregnate her to ensure she remains by his side forever.

Maisy nudges her elbow into Nico's ribs, and he slides to the edge of the cushion and clears his throat. "We appreciate you both coming today."

"It wasn't by choice," Dante grumbles.

"D!" Rose smacks her husband on the leg. "You promised to be nice."

"Yes, both of you did," Stella adds, shooting a glare at her fiancé. "You're all family, and it's about time you started acting like it."

"It's a good thing we're not outnumbered." Luca smirks eyeing the three females. "Or we'd never get away with anything." He squeezes Stella's hand, and she leans into his touch.

Dio, all my brothers are whipped. I'd grown up hearing about the great Luca and Dante Valentino and now they're nothing more than beaten dogs, kept at heal by their women. I barely recognize Nico anymore. Apparently, this love thing is contagious. It's a good thing I have zero intentions of ever settling down.

Maisy grins as she eyes the younger Valentino. Luca is nothing like Dante. Unlike his unhinged older brother, he's the smooth-talking, ladies' man. Kind of like me. Or at least he was, until he put that rock on Stella's finger.

"How about a toast," says Rose, lifting her glass. "To a peaceful future between the Kings and Geminis."

"And between the Valentinos and Rossi's," Maisy adds.

Luca and Dante nod, but both wear matching scowls. Nico shoots me a glare, and I lift my glass just like the others.

"To family," I offer sarcastically.

"That's the spirit, Marco." Maisy clinks her glass to mine, and I do my best to keep a straight face. This is all such bullshit. Even if our father didn't abandon us, I don't find it the least bit necessary to continue this charade with our half-brothers.

Nico may have agreed to this truce, but it doesn't change the fact that the Geminis and Kings will always be competitors, in the boardroom and on the streets. To pretend otherwise is just insulting.

"Luca tell them," Stella whisper-hisses, drawing my attention.

"*Cazzo, amore*, give me a minute."

"She's right, we might as well get this over with," Dante growls. "This couldn't be any more uncomfortable, and I'm ready to get out of here." He turns his feral gaze to Rose, and a smirk creeps over the scowl. "Besides I've only got a few more hours in that damned window to put a baby in my wife's belly."

"Dante!" Rose shrieks and slaps my half-brother across the back of the head.

"You know, I'm sure Nico wouldn't mind if you used the guest bedroom." A devious grin pulls at my own lips.

"Oh, my, gawd. You guys are all so embarrassing." Rose buries her face in her hands as Dante releases a wicked chuckle.

At least my half-brother's incredibly inappropriate comment has eased the rising tension in the room.

"You were saying, Luca?" Nico eyes the male across the coffee table who looks so much like our father it's unnerving.

"Right." Luca slides to the edge of the couch and runs his hand through his dark hair. Dark hair who looks a hell of a lot like mine. *Stop, damn it.* This whole family reunion thing is weird enough.

"While Stella and I were away," Luca continues, "we went to Papà's hometown in Naples."

My chest tightens for an instant as memories of home bubble to the surface. I haven't been back to Italy since the day our *Nonno* put us on that damned airplane. I shove back the images of my youth, hard. I don't need to be dwelling on those few, bright shiny moments right now.

"Anyway, I did some digging and found old account statements in Papà's stuff."

"Bank accounts?" Nico asks.

Luca's head dips, then he pulls out an envelope from his jacket's inner pocket. "As it turns out, it wasn't just letters that Papà was trying to send you." His eyes lift to mine, then pivot to Nico. "Each of you has a bank account set up in your name. Looks like he set them up when he found out about you, around twenty years ago." He hands Nico the envelope, and I peer over my brother's shoulder as he opens it.

Two bank statements are enclosed, one in each of our names like my *coglione* half-brother said.

"Fuck," I hiss as I stare at all the zeros. "Maybe he did love us."

"No shit," Dante growls.

"I don't understand." Nico shakes his head as he stares at the statements. "Why would he do all this?"

"Because he was a good man, *coglione*, just like I told you." Another growl rumbles Dante's chest. "I'm pretty sure I walked in on him the day he found out about you two. I didn't realize it then, but now that I have a better idea of the timeline, it makes sense. He told me a man must take responsibility for his actions. And that's what he did."

"Then why didn't our mamma tell us?" I snap, the question coming out harsher than intended.

"Who knows? Maybe she was pissed because Papà chose to be with our mother."

"Dante..." Luca warns, low and deadly.

"What? It's true." He shrugs and sits back on the couch, curling his arm around his wife. "I'm not trying to be an asshole."

Luca folds his hands and glances between my brother and me. "Look, this whole situation is fucked up, but we must find a way to deal with it. We all have people we care about, and who seem to care for each other." His dark gaze darts between the girls. "We have enough shit to deal with without fighting each other. So if you were sincere in your offer for peace, Nico, I'm all for it." Luca extends his hand, and I eye it warily.

An endless minute later, Nico takes it with a firm grasp. "I agree. I think we've all lost enough."

Damn, love really has changed my brother.

"Good." Dante jumps up. "If that's settled, I'd like to get home and fuck—"

Rose spears her husband with her elbow, and he buckles over dramatically, a smirk flashing across his face.

The sharp sound of four different cell phones ringing at the exact same instant abruptly cuts off the lighthearted moment.

Nico pulls out his phone before I can get to mine and mutters a curse.

"What's wrong?" I bark.

"Fucking Four Seas," Dante hisses.

The third leg of the infamous Triad has been a shitshow since Qian died. With only his sister, Jia, left as heir, the squabbling within the gang for supremacy has led to nothing but problems for us all.

"The Red Dragons want their blood," Luca adds. "Apparently, some of Jia's guys went rogue and took out their shipment of blow at the docks about ten minutes ago."

"They're out of control," Nico interjects. "I even had a meeting with Jia last week, but she wants nothing to do with any of it."

"Not to be sexist or whatever," I interrupt with an appeasing smile at the ladies, "but the Four Seas needs a strong male to step up and take control of the chaos before they burn down all the Lower East Side."

"I'm so glad you said that." Nico tosses me a wicked grin. "Because I believe I know exactly how to fix this little dilemma."

***

Read on for a special sneak peek of *Wicked King*, the next story in the Kings of Temptation series! And you can preorder it now! The release date is currently set for August 20th, but I hope to bring that up.

For all the updates make sure to join my VIP mailing list! Come hang out in my FB group Sienna Cross's Heartbreakers and you'll also get the chance to win an ARC and get exclusive sneak peeks of what's to come and the *Ruthless King* prequel story for FREE!

Each novel in the Kings of Temptation series will feature a sinfully gorgeous King and the woman who makes him fall to his knees. If you haven't read *Ruthless King*, start Luca and Stella's story while you wait for the next one!

CHAPTER 47
SNEAK PEEK OF WICKED KING

Chapter 1 – To Marry a Stranger
Jia

Today, I marry a stranger.

Worse, I marry the man who is responsible for my brother's death.

A pair of mismatched eyes bore into mine—one as brilliant as the enthralling seas of the Caribbean and the other as murky as the darkest pits of hell. His hands tighten around mine, like steel bands chaining me to a dismal future.

I heave in a breath and attempt to focus on the priest's words, but the ancient scriptures blur in the background in a muffled rush.

No, Marco Rossi is not exactly a stranger. I suppose I've known of the wicked mafia playboy for a few months now. The Italian mobster and CEO of Gemini Corporation is infamous within the dark world I've been forced to inhabit because of the blood that runs through my veins.

As a Guo, and the daughter of the former head of the Four Seas, one of the notorious gangs of the Chinese Triad, I somehow always knew this day would come, and yet, I'm still completely unprepared. How does one marry a man you despise to save your family's honor?

The melodic tune spun by the choir casts its spell across the crowded cathedral. Despite decades long hatred between the ruling families of lower Manhattan, the three legs of the legendary Triad: the Red Dragons, the Endless Night and of course the Four Seas, along with the feuding Italians: the Valentinos and Rossi's, sit shoulder to shoulder to celebrate this grand union. And complete farce.

In spite of the harmonious melody, my heart is a frantic drumroll beneath my breastbone and with the indecent sloping neckline of my pristine wedding gown, I'm certain my future husband can see its mad pounding beneath my fair skin.

Either that or he simply can't take his eyes off my cleavage. Dirtbag.

The philandering Marco Rossi is well-known among Manhattan's female elite. I'm sure he's screwed half of the city's debutantes. Likely many of the women seated in this very cathedral. He even graced the cover of *The New Yorker* last month as one of the city's most eligible bachelors. Women grovel at his feet, hang on every precious word that tumbles from his perfectly bowed lips and drop their panties without a second thought. It's disgusting really.

I hazard a quick glance at my fiancé and take in the piercing wild eyes from beneath a tumble of dark hair, wide set jaw and flawlessly carved cheekbones. Physically, he's enthralling, and logically, I understand why females throw themselves at the mafia god, but that smug smile... I want to rip it right off his ridiculously handsome face. He really thinks he's a prize. As if being shackled to him for an eternity makes me the luckiest girl in the world.

And I'm simply supposed to forget that Qian is dead because of him and his brothers?

My fingers curl into a fist at my side and the enormous

diamond glints beneath the stained-glass windows of the magnificent domed ceiling. My gaze travels from the meaningless engagement ring up my hand, to the long lace sleeves that reach down to my wrist. It's the height of summer, the temperature in the city reaching record highs, but as always, I cover my forearms and the shame they bring.

God forbid anyone ever saw… *Bà's* wrath would have only intensified.

My future husband clears his throat and his eyes dart to mine, as if somehow in that instant he's read my darkest, inner-most thoughts.

I stare up at the face of the man I'll be forced to wake up to for the rest of my life, and a wicked smirk twists his lips. Lust. Desire. Vengeance.

Something snaps inside me.

I refuse to spend the remainder of my existence at the hands of this possessive man. I suffered enough under my father's tyrannical hold, and I would do anything to ensure I never endure that torture again.

There is only one option: I'll kill Marco Rossi the first chance I get.

***

Two Months Earlier

Sitting at the drafting table with my pencil pressed to the paper, I stare out the window at the buzz of traffic below. The Meatpacking district on a Monday morning is alive with energy, a different kind than exists a few dozen blocks north in midtown. My tiny loft sits above the small warehouse space that houses my one-of-a-kind designs and the myriads of fabric samples I've managed to amass in the last year. I'm so close to finally realizing my dream.

My own fashion line.

CityZen: combining urban, chic apparel with a relaxed, modern vibe.

My storefront isn't even open yet, but I have two mannequins perched at the windows wearing my hand-sewn fashion. I've actually had a few people wander into the store looking to buy the designs.

Now, if I could only focus. I stare at the blank page, willing the image in my head to come to life on paper. I hit a wall, much like the red brick one staring at me from across the street.

Damn it. Focus, Jia.

The creak of the front door opening spins my head toward the entrance. I can't quite make out the door around the brightly graffitied brick wall that separates my bedroom-slash-studio from the living area of the industrial loft. I spent hours creating that masterpiece when I moved in—a glorious crimson and gold dragon, my spirit animal and sign in the Chinese zodiac.

"I come bearing caffeine!" My best friend's voice echoes across the high ceilings, bouncing off the metal rafters.

"You are a life saver, Ari." I reach for the skinny latte and take a sip. The first one always tastes like heaven. "You know you're not getting paid for this, right?"

She smirks. "One day, you'll be a huge designer and all the mean girls from FIT will be standing in line to get a Jia original. I'm totally content with working pro bono for now."

"I can't take advantage of you like that…"

"You're not. I'm offering my help for *free*. We had all our classes together, you know I'm no good at the creative stuff, but I am damned good at the business side. I guess Daddy was right and I should've gone to UPenn, instead." She shrugs. "Oh well, their loss is your gain." Squeezing my hands, she offers a reassuring smile. "We can do this. I know we can. I believe in you."

Unwanted emotion stings my eyes, and I blink quickly to chase it away. *Show no emotion, Jia. You must be strong and never show any signs of weakness.* My father's words echo across my mind. Even from the grave, they hold power over me. Too much power.

Tugging down my long sleeves, I give my best friend a smile. "Thanks, Ari. You don't know what your support means to me."

She peers over my shoulder, standing on her tiptoes to examine my drafting table. "I can see you're in desperate need."

I groan and spin back to the empty canvas. "I'm having a hard time connecting with my muse today."

Arianna slumps down on my bed, her cute blonde bob whipping strands of hair across her heart-shaped face. "Is there anything I can do to help?"

I love my friend. She's amazing and has been there for me since the first day we met at FIT. New York's elite fashion institute isn't exactly known for its warm and fuzzy feel. It's cutthroat and beyond competitive so I'd really lucked out when I stumbled across this gem of a human. Still… I hate getting her involved in my messy family life.

I'd filled her in on bits and pieces of our sordid involvement with New York's sketchy underground, but I'd never told her I was the granddaughter of the founder of the notorious Four Seas. She knew my brother Qian was involved with the crime syndicate but never the extent of it.

"Come on, Jia, spill." She takes a sip of her iced coffee and those expressive emerald eyes pin to mine. "Is this about your brother?"

I exhale a sharp breath and crumple down into the chair. He was killed only three months ago, caught in the middle of a shootout with the Italian mafia. I was still fuzzy on the details. And numb. My brother and I hadn't really been close since we were little. For as long as I could remember, *Bà* had treated him differently. He was being primed to take over the family business. And me? I was simply supposed to sit there, be quiet and look pretty. The best possible future for me was finding a decent match for marriage. One that would propel the Guos and the Four Seas into greater notoriety.

"Pretty much," I finally mumble to my friend. "Any way you can turn back time?"

"I wish. Then I'd go back and never agree to that date with Matty." Her lips pucker. "Not only was he a cheap bastard who wanted to split the cost of dinner, but he also tried to get in my pants on the subway." She makes a retching sound. "Come on now. If you want to get some, at least splurge on a taxi cab."

An unexpected laugh tumbles out as I watch her re-enact the story. I wish my problems were that trivial.

She waves a hand, and her smirk falls away. "In all seriousness, what can I do?"

"Nothing. I don't think there's anything either of us can do." I shrug and spin around toward my work in progress.

I've been summoned to appear in front of the Chinese Triad tomorrow afternoon. As the only living heir to the great Qian Guo, my father, not my brother who shared his name, I still officially represent the Four Seas in the eyes of the ruling families.

Clearly, I want nothing to do with their dark, illicit dealings. I have absolutely zero interest in assuming the role of head of the Four Seas. I need to focus on my legitimate business, my future. Something I never would have had if *Bà* hadn't been killed a few months before my brother.

I'm finally free, and I refuse to let anyone drag me back into the darkness again.

***

I hope you enjoyed that little sneak peek! The final book in the Kings of Temptation series, Wicked King, will be out on August 20th and you can preorder it now :) While you're waiting check out the other books in the series. And make sure you join my FB group Sienna Cross's Heartbreakers or my VIP mailing list! You'll get a FREE copy of the *Ruthless King* prequel story, *Ruthless Blood* and see how Stella and Luca first met!

ALSO BY SIENNA CROSS

<u>Kings of Temptation</u>
Ruthless King
Savage King
Brutal King

Ruthless (Ongoing on Kindle Vella)

Lords of Stonewall University (Ongoing on Kindle Vella)

ACKNOWLEDGMENTS

I'll let you in on my dirty little secret… Sienna Cross is my pen name, one I've been dying to launch for a while now. I never would've even attempted it if it wasn't for the support of my husband. He's the only one in my family who knows about naughty Sienna. Thanks for pushing me to do all the things, honey!

A special thank you to my awesome V.A., Sarah, who has been such a huge help and also vault when it comes to keeping all of this a secret. And thank you to the incredibly talented Samaiya for the gorgeous art. You really make the story come to life! And of course my beta readers, Katelin, Sarah (again!), Jena and my ARC team, you're all amazing! Some of you have been with me for years and I really appreciate all your feedback (thanks for keeping the secret too!)

And the biggest thank you to my readers! I could never do this without you :)
~ Sienna

ABOUT THE AUTHOR

Sienna Cross was kidnapped by mobsters, saved by her super-hot step-brother, then forced into an arranged marriage with a billionaire. From there, things got really interesting… She loves to write about dark, morally-gray alpha males and the captivating women that bring them to their knees. For all the inside info, join Sienna Cross's Heartbreakers on Facebook, like her page, and follow her on Instagram and Tiktok. She has a thing for stalkers ;)

www.siennacrossbooks.com

Printed in Great Britain
by Amazon

46581427R00189